One More Sunrise

MICHAEL LANDON JR.
AND TRACIE PETERSON

ONE MORE SUNRISE

BETHANYHOUSE
MINNEAPOLIS, MINNESOTA

One More Sunrise

Cover design by The DesignWorks Group, Charles Brock

Published by Bethany House Publishers
11400 Hampshire Avenue South
Bloomington, Minnesota 55438

Bethany House Publishers is a division of
Baker Publishing Group, Grand Rapids, Michigan

Printed in the United States of America

Library of Congress Cataloging-in-Publication Data

Landon, Michael, 1964–
One more sunrise / Michael Landon Jr. and Tracie Peterson.
p. cm.
ISBN 978-0-7642-0418-0 (alk. paper) — ISBN 978-0-7642-0362-6 (pbk.) — ISBN 978-0-7642-0419-7 (large-print pbk.)
1. Air pilots—Fiction. 2. Aeronautics in agriculture—Fiction. 3. Kansas—History—20th century—Fiction. I. Peterson, Tracie. II. Title.

PS3612.A5484 O54 2008
813'.6—dc22

2007034117

On Earth there is no Heaven,
But there are pieces of it.

—Jules Renard
(French writer, 1864–1910)

Chapter 1

Kansas farm country, August 1941

Joe Daley crept through the dark upper story of the farmhouse that had been his home for his entire seventeen years. His six-foot frame cast shadows on the wall as he passed the nightlight illuminating the back staircase and the family pictures staggered parallel to the steps. He started down in his stocking feet, counting ten steps, then positioned his foot carefully over the far-left edge of number eleven to avoid the familiar loud creak. The last thing he needed was any questions from his sleeping parents and brother about his predawn mission.

"Better to skip it than creak it, little brother." The loud whisper out of the shadows above him nearly caused Joe to stumble. He grabbed for the banister and turned to look back up the staircase. He could just make out his brother's grin in the glow from the small light. Rob, three years his senior, was normally his hero. Right now he was a pain in the neck.

"What are you doing up?" Joe whispered back fiercely.

"What's in the clenched fist?"

Joe tightened his grip over the small object in his left hand. "How'd you know?" he whispered louder.

"You told Bo. You might as well have taken out an ad in the *Greenville Gazette*."

Joe could hear the amusement in Rob's voice. "Let me be the one to tell Mom and Dad, Robby. Okay?" He was pleading now, but anything to get his brother back to bed and out of his hair.

"Sure thing."

Joe turned to start moving down the steps again.

"Hey, Joey! Go for the glory!" came one last comment from above.

Joe lifted a hand over his shoulder and scooped up his shoes near the bottom of the stairs. He quickly crossed the large country kitchen and checked the hands of the clock above the stove in the waning moonlight. He was slightly behind schedule. Timing was critical or his whole plan would fall apart. Grabbing two jackets from the hook beside the back door, he deposited the small item from his hand into the pocket of the smaller jacket, then stepped out into the humid predawn summer morning. A rush of adrenaline ran through Joe as he glanced at the sinking full moon. Still in his stocking feet, he bolted from the porch and raced across the yard to his dad's '38 Ford pickup.

With a vigilant eye on the horizon, Joe shoved his feet into his loafers, pushed the truck out of the yard before starting the engine, and drove as fast as he dared along the dirt road connecting the neighboring farms and cornfields. He had taken extra care with his appearance. He'd had his dark brown hair cut the day before and shaved the stubble from his chin. "Clean-shaven and well kept," his mother liked to say. He stomped on the brake when he reached the end of the cornfield, a cloud of dust swirling around the tailgate of the truck. He ducked his head to the right to look through the passenger window at the eastern horizon. A saffron hue linked earth and sky in a narrow strip and highlighted the thin, low ceiling of clouds barely visible above. With renewed urgency, he hit the gas and swung onto County Road 7. With asphalt now under his tires, Joe ramped up the Ford to forty miles an hour for the short run to his destination.

A mere two miles away, Joe's best friends, Larry Ledet and Bo Gene Conroy, were doing their part for Joe's mission under the same fading moon. Their cars were parked strategically to shine their headlights on opposite sides of a long strip of hard-packed dirt. Both young men kept their eyes on the ground as they walked along slowly, their conversation punctuating the quiet dawn countryside.

"I ain't seen a thing worth mentioning, Larry," Bo Gene said through a wide yawn. He scraped a small clod of dirt flat with the toe of his loafer and pushed back his straw boater so the wide navy ribbon around the band showed no more than a narrow stripe.

"Me neither," Larry admitted. "But we gotta make sure there's nothing out here that'll cause him a problem. Especially this time." The white T-shirt and Levi's Larry was wearing contrasted in more ways than one with Bo's madras short-sleeved shirt and pressed khaki slacks.

"I don't remember this check ever taking so long before," Bo complained.

"That's because we always do it after the sun's up, you dope."

Silence.

Larry and Bo continued slowly along the dirt strip, carefully inspecting the ground beneath their feet. Bo began to hum, then sing in a rather nice baritone, "When skies are cloudy and gray, they're only gray for a day, so wrap your troubles in dreams, and dream your troubles away."

Larry groaned. "Okay, I'll admit you do sound like the Crooner, but I'll be awful glad when Bing's got another hit and you move on from that dumb song."

"You're not going to sound so high and mighty when I'm famous and making thousands of dollars each gig. I might even get to be a movie star. You'll be begging for my autograph, and I may just turn you down." Bo finished his point by placing a homemade Savinelli knock-off pipe in the corner of his mouth.

Larry laughed and shook his head. "And I suppose you think we're on *The Road to Zanzibar* and Dorothy Lamour is waiting for us just up ahead."

"It could happen," Bo insisted, the pipe clenched between his teeth.

"Whatever you say, Bing." Larry knocked Bo's hat forward. "Let's just hurry up and finish our job. We need to get back to Betty so everything's ready when Joe shows up."

Joe killed the engine and cut the headlights as he rolled to a stop in the Johnson farmyard. He hopped out of the truck and dashed toward a two-story house silhouetted against the dark western sky. He stopped to scoop up several small stones from the ground, then took careful aim at a second-story window and let the first pebble fly. A second later he was rewarded with a sharp *ping* on the glass. No one appeared in the window. He tried again, this time with a larger pebble. Another *ping* on the glass, but no response. With one more stone curled in his palm, Joe drew back his arm and took aim. It left his fingertips at the same time he heard the window sliding up its sash. He winced at a surprised "Ouch!"

"Meg! It's me. You okay?" he called softly.

"Joe? Are you *crazy*? You hit me with a *rock*!" was her agitated reply. But he was glad she kept her voice down—he wanted to deal with her parents' questions even less than his own family's third degree.

"I was just trying to wake you up," he called back in a hoarse whisper.

"Good job. I'm awake. What are you doing here?" Meg was obviously irritated.

"I need you to come with me. Hurry up."

She leaned farther out the window. "Where are we going? The sun's not even up yet."

Joe cast another glance at the skyline, where the glow on the eastern horizon had widened since his last check.

"I know. That's kind of the point. Now shake a leg," he urged as loudly as he dared. After the slightest pause, Joe sighed in relief as he heard the window slide shut. Though it seemed like forever to Joe, it wasn't long before seventeen-year-old Meg Johnson came through the screen door, shaking her head, a scowl firmly in place. She wore a pair of clam diggers and a white T-shirt. Joe swallowed hard, marveling that she could be so beautiful and yet completely unaware of it. Her long hair was the color of summer wheat, combining the palest of straw with golden hues that tumbled over her shoulders. The color of her eyes—somewhere between blue and green—changed with her moods. Something Joe found both intimidating and wonderful.

As Joe moved quickly toward Meg, he saw her holding a white rag against her forehead. He gently pulled back her hand with the ice-filled cloth and grimaced, then leaned down to kiss her on the cheek.

"I'm so sorry, Meg. I wouldn't hurt you for anything, you know." He looked into her face, hoping she would believe him.

"I know," she said.

He let out a relieved breath.

"But tell me how I'm going to explain this knot on my head to my folks," she asked in a severe tone. " 'By the way, Dad, Joe stopped by in the dark and pelted me with a rock'?"

Joe grabbed her hand and pulled her toward the truck.

"When you put it that way, it doesn't sound so good," he acknowledged. "But now we really do have to hurry. We're running a few minutes behind schedule."

Meg sighed, still sounding out of sorts. "Where are we going? *What* schedule?"

Joe helped her into the truck. "You'll see" was all he would say as he climbed in beside her and started up the truck.

She glanced at the two leather jackets lying on the bench seat between them.

"Joe? What are we *doing*? It's too warm for jackets."

"Down here it is," he acknowledged, "but we'll need them when we get to Betty."

"You might have warned me we were taking Betty. Or maybe you were worried I wouldn't come along if you explained—is that it?" It appeared she wasn't going to give up her scolding tone yet.

Joe glanced over at her and beamed. "You can't resist me, Meg Johnson, and you know it."

Meg's mock frown said even more than her words. "I know it. I just wish *you* didn't know it." She gave him a playful punch on the arm.

The two turned at the sound of a vehicle in the distance.

Now serious, Larry asked, "Did you see the *Gazette* headlines yesterday? Sounds like that Hitler guy is sure stirring things up. Ya think Roosevelt will get us called up?"

Bo sounded just as thoughtful. "Can't say I know that. But I do know ol' Joe is going to sign up just as soon as he turns eighteen next month."

They both watched as the Ford roared up the road to the fence and bounced across the pasture.

"Actually, Bo, I think I'm going to join the army air corps myself," Larry said, staring at the pickup.

The Ford turned through the pasture gate and bumped over the grassy surface. Once again Joe killed the engine and the lights, but the area remained lit with the headlights of the two cars. Meg looked around.

"Who else is here?" she wanted to know. Joe gathered both jackets and opened his door.

"Bo Gene and Larry got here a while ago. Come on, let's go."

"What *is* the hurry anyway?" she protested as she opened her door and climbed out. But Joe slammed her door and grabbed her hand again without answering. He was practically trotting now as Meg continued with weak sounds of disapproval. Framed in the headlights stood a tandem open-cockpit biplane with a swashbuckling Betty painted across the tail.

Larry and Bo both greeted Meg, who nodded and murmured something in return. Joe handed Meg a jacket, then slipped quickly into his own as he moved toward the plane.

"She all ready to go?" Joe asked, even as he was running his hand over the wing and ducking underneath the nose of the plane to check it all out himself.

Larry nodded. "Gassed and ready. We removed the tie-downs and checked the strip for any debris. You got a clear shot for takeoff."

Meg shoved her arms through the jacket, then finger-combed her hair into a hasty ponytail. She must have caught a fleeting grin between Larry and Bo Gene.

"So you two are his partners in crime this morning?"

"Always, Meg. You know better than to ask," Bo answered with another grin.

"It'll be chilly up there. Hurry and zip up your jacket," Joe called to Meg. He helped her onto the wing and into the front cockpit. She settled into her seat while Larry removed the chocks in front of the nose gear.

"What are we doing anyway?" she probed once more.

"I want to show you something." Joe stepped into the cockpit behind her.

"But it's still dark. I won't be able to see a thing." Meg sure wasn't going to make this easy.

"Where's the girl who likes adventure?" he joked.

"She's sitting in this plane ready to take off with you," Meg said wryly as she twisted in her seat to look at him.

"And?" he prompted.

"And . . . you're the best pilot in the sky."

Joe grinned when he saw her lips curve upward and heard the smile in her voice. "You better know it," he answered. "Are you strapped in?"

She nodded and put her thumb up in the air. When Bo and Larry stepped away from the plane, Joe shouted out, "Clear!" The engine roared to life and the prop whirred in front of them. Joe reached up to his neck to feel the St. Christopher's medal Meg had given him after his first solo flight. Satisfied, he maneuvered the plane confidently onto the dirt airstrip.

Once they were airborne, Joe banked west under the clouds that by now were streaked with gold. The ground below disappeared into a huge predawn shadow, and the sky cocooned them with the promise of the coming light. He pulled back on the stick and felt the plane respond, climbing into the canopy above them.

Having Meg with him intensified the familiar elation Joe always felt when airborne. Ethereal light from behind seemed to burst over the tail of the plane and catch in the strands of Meg's ponytail dancing between them in the wind. Joe urged the plane through the thin cotton batting of clouds, at the same time executing a slow, graceful turn to the east that brought them face-to-face with the Creator's daily morning masterpiece. Indescribable peaks of pink and orange splayed out into a blush of beautiful color across the horizon. He could see Meg strain forward in her seat. Her hands came up and gripped the front of the cockpit as if to embrace the beauty before her. This sunrise was their own—for their eyes and their hearts.

Just as the sun itself made its first heart-stopping appearance, he unhooked his harness, leaned forward to touch Meg's shoulder, and spoke loudly into her ear.

"I want you to trust me," he said.

She turned so he could see her profile and nodded confidently. "You know I do!"

Once again, Joe put his hand on Meg's shoulder and raised his voice enough to be heard over the wind and the engine.

"Reach into your left pocket, Meg." She did as he instructed. With wide eyes, already damp with tears from the beauty of the sunrise, she opened the lid of the small black velvet box.

Joe cut the engine on the plane, and the silence was so profound he could hear the quick intake of Meg's breath.

"Meg?"

She unbuckled her harness and turned in the seat to face Joe, now standing behind her, his feet planted firmly on either side of the stick.

"I wanted to share this sunrise with you," he said. "In fact, I want to share all my sunrises with you, Meg. Marry me?"

She looked into his eyes, and he saw her trust, love, joy, and . . . faith.

"Yes!" she said softly. Then her voice rose. "Joe Daley, I'll marry you."

Joe whooped for joy, leaned down to kiss her, then settled back into his seat.

"We're going to see the world together, Meg! Once I'm out of basic and flying for the service, we'll have one nonstop adventure after another. Our life is going to be wonderful. I promise!"

Meg's laughter bubbled up as she slipped the modest solitaire diamond onto her finger.

"I believe you, Joe! I love you!" she called back to him as she held her left hand up in the sunlight to catch its rays.

"I love you too, Meg!" he said before restarting the engine. He was convinced he was the happiest man on earth—*and* above it.

Chapter 2

Summer 1958

A steady breeze outside stirred the leaves and swept them over the roof shingles near an overgrown branch that was beating a rhythmic cadence against the house. The noise seemed magnified, even ominous, in the dark space of the attic. With just the flashlight beam to guide her through the indistinguishable maze of the attic floor, Meg stepped carefully, throwing the circle of light around to make sure she didn't walk into any spider webs. Considering how little she ventured up here, there were plenty to watch out for, along with the mementoes of happier times tucked away in boxes and trunks and old dresser drawers. "Out of sight, out of mind" had been her refrain for too many years.

But she'd received a letter from an old friend that had stirred up memories and propelled her up the dim attic stairs when Joe wasn't around to question her. And now she was about to break her own long-held rule and lift the lid of the large trunk now sitting stoically in the light beam. Meg stood motionless for a while, then sank to her knees, slowly lifted the lid, and trained the flashlight on the remnants of her past.

In what had become a Saturday-night ritual, Meg settled into a corner of a faded couch across from a picture window in the living room. She gazed unseeing out that window and thought about all the nights she had sat here and waited.

Her eyes swept around the dark room—the two armchairs she had reupholstered three years ago, the braided rug her grandmother had given them for a wedding present. The window treatments she had painstakingly made the first year they moved into the house—heavy fabric, pleated and lined that she had found on a clearance table. She had been so proud of those drapes. "Just like the kind you can get through the Sears and Roebuck catalog," her mother had proclaimed. "Imagine that, Meg. I didn't realize you had such a talent for sewing."

The room had started out with so much potential, but now it maybe was a metaphor for her marriage. Not quite broken. But faded and taken for granted. With a sigh, she clicked on the flashlight to illuminate the book that lay in her lap. The cover of the thick volume had the words "Greenville High School 1941" stenciled in gold leaf across a dark green background. Her fingers traced over the words while her thoughts flew back almost twenty years.

She heard the wind pick up outside, that familiar sound that happened as it hit the eaves, rolled under the roof, and swirled the wind chimes on the porch. Meg carefully opened the book as if she were opening Pandora's box—afraid to let the good memories dance into the corners of her life when she had purposely kept them at bay for so many years. However, she discovered, once she turned the first page, it got easier. The flashlight moved slowly across the scrawled messages and senior pictures as she randomly paged back and forth. Familiar faces smiled at her from the black-and-white boxes that had captured them all those years ago. When she came across the *J*s, she ran the beam of the light across her own picture, captioned "Margaret Johnson," where she had written *Meg Daley, Mrs. Joe Daley, Mrs. Margaret Sue Daley,* over and over again in the hopeful handwriting of someone young and in love.

She flipped backward through the pages to find Joe's picture. So handsome. So confident. So full of life. She moved the light to the side where Joe had written his message: *To Meg, my future wife, my future everything. I love you, Joe.* Meg smoothed her hand over a small wrinkle in the glossy paper, one that ran right through Joe's handwriting.

She now started back at the beginning, letting the images from forgotten time parade past her in that ubiquitous alphabetic order. A message here, a small heart there, a picture of a young Larry Ledet, grinning for the camera in his graduation gown, the same one they all wore as they posed for posterity. In the row beneath Larry's picture was Sharon Lester. Meg flashed back to the moment in church six months after graduation when the pastor had told the congregation that Sharon had been killed in a car accident. Meg felt again the pang at the shocking news—she'd been so young, full of dreams . . . just like Joe and she.

Meg looked closely at the picture of Kathryn Mason and wondered if she'd ever made it to Hollywood. Probably not. She turned another page and found the reason she had dug the book out in the first place. A big hand-drawn heart surrounded Norma Meiers' picture on the opposite page. In Norma's familiar handwriting, *Best friends forever!* When Norma moved away from Greenville years ago, the two had tried to fill the void of their friendship with letters. But life had managed to get in the way for both of them, and eventually the correspondence tapered off to Christmas cards and quick scrawled notes about family.

And then, just yesterday, a short note from Norma saying she was coming home to Greenville and she hoped to see Meg in church on Sunday. Meg hoped Norma's visit would be long enough for them to really catch up. Meg had deeply missed her old friend and had wanted to talk to her many times over the years. But now that she was going to have the opportunity, she paused to wonder how much she actually would share with Norma. *Some things are just better left unsaid*, she thought as she turned another page.

There was one of her favorite pictures—Meg and Joe together, smiling as they sat atop a picnic table in front of the high school. Under the picture the words read, "Meg Johnson & Joe Daley. Most adventurous couple." Next to that picture was one of Bo Gene Conroy in a fedora slanted low over his forehead, a pipe in his mouth and his index finger pointed at the camera. The caption: "Bo Gene Conroy. A rising star!"

Meg turned another page and let the beam of light skip across the paper, then back again to focus on another handwritten message in the margin: "Meg—you're the one thing I envy Joe Daley for . . . be happy. Love, Luke." Meg frowned and moved the beam to the left. Luke Ramsey's handsome face stared back at her. His smile had left girls weak at the knees—the same girls who whispered about his Cary Grant eyes, deep, meltingly brown. He could have had any girl at Greenville High, Meg thought, but he dated sporadically, a homecoming dance here, a hayride or church social there. He'd asked Meg out many times, but she had been head over heels in love with Joe Daley, and no matter how many times Luke complimented her or flashed her his high-watt smile, she always refused as politely and firmly as she could. Luke was a flirt and a catch, and he knew it. He had girls speculating endlessly about who would finally capture his heart—and then his family moved away in the middle of their senior year. And nothing was heard of them since.

Restless now, Meg closed the yearbook and moved over to the darkened window. A flash of distant lightning lit the horizon and the looming clouds above it. She waited for the thunder, but the storm was far enough away that she could barely hear the rumble above the wind. Just another Kansas storm. Meg turned back to her vigil.

Chapter 3

Joe Daley was perched on his usual stool at the end of the long bar at Barney's. He sat alone, purposely removing himself from the conversations bandied between proprietor Barney Murphy and his customers as he kept their drinks flowing. For the most part, Joe kept his head down, his eyes on his beer, and his thoughts to himself. When he occasionally did glance up, he was face-to-face with his own reflection in the mirror on the wall behind the bar. An "I Like Ike" bumper sticker plastered on the glass rode the top of his head like a hat. The shaggy-haired man staring back at him from the mirror was all too familiar—flat eyes, dreary expression, shoulders slumped over his glass. Joe rubbed knuckles along his bearded jawline; then his image vanished as Barney stepped between him and his reflected twin.

"Looks like you need another one, Joe," Barney noted jovially. He didn't wait for a reply, just snagged the empty glass to refill from the tap and settled it back in front of Joe. He nodded his thanks and once again gave his mug all his attention.

"Hey, Barney. Got a drought going over here—need somethin' to quench it."

Barney made his way to the middle of the bar, where forty-year-old Abe Gunderson sat on a stool digging through a bowl of peanuts. He was a regular at Barney's, had been for a dozen years, and no one called Abe by his Christian name except maybe his mother. To Barney and everyone else around, he was simply Gunny.

"I'll fix you right up, Gunny," Barney said as he slipped a full mug in front of the man.

"You know what makes you an excellent barkeep, Barney?" Gunny grinned crookedly up at him.

"What's that?" Barney poured more peanuts into the bowl.

"You know the needs of your customers." Gunny picked up his drink, tipped it slightly toward Barney, and studied the amber liquid before downing half the frosty tumbler.

Barney wiped down the bar. "That's my job. To lighten loads and lift spirits. And to keep everyone perched on a barstool as long as I can!" His chuckle didn't quite obscure the seriousness of his statement.

"You do a great public service," Gunny affirmed, punctuated by another long swallow.

Barney grinned. "And you, pal, are on your way to paying my electric bill again this month. I'll keep pouring 'em as long as you keep drinking 'em."

This time Gunny's grin was sardonic. "A man wants to feel like he's contributing to something, Barn, even if it's only to your electric bill."

A small feminine hand knocked on the bar in front of Joe, drawing his gaze up into the kind eyes of Marsha Peterson, Barney's only employee.

"How're you doing tonight, Joe?" she asked.

Joe pressed his lips together in an attempt at a smile. "Made it through another week, Marsha—how about you?"

"I'm good. Busy—but good." She reached under the bar and withdrew a small black apron. Marsha, just shy of her twenty-ninth birthday, tied the apron around her slim waist and tucked short blond hair behind an ear. She smiled at Joe and then made her way toward Barney. "We're down to just one case of Hamm's in the back, Barney."

Gunny raised his glass to Marsha. "To the hour of the wom—wait. To the beer of the—no—to the *woman* of the *hour* who keeps track of the beer!" Gunny finished triumphantly, sloshing his drink on the bar. Barney was there in a second to wipe it dry.

"Such a sentimental tribute, Gunny. Careful, or you'll make me cry," Marsha quipped as she stuffed several books of matches and drink coasters into the pockets of her apron.

Joe drained the last drop in his mug and watched Barney miraculously reappear to refill it. He looked above the bar to the television positioned overhead. In various shades of gray, Chet Huntley and David Brinkley were wrapping up the evening news with their signature sign-off. From his stool, Gunny lifted his glass and chimed in with them.

"Goo' night, David. Goo' night, Chet," Gunny mimicked sloppily.

" 'Goodnight, Irene, goodnight, Irene, I'll see you in my dreams.' " A strong baritone sang out from the middle of the room. Joe turned his attention back to the mirror where he could see Bo Gene Conroy standing next to the pool table in the middle of the room, using a pool cue as his microphone. Stockier than he'd been in high school, Bo Gene's jet black hair, slicked back with Brylcreem and faithfully dyed every four weeks, hung onto his neck. Dressed from head to toe in black, Bo flipped up the collar of his leather jacket and finished his short chorus of "Goodnight, Irene." He bowed to applause from his fellow patrons and then turned back to the pool balls scattered across the green felt. A hometown boy through and through, Bo was also a people magnet. With his booming voice and infectious laugh, he was always the life of the party—the guy who could take a humdrum evening and make it fun.

"This one's for the next round, Ralphie boy!" Joe heard Bo announce. "Eight ball in the corner pocket." It slid neatly in, followed by the white cue ball.

Bo's opponent, Ralph Hutton, still in his overalls from a day's work on his farm, grinned and held his stick in the air. "You scratch—you buy. Good thing you got a good voice, Bo Gene, 'cause you can't shoot pool to save your own sorry hide. Should I rack 'em again?" Ralph offered.

"Three losses is my humiliation limit for one night," Bo said with a little wave to Ralph as he ambled toward the bar and planted himself next to Joe.

"A beer for me and one for Greenville's own Willie Mosconi over there," Bo Gene said to Marsha, motioning with his head toward his pool mate. Nodding toward Joe, he ordered, "And pour another one for the Red Baron of Bugs."

Inwardly Joe recoiled at the nickname but came up with a thin smile. "Thanks, Bo Gene. Next round's on me."

Marsha settled the drinks in front of them. "Let me know if you need anything else, Bo," she offered with a smile before she moved on to her next customer.

"How's the bug business, Joe?" Bo asked, leaning toward his friend.

"Riveting, Bo Gene. There's a new spray that's got only half the drift of the old one."

"Is that good?" Bo asked in all seriousness.

Joe lifted a shoulder. "Not if you're a bug."

Bo chuckled and slapped a hand on the bar. "You're a great straight man, Joe."

"At least I'm great at something. How're sales these days?"

"Everyone needs a vacuum cleaner, my man, and mine sucks up dirt better'n anything west of the Mississippi. What other product can you say that about and it's a good thing?" Bo grinned and struck the counter again. "When're you gonna be a pal and buy a Hoover from me, Joe?"

"A new vacuum isn't high on my list right now, Bo."

"You got money trouble?" Bo asked.

"I've got two kids. Same difference."

"I'll tell you what. When I debut on *American Bandstand* and they pay me all that money, I'll *give* you a Hoover." Bo Gene slid his slightly rotund form off the barstool. "But for now, it's show time!" The man grinned around at his audience as he crossed the floor toward the jukebox in the corner. He dropped a nickel in the slot, and the strains of Elvis Presley's hit "All Shook Up" filled the place. Bo Gene launched into his best Elvis impression, singing the lyrics along with the entertainer at the top of the *Billboard* listings. Bo's hips gyrated along with the music in an exaggerated manner that would have made Ed Sullivan blush. The men in the bar hooted and hollered and egged him on. Marsha stopped serving for a moment and watched Bo's performance with a slight smile. Joe looked from her to Bo in the mirror and watched the way he made "happy" look so easy.

"Look-it that guy go! He should be on *Name That Tune*!" Gunny chortled loudly.

Joe turned his attention from the floor show in the mirror to his drink and willed time to slow down. In fact, he'd be satisfied if it would just stay suspended for a while so he could sit on this stool and pretend his life outside the doors of Barney's didn't exist.

Larry Ledet looked much as he had in high school, save for a few smile lines around his eyes and that classic military-style haircut he'd sported since service days. He drove his '56 Ford

Interceptor patrol car slowly along Main Street. The black-and-white cruiser, in pristine condition, was his pride and joy. He was conscious of the fact that the town of Greenville had spent a lot of money to purchase the car and get their police department up to snuff. Outfitted with standard equipment, the vehicle was right up there in importance with his police badge, and he kept a chamois under the front seat in case he needed to remove any marks while on duty. When he referred to the Ford as "she" or "her," his wife, Anne, teased him about his "other woman." But he knew Anne was proud of his stature in the community, and he took her ribbing in stride. She kept his uniform crisply pressed and made sure the collars and sleeves of his uniform shirts were never frayed or faded.

Larry automatically swiveled his gaze from one side of the street to the other as he drove past the mainstay businesses in town. Most were buttoned up tight for the night. Greenville Hardware, Butterick's Fabric Store, and F. W. Woolworth all boasted summer sale signs in their windows. Viv's Diner, home of the best pie in Kansas, was positioned strategically across from the Regal Cinema and Jeeter's Tastee Freez. It had occupied the same corner since 1935, when owner Roy Jeeter's official opening was to cut the ribbon wrapped around a ten-foot plastic vanilla ice-cream cone in front of his little shop. The cone had long since become a city landmark—and seeing it meant Larry had reached the end of Main. He glanced at his watch, then eased the Interceptor into a U-turn.

Within minutes, he was on his way back down Main to Barney's Tavern. He parked in front of the brick building sitting apart from the other businesses in town and got out of the car, thankful that no one was in sight. He walked quickly to a faded yellow truck parked in front of the bar, lifted the hood, unscrewed the distributor cap, and pulled out the coil wire. A moment later, the distributor cap back in place, he lowered the hood and shoved the coil wire into his pocket.

Larry entered the tavern to a barrage of greetings. He smiled and nodded toward Bo Gene, who was as usual entertaining the crowd. Bo sang out the last few lyrics of "Heartbreak Hotel" and took a bow to enthusiastic applause and somewhat inebriated catcalls. When Bo noticed Larry, he curled his lip just like Elvis. "Thank you, thank you very much," he said in a mock sultry voice.

Larry sauntered past him. "Hey, Bo Gene," he said, "I heard you're singing in church tomorrow morning. You best not be doing any of that gyrating in God's house or the ladies'll run you right out the vestibule doors."

"Don't you worry about it, Larry. Elvis sings gospel in church all the time. If it works for him, it'll work for me." Bo grinned. "I'll keep my swivel in check."

"Are you really singing in church tomorrow, Bo Gene?" Marsha queried, balancing a tray of drinks on her hip as she headed toward a crowded booth.

Bo looked at her and his cheeks flushed red. "Yeah, I'm gonna sing 'Amazing Grace.' "

"I'll look forward to that."

Joe, looking in the mirror behind the bar, shifted his gaze from Bo back to his own reflection. "Can't save a wretch like me." He grinned sardonically.

Larry took the stool right next to Joe as he did every Saturday night. The two were the same age and had known each other all their lives. But Larry's youthful appearance, clear eyes, and stalwart bearing made the contrast between the two men, in the middle of their third decade, very evident. He leaned on the bar and looked at Joe.

"Saw you make your run over the Sorenson place today when I was coming home from Emporia around three this afternoon. You're usually through spraying by that time, aren't you?"

Joe shrugged. "I like to be. Hot air currents and all. But they didn't have anyone out there flagging the field. Chewed up two hours of my time trying to find someone."

"Give me a heads up next time, and I'll flag for you," Larry told him.

Joe propped his elbow on the bar, dropped his chin in his hand, and gave him a long look. "You're the chief of police—not some field-flagger, Lar."

"Got your usual for you, Chief," Barney said as he swiped a damp rag over the bar just in front of Larry.

"Thanks, Barney."

"Put the chief's on my tab, Barn!" Gunny said, listing over the bar like a ship in rough water.

Larry looked from Gunny to Barney. "Have you got his keys?" he leaned over to whisper.

"Yeah. He'll sleep it off in the booth and drive home tomorrow like he usually does." Barney reached below and pulled out a bottle of frosty Hires root beer. He put the soda and a bowl of peanuts in front of Larry.

"Hey, Larry," Barney said, "my nephew Johnny is supposed to write a history paper about a real war hero. Would you mind if he stopped by the station and talked to you?"

"I'm no hero. Just did my part." Larry shifted uncomfortably on the barstool and lowered his gaze. He took a sip of his soda.

"Some of us didn't do no part at all," Joe said, tongue thick. "We're just plain worthless, so you had to pick up our slack—and not just once! You had to do it twice."

"Give it a rest, Joe," Larry murmured, and then looked at Barney. "Tell John to stop by anytime. I'll answer whatever questions he has."

"Thanks a lot, Larry. He's a good kid—wants to be a pilot someday. When I told him you flew in the Second World War and the Korean War, he started a list of questions right then and there."

Joe turned his empty mug over on the bar. Larry laid a casual hand on Joe's shoulder. "Say, Joe, what do you say we call it a night?"

Joe shrugged. "I thought I'd see who's on with Jack Paar tonight." He looked at Barney. "Aren't you going to turn on *The Tonight Show*?"

"It's Saturday. Paar ain't on Saturdays. You know that," Barney replied.

Joe stared at the blank screen of the television, then slowly nodded.

"C'mon, Joe. Let's get going. Anne will be looking for me, and I'm sure Meg's wondering where you are," Larry said, sliding off the stool.

Joe got off his stool on unsteady feet and started toward the door.

"My wife's no fool, Larry. We both know that."

As Larry and Joe stepped outside, Joe paused for a minute to let the world stop spinning and noted with detached interest that it had started to sprinkle. A gusty breeze rocked the metal frame of the sign suspended above Barney's door. With Larry right by his side, Joe weaved his way toward his truck.

Joe's yellow '45 Ford was in about as sorry a state as Joe. The paint had oxidized in the Kansas sun, and the tires were worn nearly bald. While Larry watched, Joe climbed into the cab and tried twice to get the key in the ignition. When he finally succeeded, he turned the key, but the engine didn't even turn over. He lowered his forehead to rest it against the steering wheel.

"Blasted truck," Joe muttered. "Can't ever depend on it."

"Come on before it really starts to come down," Larry said, wiping a few drops of rain from his face. "I'll drive you home and bring you back to get your truck before I go to church in the morning."

Joe hesitated, the defeat of his life all over his face, and then opened the door. He sat with his legs dangling over the running board. "You ever wish you could start over, Larry? Just turn back the clock and catch all the breaks you never saw coming the first time?"

"I don't think there's a man alive who wouldn't wish that," Larry answered, lightly touching Joe's arm. "I've got hot coffee in the patrol car. I even washed out your cup and threw it in the glove box."

Joe climbed out of the truck, and Larry reached behind him and pulled the keys from the ignition. They started toward the Interceptor.

"You gonna tell Barney's nephew all your war stories, Larry?" Joe asked.

"I'll tell him a few. I'll start by telling him about the guy who taught me to fly," Larry answered as he slipped Joe's car keys into his pocket and pulled out his own. "And I'll make sure he spells your name right, Joe."

Chapter 4

A loud thud and thump sounded outside, and the wind chimes rang out loudly. Meg frowned and got to her feet, shoved the yearbook under the couch cushion, and made her way to the window in time to see two aluminum lawn chairs tumble across her porch and down the steps. She took note of the scattered flats of flowers she had intended to plant. Then the braided rug near the front door slid across the porch, following the path of the webbed lawn chairs.

Meg decided to corral the chairs and rug—not the first time she'd had to chase down porch furniture because of blustery weather. This was Kansas, after all. She pulled open the front door and was hit by a gust of wind carrying the smell of rain and wet dust. Instinctively she ducked her head into the wind, squinting against the inevitable loose dirt that would sting her eyes if she wasn't careful. She thought back to the last weather report she'd heard on the radio around suppertime. Had they mentioned thunderstorms? She couldn't remember—had been too busy with her two kids to really pay attention.

The wind carried the first fat splashes of rain onto her in spite of the roof hanging over the porch. She brushed them off her face as a flash of lightning gave her a brief glimpse of those errant chairs rolling across the yard. She paused on the porch just long enough to consider chasing them. A little rain wouldn't hurt her, and those chairs were only two years old. She decided to brave it, although the rain was coming down harder now. But then another strobe of lightning had her squinting into the distance. The light show had become incredible. From the inside out, gray thunderheads against the black sky were illuminated with jagged bolts of lightning that danced and streamed from heaven to earth like blazing gold ribbons. The electric display lit the sky for seconds at a time, enough for Meg to see something that sent a vibration of fear straight down her spine. A black funnel had dropped from the fat swath of gray clouds, and it seemed to dip and curve and move in concert with the whine of the wind.

She quickly turned to get inside to her sleeping children. And then the wind abruptly stopped, leaving only the smattering of raindrops hitting the wooden porch. *The calm before the storm*, she thought as she nearly yanked the door off its hinges and ran toward the stairs. She heard the wind come back with a vengeance—redoubling its efforts against her house. She thought of Joe, briefly—a flash as quick as the lightning. Had he seen the storm, heard any kind of warning on the radio?

She took the stairs two at a time to get to the second floor, where her children slumbered. "Danny! Get up!" she yelled as she gave a quick rap on his bedroom door. Fifteen-year-old Danny stepped into the hallway just as Meg disappeared into another bedroom—only to reappear moments later tugging on the hand of nine-year-old Christy.

"We need to get to the storm cellar," she said to both kids as she made her way to the stairs, trying to keep her voice matter-of-fact. Christy sleepily lagged behind and Meg pulled her forward, even as she used her other hand to nudge Danny ahead of her.

"Hurry up, kids—I don't know how much time—"

"Is it a tornado?" Christy asked as she quickened her steps. Meg could hear the hint of fear in Christy's voice and looked down at her daughter's bare feet. *No time for shoes. . . .*

"Yes."

"Is Dad home?" Danny asked.

"No," she said briefly, "not yet."

"Does he have a storm cellar at his meeting place?" Christy asked. More fear now. "Will he be okay?"

Meg hustled them down the stairs. "He'll be fine." She heard the nerves in her own voice, felt the breathy panic that was creeping over her as they hurried across the living room. She saw her flashlight—still on—lying on the couch and grabbed it. Winded by nerves and fear, she dragged in a deep breath and answered, "Daddy knows what to do in case of a tornado."

The wind and rain whipped at them as they ran out the front door and down the porch steps without pausing. The beam of her flashlight bounced over the grass, and Meg heard the door slam behind them as a gust caught it. Had it slammed open or shut? Was it still in one piece? She did not risk a look over her shoulder.

Lightning laced the sky and thunder chimed in just in case they weren't serious enough about getting to safety. Meg scooped Christy into her arms and ran after Danny. He now was leading the way to the double wooden doors that angled into a hump in the earth beside the house. He pulled on the doors, struggling to open them against the heightening wind.

"Get in!" he yelled. Meg pressed the flashlight into Christy's hand, and the little girl scrambled down the steps into the dark.

Meg helped Danny with the doors, and together they pulled them shut against the storm.

"Mommy?" Christy's voice came from below as Meg picked her way downward with Danny on her heels.

"Right here, sweetie," she said as she stepped onto the hard-packed dirt floor.

"My light's going away," Christy said, and as if to punctuate her statement, the flashlight died with its fragile circle of light. "Mom?"

"Hold on, squirt," Danny said. In a moment he switched on the flashlight they kept in the cellar. Meg cast a quick glance at Danny and at the shelves behind him. Were there extra batteries? Probably not. She had asked Joe to replace them the last time they had been down here. *I should have done it myself. . . .*

"Light the lamp too, okay, Danny?" Christy said fretfully. "It's creepy down here."

Danny threw the light onto the opposite wall, where Mason jars stretched across more wooden shelves. Dill pickles, jams and jellies, tomatoes, relish, and green beans were lined up neatly in rows, labeled and dated in Meg's precise handwriting. Danny plucked a small hurricane-style oil lamp from a shelf along with a box of matches. In a moment, the subterranean room glowed. Meg hunkered down along a wall and stretched her legs out in front of her.

"Come on. Sit here with me," she invited. Christy plunked down on one side of her, Danny on the other. They heard the shifting wind beat on the cellar doors, trembling and shuddering and threatening to fly open. Meg sent a ragged prayer toward heaven as she simultaneously worried about her mom and Joe's folks—and Joe. *Where is he right now?*

The rain made a steady drumming sound on the hood of the patrol car as Larry motored past the outskirts of town. He glanced over at Joe leaning heavily against the passenger door, his coffee cup loosely balanced on his lap.

Larry judged the wind to be about thirty knots or so—not terrible, but enough to feel inside the patrol car. He had a healthy caution about Kansas weather. He'd lived through two wars, faced the enemy, flown in adverse conditions, and landed with a blown nose gear once. He wasn't scared of many things at this stage in his life, but he was mighty respectful of tornadoes. They were indiscriminate in their wrath, and he'd heard enough stories over the years about families devastated by nature to never take subtle weather changes lightly. He pressed down on the gas pedal to step up the speed. He heard Joe curse under his breath as he took a curve rather fast—figured Joe had spilled his hot coffee . . . again.

"You hear any weather forecast today?" Larry asked as he reached for the volume on his police radio.

"What's to hear? Hot, humid, maybe some wind." Joe stared out the windshield. "I predict rain," then snorted at his own joke.

"Weather like this could spawn a twister," Larry said soberly.

"Not that likely at night," Joe said, a touch of lucidity returning as he shifted in place and looked out the window again.

"Not likely—but possible," Larry observed as he watched the trees sway in the wind.

By the time Larry made the turn onto Joe's rural road on the edge of Greenville, the rain had stopped and the wind had calmed. The gravel crunched under the tires as the car pulled to a stop in Joe's driveway. With the car idling, they both looked at the dark windows of the house, Joe's signal from Meg it was okay for him to come in—the kids were asleep. Though they'd never discussed it, Larry knew the message too. He had spent many a Saturday night pouring Joe another cup of coffee in the front seat of the cruiser if a light happened to be on in the house when they pulled up.

In spite of the dark house, Joe lingered.

Larry looked at him. "Need help?"

"No." Joe didn't move.

Larry, usually a patient man, was anxious to get home. "I'm thinking I should get going and check on Anne and Emmy," Larry finally said. "Wind might have caused some damage at my place."

Joe nodded slowly. "Might have," he mumbled as he struggled with the door handle. "Thanks for the ride."

Larry watched Joe's unsteady gait across the yard toward the house and then backed up the drive.

Joe was surprised, but not disappointed, that Meg wasn't at her post in the living room. *Good*, he thought. *One less conversation I'll have to have.* He made his way up the stairs, hand gripping the banister for support, shushing himself when he stepped too hard on the tread that groaned under his weight. In his bedroom, he glanced at the bed and took a minute to realize it was still made. *Where's Meg?*

"Must a' missed her," he muttered as he sat down heavily on the bed and struggled to get his work boots off. Toeing the heel of one boot, he pushed hard against the other but couldn't budge it.

"Meg!" he hissed in frustration. "Meg!" A little louder now.

Wearing one boot, he made his way out into the hallway and saw that Danny's bedroom door was open. He looked in—no Danny. He walked unsteadily to Christy's room. He could tell she'd been in bed—but the room was empty. His mouth felt dry, throat parched. His nerves felt all notched up in spite of the beer buzz he still had going. *Whole families don't just . . .*

disappear. He made his way back down the dark stairs. Going down was definitely harder than going up, he decided. Longer way to fall.

The front door opened and the night seemed to give back his family. Meg had an arm firmly wrapped around Christy, who stood wet and shivering in her nightgown. Without warning, the girl flipped on a lamp near the door, and Joe stood at the bottom of the steps and blinked against the light.

"Daddy! You're home!" Christy said and launched herself at him. Joe stumbled back but recovered his footing as he looked over the top of her head to find Meg assessing him.

"We were in the storm cellar, Dad. Mommy saw a tornado!" Christy's words tumbled over each other. "A tornado was coming at us but missed us, I think. Don't you think? Did you see it? Did you hear the wind? Did you have a storm cellar at your meeting?"

Joe opened his mouth . . . but couldn't find the right answer. His head was swimming, and the room seemed to float and shrink around him.

Danny walked toward him, his mouth a thin line of anger. "Where's your other boot, Dad?"

Joe looked down at his stocking foot—hole at the big toe, no less. "Uh, um, upstairs."

Danny flicked a glance at his feet again, then whirled and started up the stairs.

"Good night," he threw over his shoulder.

"Thanks for your help, honey," Meg answered Danny as she disengaged Christy's arms from around Joe's waist.

"Welcome" was the sarcastic reply that drifted down the stairs—then a firmly closed door.

"C'mon, sweet pea. Let's get you into a dry nightgown and back to bed. Tell Dad good-night."

" 'Night, Daddy. I'm glad you're fine," Christy said as she ran up the stairs. Joe had to turn away when Meg looked at him. He studied the hole in his sock.

"I'll get Christy settled," she said. "Are you okay to . . . ?" Her voice trailed off, and it was her turn to look away.

"Yeah. Fine," he said and watched as she trudged up the steps after their daughter.

Joe tossed his shirt in the general direction of the bedroom chair and crossed to the dresser he and Meg had bought right after they married. The wood grain across the top was scratched from years of loose change and other things he managed to cart home in his pockets. He shifted slightly on his feet and grabbed the top edge, trying to maintain his balance, then carefully lifted a long chain with the medallion from around his neck.

Sober or not, he could clearly recall the day Meg had given it to him, her face flushed with love and pride after he'd soloed. *"It's a St. Christopher's medal, Joe—he's the patron saint of travel safety."* He also remembered her arms around his neck as she explained its meaning, the trust in her eyes that was the true gift.

With a finesse that belied his inebriated state, Joe now placed the medal down on the dresser in front of a picture of Meg in her wedding gown. He didn't actually look at the photograph, but he could remember the feel of the gown's smooth satin, the smile for him that made the dress her own, though it was a family heirloom that had graced several wedding ceremonies.

The chain curled haphazardly, and he took the time to straighten it out. Although he'd never admit it about himself, Joe knew most pilots had some superstitions. He knew Larry had never flown a combat mission without the silver dollar his granddad had given him, tucked into his sock, and Chip

Armstrong always tapped the tail of his Kaydet aircraft three times before he'd climb into the cockpit. His own dad had worn the same leather jacket on every mission he'd ever flown—even after he'd worn a hole through the elbow and the zipper had rusted into immobility.

Joe gave a last, satisfied glance at the medal and slowly made his way to the bed. He sat down on the edge, still wearing one boot, and wondered if his medal would have gotten him through the war. *Would have been nice to know. . . .*

Chapter 5

Joe knew he was destined for this moment. This day belonged to him, and he'd known it in his gut from the time he'd slipped his medal over his head, climbed into the cockpit, and felt the main wheels leave the solid world behind. The sensation of flight enveloped him with a familiar and comfortable ease. He looked down at the expanse of water below and remembered that first time. . . .

. . . The feeling of soaring surrounded little Joe, and he felt at home. It was so familiar, so comfortable—so right.

His dad's voice was in his ear. "Be cocky—but not careless, son. Confident—but never cavalier. Be brave, Joey—but don't be foolish enough to let go of your fear. . . ."

Joe shook his head once and felt the girth of the stick in his gloved hand. He shifted to move the parachute strapped to his back away from his left shoulder blade. The wings of his F4U Corsair sliced through ash gray clouds hanging low over the steel blue Pacific. The steady, monotonous drone of the aircraft's engine reassured him that he'd make it back to the carrier in one piece. He looked out at the wings riddled with bullet holes, then pushed scratched goggles up onto his helmet as he scanned for the enemy. He swiveled from side to side, eyes peeled for the familiar but deadly red circles on the wings of the Japanese Zeros that were hunting him as fervently as he was hunting them.

And then he spotted them—a foursome of Zeros high and to his right. He could tell they hadn't spotted him yet, and he executed a forty-five-degree turn and plunged down toward the ocean rolling below him. He needed the element of surprise if he was going to take on all four. He felt the belly of his plane all but skim the crests of the waves that stretched toward him, then got the Zeros back in his sights. He started to climb behind them—a sneak attack if he was lucky. Suddenly he felt the staccato of bullets behind him and whipped around to see a Zero on his tail. There were five!

Joe pulled back on the stick and scrambled upward, and the formation of the four Zeros broke ranks and scattered like birds in the wind. Divide and conquer. Joe banked steeply west as the Zero on his tail took aim and ended up spattering one of his own wingmen with machine-gun fire. Joe watched the Zero burst into flames before it fell into the water. Another Zero was on him again—more vengeance this time, he could tell. Joe dove toward the ocean in his F4U, looped back around, and came up behind another enemy aircraft. He triggered a round of bullets like hail on a steel-plated drum.

He leveled off only to find two of the Zeros double-teaming him. They were attacking from either side; they also had a Zero below him. He had nowhere to go but up. He forced himself to stay the course—let the planes come to him, pray the bullets would miss their mark. He waited . . . waited . . . then yanked the stick back so hard he worried briefly it had come off in his hand. He sent the Corsair heavenward and heard the explosion below as the planes collided. By Joe's count there was one Zero left. And it looked like its Japanese pilot had decided to duck out of this one. Joe took off after him, his adrenaline pumping, immortality fixed in his mind. The hunted had become the hunter. With the Zero dead ahead, Joe picked his moment—fired, and sent his enemy into the sea to join the rest of them.

Joe shouted along with the splash and felt the rush of victory. The sun broke through the clouds, creating a glare that bounced off the glass of the cockpit. He averted his eyes, then looked up into the azure above. Not a cloud to be seen. The engine of the Corsair started to sound more like the thrumming beat of a snare drum in a victory parade.

Joe felt his chest swell with pride as he looked out at the citizens of Greenville lining Main Street to welcome him home. American flags waved from the hands of every man, woman, and child as they cheered him, the returning hero. He saw three lovely young women standing on the sidewalk making a special effort to show Joe how much they admired him. A tall redhead pursed perfectly painted red lips and blew him a kiss; a lovely brunette waved and pressed her hand over her heart when he looked at her; a slender blonde gave him an exaggerated wink and smile.

He was *so happy* as he sat high on the top of the backseat in the convertible that cruised slowly down the street. He could feel the cool leather of the seat beneath his hand, the warm sun on his face. He sniffed at the air and smelled hot dogs and cotton candy. He tapped his foot in time to "The Star-Spangled Banner" played perfectly by the Greenville High School Marching Band as they stepped in unison in front of him. The drum major thrust his long silver mace up and down, over his head, and Joe watched it bob to the cadence of the drums.

Robby, behind the wheel of the red convertible, turned in his seat with a grin.

"Go for the glory, Joe!"

His mom and dad walked on either side of the car, waving to the good folks of Greenville. His dad, wearing his old navy uniform, looked over at him with unmistakable pride in his eyes. His mom seemed to be enjoying the momentary spotlight reflected from her son. She wore her best pillbox hat and waved a white-gloved hand to the women she knew from church. He looked at Meg, sitting almost at his feet in the backseat of the car, and she was wearing his St. Christopher's medal around her neck. Her blond hair blew back away from her face as she smiled up at him with pride and love.

"I love you, Joe. You're my hero. You're everyone's hero!" He could see her lips form the words, though he could not hear them. He spotted Christy and Danny standing in the crowd at the edge of the street with their friends.

"Hey, Dad! That's my dad! He's an ace! My dad's an ace!" Danny shouted. Christy waved and shouted right along with him. "Take me in your arrow plane, Daddy! Let's go for a ride through the clouds!"

Larry was there next to Anne. He waved his American flag with one hand and gave a big thumbs-up with the other.

Joe was staggered by his own sense of happiness as confetti rained down. He watched the bits and pieces of colored paper swirl in the air in front of him, dancing across Meg's hair, settling on the shoulders of her light blue dress, fluttering past him as they covered the white leather seats of the Cadillac. He looked again at the people on the streets—waving their flags, chanting his name, hands locked over their heads in the universal sign that he was the winner of the fight—and he relished every moment.

Joe wanted to hang on to the dream even as he surrendered to reality. He felt as if he had pennies sitting on his eyelids. He opened them slowly and tried to focus. In spite of the curtains at the window, the sun lit the room with a gauzy haze, suspending dust particles over the bed. As usual, the remnants of his frequent dream reminded him once again of his failures in life.

He took a mental inventory: his head throbbed, his right arm was asleep, and his throat was as dry as parchment paper. All in all, typical for a Sunday morning. Gingerly he sat on the edge of the bed to test the depth of his headache and balance and then listened for any stirrings downstairs. All was quiet in the house, but his body screamed for two things: Bayer aspirin and strong coffee.

Joe was almost to the kitchen when he heard Christy giggle. The sound literally stopped him in his tracks. He'd thought he was alone in the house, that Meg and the kids had already left for church. A moment of panic seized him. What if they weren't going this morning? He wanted—no—he *needed* the time alone. He needed to ease into the day without the pointless conversation and veiled incriminating looks from his family. He thought briefly about heading back to the bedroom, crawling under the quilt, and pretending he was still asleep. But he really needed that aspirin, and he could smell the coffee. Meg made great coffee.

He stepped into the doorway of the kitchen. Meg and the kids were at the round maple table, finishing breakfast. He was momentarily surprised that this was his family. Meg, in a pretty dress Joe knew she'd made herself, looked much like she did when he married her. She tucked a strand of that long blond hair behind her ear as she listened intently to something Christy was saying. Danny was dressed in his best white shirt. Hunched over his plate, he shoveled in his breakfast as if someone were going to snatch it away. *He looks so much like Robert.* Joe banished the thought as Danny looked up and noticed him.

"Morning," Danny mumbled.

Joe cleared his throat, then winced at the sound in his own head. "Morning."

"Good morning," Meg echoed as Christy crossed the kitchen to hug Joe.

"Guess what, Daddy?" Christy asked.

He slowly shook his head, then thought better of it as the room tilted. And it was too early for riddles. "Don't know."

"I found one of our porch chairs sitting on the side of the road like someone put it there to watch a parade," she said. "But I couldn't find the other one."

Right. There was a storm. He let his arm slide around Christy's shoulders as she wound her arms around his waist. He had a fleeting thought that her hair smelled like Meg's—Breck shampoo.

"Any damage?" he wondered.

"Not that I could see," Meg replied as she finished off the rest of her juice.

"If you hurry, Daddy, you can go to church with us," Christy invited hopefully as she gazed up at him.

For a second, Joe felt the misplaced optimism of his family hang in the air. As if he might actually agree to go—when everyone knew he wouldn't.

But before Joe could answer, Meg jumped up and started clearing the table.

"We have to leave before he can get ready, honey. Maybe Dad will be able to come with us next Sunday."

Joe could feel her gaze on him. He was acutely aware, in the bright light of morning, of how he looked. Disheveled hair, yesterday's T-shirt, bloodshot eyes. His hand flew to his head when the phone on the wall rang, two long rings followed by one short. The pattern started again, and he closed his eyes against the shrill sound.

"That's our ring, Daddy. Aren't you going to answer it?" Christy asked.

Joe looked over at Meg, who was stacking the dishes in the sink. "Mom can get it," he said.

"It's awfully early on Sunday for someone to be calling," Meg mused as she made her way to the phone. Listening to her end of the conversation, Joe could tell his mother was on the other end of the line. He immediately tuned out and thought about his original objective—aspirin and coffee.

"My teacher told us in some big cities, houses don't have to share. Each family gets their own phone number," Christy was saying. "Do you think that'll ever happen here in Greenville, Daddy?"

"I wouldn't hold my breath," Joe said. He was moving carefully across the kitchen for the aspirin bottle Meg had pulled from the cupboard and put next to the stove and the coffeepot. He was just pouring himself a cup when Meg hung up the phone.

"Your mom says your dad's cold has gotten worse," she reported. "Those summer colds seem to hang on forever. Anyway, they aren't going to church this morning, but she needs the humidifier they loaned us when Christy had that bad cough last month."

Joe didn't know what any of this had to do with him—and didn't care. He popped the tablets into his mouth and washed them down with coffee.

"Is Larry taking you to pick up the truck this morning before he goes to church?"

You know he is, he thought. *He always does.* "Yeah, he is," Joe said, trying to sound cooperative while ignoring the throbbing at his temples.

"Good. Then maybe you can take the humidifier over to your parents after that."

My parents? This morning? No way.

"Can't you just drop it off on your way?" he asked, trying to keep his voice from sounding whiny.

Meg gathered up her gloves and handbag from the kitchen counter. "I'm going to be a greeter this morning, so I'll need to be there early."

Nicely played. Ding. Round one. Meg.

"Or if you prefer, I'll take it over to them, and you can take the kids to church and hand out the bulletins," she offered without looking at him. But he could see the expression on her face anyway.

Ding. And round two goes to Meg.

"I'll take 'em the humidifier," he said flatly.

"Good. It's in the upstairs hall closet. Come on, kids. We've got to get going. Make sure you turn the burner off when you're done with the coffee," she said over her shoulder.

Joe waited for them to go out the kitchen door, then went to the window and watched as Meg opened the door to a worn Bel Air he had accepted as payment for some spraying he'd done a few years back. As the three of them climbed into the vehicle, Joe had the unbidden thought that the car had just devoured his family. *Devoured*—one of Christy's "look-it-up words." He glanced at the table and pictured her sitting there with Meg a few days ago, their two blond heads together over a dictionary. Meg was helping their avid little reader find words she'd read that she didn't understand.

Christy had her finger on a word in the book and grinned up at him. "I'll bet you can't spell *superfluous,* Dad."

Danny had just walked into the kitchen to scavenge the contents of the Frigidaire, as he did most evenings after dinner. "I'll bet you don't know what it means, squirt," Danny teased, ruffling her hair as he passed.

"Yes I do. It says right here it means 'not essential and not required,'" Christy shot back triumphantly.

Joe watched out the window as the car pulled away from the house, taking away his wife and children. He reached for the bottle of Bayer, shook out two more aspirin, and thought, *I'm superfluous.*

Pastor Don Anderson stood behind the pulpit at Greenville Community Church and smiled at the congregation.

"And now Bo Gene Conroy is going to bless us with his favorite hymn, 'Amazing Grace.'" Meg, with Christy and Danny on one side of her and her mother on the other, watched as Bo slid out of a pew and made his way to the front of the church. He struggled to button the suit coat he wore, pulling the jacket snug across his middle.

Meg's mom leaned over and whispered, "That suit could use a good pressing. Bo Gene needs a wife."

Meg nodded, knowing it wouldn't do any good to argue with her mother. Sylvia was a worrier. She worried about Meg and her family. She worried about her neighbors and casual acquaintances. She worried about what people thought and what kind of appearance she kept. *And what kind of appearance her daughter keeps. It's gotten worse since Dad passed away*, Meg thought, then turned once more to look over the people gathered in the church. She still hadn't seen Norma and hoped something hadn't happened to make her change her plans.

Her mother nudged her. "Quit fidgeting," she said quietly. Meg sighed and turned to face the front as Bo Gene positioned himself in front of the congregants. He slipped a finger into the collar of his white button-down shirt to pull it away from his neck, then looked at Clara Jenkins at the organ and gave her a little nod.

But as soon as Clara struck the first chord for the hymn, everyone in the church knew their soloist was in trouble. He recoiled at the volume of the organ, and before she had completed the introduction, he croaked out the first word of the well-known hymn—which suddenly seemed to have a double meaning. Meg tried to keep her face expressionless as she thought it would be *amazing* if Bo could get through the song.

Larry was seated between his wife, Anne, and thirteen-year-old daughter, Emmy, in the pew ahead. As Bo sang the first line, " 'Amazing grace, how sweet the sound,' " Meg watched Larry slip his arm around Anne and whisper in her ear, "I beg to differ." Both women looked down at the same time to cover their smiles.

" ' 'Twas grace that taught my heart to fear, and grace my fears relieved,' " Bo warbled as the door to the sanctuary opened.

Meg turned in the pew to see Norma Meiers make her way into the church with three boys following behind her. *She has children? Why didn't I know that? They look to be about Danny's age.* When Norma settled into a pew a few rows behind her, Meg caught her eye and beamed a smile in her direction. Norma's answering smile was warm and happy.

Christy leaned over and poked Meg's arm. "Who is that, Mom?"

"She was my best friend all through school," Meg whispered back. She turned her attention back to Bo as he battled on with the hymn. At the organ, Clara seemed to be in as much pain as Bo.

" 'When we've been there ten thousand years, bright shining as the—uh, sun.' " Bo strained to hit the high note, and his face contorted along with his pitch. Clara suddenly picked up the tempo, and Bo was singing "Amazing Grace" in double time. When he finished the hymn, the collective sigh of relief from the congregation followed him back to his seat.

Pastor Don took the podium again and looked out at the familiar faces. The membership wasn't large, but it was faithful. "Thank you, Bo," he said with genuine warmth as he looked at the red-faced man. "That song was written by a man, a former slave trader, who knew firsthand what that amazing grace meant.

That grace is what all of us here need today." He looked around the assembly once more.

"Today I want to talk to you about possibilities," he began. "A man getting swallowed up and living in the belly of a whale *possibilities*. The Lord talking through a donkey *possibilities*. The parting of a sea *possibilities*. A man wrestling with an angel *possibilities*. What limits are you putting on God? What possibilities are you open to this morning?" he asked.

Meg looked down at her wedding ring and adjusted the diamond so that it was centered on her finger.

Chapter 6

Joe drove the truck along County Road 7, intent on getting his errand done so he could get home and have some time alone before Meg and the kids got back from church. Lucky for him they usually stayed after the service to talk to the other faithful members of the flock. That gave him three whole hours every Sunday to be totally on his own—three and a half if Pastor Anderson became inspired. No need to avoid eye contact with Meg, respond to Christy's exuberance, or deal with Danny's bewilderment and anger.

Ten minutes later, Joe made the turn from the asphalt to the dirt road leading to his childhood home. Now he drove slowly along the narrow road, reluctant to face his mother and the questions he knew he'd see in her eyes.

The trees that lined either side of the drive were heavy with foliage and dipped in the center, leaving only a strip of sunlight that fell across the hood of his truck, seeming to split it in two. *So many memories along this shady lane. Don't think about them. There's no point in rehashing the past.* But he couldn't help it. He stared out the windshield in the present but saw two boys from the past running as fast as they could, black PF Flyers slapping at the dirt as they raced to the biggest and oldest tree. "Last one to the big tree is a rotten egg, Joey!" Thirteen-year-old Robert slapped its trunk and turned with a grin to watch his ten-year-old brother dive for the same tree, skinning the palm of his hand in the process. "You're never gonna beat me, Joe. Never, ever. I'm the big brother and you're always gonna be slower. It's just how it is." Chest heaving, the little boy blew on his injured palm to try to cool the burning sensation of torn skin. Robert clapped him on the back. "Let's call it a war wound—okay? Come on—maybe Ma'll have some cookies just out of the oven—for a rotten egg like you!"

The boys turned back to the road toward a large farmhouse. "I'm gonna beat you someday, Robby. You just wait and see."

Robert had laughed. "Not unless I'm planted six feet under, little brother."

The strip of sunlight that had been riding the hood of Joe's truck widened and then disappeared completely as he left the cover of the trees. The two-story farmhouse sat a hundred yards away. Joe thought it looked forlorn and forgotten. Almost as if the house knew it had outlasted its reason for being. *When was the last time I was here? Two months ago—three? Paint's peeling on the shutters. Dad's never let that happen before. I hope he's in bed so I don't have to see him.* Then the ever-present guilt climbed on his shoulder and whispered in his ear.

He parked the truck in the same spot he had parked as a teenager and looked up at the American flag that flew on the flagpole in front of the house, the flag his dad had been given when he retired from the United States Congress. The house might look worn down, but his dad always treated the flag with reverence and made sure it was in pristine condition. Humidifier under his arm, Joe made his way to the screened-in porch. After reaching his hand to pull open the door, he had second thoughts and knocked. *Strange to knock on the door of a place where I lived for over half of my life. Just open it and go in. They're my parents, for crying out loud. Why is this always so uncomfortable?*

Lois Daley pulled open the door and her eyes widened. "Joe! What a surprise! A nice one." She stepped back so he could enter. "You know you never have to knock on this door. It's your home too," she added, her tone warm.

"Hi, Mom." Joe stepped inside and gave her a hug with his free arm. He was always surprised that she seemed so small to him now. Small and somehow fragile. He stepped back and took in her appearance. Lois Daley had been what his dad liked to call "a real looker." Even now, at sixty-five, she was an attractive woman. She wore her soft gray hair—no Lady Clairol for her—in a short bob. Her dress reminded him of the ones she wore while he was growing up—complete with apron and its blue gingham pockets.

He saw how happy she was to see him and felt that immediate surge of guilt that he didn't make the effort more often. It wasn't his mother he resolutely avoided—it was his father. So his mom suffered because of the strange but insurmountable wall between Harold Daley and his son.

Joe automatically wiped his feet on the rug in the mudroom before he walked into the kitchen, relieved when he looked around and determined that his father wasn't anywhere in sight.

"I told Meg she could bring that humidifier by after church—but this is so much better because I get to see you," his mother said with a pat on his arm.

After church, huh? Ding. Meg wins round three, and I didn't even know I was still in the ring.

"Your dad's in bed," she explained. "You know how ornery he can be when he's sick. I've practically had to hog-tie him to the bedframe. He's not very good at resting."

"No—he never has been."

Joe could feel her looking at him with a mother's critical eye. He was acutely aware of his haggard appearance and her worried expression.

"How's everything?" she asked.

Joe looked over the top of her head when he answered, his eyes looking everywhere but into those all-knowing eyes.

"Fine, Mom. Everything's fine. Business is pretty good right now. I'm putting in a lot of hours, but I'm not complaining." He knew he was talking too fast, but anything to keep his mother on safe subjects.

"That's wise. I'm not sure the good Lord has much patience with complainers," she said, softening her comment with a smile. She gestured to the humidifier Joe had placed on the table.

"I hate to ask, but could you carry that upstairs to the bedroom for me? The arthritis in my knee is starting to give me fits, and I don't climb the stairs unless I have to."

"He might be sleeping. I don't want to bother him."

"Your father asleep during the day? Not a chance," she declared as she went to the counter and picked up a glass of prune juice.

"If you can manage both, bring this to him as well, and make sure he drinks the whole thing." Joe knew better than to argue. Besides, she asked so little of him. He picked up the humidifier and she handed him the glass.

Joe stopped at the threshold to his parents' bedroom. It had been years since he'd been in this room, but nothing had changed. His graduation picture was on the wall above the bed next to a picture of Robert in his navy uniform. The old oak bureau held a collage of pictures—Meg and Joe on their wedding day, a baby picture of Christy, and one of Danny as a toddler. A glass jar filled with loose change just like when he was growing up. "*You've done your chores all week long, Joe. I'm proud of how hard you worked. Go get your allowance from the money jar,"* his dad would tell him. Joe worked hard for the allowance money, but not because he wanted to buy anything. *I just wanted to make him proud.*

His dad stood at the window with his back toward the door, wearing a blue flannel bathrobe that looked too warm for the July morning. Just seeing his dad in the room triggered a parade of memories—crawling into that four-poster when he'd had a bad dream; his dad showing him how to tie his first necktie; his mom placing the clay pot he'd made for her on the dresser; hiding under the bed after Robert found out Joe lost his best baseball mitt.

Robby dropped to his knees, reached under the bed ready to haul me out and pound me a good one—and then Dad came in and stopped him. "Simmer down, son. You don't hit your little brother no matter what he's done. Joe will do your chores for a week. That's the end of it." And it was. The old man's word was law.

Joe took a moment to study his father. *He used to be taller—didn't he?* His gray hair looked thinner, his shoulders rounding in the way of the aged. Joe was startled when his dad addressed him, even though he hadn't turned from the window.

"I saw you drive up," he said in a voice husky from a bad cold. "That old Ford looks like it's running pretty good."

"It has good days and bad days," Joe said as he crossed into the room. "Kind of like me." Harold turned as Joe put the humidifier down on the dresser, then moved forward a few more feet and held out the glass of juice.

"Mom sent this up for you. I'm supposed to make sure you drink it."

"I've been married to your mother for forty-two years, and I've never been able to convince her I don't like prune juice. She thinks it cures everything from the common cold to a bellyache." He shuddered but took the glass with a wry grin.

Joe shifted uncomfortably and rocked back and forth on the balls of his feet. *It shouldn't be this hard to find things to say to my own father. . . .*

Harold turned back to look out the window.

"I've been watching a blue jay for the last hour. She's making a nest in the branches of the old maple," he said, "the one Robby ran into with the tractor. Remember that?"

"I remember," Joe answered quietly.

"I saw him do that, you know. Right from this very window. I heard the tractor coming up the lane and looked out in time to see him swerve to miss a rabbit and go right into the tree." He kept his gaze on something beyond the window and took a sip. "I watched you from this window the morning you pushed the truck down the lane to go propose to Meg, and I was looking out this window when the government car pulled up with the navy chaplain to tell us that Robby had been shot down. I ran down the stairs and tried to get to the door before your mother—but she beat me to it." His dad's voice had grown more gravelly as he talked.

Joe felt his heart tighten at his brother's name. *As usual I don't know what to say. I'm sorrier than I could ever tell him that Robert died—even more, that he died and I'm still here. I'm sorry the navy thought I was a reject and wouldn't let me in. I'm sorry I'm such a disappointment, Dad. Sorry, sorry, sorry!*

Harold walked away from the window and sat down on the edge of his bed.

"You're staying busy these days?" he asked.

"Yes, sir. I picked up a couple extra farms that Chip Anderson didn't want. He'd rather play in the sky than work the crops. He only dusts to support his flying habit."

"Still finds the joy in the flight, does he?"

"He's young. I guess he does," Joe answered.

"How about you? You still find any joy in the flight?" his dad asked quietly.

Joe looked beyond his dad and saw a bird glide past the window. He glanced at his watch. "I'd better get going."

"Thanks for bringing the humidifier over." Harold drained the juice in one long swallow. With a grimace, he handed Joe the empty glass. "Take this back to your mom."

"Why do you drink it if you hate it so much?" Joe asked inexplicably.

"Your mother expects me to drink it, and I can't bear to disappoint the people I love," he said without looking at him.

You mean the way I do—every day—every way. We can't all be you, Dad. We can't all be Robby. Some of us are just plain . . . disappointments.

With the Sunday service over, the fellowship hall filled up with those who loved being part of the family of God and those who attended church merely as a means to an end—for the delicious coffee cake that was served immediately following the benediction or for the community status that churchgoing provided. While Christy and Danny joined others in line at the serving table, Meg was part of a group of women huddled around Norma.

"When did you get back into town, Norma?" Anne asked.

"Just yesterday," she answered, then looked at Meg. "You got my letter saying I was coming?"

Meg smiled and nodded. "It put me in a nostalgic mood. I dug out our old high school annual and looked at the pictures last night."

"We used to have a lot of fun, didn't we?" Norma said. "Boy, we must have driven your mom crazy."

Meg grinned. "I'll say we did." She looked around the circle of women. "Once when we were maybe fourteen, Norma covered my mom's Ivory soap bar with clear nail polish. Mom couldn't figure out why she wasn't getting any lather from that soap. She even wrote to the company and complained."

"And then she banned me from the house for two weeks when she found out," Norma continued with a laugh.

"You *were* a bad influence," Meg teased.

Norma lifted her brows. "*I* was a bad influence? You talked me into sneaking out of the house for a midnight picnic with Joe and that guy Roger—what was his last name? I ended up with a poison oak rash that I couldn't explain to Granny."

Meg laughed. "I loved picnics in the moonlight."

"Me too," Norma said with a reminiscent smile. She glanced around the fellowship hall.

Clara Jenkins followed her gaze. The boys were standing together in line for some lemonade. "I didn't know you had children, Norma," she said.

"I didn't until a few months ago," Norma responded. "They're my foster children."

"Is your husband here visiting with you?" Anne asked.

Norma shook her head. "No. Bob didn't come with us." She paused and looked around the little group, then said, "The truth of the matter is that we . . . we aren't living together right now."

Meg raised her eyebrows in surprise. Clara pressed a hand over her chest as if shocked to her very core.

"You're not a . . . *divorcée*?" Clara asked, lowering her voice as she uttered the word.

"We're separated, Clara," Norma admitted and forced a smile. "A mutual decision that seems best right now."

"I'm sorry, Norma. I shouldn't have brought it up," Anne said, sincere apology in her voice.

Norma put a hand on her arm. "There's no need to be sorry, Anne. It is what it is. It would have been strange for you *not* to ask about my . . . my husband."

Again Norma turned her eyes toward the boys as they walked away from the line with their drinks. The other women did the same.

"Must be a challenge to suddenly find yourself the mother of three boys," Meg said frankly. "One fifteen-year-old boy is enough for me most days. Danny's a good kid, *but* . . ."

Several of the women chuckled and nodded. Norma smiled. "I do have times when I wonder what I was thinking when I took on these boys," she said, "but then one of them says or does something to let me know how hard their life was before, and I know I made the right decision."

"How old are they?" Anne wondered.

"Frankie is twelve and JP's thirteen. Zach just turned sixteen last week," Norma said. "I'd love for them to meet Danny and others who are their ages."

"Of course," Meg agreed. "Maybe if you have time while you're here, they can all go to the Regal together for a matinee. Danny loves movies."

"I think there'll be time," Norma said with a little smile. "I've decided to stay here in Greenville with the boys. I still have the farm that Pops and Granny left me, and we're going to live there."

"Norma! That's wonderful. I'm so happy you're staying," Meg exclaimed.

"Me too. It feels like this is where we're supposed to be. The boys have been through so much in their short lives, and I want this to be the place they can get a fresh start."

"The boys haven't been in *trouble* or anything, have they?" Clara asked, obviously worried.

"Yes. They've been in trouble," Norma admitted bluntly, "and they've made mistakes because of their prior circumstances. But—"

"A mistake is breaking a window," Clara said pointedly, "but *trouble* is something else entirely. Trouble is something Greenville won't abide."

Norma met Clara's direct gaze with one of her own. "I don't *abide* trouble either, Clara."

"Are the boys happy about the move?" Meg asked quickly.

"I think they will be. It's going to be a big change from Kansas City, but I'm confident they'll do well here. There were too many temptations and too many bad memories for them in the city. I think the farm will be a place for them to find healing—and come to realize they too have a lot to contribute to the community."

"It sounds like you've got your hands full," Anne said.

"I've got my *heart* full with the boys," she answered evenly. "And I intend to keep my heart full as long as God allows me to fill a need for troubled kids."

The chatty conversation of the women had been replaced by a thoughtful—somewhat worried—silence.

Norma looked at the long serving table where people were filling their plates. "That can't be Lilly Anderson's famous coffee cake, can it?" she enthused.

"The one and only. Pastor Don's mother still makes it every week."

"She seemed ancient when we were kids," Norma mused in amazement. "She has to be in her nineties by now."

"Ninety-six," Meg answered. "I asked her for her recipe about a year ago, and she told me I'd get it on her one hundredth birthday. By then she thinks she might not feel like baking anymore."

Norma grinned at Meg. "It's so good to be home."

Chapter 7

Joe turned his truck down the familiar road he drove six days a week, weather permitting, and draped his wrist over the steering wheel. He blew out a long breath and fixated on the fact that it was Monday. He hated Mondays and the pointless routine of everything. Monday was also the farthest workday from Saturday night—and Barney's.

He passed landmarks he knew intimately from years of traveling the same path. A broken-down tractor at the edge of Clyde Evans' field; the grain silo that the Greenville High class of '51 had painted orange one Halloween; a kite tail that had wound itself around a telephone pole at least three summers ago; a pothole in the two-lane road that grew larger with each heavy rainfall. Joe thought for a moment about how his life was just like that pothole—slowly eroding away and becoming nothing more than a hazard to those around him.

With a practiced glance, he looked up at the sky, where a couple of white clouds floated aimlessly against the blue backdrop. Clear and a million—the flyers' phrase flitted through his mind as he turned west at the sign: "Ernie's Air Field—2 miles. Dawn to

Dusk." At least the weather wouldn't be a headache today, and he could get all three fields dusted before the midday heat and wind kicked up.

The airfield boasted two separate hangars, a small shack that doubled as an office building, and a fairly well maintained dirt strip that ran along the edge of a large cornfield. An acre of concrete provided a place to tie down as many as six planes at a time. Joe turned his Ford into the drive that led to the airstrip and took a quick inventory of the planes on the pad—a Cessna 170, a high-winged Piper, and one other Stearman biplane besides his own. A shiny new truck backed out of a parking space beside the office, "Vanguard" stenciled prominently on the doors. Joe pulled in as the Vanguard truck drove away. The two men in the cab looked at him and nodded as they passed. Joe parked and made his way into the small office building past a sign that read FBO.

Ernie Colfax had never met a stranger. Some sixty years old, Ernie talked to everyone—about everything. Joe disliked what he considered useless chitchat that Ernie always put him through, but he couldn't avoid it. Ernie was the fixed base operator, which meant he ran the show, made the rules, and kept the place stocked with the pesticides and fertilizers that Joe used to dust the fields.

Ernie looked up from his books and smiled. "Mornin', Joe," he said.

"Ernie" was Joe's acknowledgment as he made his way to a pot of coffee on a hotplate in the corner of the shabby office. "How many you got booked for me today?"

"Three." Ernie was looking out the window that gave a perfect view of the windsock near the long dirt strip. "Not a breeze stirrin' out there," he said, waving toward the sock hanging limply from the pole. "Should help keep the drift down—more dust on the crops, ya know," he added with a chuckle.

Joe followed his gaze and took a swig of coffee, then made a face. "You know, this stuff's thick as motor oil. Is it yesterday's? You might try starting from scratch each morning. One scoop of Folgers for each—"

"When ya start paying me for it, you can start complainin' about it," Ernie said, but his tone was jovial. "Did you hear about ol' Jason Cline?"

Joe tried to fight down another swallow of his coffee and shook his head. "What about him?"

"His last run Friday was too low, an' he clipped a tail on the standpipe over at Chalmer's field."

"Was he able to land her all right?" Joe asked, looking up from his cup.

Ernie nodded slowly. "He got her down, but it wasn't pretty."

"Long as he walked away, it was pretty enough."

"Yes, sir. I figure that's what Jason was thinking. But it put his Kaydet out a' commission for a while. I heard he ain't got the money to fix her up right now. You might be gettin' more business over at Emporia if you want it. When folks call looking for someone, I figure I'll split up the work 'tween you and Chip," Ernie said.

"You might have to round up some flagmen to work the fields. I have a hard time getting anyone worth two cents out there. I'll pay the going rate if someone wants the job." Joe turned toward the door. "I need some fuel."

Ernie settled a baseball cap on his nearly bald head and came around the counter to follow Joe out the door. "There were some men here earlier," he said, hurrying to catch up. "Ya ever hear of Vanguard?" They started across the cement pad toward the planes.

Joe shook his head. "No. They selling chemicals or something like that?"

"No sirree. They're selling themselves. They're thinking of comin' to Greenville and starting one of those big-shot outfits. 'Corporate farming' they called it. Said it could be a 'real boon' to our town."

Joe lifted an eyebrow. "Boon? What're they talking about?"

Ernie shrugged. "Beats me. But the way they said it, made me think it must be something good."

Ernie's signature bowlegged gait carried him on toward a five-hundred-gallon gas drum on the edge of the tie-down pad. Joe walked to a Stearman open-cockpit biplane. Sun reflected off the bright yellow wings and deepened the cobalt blue of the fuselage. The sight of the plane always pumped him with mixed feelings—pride that he owned her (co-owned her with the bank anyway), a certain thrill that he would be airborne in a matter of minutes, and an inevitable sadness and sense of failure. This aircraft had been a military trainer preparing countless aviators for combat, but he hadn't been one of them.

Joe pushed the thought from his mind as he did his preflight. He ran his hand along the leading edge of the single-blade prop, ducked under the nose, and let his discerning and experienced eyes rake over the wing wires, the fuselage, and the wheels. When he straightened up again, he found himself under the steady gaze of local farmer Hiram Edwards.

"How ya doin', Joe?" Hiram greeted him.

Joe lifted a shoulder in a shrug. "I'm surviving, Hiram. You?"

Hiram pulled a worn straw hat off his head and clasped it tightly between hands callused from years of hard work. A life working in the cornfields had lined his face with creases borne from weather. Both sun and wind had shaped the permanent lines that gave him an air of rural experience.

"I guess you could say I'm okay today—mostly because Sara is having one of her good days. How she's doing determines how my days go." He fixed a look somewhere over Joe's shoulder. "Guess that's how it should be after forty years of livin' together."

"Meg told me she finished her latest round of treatments," Joe said, looking at his watch.

Hiram nodded. "It's hard on her. I'd say the cure is nearly worse than the disease."

I'm burning daylight here. Cut to the chase, Hiram. . . . "Can I do something for you, Hiram?"

The man hesitated, then cleared his throat. "I'm hoping you might be able to spray my fields next Monday. I've seen rootworm beetles all over the corn, and if I don't get that taken care of right off, I'm gonna have some serious pollination problems next spring. I already talked to Chip, and it'd be two weeks or more 'fore he could fit me in."

"I'm headed over to Clyde Evans' right now. He's got the same rootworm problem. Probably need to use something stronger to kill the eggs in the soil for the next planting season. I think I can fit you in Monday."

Joe watched Hiram fidget with his hat. When the man looked up at him, Joe could see honest misery in his eyes.

"I wonder if I can pay you when the crop comes in, Joe. Things are a little tight right now 'cause of all Sara's doctor bills. The treatment is real expensive, and I'm having a hard time balancing it all. I . . . well, I gotta have a decent crop or I could lose everything."

Joe tried not to notice the toll it took on Hiram just to ask. *It's not my problem. I'm running a business—not a charity.* "I sympathize with you, Hiram. I do. But I have to have the usual half up front before I can spray. I've got costs too, you know, and I can't be changing the way I do business for every personal situation that comes along. I'm sure you understand."

"I wouldn't ask if I had a choice, Joe." Hiram's voice shook.

"And I wouldn't say no if I had a choice. If you can work something out by Monday, you let me know. I'll keep a slot open for you."

Hiram gave another quick nod, settled his hat on his head, then walked away. Joe removed the tie-downs and chocks around the wheels and climbed into the rear one of the tandem cockpits.

Joe taxied the Stearman over to the fuel drum, where Ernie waited for him and shut down the engine. He climbed off the wing.

"I need it full, Ernie. Anyone checked the strip this morning?"

"You're the first, Joe. I'm not even sure Chip is flying today."

Joe nodded and walked toward the dirt runway. With his eyes on the ground, he thought about the countless times he'd made this obligatory walk to check for debris, ruts, maybe an errant branch or anything else that didn't belong. Pilots called it FOD—short for "foreign object damage"—stuff that could cause a pilot to have a blowout, veer off the strip, even flip a plane if the wheels connected with something big or hit an unseen hole. Something like that tree branch he spotted lying across the dirt toward the right. As he bent over to pick it up, the St. Christopher's medal he still wore on a chain slid out from the collar of his shirt. He tucked it back out of sight as he carried the branch to the wide edge of the strip and tossed it into the cornfield.

He turned to head back to his plane, where he could see Ernie was still hand-cranking the gas into the wing. Just past Ernie, Chip Armstrong was parking his truck alongside Joe's old Ford. Joe had hoped to get in the air without seeing Chip today, but no such luck. He made his way back to the Stearman.

Chip Armstrong was one of those perpetually cheerful people who found something wonderful in almost every situation, every day of every week. At twenty-three, he had yet to be disappointed in life. He drove Joe crazy.

"Looks like I got here at the right time, huh, Joe? No need for me to walk the strip now that you've done the work for both of us." Chip grinned and slapped Joe so hard on the back he nearly knocked him off-balance.

"Luck of the draw, Chip. I just got here first is all—the strip is clean. Watch the rut at your three o'clock 'bout midway down. It's growing," Joe said and purposely looked at Ernie. "You need to get that thing graded, Ernie."

"Sam's coming over first of next week with his dozer. He'll scrape the strip and fill in the ruts again," Ernie answered. "I topped you off with fifty gallons, Joe. You must've been running on fumes last week."

"Yeah, I planned on getting gassed up Saturday after my last run," Joe said, "but something came up."

Chip shrugged on his leather jacket. "Got gassed up at Barney's instead, right, Joe?"

Joe tossed a look Chip's way. Ernie shifted uncomfortably on the balls of his feet as he looked from one man to the other. It was clear by Chip's unconcerned air that he hadn't meant anything by the offhand comment.

Joe forced a smile. "A man who works hard plays hard."

Chip tied a scarf around his neck and nodded. "Absolutely. That's sure the truth. I hope when I find a good woman and settle down with kids and the house and the whole nine yards, I'll find someone as understanding as your Meg must be. A pilot's wife has to figure she's gonna come second to the job. No woman can compete with flying—am I right again? I mean, we have the greatest job in the world! No stinking office for us—the sky is our office. The view always changes. The thrill is always there! Work hard—play hard." He slapped Joe on the back again. "I'll be pulling the Kaydet up for some gas, Ernie. Hang tight."

Joe watched Chip swagger away. *Was I ever that young? Was I ever that enthusiastic? Man—he bugs me. Nobody can be that happy all the time.*

Joe dropped into his seat and tugged on his goggles. They settled in a rut worn into the leather of his helmet. He reached up to touch the medal, then locked his double shoulder harness. He looked right and left, spotted Ernie standing back several yards away, and yelled, "Clear!"

Heel-and-toeing the gray rudder pedals and brake, Joe maneuvered the Stearman to the strip. He lined up the center, then pushed the throttle for speed. The throaty roar of the radial engine filled the quiet morning as Joe rolled down the strip for takeoff. The nose of the Stearman was so high it was impossible for Joe to see over it, so he maneuvered the plane by a constant S motion, looking from side to side until he finally eased the stick back and felt the wheels leave the ground.

Once airborne, Joe used visual flight references on the ground to set his course. A wide turn to the south, and he was on his way to his first job of the day. He used the back of his glove to wipe some oil spray from his goggles and thought about that military aviator's cap he'd never gotten to wear, all the places he had wanted to see, all the sights he and Meg were going to visit together. The adventures they had planned.

What had once been his passion had turned into nothing more than a way to make a living. His shattered dream of being a military pilot had invaded all he'd loved about flying—and he mourned the loss of that love. Oh, there were occasional glimpses, moments that reminded him of how he used to need to fly as much as he needed to breathe. A blazing streak of color on the horizon, a sense of freedom that filled him when the wheels left the ground, the view from above that made everything below seem ordered and symmetrical—perfect. At unguarded times he remembered how much he had loved flying with Meg—two of them alone in the world, shooting through the sky, sharing the thrill.

Now he looked down on the same valleys, roads, and patchwork-quilt fields day in and day out. He truly was the Red Baron of Bugs.

Stop the world—I want to get off.

Meg pulled the wagon full of marigolds to the front of the house, where she had already turned and loosened the dirt around her wilting spring garden. She'd managed to salvage some of the plants from the flats that had been blown about on Saturday night, and despite their somewhat bedraggled appearance from the storm, she was hopeful they would be hearty enough to withstand the summer sun and last until the first frost of the season. Wearing worn blue pedal pushers and a sleeveless yellow blouse, Meg knew she looked more like a teenager than a married woman with two growing children. She'd pulled her long hair into a ponytail that trailed over her shoulder when she bent over to kneel in the soft dirt.

She had barely turned the first spadeful of soil when she heard the sound of an approaching vehicle and turned to watch an unfamiliar truck pull into her driveway. She sat back on her heels and put a hand over her eyes to shield them from the glare of the sun as she looked at the shiny two-tone model, a new Chevrolet. When the door opened, she got to her feet and brushed off the dirt that clung to her knees. She looked up to see a tall, well-dressed man in sunglasses who was striding toward her.

"Hello," he called as he got closer.

"Hello," she answered. "Can I help you?"

He stopped a few feet from where she was standing. "There never was much help for me," he said with an ironic smile. "How are you, Meg?"

She frowned. His voice was familiar somehow, but she couldn't place him. And then he took off his sunglasses and flashed a wide smile at her. Her brows shot up in surprise. "Luke? Luke Ramsey?"

His smile broadened. "In the flesh."

He was every bit as good-looking as she remembered—in fact, the years had given him a maturity that had only enhanced his features. He was taller, broader, nicely dressed, and seemingly confident—more attractive now than he was in the yearbook picture she had just looked at Saturday night.

He stretched out a hand, and she wiped the dirt from her own across the seat of her pants without thinking.

Luke laughed as she offered that hand. "Meg—Meg Johnson. You're just as I remember," he said, "and you don't know how happy that makes me." He shook her hand, holding it a little longer than necessary.

Meg blushed and practically snatched back her hand. "What are you doing here? I mean—" She was embarrassed at sounding so awkward and ill at ease.

"*Here* here? Or do you mean Greenville?" Luke asked.

She gave a small shrug and tried to pull herself together. "You know, I mean, back here in town. It's been years and years—"

"Seventeen since I left," he said. "About time I came back to pay a visit to the old hometown, don't you think?"

"Oh, sure. It's just . . . you know . . . after you . . . your dad, I mean your family left town . . ." she stammered, finally letting the statement fade away.

"To tell you the truth, I never thought I'd be back here either," Luke admitted, "but things change. Circumstances change. Blame gets put in proper perspective—which in this case is squarely on my father's shoulders."

"How is your . . . your father?" she asked.

Luke's practiced smile was quick as a flash. "I don't know."

"Oh. I'm sorry. He isn't—"

"Could be. I really *don't know.*" Luke looked toward the house. "How's Joe? Still crop dusting?"

She frowned. "You know he's a crop duster?"

He smiled slowly and lifted a shoulder with a nonchalant air. "I keep up with things."

Meg didn't know why he made her feel so uncomfortable. Maybe it was her dirt-stained gardening attire compared with his blazer and wrinkle-free pants.

"And what about you, Luke? Are you married?" she asked.

"I haven't found the right woman yet." His voice was casual, but his expression seemed to be saying something else. "I guess you could say I'm married to my job," he finished.

"Which is . . . ?"

"I'm regional manager for the midwestern territories of Vanguard Industries—which basically means I'm in charge of the midsection of the country."

"Sounds important—what's Vanguard?"

"Corporate farming," he said with a touch of pride, "the future of agriculture in this country."

Meg heard a plane overhead and instinctively looked up at a commercial passenger plane passing directly above them. She dropped her gaze and caught him staring at her. She laughed self-consciously. "Pilot's wife, you know. Force of habit. Every time a plane goes over I can't help myself."

"How nice for Joe to be looked up to," he noted with a small grin, ". . . to be thought about like that."

Meg smiled. "He probably doesn't even know I do it."

"His loss, then," Luke observed with one eyebrow raised.

Meg looked again at the sky as the plane's engine droned into silence.

"Listen, Meg, Vanguard Industries looks to me for recommendations about where they should establish new corporate farms, and I couldn't think of a better area than right around Greenville. There's a lot of unused and underdeveloped land here, and my company could put a substantial amount of money and resources into expanding and enriching the ground in order to farm it to its maximum potential." His obviously practiced speech was warmed by his enthusiastic tone.

"And the family farms that are already established here in Greenville? What about them?"

"There are all kinds of options for those folks. We can buy their land outright—and in most cases, the farmers stay on and work the fields just like they've always done without all the headaches and pressures of ownership."

"Did you stop by to get *my* permission?" she asked. *There's that smile again.*

"We'll need crop dusters to work for us—and since everybody says Joe's the best duster around, he could be instrumental in our setup here."

Meg's surprise must not have been lost on Luke.

"Look, Meg, I'll admit there's some history between my dad and Harold Daley," he said, "but I know right from wrong, and I'd like to right the wrongs my father caused. Pay back this community for his mistakes."

"I don't think anyone here expects that from you, Luke," she said. "You were just an innocent bystander in what went on a long time ago."

He shrugged. "He was my father, and I carry his last name. I'd like people to hear the name Ramsey and not think dark thoughts, you know what I mean?"

Meg heard her children approaching on their bikes, Christy's laughter and Danny's murmured response. In moments they wheeled their bicycles onto the gravel driveway, coming to a stop beside Meg and Luke.

Meg kept the introductions brief. Christy blushed when Luke shook her hand and told her she was just as pretty as her mom. Danny couldn't take his eyes off Luke's shiny new truck as they walked their bikes to set them next to the porch. Luke watched them disappear into the house.

"Christy looks like you," he mused, "and so does Danny. I don't see any of Joe in either one."

"Oh, there's plenty of Joe in both. Stubborn to the core." Meg tilted her head to the side and studied him. "You knew Joe wouldn't be home when you came by today."

Luke shoved his hands into his pockets. "I figured he'd be gone, and I wanted to talk to you before I approached him with this," he confessed. "It's a great opportunity for him, Meg. For both of you. Vanguard would be a steady paycheck, and Joe could find himself being supervisor over the other pilots we hire for dusting."

"People are used to the way things are around here," Meg said. "Farms get passed down from one generation to the next. In fact, an old classmate of ours is a perfect example. You remember Norma Meiers?"

"Sure. I've actually had some business dealings with Norma recently in Kansas City," he said casually.

"She's back here to stay now," Meg said.

"So I heard."

"I just think that you'll have a hard time convincing people to consider such an enormous change, Luke. We're just not used to it around here."

"Sometimes people just need to be offered a choice. Something different. Something better. Change is a good thing." He smiled as if to soften his proclamation. "Well, I better let you get back to your gardening."

"It was good to see you, Luke."

"You'll be seeing me again. I'm at the hotel in town for the duration."

"The duration?"

He flashed his charming smile. "The time it takes me to get this community on board with the best break they'll ever be offered."

"I'll tell Joe you were here," she said.

Luke nodded, then slipped his sunglasses back on. "You know, Meg, you're even lovelier than you were in high school," he said in a low voice. "Tell the lucky man I'll be in touch."

Meg felt herself shiver as she watched him saunter back to his truck and climb into the cab. *Lovelier than high school . . .* She shook her head. Here she was, hair pulled back, no makeup, not even lipstick. Dirt under her fingernails and a pair of old pedal pushers that had seen better days. *Mom would be absolutely horrified*, she thought as the sound of Luke's truck faded into the distance. She looked at her house with its fading paint, the porch rail missing two slats in front. With a sigh, she turned back to the flower garden. *Something different. Something better. Could change be a good thing?*

Chapter 8

Joe pulled the truck into his driveway and hesitated before killing the engine. In the hazy twilight of the evening, he could make out Meg in the kitchen window, head bent over some task. This was the time of day he most hated. And he hated that he felt that way. It was the stopping. The time to reflect. The time to regret. The motionless chunk of time every night that had him revisiting pieces of his past, parts he wanted to forget but that lurked in the corners of his mind and popped out whenever he let his guard down. It was why Joe spent so much of his time simply moving.

He fought the urge to back up the truck and take off again. He turned the ignition key off, and the truck dieseled to a shaky stop. The engine sputtered a few more times for good measure. *The machine reflects the man. Perfect.*

Meg heard the front door open, then close. Christy had just finished setting the table.

"Daddy's home!" she called, her expectations about Joe not yet fully formed like the rest of the family.

Meg pulled a casserole dish from the oven. "I know. Go tell Danny supper's ready." Meg heard Christy greet Joe on her way through the living room and his muffled reply. She turned from the stove as her husband walked into the kitchen. She watched him glance at the table and saw his look of resignation. *He looks trapped.*

"We waited for you," she said as cheerfully as she could manage.

Joe dropped his keys on the counter, then crossed to the sink to wash his hands. "I told you not to wait on me for supper anymore," he said gruffly.

"We don't mind. It's the only time we're all together lately." She took off her apron and hung it on a hook by the stove. "How were your flights?"

"Uneventful," he answered as he pulled out his chair and sank into it.

Meg carried the casserole to the table and sat opposite Joe.

"You always say an uneventful flight is a good flight."

"Yeah, that's what I say."

Meg's heart constricted as she realized Joe had not looked at her since he entered the room.

Danny came in with Christy on his heels. As soon as the kids took their seats, Meg bowed her head and began to say grace. Christy and Danny automatically joined her in the mealtime practice, but Joe's hand hovered over his fork while she finished her sincere thanks for the meal and the time together as a family. When she looked up from her prayer, Joe had already started eating.

As usual, Joe was on the periphery of the conversation at the table. He didn't seem to pay much attention to the talk of the new movie at the Regal, or that the creek was higher than it had been in years, or the latest gossip about the kids' friends. Meg was talking about the flowers she had planted out front.

"I think the marigolds make the old flowers happy," Christy added. "Don't you, Daddy?"

"I guess I didn't notice them," he said. "Sorry."

"Danny didn't see them either. He just about rolled his bike right over them when we got home from the park today, 'cause he was too busy staring at the truck Mom's friend was driving," she said.

"It was a beaut, all right. One of those brand-new Chevys. First one I've ever seen with two different colors like that," Danny said between mouthfuls. "I'll bet it cost a ton of money."

Joe looked over at Meg. "Who was it?"

"You're never going to believe this—but Luke Ramsey showed up here this afternoon," she said.

"Luke—as in *Frank Ramsey's son*? That Luke Ramsey?"

Meg nodded. "I was pretty surprised to see him."

Joe shook his head. "Surprised? I would think stunned would be more like it," he said, his tone caustic. "I figured after my dad blew the whistle on his old man, we'd never see any of the Ramseys in Greenville again."

"What's this about Grandpa?" Danny ventured.

Meg looked at him with a quiet admonishment. "Adult conversation, Danny."

Danny looked from one parent to the other, then turned his attention back to his nearly empty plate without another word.

Joe dropped his fork onto his plate, and it clattered in the quiet moment. "Why didn't you tell me when I first got home? Luke Ramsey isn't an everyday visitor, Meg. You waited until Christy brought him up to admit he just *happened* to be back in town and just *happened* to stop by—our house? *Our house* of all places?"

Joe's accusing look said far more than his words. "It's not that I was avoiding the subject," Meg said with a frown.

"Can I be excused, please?" Danny asked, looking at Joe. But Joe didn't respond. He was still glowering in Meg's direction.

"You're both excused," Meg said quickly. "Please take your plates to the sink." Christy and Danny scooped up their dishes and dutifully carried them over.

"I thought Mr. Ramsey looked just like a movie star," Christy said innocently as she started out of the kitchen behind Danny. "And he smelled like you used to smell when you went to church with us, Daddy. Old Spice."

Joe pushed his plate away and looked across the table at Meg. "Guess that's a lot better than fertilizer and pesticides, huh?"

"You're being silly."

"Did you know he was coming?"

"Of course not! I told you, I was surprised. Very surprised," she said. "He works for a company called Vanguard Industries. They're some kind of corporate farming outfit, and they're thinking of starting an operation here—around Greenville. He wants to talk to you."

She got up from the table and grabbed her apron from a hook on the wall, then began to tie it around her waist. She could feel Joe's eyes on her.

"Why does he want to talk to me?" Joe demanded as she started to fill the sink with water to wash the dishes.

"He knows you've got the crop-dusting business, and he heard you're the best. They'll need pilots to dust their fields. He even said you could be in charge of the other pilots."

Joe got up and crossed to the sink. "If he knew I still had the business, why did he show up here in the middle of the day to talk to me when he knew I'd be flying?"

"I, umm, I guess . . . what I mean is that I asked him that," she said, "and he said that . . . he said he wanted me to know he'd be, you know, talking to you about this."

Joe raked his hands through his hair. "He always was real considerate . . . of you."

"He's really not worth talking about," Meg said, turning back to her task.

"But he's worth *thinking* about—right?" The tenor of his voice was growing tighter with forced control. " 'To Meg—the one thing I envy Joe Daley for' . . . sound familiar?"

Meg frowned. "What are you talking about?"

"I found our high school annual stuffed under the couch cushion yesterday when you and the kids were off at church. The page with Luke's picture on it was dog-eared."

"I closed the book quickly on Saturday night when I thought a *tornado* might be headed for our house," she said, doing her best to keep her voice even. "Bending a corner on a book wasn't a priority."

"So you admit you were looking at Luke's picture?"

Meg's eyebrows drew together. "I was looking at everyone's picture in the yearbook—especially the pictures of you and me. Why are you getting so worked up about this, Joe?"

He paced back and forth across the kitchen. "I'm *worked up* because I came home to find you wearing a new shade of lipstick and smelling like flowers." His voice rose with every word. "I find out from my daughter that you entertained an old classmate of ours—who probably hates me—and who, by the way, had a huge crush on you in high school. Apparently he still looks like a movie star, and he's driving a shiny new truck!"

Meg could not keep the flash of anger from her voice. "Let's not forget that he smelled like Old Spice!"

Joe whirled around and pointed his index finger at her. "That's right! He smelled like Old Spice—not like bug killer!"

"You're talking crazy, Joe." Meg knew she had to get things back on a more even keel. "I wasn't entertaining anyone. Luke showed up unannounced this afternoon, and there was nothing

I could do about it. And, by the way, I put this lipstick on every night before you come home!"

"And apparently you sit around on Saturday nights and look at old yearbook pictures wishing you could turn back the clock—is that it?"

"I'm not the one who is sitting around wishing I could turn back the clock," she said, her voice edged in hurt and anger, "and when I sit around on Saturday nights, Joe, I'm waiting for you!"

Meg regretted her words as soon as they were out of her mouth. She knew Joe would stew over them for hours—building hidden meanings and his perceived failures into a giant wall of silence that would take days to break through. She stood at the kitchen window and watched Joe slam the door of the truck and shoot backward down the driveway, tires throwing dirt and rocks into the air. *At least the airstrip is closed and he won't go flying. Thank you for that, Lord.* She watched the taillights of the truck disappear. Her thoughts were interrupted by Danny as he walked into the kitchen.

"Where did Dad go?" he asked.

Meg looked at the expression on her son's face. "He just had an errand to run."

"He left because he's mad," he muttered as he started to clear the rest of the dishes from the table and carry them to the sink. "He's always mad."

"He's not always . . . mad," she argued.

"Sure seems that way to me."

Meg sighed. "He's just going through something, honey."

Danny shrugged. "Then he's been going through it for as long as I can remember."

Meg didn't have a response. She watched as her son walked out of the kitchen. *Something different. Something better. Something's got to change.*

Joe slammed the truck into a parking place on the street in front of Ray's Package Store. It was one of the few establishments open in the evening on a weeknight. He didn't normally frequent Ray's place, but tonight he was making an exception. He needed a beer, and Ray sold them by the six-pack. *Who does Luke Ramsey think he is anyway? Shows up at my house, unannounced, in the middle of the day and chats up my wife! Man, I hope there's some justice in life and he doesn't look as good as he used to. He was always so full of himself—plenty of nerve. Even in high school—telling me how lucky I was that I had the prettiest, sweetest girl in school. Telling me that he'd trade places with me in a second to have Meg on his arm! Telling me stuff I already knew.*

A bell over the door announced Joe's arrival. Ray Brantford was behind the counter and greeted him by name. The store, stocked primarily with alcohol, also carried basic necessities and toiletries. Ray had found over the years that even a housewife who was hell-bent against liquor would find her way into his little establishment when in need of a tube of toothpaste or a bottle of aspirin for that surprise headache when Woolworth's was closed. Ray had taken one look at the scowl on Joe's face and seemed to know the man wasn't after a candy bar.

"Got a six-pack of Pabst Blue Ribbon on sale, Joe," Ray said. Joe nodded and headed toward the back wall of the store.

The bell over the door rang again as another customer entered. Joe reached into the refrigerated cooler Ray kept in the back and grabbed the Pabst. With the six-pack under his arm, Joe made his way to the cash register. He turned the corner at the end of an aisle and ran right into Ray's new customer. It was a moment before he realized it was Luke Ramsey.

Another roll of the dice on the Joe Daley board game of life, huh, God? You must get such a kick out of watching me squirm.

"Joe?" Luke said as he thrust his hand out. "How *are* you?"

Joe was looking at a salesman, he was sure. He shifted the six-pack and shook the hand of someone he had never planned to see again. "Good enough, Luke. Meg told me you were in town."

"It was great to see her. She hasn't changed a bit. Just as pretty as I remember. I met your kids too. You're a lucky man," Luke said. Joe was suddenly very aware of the beer under his arm.

"Yes, I am. Got a great family. Good business. My own plane." His voice trailed off as he looked at Luke. *Guess there is no justice. Looks as good as ever—hasn't aged a bit. Expensive clothes, fancy watch, silver cuff links with his initials. Nice. Those teeth could be in a toothpaste ad.*

"I'm sure Meg told you why I stopped by today?"

She tried. "She said you worked for that outfit Vanguard. A couple of your people paid Ernie a visit out at the airstrip today," Joe said.

Luke nodded. "Steve and Earl. They're doing some legwork for me," he said. "Vanguard is a great company, Joe. We could do some amazing things for this town. I'd really like to talk to you about it."

Joe paid for his beer and pocketed the change. "I'll check my schedule and get in touch with you, Luke. This time a' year, you know, lots a' work for me. In fact, I can barely keep up with the demand . . . business is so good."

He checked inside the bag. "I need an opener, Ray," he said as Luke put a tube of toothpaste, a toothbrush, and a can of shaving cream down on the counter in front of Ray.

"That do it for you?" Ray asked Luke as he dropped the items into a small bag.

Joe stood impatiently by. "Ray—can opener for the beer?" Joe asked again.

"Hang on, Joe. I'll get you one," he said and then looked at Luke. "Got beer on sale tonight."

Luke flashed a smile. "I don't drink, Mr. Brantford, but thanks anyway."

Ray scrutinized him a little closer. "Luke," he said slowly, "I remember you. Frank Ramsey's son—right?"

Luke shifted his weight and picked up the bag. "That's right. In name anyway. I don't make any claims to the man anymore."

"Probably best in this community," Ray agreed as he reached under the counter and retrieved a metal can opener. Joe grabbed it and headed for the door.

"We're open every night—except Sundays, of course," he heard Ray say to Luke.

"You've got a great place here, Mr. Brantford. Better stocked than some of the stores in Kansas City," Luke said sincerely. "Have a good night."

"Thanks. Come back anytime."

"Hey, Joe, hold up a second, will you?" Luke said, hurrying out the door. The sound of Ray's bell cut off when the door closed.

Joe stopped and looked at him. "I'm running a little late, Luke, and I hate to worry my wife."

"I was hoping to talk to you. . . ." Luke's voice trailed off and he jiggled the keys dangling from his index finger.

Joe looked past Luke at the Chevy parked right in front of his old broken-down Ford, the one with "Gre nvil e Crop Dust ng Ser ice" painted across the door. The two tones of the blue paint on Luke's truck gleamed under the streetlight at the curb. *No wonder Danny almost trampled Meg's flowers.*

"Nice truck," Joe observed.

"Vanguard bought it for me. It's a great company, Joe. It could do wonders for Greenville and for you."

Joe shrugged. "I'm not looking for wonders, Luke."

"Look, I know I'm the last person this town ever expected to see again."

Joe just stared at him. "No, I think that would be your dad."

"Just so you know—I have a great deal of respect for your father. He's a man of real character and integrity—two things that my father obviously was lacking."

"Nice of you to say." Joe's skepticism was evident in his voice.

"I know how it feels to be gripped by a memory," Luke said, his voice not concealing his bitterness, "and I'm not asking for anyone to forget. I'm just asking for a chance to make things right."

"It's a free country, Luke. You got every right to make your pitch here if you want to."

Luke seemed to relax, then smiled. "That mean I can make my pitch to you?"

"Well, like I said, I'm pretty busy right now," Joe said evasively.

"I'll be in town for a while." Luke produced a business card from his shirt pocket and offered it to Joe. "I'm sure we can find a time."

Joe shoved the card into his pants pocket and made his way to the truck. "I gotta get going. Good to see you again." *Just take me now, God, before he watches me climb into that old heap of you know what.*

"Give Vanguard a chance, Joe. We might be able to swing a new truck for you."

He forced himself to smile. "And give up this fine old piece of machinery? We've been together as long as me and Meg." He winced as the door creaked when he opened it and all but tossed in his six-pack. He slid inside and willed Luke to walk away, but the man stood and watched as Joe turned the key—and the engine barely coughed. *Not now. Don't do this now.* He tried again and this time had some luck. In a matter of seconds, he was looking at Luke Ramsey in his rearview mirror.

I guess the fact that his old man was a crook didn't change Luke's future one bit, Joe thought. Last time he'd seen Luke was in chemistry class January of his senior year. There one day—gone the next. Luke had always been a thorn in his side—his competition all the way through school in sports, grades, and girls. But Joe had been the victor when it came to Meg. After Luke's family had left town in disgrace, Joe hadn't given him a second thought. He had his future all mapped out with Meg by his side, and Luke didn't matter to him one little bit. *But the future fell apart and now Luke's back. Apparently successful, self-assured Luke. If I didn't have bad luck I'd have no luck at all.*

Technically, the airfield closed at dusk, but Joe drove past the sign anyway and into the parking area. The full moon provided just enough light. Using the can opener Ray had given him, he opened the first of the six beers he planned to drink. He rolled down the window and listened to the serenade of the crickets in the nearby fields. The planes parked on the cement apron near the hangar loomed like giant toys in the dark. He laid his head back against the window behind his seat and proceeded to drink away another night of his life—away from the prying eyes at Barney's. Away from his wife with the perpetual worry etched across her face. Away from his kids whom he barely knew. *One less night to think about what a colossal failure I am. I wish I could just go . . . away.*

Chapter 9

"Hey, Joe! Wake up. Come on, wake up!" Ernie said as he knocked on the door of Joe's truck. Joe opened his bloodshot eyes and squinted in Ernie's direction. "What are you doing here, Ernie?" he mumbled.

"What am *I* doing here? What are *you* doing here?" Ernie countered. "It's barely dawn. You never take off this early."

Joe straightened in his seat and quickly pulled the visor down to shield his aching eyes from the brightening daylight.

"I got a busy day. How long until that sludge you call coffee is ready?"

"Give me fifteen minutes. I haven't even unlocked my office yet," Ernie said as he looked toward the strip and the windsock that was fluttering off the end of the pole. "There's a breeze picking up. Looks like five to ten knots. I heard over the radio from flight services that some weather might roll in midday. Keep an eye on it."

As Ernie trudged toward his office, Joe chanced a look in the rearview mirror. He grimaced at his reflection and tried to flatten out his hair that was standing on end. He knew he should call Meg, but somewhere in the back of his mind, he hoped she had gone to sleep last night and woken up thinking he'd left early. He knew she'd be up soon so she could have a little time to herself before the kids got up. She read her Bible, spent some time in prayer. *I wonder if she's given up praying about me.*

With every uneven bounce down the dirt strip, Joe remembered why drinking the night before he flew was a bad idea. It wasn't so much the nagging headache riding the space behind his eyes. It was the sluggish way he felt in the seat, the slightly foggy view through the windscreen, the way the world seemed to shift and wobble even when the wings were steady.

He took a deep breath and gripped the stick as he felt the wheels leave the ground. Aiming the aircraft into the dawn, he looked for those landmarks that would get him to his first job of the day. He usually cruised at three thousand feet—give or take a couple hundred. Low enough to feel connected to the familiar references on the ground, high enough to recover in case something went wrong. He could already see cumulus clouds building miles away to the north, but he figured he'd be done with his morning runs before the clouds would become an issue.

He executed a ninety-degree bank to the west and looked for the Malloy farm below. From the air, the two hundred acres of wheat looked like precise lines on a graph. Joe circled the farm, eating up altitude with just a few passes. He saw Adam and Helen Malloy already in the field, white flags in hand. Joe waggled the wings on his last pass over the field, and the Malloys waved the flags to let him know they were ready. Helen stood at one end of the field with Adam at the other, large bandannas pulled over nose and mouth to keep as much of the chemical out of their lungs as possible. With every pass Joe would make, the Malloys would reposition themselves, letting him know where the next dusting of spray would go. Joe made a wide pass and then lined up the Stearman to approach the field from the north. He didn't need to check the altimeter for his altitude. He dropped down until he heard just the right pitch from the wind rushing through the wing wires and started his first pass across the field. Flying a mere six inches over the crop, he pulled what pilots called "the money handle" on the hopper in the front cockpit, releasing the pesticide in a fifty-foot swath over the field. His accuracy depended on altitude, the wind, and his innate sense of timing. He got to the end of the field, closed the hopper, and pitched the nose up to climb two hundred feet. With natural skill, he looped back around and began again. As much as he despised the nickname, he knew he *was* the Red Baron of Bugs.

The wind was picking up. Joe heard the difference in the plane's performance as much as he felt it. He had been so intent on the task at hand, he hadn't realized the clouds had moved in and settled over the farmland like an enormous white sheet unfurled on a clothesline. Joe had planned to simply return to the airstrip, refuel, and take off again for his next job, but the way the breeze had picked up, he decided to call Tom Simpson and reschedule. With the wind, he'd end up overspraying or not spraying enough—and waste his time and the Simpsons' money. He hoped to land before the sky opened up. Flying in an open cockpit through pelting raindrops wasn't the most comfortable feeling in the world. If the weather did hold, he thought, he'd do some regular maintenance on the plane. *As long as I don't have to go home early and face Meg and the kids.*

Joe kept the plane below a deck of stratus clouds as he turned back toward the airstrip. The rolling waves of the clouds cast dancing shadows over the landscape below him. He made a wide, slow turn and found himself looking over the side of the plane at cornfields—row upon row of stalks lined up in military precision. *There's Hiram's place. Corn looks like it's more than halfway to harvest height. Not my problem . . .*

Joe lifted his gaze to the clouds above, spotted a big hole in the billions of crystallized droplets suspended in the atmosphere, and pushed the Stearman through to a spectacular display of blue, where a few fat, slow-moving clouds skimmed the edges of his wing tips. *"Daddy? Does it feel like you're going through cotton candy when you fly your arrow plane through a cloud?" When did Christy quit saying "arrow plane"? Three years ago? Four?* Suddenly, from out of nowhere, he saw a huge bird heading straight for his plane. The snow-white thirty-pound bird had a wingspan of at least seven feet, and a deep call resonated from his jet black beak. *A trumpeter swan!*

Joe's reaction was instantaneous. He yanked back on the stick to force the plane higher to miss the bird—and flew right through a spherical rainbow of diffused color that formed a shadowlike wall on a cloud right above him. The nose of the Stearman slipped inside the dense white fog, and a sheen of moisture immediately slicked his features. His mind was still trying to play catch-up to his action when in the next splintered second he saw something else hurtling at him . . . brilliant white . . . winged. *What . . . ?*

The impact was sudden and caused a violent shudder throughout the plane. Shards of light exploded all around Joe, and he yelled out in surprise—too stunned to be scared. Yet.

A line of blue smoke whipped back from the nose of the plane and the guttural, comforting sound of the engine abruptly disappeared. Joe swiped at oil spatters on his goggles with his glove. *I must have hit the swan's mate. They travel in pairs! Stupid! How was your day, Joe? Eventful, Meg—a bird slammed into me at thirty-six hundred feet. Is that lightning?!*

Joe's heart picked up the pace as he tried to restart the engine—then his heart went from a trot to a gallop when the plane didn't respond. *Come on, c'mon, c'mon, start—START!*

Nothing but the sound of the wind playing fiddle with the wing wires. *I'll just have to land her like a glider.* But the stick was as unresponsive as the engine. He felt himself lift in the seat as the plane nosed over into a dive. Logically, he knew without the stick and rudder, he had no control over the dive. *I'm going to die!* The plane started a downward spiral, ripping and tearing through clouds that seemed to be ablaze with an ever-changing scattered, lustrous light. Joe had the unbidden thought that a thousand flash bulbs were going off around him—and his eyes actually ached from the radiant brilliance. The strobe effect of the light pattern swooping around and below him lent even more of a surreal air to his dilemma. Though in his heart he knew it was pointless, he fought with the stick even as he kept trying to restart the engine. He knew his life would be over in minutes—seconds maybe. He still couldn't see the ground. *Maybe I'll die from a heart attack before the impact can kill me.* He squeezed his eyes shut and prayed aloud his first honest, heartfelt prayer in years. "Help me, God, please—I don't want to die. Just give me one more chance! One more day!"

Joe opened his eyes and found the silver-edged light show had intensified. It was as though he were riding the edge of a lightning bolt that had spun out of control—and then it abruptly disappeared. He could just make out dark shadows on the edge of the cloud—and then the nose of the plane burst through the last traces of crystal moisture.

A cornfield stretched far and wide below him, and Joe screamed at the speed of the ground rushing up at him. He made another frantic attempt at starting the engine—and this time it caught. Almost afraid to believe it, Joe tested the stick and felt a sweet response. He was still diving at the earth and was close enough to see the individual ears of corn stretching toward the sky. He used all his strength to pull back on the stick, willing the plane to respond, even though he was only fifty feet off the ground.

"Please. God. One. More. Day for the Red Baron of Bugs!" he yelled above the engine. *Like a run over a cornfield—pull up! Up! C'mon!* The nose turned upward, and he felt his weight press into the seat even as the tail wheel clipped a row of corn husks. Giddy with relief, he pulled back on the stick for a slow, steady climb.

"Thank you, God! *Thank you!* I promise—I promise I'll live every day as if it's my last!"

Joe eased up on the power and rolled onto the base leg of his final approach. He held high until he was almost lined up with the dirt strip, then kicked hard on the right rudder, pulled the stick to the left, and dropped the nose of the Stearman. The plane slipped sideways through the air. Just over the end of the strip, Joe neutralized the controls and leveled the wings—and landed perfectly despite the heavy crosswind whipping the dirt from the field into a dust devil all around him. He kept his speed up and taxied from the airstrip to the cement apron without letting the tail wheel touch the ground.

As he rolled the Stearman to a stop, Ernie appeared beside the wing and watched as Joe pulled off his goggles and helmet and quickly climbed out of the cockpit.

"That was some landing! Yessiree. Some landing! I was worried 'bout that crosswind, but I see I was wastin' my time," Ernie said, his smile like a proud parent's.

"Can you set the chocks and tie her down for me, Ernie?" Joe asked as he jumped off the wing. "I need to get home."

Ernie assured him he would see to the Stearman, but Joe didn't even hear him. He was too busy running toward his truck.

Chapter 10

Meg snapped a clothespin onto the last sheet on the line just as the wind caught it and billowed the damp cotton across her face. She stepped back from the tangle of material and then cast a critical eye on the fourth load of laundry she'd hung out to dry that day. Somewhere in her mind she knew she had overdone it—washed the same sheets she'd washed only three days before. She should have been exhausted, considering she'd been on the move from the time she had discovered Joe hadn't been home all night until now. Her fingers had trembled as she dialed the number for Ernie's airstrip that morning before the kids got up. Once Ernie had assured her that he'd seen Joe that morning, she'd gone from being worried sick to being sick with anger. With the kids out of the house—"*It's a beautiful summer day—go outside*"—she had channeled her hurt and anger into a whirlwind frenzy of organization and cleaning that would have made her mother proud. *Drop by today, Mom, and you'll be impressed—you could eat off my kitchen floor it's so clean . . . not a dust bunny to be found. . . .*

She was picking up her laundry basket to head inside when she heard the unmistakable sound of Joe's truck pulling into the driveway in front of the house. She dropped the basket and made her way through the back door.

Meg peered out the kitchen window over the sink and could see that Joe's truck was indeed parked in the driveway—and it was empty. She waited in the kitchen, arms crossed over her chest, foot tapping impatiently, mouth in a stern line that suggested she was ready to do battle. She waited to hear the familiar squeak of the front door—but she didn't hear it. One, then two, then three minutes passed, and her shoulders actually got stiff from her posture. *How long can it take to get from the driveway to the house? I do it with groceries in each arm and could have made two trips by now. Where is he?*

She looked out the window again. *What's he doing? Hiding? Waiting for me to go to him?* She crossed through the kitchen and started through the living room. *Fine—I'll go to him. He's got plenty to answer for, that's for sure.* She stopped in the middle of the living room—wondering again why he wasn't coming in the house. She shook her head. *If he's mad, he can sit out there till suppertime.* She turned on her heel, fully intending to go back into the kitchen, but heaved a sigh of frustration. *This is ridiculous! I know he's out there. . . .* She pushed through the screen door and stepped out onto the porch.

Joe sat in the rocking chair beside the door, forearms resting on his knees, eyes on the horizon. Meg let the door bang shut behind her. He turned and looked at her—his eyes hazy and unfocused.

"I've been thinking about Robby," he said quietly. The statement took her completely off guard. She drew her brows together.

"What about him?" she asked, trying to tamp the anger she'd held simmering all day long.

"Right before our wedding, he took me aside and helped me with my tie. I was nervous and pretty sure you were getting the raw end of the deal marrying me. He said, 'Think about Dad when you're not sure what you're doing, Joey. Think about how good he is with Mom—and us. Think about that and you can't miss.' I wonder if he had lived through the war, who he would have married. How many kids he'd have by now. . . . Would our kids be close cousins who couldn't imagine Christmas or Easter without big family dinners?"

"Joe . . ."

"I'll never forget watching my mom make and remake Robby's bed as if he was going to walk back in the door any minute and his room needed to be perfect."

"I remember," she said softly.

"I went to find my dad—tell him how he needed to be with Mom—but he was alone in his den, his back to the door . . . and I saw his shoulders shaking. He was sobbing so hard it shook his entire body, but he wasn't making a sound."

"You never told me that," she said.

"I wasn't meant to see it, and I never said anything to him about it.

"All I could think about was revenge. I should have been thinking of you—after all, we'd only been married a few months, but I just wanted to get overseas as fast as I could and single-handedly avenge my brother's death. It ate me up, Meg. I just knew I had to go make it better—give my family some peace—some sense of justice. I couldn't bring Robby back, but I could go and be the war hero that I knew I could be. I would come home in one piece and be such a good son—I would help make up for Rob's absence."

"And then, of course, the doctor told me about my heart—said I couldn't go, even though I was volunteering," he said. "Hard to imagine one number and letter—4-F—having such an impact on someone's life, isn't it?"

"It's not something you chose, Joe," she said, feeling like a broken record. She'd said it hundreds of times before.

"My father was a war hero, my brother was a war hero, and I couldn't even go avenge my own brother's death and help defend my own country," he said. "When the other dads were talking up their boys' service, my own father, a United States congressman, for crying out loud, couldn't say a word about his only living son. What was there to say? His son had taken a job as a glorified bug killer? I wonder sometimes if my dad remembers anything about me besides how I've disappointed him.

"It's the one thing I'm good at, Meg. Disappointing the people I love . . . especially you." He turned toward her, and she was astonished to see tears pooling in his eyes.

"What's happened, Joe? What's going on?" she asked.

"I . . . a bird hit the plane today when I was on my way back to the airstrip. A *big* bird—trumpeter swan, I think." Joe didn't have to go into the mechanics of what that meant. Meg had been a pilot's wife for a long time. She knew the possible ramifications of a bird strike.

"You lost the engine?"

"For what seemed like an eternity, I lost everything. No engine, no stick, no rudder."

"And then you got the engine started again?" she prompted, taking a step toward him.

Joe looked past her and she could see he was reliving the moment.

"I saw the ground rushing at me, and I knew I was going to die. I prayed to live—begged God for another day. I said I'd try and live every day as if it's my last." He leaned toward her, looking sincere.

"I was riding a flat spin with no control, with a hard piece of ground coming up fast. I think the only reason I'm here is because God answered my prayer. He granted me a miracle, and now I have to hold up my end of the bargain.

"I barely remember how I got home. All I could think about was you and the kids. I wanted to get here and tell you how much I love you! I couldn't wait just to hold you. I pulled into the driveway—started to run into the house and it suddenly hit me. Why should you trust anything I say? Why believe me now? After all the years that I've made things so miserable for you—all the ways I've failed you."

I love this man. Heaven help me, it's never changed. I've always loved this man. She reached out her hands, and he grabbed them—then stood and pulled himself up. He wrapped his arms around her and held her tightly, speaking softly into her ear in a voice husky with emotion.

"I am going to be a better man, Meg. I'm going to quit thinking about what I don't have and start concentrating on what I do have—like you and the kids. I promise I'm going to try harder—a *lot* harder—to do that."

She stepped back, put a hand on his chest, and gently pushed back so she could see his face. "I'd like to believe that, Joe, but the truth is, I find hoping for that more exhausting than just accepting the way you are."

"This time is different. I know it is," he said sincerely.

This time. The words rang warning bells in her head. *This is a familiar road, and I know what's at the end of it,* she thought. *Hopes are dashed, and my heart takes another beating.*

She hesitated. "I'm glad you're home."

He cleared his throat. "Me too."

Meg turned toward the street; she could hear the strains of Christy and Danny making their way home.

"I hear the kids. . . ."

Joe looked toward the street just as Christy turned her bike into the driveway and got off to walk it through the loose gravel.

"Christy!" he said as if he hadn't seen her in years, not hours. He hurried down the porch steps toward Christy—opening his arms wide.

Please, please, please, God. Meg wasn't even sure what she was praying for.

"Hi, Daddy!" Christy called with a smile. Without hesitation, she laid her bike down and hurried into his embrace. Meg watched as Joe picked her up and twirled her around. *Just like when she was little. As usual, Lord, you know what I'm praying for even when I don't. Thank you.*

Meg watched Danny turn his bike onto the driveway and look at his dad and Christy. She saw the bewildered look on his face as Joe twirled Christy around, hugged her, and then set her back on her feet. Joe looked at Danny, who still hadn't moved. Without realizing it, Meg held her breath. Joe crossed to Danny and put his hand on his son's shoulder. *He's older, Joe. He's familiar with disappointment. He knows more than you think.* Joe said a few words to Danny. And then much to Meg's amazement, she watched her husband embrace her son for the first time in a very long time. Danny stood stiffly with one arm at his side and the other on his bike. But he allowed Joe his hug.

Joe walked with the kids up the drive and waited as they parked their bikes near the porch. Christy was happy, bubbling, talking about the friends she saw at the park. Danny looked at Meg and raised his eyebrows but followed Joe into the house. *He obviously thought he was going to die today—and now he's celebrating the fact that he's alive. Thank you, God, that he's still here with us. Help me to be grateful for his change of attitude without weighing it down by his broken promises of the past.* Meg heard Christy laugh as she opened the door to go inside. She tried to ignore the tiny seed of hope that had taken root in her heart when Joe had promised to be a better man. *He looked at me with such sincerity. Eyes don't lie. How do I ignore that?*

All through dinner his mom and Christy had been talking with his dad as if nothing was unusual. *He never talks much during supper! It's like he's barely present.* Danny didn't know what had gotten into his dad tonight—but he wasn't as easily fooled as Christy. *Heck, Christy still believes in Santa Claus and that Dad goes to meetings on Saturday nights.* Danny sighed. He'd been that young once and easy to fool.

He hugged me like I was a little kid or something, his thoughts continued. *Maybe next he's gonna want to go out to the garage and help me with my puzzle like he used to. Something's going on—but what?*

"I was thinking that after church this Sunday, we'd take a drive and have a picnic. How does that sound?" Joe asked. Danny knew there was little chance of that actually happening. His dad was always nursing a headache on Sunday morning.

Christy clapped her hands. "Did you hear that, Danny? A picnic!"

She actually believes he's gonna follow through on this. Must be nice to be so young.

"Sunday is a long time away, squirt," Danny said as he shot a look at Joe, then quickly dropped his eyes to his plate. He knew without even seeing it that his mom would be giving him the "mom eye." That special talent God gave mothers to stop their sons in the middle of a sentence with just one piercing look. But he didn't care. He wasn't going to be so naïve anymore. He knew the truth. He knew his dad was at Barney's Tavern on Saturday nights. He'd heard him stumble against the wall, heard him mumble with a tongue thick with alcohol. He'd been awake more than once when his mom had tried to ease his bedroom door shut so he wouldn't see his dad weave past his door. Everyone knew . . . but Christy. The man who had been an observer at this supper table for as long as Danny could remember had suddenly become a participant. He couldn't figure out why—but it didn't really matter. Whatever had caused him to have this interest in the family, it wouldn't last. Danny listened as Christy and Joe talked about their plans for the coming picnic and a thought crossed his mind. Suddenly, his eyes glistened; he blinked back tears that threatened to expose the little boy inside who wished he could still believe in Santa Claus.

The house settled into itself for the night. Joe put the empty milk bottles in the box on the porch so Jerry, their milkman, could replace them in the morning. He turned out the lights, then stood at the bottom of the stairs and listened to the sound of his family going through a ritual he usually avoided: Meg asking if they'd brushed their teeth, Christy wanting to know why she couldn't stay up as late as Danny, who had the privilege of reading for half an hour, and Meg's patient response, "When you're a little older."

A gusty wind—the same wind that had plagued him upon landing earlier in the day—blew under the eaves of the house, producing a concerto of comforting sounds as Joe headed up the steps.

He stopped outside Christy's door and saw her kneeling next to her bed with Meg right beside her. Their heads were bowed, and he stayed in the shadow of the hallway and listened to Christy's prayer.

". . . and God bless Mommy and Daddy and Danny and everyone I love, and thank you, God, that Daddy wants to take us on a picnic next Sunday. And maybe fishing too. Amen." He watched Meg drop a light kiss on the top of Christy's head and utter a soft amen. *I've missed so much. . . .*

Joe moved to Danny's door and gave a little knock.

"Good night, Mom" came Danny's response from behind the door. "I love you."

Joe cleared his throat. "It's me, Dan. Just saying good-night."

"Oh. 'Night" was Danny's muffled reply. Joe turned away from the door to go to his own room. *I love you, son.*

It had been more than an hour since Joe heard Meg slip into the soft, even breaths that told him she had given herself over to sleep. In the early days of their marriage, he had purposely stayed awake until he heard that change in her breathing. He had felt so protective of her, and he liked the reassurance that she was safe and secure beside him. Now, lying in the dark with just a sliver of moonlight stretching across the ceiling of the bedroom, he tried to remember the last time he had felt those stirrings of protectiveness for his wife and children. He was ashamed to admit it had been too long for him to remember. *I thought I was going to be a human plow in some farmer's field today. Otherwise, I'd be sleeping in this bed with my wife and turning my back on our life like I've been doing for years.*

Joe kept his eyes on the stripe of silver light above him. He didn't want to close them and give in to the physical exhaustion of the day. He had to stay on guard against sleep. If he slept, he might lose the tenuous hold he had on the joy of having this second chance at life. He might lose the feeling that he had experienced a miracle.

Feeling as if he was losing the battle to stay awake, he slipped out of bed and walked over to the window. He drew back the curtain and peered out at the sky decorated with starlight, which paled in comparison to the light show he had experienced falling through the clouds earlier that day. He dropped the curtain back into place and sat down in a chair across from the bed. In a matter of minutes, he felt himself sliding toward sleep. Even as he gave up the tug-of-war with consciousness, he wanted the night to go on forever so he could delay the moment when he looked in the mirror in the morning. *I'm afraid the old Joe will be looking back at me.*

Chapter 11

Joe leaned low over the bathroom sink and splashed cold water over his face in an effort to chase away the cobwebs of sleep. He had dozed fitfully in the chair until his aching back had woken him and he'd crawled under the covers just before dawn. Even though he had finally slept, events in the Stearman replayed themselves again and again in his unguarded dreams: the first beats of panic, then the terror, the disbelief—the relief. He stood up, and beads of water dripped off his chin as he looked at his reflection in the mirror for some sign of the man who just yesterday had believed in miracles. But already, in the morning light, the previous day was veiled in a surreal fog in his mind—the urgency of his emotions had slipped and faded to something more rational, more reasonable. His visceral reaction to the flight had been real—and justified. It wasn't often a man faced his own mortality in a ninety-degree dive. *I hit a bird. The engine quit. The plane went into an unrecoverable spin. Yet here I am—the Red Baron of Bugs lives to tell the story.* He knew that today was supposed to be different. *No, wait*—I'm *supposed to be different.*

"Meg!" he shouted as he searched frantically through the drawers of the dresser. He could hear her in the hallway outside the bedroom mediating an argument between the kids.

He felt an irrational surge of panic at the thought it might truly be missing and looked up anxiously when Meg entered the room.

"What is it?" she asked.

"My medal's gone. I can't find it anywhere," he said as he moved her picture and pawed through the loose change and papers on the dresser.

"That's ridiculous. You've put it in the same spot every night for years," she said.

"I know," he said impatiently. "But it's not here. Maybe one of the kids took it."

Meg opened a bureau drawer and began to look through it. "Don't be silly. They wouldn't touch it," she said. "Maybe it's stuck in your shirt from yesterday."

Joe went to the hamper in the corner of the room and pulled out the shirt to shake it. "No. It's gone. Seventeen years I've had that thing and suddenly—gone!"

"Maybe it came off in the spin?" she offered.

He shook his head and dropped to his knees. He swept his hand around on the worn oak floorboards under the bureau. "I've done plenty of loops and barrel rolls and spins, and it's never happened before." *There's a first time for everything. Didn't I learn that yesterday?*

The bedroom door swung inward and knocked Joe, still on his hands and knees, right in the head. Christy peered around the door with an apologetic look on her face when she heard Joe holler out.

"Sorry, Daddy. Are you all right?"

He got to his feet, his hand resting gingerly on the top of his head. "Fine," he answered tersely.

"Can we still have our picnic on Sunday?"

"I don't . . . what? Yeah, sure."

Meg moved across the room and quickly began to scoot Christy out the door. "Go tell your brother his room better be clean or he's not going anywhere or doing anything today."

"But he hates it when I tell him to do something," she grumbled.

"Well, tell him anyway," Meg retorted.

"Can I go with Katie to the creek today?" Christy asked.

"Only if Danny goes with you and you're both home by suppertime," Meg told her.

Christy ducked back out the door, and Meg put a hand on Joe's arm. "I know how much the medal means to you," she said. "I'm sure it'll turn up somewhere."

"Seventeen years. I've worn it for *seventeen* years!"

"You know I'll keep looking for it, right?" she asked as if she could read his mind.

He rubbed a hand over his tired eyes. "I know."

"You didn't sleep much last night, did you?" she asked.

"No."

"You were probably just keyed up about what happened yesterday."

"Probably. But I don't want to dwell on stuff like that—it doesn't do anyone any good."

She gave him a long look—and then he saw the shadow of disappointment flicker across her face as she left the room.

Joe tucked in his shirt and picked up his watch from the bureau. *At least this is where I left it.* He slid the watch over his wrist. He heard Meg tell the kids to be careful at the creek and the front door banged shut. He had the fleeting thought he should have made the effort to tell them good-bye. *Be a better man. . . .*

Joe entered the kitchen and made his way to the stove just as Meg hung up the phone. "That was Norma. We're getting together today," she said, "unless you need me to do something for you . . . ?"

Joe shook his head. "I need to get out to Ernie's and check on the plane. I don't know what kind of damage it took when I hit the bird yesterday, but I'm guessing it could be extensive—and expensive." He looked at the empty burners on the stove.

"No coffee?" he asked.

"I can't get the burners lit. This is the third time in as many days that I can't use the stove. I think we may need a new gas line," she said.

"We need a whole new range. Everything around here is falling apart. And now—if the Stearman is damaged, we're really going to have to tighten our belts."

"Can we tighten our belts *after* Danny's appointment with Dr. Lindstrom this week?" she asked hopefully.

"Who?"

"Dr. Lindstrom. The orthodontist."

"Oh. The braces guy—that's this week?"

She nodded. "The initial appointment is fifteen dollars, but it goes toward the braces if he still thinks Danny needs them."

"It's how he makes his living, Meg. Of course he's gonna say he still needs them. Can't this wait until later—maybe after school starts?"

"No, Joe, it can't. Danny is already a year older than most kids who get braces."

"Fine. But have Lindstrom bill us."

"He has a strict cash-only policy."

Joe collected his truck keys and a black lunch pail from the counter. "Yeah? Me too, but that doesn't mean people do it. And if you ask me, this braces thing is a racket. Danny's got a space between his teeth, and that means he needs a mouth full of metal. It's a racket!"

"So can Danny get the braces if he needs them . . . or not?"

Joe sighed. "Take him to the appointment. Otherwise, I'll be the father who let his son grow up with a gap in his teeth you could drive a truck through. I've got to go."

He was halfway down the driveway when he realized he hadn't even given Meg a proper good-bye. *Nothing out of the ordinary there. She's used to it. A man can't change overnight—and let's face it. She didn't really believe I would—or could.* Joe tossed his lunch box into the cab of the truck and settled behind the steering wheel. He turned the key . . . and heard a click. He tried again and another click. He slammed his hand against the steering wheel and swore under his breath. *How am I supposed to be a better man when I can never catch a break?* He turned the key again and pumped hard on the gas. The engine sputtered and caught. *It might be a new day, but it's the same routine, the same truck. The same man in the same life. . . .*

Ernie stood at the nose of the Stearman next to Joe, and the expression on his face carried a newfound respect for the term "bird strike." Joe traced his finger along a V-shaped hole in the leading edge of the prop where a piece of the wooden blade was missing.

"I'm missing a good eight inches of my prop." Joe leaned a little closer. "The wood's not even splintered."

Ernie nodded sagely. "You're gonna need a whole new prop. *How* big did you say that bird was?"

Joe stepped back and crossed his arms over his chest, his eyes closely examining the plane. "I never actually saw it, but I figure if it was anything like its mate, it was probably between thirty and forty pounds."

"I've seen plenty of bird-strike damage in my time," Ernie said, "but nothing like this."

"How do you mean?" Joe followed Ernie around the plane as the man gestured at the wings.

"Those slices through your wing wires are in three different places like they been run through with a blade. Same thing with that tear we found on the upper wing. A clean cut—nothing ragged or jagged about it. And where's the blood? You hit a bird that size, and there should be plenty a' blood spatters along the fuselage—or at least on the windscreens of the cockpit. 'Bout the only thing I can think of is that the plane's got more damage than the bird. You were a lucky man, Joe. It could a' been a lot worse."

Trust me, Ernie. It was a lot worse.

"You want me to give a call over to Boeing in Wichita and see if they got the parts you're gonna need?" Ernie asked.

"Yeah. Thanks. Let me check the number on the back of the blade before you call," Joe said as he pulled a ladder over to the nose of the plane and climbed up so he could get behind the prop and find the model number. But it wasn't a number he spotted on the back of the prop when his eyes were even with the blade. It was a single white feather that was easily a foot long. The feather was wedged between the prop and the cowling. He reached for it, slipping his hand behind the feather and the cowling, and then yanked it back when he felt a sharp pain. He drew back his hand and saw a cut across the pads of two fingers. He wiped the blood off on his pants, then carefully reached for the feather again, this time pulling it from the quill at the bottom. When he withdrew it, the dazzling white feather gleamed in the sunlight. He climbed off the ladder and held it up for Ernie.

"That's the biggest darn bird feather I've ever seen," Ernie commented. "You catch your hand on something?"

Joe turned his hand over and saw that he was bleeding again. "Must be a sharp edge behind the cowling."

Ernie's eyebrows shot up and he laughed. "Or maybe that's a feather from a really sharp bird." Joe could still hear him chuckling as he walked back toward his office. "Write down the model number for the prop for me, will ya?"

"All right," Joe said and fumbled in his pants pocket for something to write on, then withdrew the small business card Luke had given him. He studied the card with Luke's name and the Vanguard logo, then pulled a pencil out of his shirt pocket and began to climb the ladder again. *Be a better man. . . . Vanguard can do great things for you, Joe.*

Viv's Diner had only a handful of patrons when Joe entered and spotted Luke in a corner booth. He gave his boots a cursory scuff across the doormat protecting a small piece of linoleum floor that was yellowed and buckled with age. Calendars, all depicting some December vista, hung on one wall in rows that dated from the previous December of 1957 back to December of 1917—the month that diner owner Viv Hatfield's husband had been killed in World War I. The forty calendars flapped in the breeze on a windy day anytime the diner door opened. Viv, whose trademark beehive hairdo could withstand a hurricane-force wind, waved at Joe from behind the lunch counter.

A white Formica tabletop stretched between Luke and Joe like a bridge that neither was sure how to cross. Years of names had been etched into the surface of the Formica—the handiwork of teens with pocketknives. Joe knew the graffiti by heart—where each name was placed and, for the most part, knew the faces behind the names. He shifted on the cracked red vinyl seat and tried to relax as Luke spent a few minutes tripping down memory lane.

"It's been strange being back here in town," Luke said with a half smile. "Seems like forever ago that we left—but then I come in here and sit in this booth and it seems like yesterday."

"At least you've seen the big world out there," Joe said. "That's something I haven't done."

"You know, I would have been happy to have stayed right here in Greenville," Luke said, then lifted a shoulder in a shrug. "But . . . life had other plans, I guess, and I had to play the cards I got dealt."

"Seems like you've done all right with that hand," Joe observed.

"Not bad, I guess," Luke said modestly, "but truthfully, I'd trade any financial success I've had for a family like yours."

Luke purposely looked over at the end of the booth at a large heart carved into the tabletop; in the center it said, "Meg & Joe forever." Joe followed his gaze and a small smile tugged at the corner of his mouth.

"Man, I wanted to be you in high school," Luke said. "It seemed like you had everything going for you. Great parents, good athlete, popular with everyone and—"

"Meg," Joe added.

Luke nodded. "And Meg." He flashed a self-aware, half-embarrassed smile at Joe. "You know, I had a crush on her for a lo-ong time, but she wouldn't even give me the time of day. I doubt she knew any other boy in the school existed except you."

Viv approached with two glasses of water. "Luke Ramsey, I don't think there's anything left on my menu you haven't tried as often as you've been in here," she said with a pleased smile.

"Then I'm just going to have to work my way through your menu again, Viv," he responded, "and I'll start with the special."

"Okey-doke," she said. "Joe?"

"I'll have the same."

"It'll be up in two shakes," she said and then moved behind the counter like a woman on a mission.

Luke reached into an expensive leather briefcase beside him on the seat. "I've got a couple brochures here I want you to have, Joe. Gives some stats about Vanguard and the positive impact it's had on similar farming communities like Greenville."

Joe saw the flash of Luke's shiny cuff links and wondered idly if the man ever wore anything other than long-sleeved shirts. He tugged at the tail of his short-sleeved pullover and regretted not putting an iron to it. Suddenly he felt rumpled and out of his league. *In high school it was always me beating him out—but now here we sit. Me with my hat in my hand—and Luke holding all the cards. Talk about a tough hand to be dealt. I go to work for Vanguard—for Luke—and I wonder how many times I'll be putting Meg in a room with this man. How many social get-togethers she'd see us side by side and compare—see that she picked the loser. Who needs that? I don't need that. . . . I don't need this job.*

And then Luke slid a picture across the table toward him. Joe's eyes widened at the sight, and he leaned closer and whistled under his breath. "That's some statistic," he said as he looked at the picture of a shiny new plane.

Luke grinned. "I thought that would get your attention. That's a G-164 Ag Cat. Pretty, huh?"

"Pretty sleek," Joe agreed. "Looks powerful."

"That's the prototype, but Vanguard has put in an order with a company called Grumman for forty of those babies," Luke said. "And some of them will be parked right out at Ernie's airstrip if this deal all comes together."

"How many pilots you figure you'll need?" Joe asked, unable to take his eyes off the photo of the plane.

"I think I should be asking you that, Joe. You're the one with the experience in this area—and you know the fields and how often you have to spray."

Joe shook his head. "I don't know. Right now I'm my own boss, and all I have to worry about is my own hide."

"True. But right now you have to worry about your own repairs and your own bills—and coming up with enough work to meet your monthly expenses for your family," Luke said. "It can't be cheap to raise a family these days."

"I've been managing."

Luke folded his arms on the table and leaned toward Joe. "Wouldn't it be nice to do more than just 'manage'?" he asked. "With Vanguard you'd have a brand-new plane, could set your own hours, a salary that would be guaranteed every month regardless of weather or how many fields you sprayed. We offer health insurance for your family, and of course there would be the company truck."

Joe's eyebrows rose. "Company truck?"

Luke nodded. "Of course. You'd be considered a manager, and all managers get a new company truck—just like mine."

Viv arrived with their meals. "Dig in while it's hot," she said and then hurried off again.

Luke tucked right into his meatloaf, but Joe pulled the picture of the plane a little closer. "Wonder what her max speed is."

"A hundred twenty-eight knots," Luke said with his fork poised in the air, "and she carries fifteen liters in the forward hopper."

"A hundred twenty-eight knots," Joe whispered, then slid it back.

Luke raised a hand to stop him. "No, you keep it."

Joe finally tore his eyes away from the picture and looked up to Luke flashing that perfect smile. Joe found himself smiling in return, then joined Luke in digging his fork into the meatloaf.

It was after eleven at night when Joe finally climbed the stairs through the quiet house to his bedroom. He was pleased to see that Meg was still awake, propped up in bed, with a half dozen magazines spread across her lap.

She looked up from the magazines, and he was immediately aware she was trying to gauge his mood just by looking at him. He thought he'd make it easier for her and attempted a smile.

"Hi," he said.

She answered his smile with one of her own. "Hi." She began to collect the magazines.

"Did you get all the repairs done on the plane?" she asked as he shrugged out of his work shirt and threw it over the chair in the corner.

"Yeah. I was lucky that Chip picked up the prop for me when he was in Wichita," he said as he crossed to the dresser. "Ernie had everything else at the airstrip." He pulled some change from his pants pocket and put it on the dresser.

"That's good, then, and you got something to eat—because if you didn't, I can heat up—"

"No, it's okay. I had something," he said, then as an afterthought, "Thanks, though." He took off his watch, put it next to the loose coins, and then automatically reached for his medal—and stopped. His hand dropped to his side.

"You didn't find it, then?" she asked with a trace of worry in her voice.

"No," he said. "Guess that means you didn't either?"

She shook her head. "I'm sorry. I turned this room upside down after you left this morning. Wherever it is—it's not in the house."

A shadow passed over his face and he sighed. "I was kind of hoping all day—you know—that I'd come home and you'd say, 'Look what I found—it was right here all along and we just didn't see it.'"

"There's a little place in Emporia that sells the exact same kind of—"

"It wouldn't be the same," he said with a quick shake of his head as he toed off his boots.

"I know," she said sympathetically. "I just thought it might help."

He forced another wobbly smile. "I appreciate it, I really do." As if to emphasize his point, he tried to be casual as he walked over to the bed and dropped a kiss on the top of her head. "Thanks."

He saw her look of surprise and then the quick way she tried to cover it. *Surprised by a simple kiss,* Joe thought. *Well, why shouldn't she be surprised? I haven't exactly been Mr. Affectionate lately. Longer than lately . . . be a changed man . . .*

Joe started toward the small bathroom that adjoined their room.

"The pajamas on the hook are clean," Meg said as she dropped the magazines next to the bed.

"Okay." He closed the door, leaving just an inch or so cracked as he grabbed his pajamas that were hanging on the back.

"We had that appointment with Dr. Lindstrom today," she said from the other room.

Dr. Lindstrom? Who . . . oh. "How'd that go?" he responded as he pulled off his dirty clothes and stepped into the pajamas.

"He thinks we should wait just a few more months for Danny's braces because all his wisdom teeth aren't in yet," she said, and he heard her yawn.

No, don't yawn—wait—just wait. . . . "That's good." He ran a stripe of toothpaste over his toothbrush, turned on the faucet, and made an attempt to achieve that "minty fresh breath" he hoped he'd need.

Clean pj's—check. Teeth brushed—check. Hair—

He straightened up and looked in the medicine cabinet mirror over the sink. *Lights definitely need to be off,* he thought as he looked at his sorry reflection. He tried to smooth down his hair with a wet hand, saw the bags under his eyes and the five-o'clock shadow that was six hours old. *How to work a miracle in thirty seconds,* he wondered.

He opened the medicine cabinet and moved aside a bottle of antacid, a half-empty bottle of aspirin, and some mentholated rub for cold and flu season. Hiding in the back corner on a shelf was a bottle of Old Spice aftershave. Joe pulled it out and worked off the cap. He splashed some into his palms and then onto his cheeks. *Better—at least better smelling.* He closed the door to the medicine cabinet and came face-to-face with himself again. He started to button up his pajama shirt and then changed his mind, leaving it open. Shoulders back, chest out, chin up—he tried out his best dazzling smile in the mirror—and then leaving it frozen in place, he pulled open the door to give Meg the full effect. But she was fast asleep.

Lying on her side, lips parted in the relaxed state of sleep, Meg looked so young and so beautiful. Disappointment and frustration vied for top billing as Joe buttoned up his shirt and carefully pulled the sheet up over Meg's shoulder. He switched off the lamp next to the bed and went to the chair by the window that was bathed in moonlight. He started to move his shirt from the arm of the chair and then remembered that the picture Luke had given him was in the pocket.

He relaxed into the cushions, let his head rest against the high back of the chair, and held the picture of the plane up in the moonlight. For a moment, he let himself daydream about taking his family for a ride in a truck that didn't rattle, groan, and moan with every mile. He'd pull up at the airstrip in the new truck and show them the new plane—his new office—with his name over the door, of course. Danny would love the truck, but he'd love the plane even more. Christy would want to go for a ride in Daddy's new "arrow plane," and Meg . . . Meg would smile at him just as she used to . . . as if he were the only man in the world. For just that moment, he imagined what it would feel like to be . . . successful. *Can a new direction create a new man?*

Chapter 12

With the Stearman lined up at the edge of the airstrip, Joe sat in the cockpit and watched the flash of the new propeller as it spun and powered the loud, guttural growl of the engine. He snugged down the harness to be sure it was secure. The instant he put his hand on the throttle, a bead of sweat trickled down from his forehead. His eyes shifted and landed on the gleaming white feather he had found behind the prop, now wedged crosswise behind the altimeter—a reminder of a dive and a spin and a bird that came out of nowhere. *Vigilance is the key.* Wham! Silence assaulted Joe, and he was suddenly free-falling back through the clouds. Flashes of light interspersed with images of the ground rushing up at him. *"Help me, God, please—just give me one more chance!"* Joe squeezed his eyes closed just before impact—but when he reopened them, he was still staring through the prop down the dirt strip.

Joe's breath came in short puffs of nervous air that left him feeling weak. His hand went to his neck, still searching for the missing medal. He swallowed back the panic he felt at having to fly without it—even though he knew it was just a piece of metal.

Some kind of crutch he'd been using for years as a substitute for what? *It's not the medal that makes the man—it's the confidence.*

Still, he sat in the cockpit without moving as he tried to will his hand forward on the throttle; it would not budge. *What's happening to me?*

Before he even knew he was going to do it, he unbuckled his harness. Joe taxied off the strip, shut down the engine, and climbed out of the cockpit. He felt like a fool standing beside the plane, but he knew as sure as he knew his own name, he couldn't fly right now. He'd have to call Tom Simpson and apologize—again—for not making it over to his place to spray his fields. *Maybe I'll tell him the repairs aren't done. He can't fault me for that. I'll have a better perspective on this later. Tomorrow. The day after?*

Joe knew Ernie would be out of his office any minute, wondering what he was doing, and he dreaded having to explain this sudden deficit of confidence he had. He knew Ernie understood the rituals of flying—he wouldn't fault him for the way he was feeling—but he would expect him to rise above it and get the job done. How could he tell Meg he was the poster child for disappointment yet again? "*Maybe it came off in the spin?*" *Could that have happened?* Maybe Meg was right. Maybe the chain broke and fell out of the plane. Maybe if he looked hard enough, he could find the medal Meg had given him. *Maybe I'll win a million dollars by sunset. Yeah, right.*

It didn't matter that it was a crazy long shot. What mattered was that he couldn't make himself take that plane up right now. He had to *do* something proactive to fix this mental block, and if that meant looking for the proverbial needle in a haystack—then that's what he was going to do.

Joe looked at the compass on the dash of his truck as he sped along the two-lane highway. He wondered briefly what Ernie had made of the flimsy excuse he'd given for not flying—a forgotten appointment. Whether he'd believed him or not, Ernie had assured him he'd call Tom.

Trying to reconstruct his flight path from the ground would be tricky. It was one thing to go "as the crow flies" but quite another to be confined to roads and byways. He called up a mental map of his return trip to the airfield right before he hit the bird, trying to remember the landmarks below him just as he had gone through the barrier of stratus clouds. Whose field? Whose house? Whose grain silo or windmill churning because of the high winds? Suddenly, it wasn't the landmark he remembered as he climbed through the cloud bank—it was the field he had been facing in a ninety-degree dive. He was positive it had been Hiram Edwards' field. For a second, he thought about turning around. *Of course it would be Hiram's fields—just my rotten luck.* But he didn't turn around—the draw of finding his medal outweighed his pride.

Joe rolled to a stop in the yard in front of Hiram's farmhouse. He hadn't been to the house in years—only seen it from a bird's-eye view when he had done the occasional spraying job for Hiram. The optimistic sunny yellow paint and bright blue shutters on the house seemed incongruent with the stress, fear, and uncertainty that Hiram and Sara had been dealing with since Sara's diagnosis of cancer a year ago. *Or has it been two years? I don't remember.*

Joe hated personal interaction with his customers; he had always preferred to do business by mail and phone. He'd tell his customers to make their appointments by phone and mail him a check. Which was why having to go to Hiram's door and actually asking the man if he could search his cornfield was almost as hard as flying the Stearman without his medal.

Almost . . . but not quite.

Joe made his way to the door—and then stopped. *What in the world am I gonna say? What if I wake Sara—I hear she sleeps a lot these days. What if Hiram tells me no? He's got every right to be mad—I turned him down flat in his time of need.* He willed himself to the door. *Knock. Just do it. Knock on the door! Just ask and get it over with.* Joe rapped his knuckles on the door and stepped back. It was only moments before he could hear footsteps approaching.

"Joe! What a nice surprise," Sara said with a lilt to her voice.

The last thing he was prepared for was that Sara would answer the door. He could barely make out her image behind the screen and silently berated himself for his stupid idea. *Hiram probably told her what a selfish jerk I was, and she's going to slam that door—just like she ought to.*

Sara opened the screen, and Joe took a step back at her robust, healthy appearance.

"Sara! I didn't expect—I didn't think—wow! You look wonderful."

And she did. Gone was the gaunt, gray pallor of her skin and the haunted, worried look in her eyes. Instead, her cheeks were flushed with the color of fresh-picked peaches, and her eyes were radiant with joy. Even the wispy white hair she'd kept so little of during her regimen of medical treatment had thickened into the hair of a much younger woman. Joe had seen her in town only two weeks ago, and he was staggered by the difference in how she looked now.

"Thanks, Joe," she said as she stepped outside. "I'll tell you a secret. I feel even better than I look!" She smiled. "I feel like I'm only fifty years old again. I feel good enough to put up enough corn for three winters when Hiram gets it harvested!"

"Last time I, uh, talked to Hiram, he said you'd had a good day, but this"—Joe gestured to her—"this is a . . ."

"A miracle! It's a miracle. I went to the doctor yesterday, and he gave me a clean bill of health! Don't ever doubt that prayers matter, Joe!"

"I won't. I . . . don't," he said.

"I'm not sure I can explain what it feels like to have a second chance at life, but I can tell you I'm going to be grateful for every minute God has seen fit to gift me with."

Second chance at life. "Seen fit to 'gift you with'?" Joe asked.

She nodded. "I can't think of a better way to put it—can you?"

"No. I guess I can't. I'm so happy for you, Sara," Joe said sincerely. "Meg will be too."

"Thank you, Joe," she said warmly. "I suppose you must be looking for my man."

"I was, actually."

"He said he was going to the north field to double-check the irrigation ditch," she said. "You can go on out there and find him. Look for the tractor—he'll be close by."

"Okay, thanks." Joe turned to leave.

"Oh, and Joe? Will you tell Hiram that I've got an applesauce cake just out a' the oven? You're welcome to come in and have a slice with him," she offered.

He nodded with a smile. "I'll tell him."

The corn in the field was at least as tall as Joe as he walked through the rows, stopping every now and again to look closely at the nearly mature ears on the stalks. *I don't see any rootworm beetles,* he thought. *This corn looks near perfect.*

He spotted Hiram's tractor near a culvert running between plotted acres. As he made his way slowly through the rows of corn—*corn free of bugs*—he felt ridiculous. In actually walking through the acreage, he realized how futile his mission really was. He did a quick about-face. *What on earth was I thinking?*

That I'd just wander into the cornfield and pluck my wayward medal off an ear of corn? I have to get out of here before anyone sees me. Sara doesn't know what I wanted. She'll just tell Hiram I stopped by, and no one will be the wiser. . . .

"Joe! Joe Daley?" Hiram called out.

Joe stopped and closed his eyes in a moment of pure frustration, and then he turned to find Hiram striding toward him.

"How ya doin', Hiram? Sara told me I could find you out here."

Hiram grinned. "She looks good—doesn't she?"

Joe smiled back. "She really does. She told me the doctor said she's cured."

Hiram hooked his thumbs in the pockets of his overalls and nodded. "Yes, sir. The doctor gets to say it—but it's the good Lord that did it."

"You both must be so relieved."

"Relieved, giddy, blessed, thankful—you name it—we're feeling it," Hiram said. "You wonder about miracles, and then you're blessed with two of them inside of a week!"

"Two. Miracles?"

Hiram swept his hand over the corn. "Look at these ears a' corn, Joe. Not a rootworm beetle to be seen!"

"You get Chip to spray for you, then?"

"Nope. Didn't have the cash money to pay him either," Hiram said, and Joe felt a sweeping sense of guilt.

"I'm telling you the corn is the other miracle. One day it's infested something awful—and the next I couldn't find a bug if someone was gonna give me a dollar for it."

"That's . . . impossible," Joe said.

"No, sir, that's miraculous. Only explanation I can come up with. I'm keen on believing God's smiling down on me and Sara right now, Joe. This is going to be my best harvest in ten years! Ten years! Of course, the best part is that my girl will be right there to see it!"

Joe was speechless. He had almost forgotten how awkward he had felt walking out to find Hiram in the field. And then Hiram asked the question he didn't know how to answer without sounding ridiculous.

"What brings you out here?" Hiram asked.

"You know, Hiram, it's been so long since I've actually walked a field, I thought it would be a good thing for me to get back to some basics and get a feel for the crops I spray." *Who knew I'd be so good at lying on the fly? Let's see if you buy that, Hiram. . . .*

"That makes sense," Hiram acknowledged.

It does? Good. It's all I've got right now.

"You might be looking at basics, but I can show you something darn unusual if you're of a mind to see it," Hiram said.

"Okay. What d'ya got?" Joe asked. Hiram gestured for him to follow, and Joe actually found he had a hard time keeping up with the old farmer in the faded overalls.

"What do you think of this?" Hiram asked as they stepped from between the tall stalks of corn into a huge area of the field that looked as though the corn had been shucked, removed, and then tilled down to nothing but tiny green stalks resembling new spring growth. He shook his head in amazement.

"I think it's pretty strange. How did you do this?"

"I didn't do it. I just kind a' stumbled across it the other day when I was out here checking on the corn," Hiram said. "Stumbled on something else too."

Joe squatted down in the dirt and ran his hand over the stubs of green. "What was that?"

"I believe that was me."

The man's voice was one Joe had never heard before, deep and pleasant. Almost melodic. He straightened up and looked at the biggest man he'd ever seen. Stretching well over six feet tall, with a neck that seemed as thick as a tree trunk and arms to match, a man of indeterminate age stood just a few feet away with an old horse harness tucked under his arm like a toy. Hiram beamed like a proud father as he stepped toward the stranger.

"Ferguson! There you are. I want you to meet Joe Daley," Hiram said.

Joe stayed where he was, but Hiram gestured toward him. "Come on, Joe. He's big but he's harmless, isn't that right, Ferguson?" Hiram looked up at him with a twinkle in his eye.

Joe crossed the few feet between them and stuck out his hand.

"It's nice to meet you," Joe said and felt his hand disappear into Ferguson's as they shook.

"And you too, Joe," he answered in that unique voice.

Bo would kill to have a voice like that, Joe thought. Ferguson dropped Joe's hand, pushed a thick mane of hair off his forehead, and then pulled a little at the collar of his shirt.

Where does he get clothes that big? "Are you just visiting, or are you new to Greenville?" Joe asked.

"He doesn't know," Hiram said cheerfully. "Fact a' the matter is, I found him lying right here in this clearing. Buck naked." Hiram turned to Ferguson. "Hope you don't mind me mentioning that part." Ferguson shook his head with a smile. Hiram turned back to Joe. "Best we can figure is something bad happened. A blow to the head. Somethin' that made him unable to remember his particulars—Sara's of the opinion he has a good case of amnesia."

"At least you remember your name," Joe said.

Ferguson smiled. "I've found that a name is important."

"Uh, yeah. I'd have to agree with you on that," Joe said.

The three men stood in silence for a moment. Ferguson shifted the harness from one arm to the other. Joe studied the dirt under his feet. *Tell them why you're really here. That you came to find a tiny medal that fell hundreds of feet from the sky. Yeah. They'll look at me like I'm on the slow train to Nutville. Maybe I am.*

Hiram cleared his throat. "Joe felt the need to walk the fields today," he explained to Ferguson, "stand in the crops he usually just sees from a bird's-eye view."

"You're a flyer?" Ferguson asked with interest.

Joe nodded. "Crop duster. I spray most of the fields around here."

"I saw Ernie Colfax at the diner yesterday, Joe," Hiram said. "He says a huge bird banged up your plane pretty good."

"It did some serious damage, that's for sure," Joe agreed.

"This . . . bird encounter you had. It was recent?" Ferguson asked.

"Recent enough I still sweat when I think about it. I was in a cloud bank and never saw it coming."

Hiram said, "Guess you were able to land all right, then, in spite a' the damage?"

"I can't say there weren't some tense moments when I lost control—but I managed to recover it," Joe explained. "When I saw the chunk that was missing from the prop and the other damage, I'd say I was awful lucky to get her back on the ground."

"I'd say that was an answer to prayer," Ferguson said with a smile.

The comment took Joe completely by surprise—and he couldn't even muster a response.

"That'd be my take on it," Hiram said. "Don't you agree, Joe?"

Joe was still studying Ferguson. "Hmm? Oh, yeah. I agree."

Ferguson hefted the horse harness to his other arm. "Hiram, I was wondering if this is something I might have."

Hiram scratched his head. "Don't know why not. It's worthless to me. It broke about five years ago, and I haven't seen it since. Where'd you find it?"

"It was all but buried under the dirt in the next field. The clasp was the only thing sticking out of the soil. I saw the sun reflecting off the metal, or I would have passed it right by," Ferguson told him.

"You're welcome to it."

"Thank you." Ferguson smiled, then disappeared back through the cornfield with the harness tucked securely under his arm.

Hiram waited until Ferguson was out of earshot and then shook his head. "When I found the big guy in my field, I don't mind admitting that I was little scared a' him, what with the scrapes and scratches. But he didn't seem any worse for the wear, and after spending just a few minutes talking to him, I knew in my gut he wouldn't hurt a fly. You look in his eyes, and you see a gentle soul who's grateful for the food, shelter, and clothes."

"Where'd you ever get clothes that big?"

Hiram grinned. "We sure didn't have anything here to fit him, but Sara fashioned his shirt from an old tablecloth and then used a pair of waders as a pattern to make him a pair of pants from a canvas tent I used in my younger days."

"And you really aren't worried about having him around?" Joe asked.

"No, like I said, he's a gentle man, even if he is a little . . . eccentric."

"Eccentric?"

"I'm starting to think that wherever he's from or whoever he is, Ferguson was a junk collector. Saw him yesterday with an old birdcage that's missing the door. Don't know how he's gonna keep a bird in there." Hiram tucked his thumbs into the bib of his overalls. "But then again, one man's junk is another man's treasure. Ain't that right, Joe?"

"I guess so," Joe agreed, then remembered he had a message for Hiram. "I forgot to tell you Sara said the applesauce cake is done."

Hiram's eyes twinkled. "Makes my mouth water just to think about it. Come back to the house with me and have some, Joe."

"I better pass, Hiram, but thanks. I've got a field to spray today."

"Well, then, I'll walk back that way with you," Hiram said as he started into the path through the tall corn and disappeared. Joe slowly followed him, but just as he was passing the first tall stalk of corn on the edge of the wide opening, he saw the sun glint off the husk. He stepped over to the ear of corn, and his knees nearly buckled with his discovery. There—caught on the edge of the corn husk—was his St. Christopher's medal.

His surprise—and excitement—and disbelief rolled into his gut and he yelled out, loudly, with a hysterical laugh. His hand shaking, he lifted the chain from the corn and examined it. "Well, I'll be a son of a—"

"Joe?" Hiram hurried back. "I heard you yell. You all right?"

Joe grinned at him and closed his palm around his medal. "I just can't get over how great your corn looks, Hiram!"

Hiram grinned back. "It does look like miracle corn—doesn't it?"

"It sure does," Joe said. He had a definite bounce to his step as he followed Hiram back through the corn.

Chapter 13

The sound of mallets crashing into drywall reverberated throughout Norma's house, punctuating the birdsong of the quiet countryside. Meg and Norma, covered in a fine sheen of chalky white dust, worked side by side tearing down an interior wall that separated one upstairs bedroom from another. Ankle deep in chunks of drywall and torn pieces of wallpaper, they had managed to expose a hole large enough to walk through between two-by-four studs.

Norma took a big swing at the wall and crashed through a parallel section. "This sounded," she said breathlessly, "like a better idea yesterday."

Meg's own swing cut out another chunk of the wall. She peered through the hole, chest heaving. "Too late now," she quipped. "And Rosie the Riveter doesn't have anything on us."

Norma gave a short laugh and attempted to bring her mallet up again but then let her arm swing limply at her side. She used her free hand to wipe the sweat off her forehead. "If I don't take a break, my arms are gonna fall off," she said as she dropped the mallet to the floor.

Meg issued a relieved groan and dropped her own tool. "You mean you can still *feel* your arms?" she asked. "Mine went numb fifteen minutes ago."

Norma tried to brush the drywall dust from her hot, sticky arms. "Why didn't you say something?"

"And let the city girl outdo the country girl? No thanks," Meg said as she dropped to the floor.

Norma laughed and made her way to an open window where a pitcher of water and two glasses rested on the sill. She started to fill the glasses.

"What on earth were we thinking, sending my boys to the movies and your kids fishing?" Norma asked.

"While we throw our shoulders out and possibly suffer other permanent damage," Meg added.

Norma handed Meg a glass of water.

"That's parenthood for you," Meg quipped as she gulped down the water without stopping.

Norma moaned tiredly as she lowered herself to the floor next to Meg. "Parenthood. Everything seemed awfully simple when we were kids."

"It *was* simple," Meg agreed.

Norma took a long drink, and silence fell between them.

"You haven't said much about Bob," Meg finally said carefully.

"I know," Norma answered, her voice low. "It's a strange thing to talk about. I never pictured my life turning out this way."

"I'm sorry, Norma," Meg said quickly. "I shouldn't have brought it up."

"No, it's fine," Norma assured her. "I've wanted to talk to you about it since I've been back, but I worried I'd ruin the perfect image you have of me."

Meg cocked her head to the side and smiled. "No worries there."

"Even though my story had *ugly* written into it . . . it does have a happy ending."

Meg smiled encouragingly. "I love happy endings."

"When I went away to Kansas City for college, I have to admit what I really wanted more than an education was to find what you and Joe had. I wanted someone I could love and who would love me that completely. I met Bob a few weeks into my first semester when we were both on the school activities board. I know I wrote you about him, but I never could quite capture him on paper. He was a senior—and seemed so worldly-wise and self-possessed. He had the kind of magnetic charm that drew people to him—especially girls. Imagine my surprise when he started to notice me. I wasn't even in his league. Rumor had it that he came from a wealthy family. He drove a new car, had new clothes, and had a seemingly endless bank account to treat all of us on the board to lunches and dinners.

"The first time he asked me to have dinner alone with him, I panicked. I didn't look like the other girls I had seen him date. For starters, I was sure I didn't have anything to wear. I was just a hick from a little farming town who'd been raised by her grandparents. I had resigned myself to the likelihood that this would be a one-time-only date and then he'd see his error in judgment."

"But he fell head over heels for you instead," Meg interjected.

"Yes. Much to my astonishment, he did. And I was head over heels for him by the end of that first date. I didn't really believe him when he said he loved me just as I was. He said he appreciated that I was different from the other girls. He thought I was innocent and sweet.

"But what he called sweet, I began to think of as boring. I started to obsess that he would get tired of the little good girl from Greenville. I met all his friends—the majority of whom were flat-out snobs, I tell you. I don't think Bob saw them that way—these were the kinds of people he'd known all his life. But I knew what they thought of me, and I set out to change it. At first, I refused the cocktails they'd offer, but gradually I learned that if I accepted the martinis or the gin and tonics, they thought I was more fun. I was changing to impress people who could care less about me, and I found if I drank enough, I could forget how phony I had become." Norma got up to get them both more water.

"Bob and I eloped, and I was glad we did. If we'd planned a real wedding," she continued as she poured their glasses full, "I was afraid he could have had time to reconsider the whole thing. When we got back from our honeymoon, I realized how much money he really had. We bought a beautiful new home and filled it with expensive . . . everything. I pointed and he bought. It was almost as intoxicating as the alcohol. Suddenly having so much, now I worried even more about having so much to lose. Instead of attending the cocktail parties, I was giving them. The weekdays were filled with luncheons and charity events. And more drinking. Wine with lunch, cocktails at dinner. I had taken the game to heart, and I was winning. I went from judging snobs to judging those who weren't—a champion at it who looked down her nose on anyone who didn't wear the right clothes and live at the right address.

"After a few years of marriage, Bob and I were practically social royalty . . . but we felt like something was missing in our lives. We wanted children, and of course, I presumed if I wanted a child, I'd get a child. Except it didn't work that way. As it turns out, I can never bear a child naturally."

"Oh, Norma. I'm so sorry."

Norma put her hand up. "Please, don't feel sorry for me. I've cornered that market all by myself. Bob tried to talk me into adopting a child, but I was petulant and selfish. If I couldn't have 'a baby of my own,' I said, I wouldn't have any children at all.

While Bob watched me spiral out of control, I made sure I didn't have a single minute to think about my poor, sad misfortune.

"You know, Meg," Norma said, turning to look at her, "it didn't dawn on me to pray for some kind of peace. In spite of all I knew from my childhood, any awareness of God didn't even dawn on me at all during that time. I didn't lash out at Him, I didn't consider Him unfair. I just didn't factor Him in at all. I didn't call Granny and Pops on Saturdays anymore. I was sure they'd hear things in my voice that would make them sad. When Pops died and I came back for his funeral, I couldn't even look Granny in the eye. I said the proper things, made the proper offers, and then got out of here as fast as I could."

"I remember that. We didn't even get a chance to say more than hello at his service," Meg said quietly.

"I had to get back to Kansas City and the circle whose hearts were just like mine. Empty. When Gran passed away not long after Pops, I couldn't come back. I planned to . . . then one drink led to another, and I washed all the plans right down my throat with a fifth of vodka and some ice."

"That's why you hired a company to come and clean out the house?" Meg asked.

Norma nodded. "Bob threw himself into his work—and I threw myself cocktail parties. Looking back, I couldn't even tell you when I crossed that invisible line from being a social drinker to an alcoholic. I just know that I needed a drink to start my day and one to end my day and a few to get me through the hours in between. Someone made an offhand comment to Bob about my drinking—which I overheard. Bob laughed it off, but I worried he would start to watch me more closely, so I barely drank anything in public. I did the majority of it alone. I hid bottles in my dresser drawers, in potted plants, and even hid one in the toilet tank."

Norma shook her head slowly. "It was fashionable in our circle to 'take on a cause,' so I agreed to help with a fundraiser for a local orphanage. I met the children and took the tour of the group home and felt myself pump up with importance. Twice when I met with the director, a little girl named Jenny followed me around like a lost puppy. She told me I reminded her of her mommy."

"That's sweet," Meg said.

"Oh, I thought so too at first. But when I went back to give the check to the director of the facility, I learned that Jenny had died. She ran away in January and froze to death in an alley a mile or so from the orphanage." Norma shook her head sadly. " 'All she wanted was a mother,' I whispered. I didn't even realize I'd spoken the words aloud. The director agreed with me and said if Jenny had been blessed with a wonderful woman like me for a mother, her life wouldn't have ended in tragedy the way it did. She went on to say that Jenny's mother was a useless, no-good alcoholic who put her addiction over everything—including the five-year-old child she had abandoned."

Norma's eyes welled with tears. "When I heard those words I wanted to die. I was consumed by shame. What she thought was a compliment ended up being a knife in my heart. It's no wonder I reminded Jenny of her mommy—*I was just like her.*"

Meg could feel tears in her own eyes—for that little girl and for her friend.

"I left the orphanage," Norma said, "and don't even remember walking in the door to my warm, comfortable, enormous house. On my knees in my bedroom, I finally talked to God. I asked Him to help me. I asked Him to forgive me. And I asked the Lord to use my life for His glory.

"I know what it means to be born again, Meg," Norma said, looking again at her. "That day I was cleaned from the inside out and forgiven. I haven't had a drop of alcohol since then—and with God's continued help, I never will again."

"That's your happy ending," Meg said softly. "Ending . . . and beginning."

"Amen to that, sister!" Norma exclaimed.

"And Bob?" Meg ventured.

"Poor Bob." Norma shook her head. "He didn't know which end was up. He knew I was an alcoholic—he'd just never said it out loud. We hadn't ever talked about it because I was keeping things together—functioning on some level in spite of the drinking. At least it was something he understood. And then I did a complete about-face—which he *didn't* understand. My newfound faith, my mission to be of service to children like Jenny. He thought—maybe even hoped—it was just a passing phase.

"Bob wasn't interested in being a foster parent, but I was relentless about it. He finally gave in just to get me to stop badgering him. When Zach came to live with us, Bob started working more. When JP and Frankie, two boys from another family, joined us, Bob barely came home.

"Becoming a parent is daunting anyway," Norma continued with a sigh, "and then when we were faced with the problems that came with the boys—it was beyond draining. Zach took things from us—money, clothes, a watch. When we'd confront him about it, he'd lie right to our faces. He started smoking when he was only nine, bumming cigarettes from older boys, stealing them whenever he could. Then, I'd find food hidden all over JP's room—in drawers, under the bed, in the closet. The poor kid had always worried where his next meal was coming from, and so he was just stashing it for what he thought was inevitable—the time when we wouldn't provide him a meal. Frankie cowered whenever he heard a loud noise or someone raised their voice. It was impossible to get him to answer a simple question.

"It just all turned out to be more than Bob could handle. He had agreed to take on the kids because of me—but didn't have the same commitment to seeing it through as I did. He wanted to send them back, but I couldn't do it. Even though I had—and still have—days when I feel completely at a loss." Norma's eyes glistened with unshed tears as she released a pent-up breath. "Okay—I made it through the worst of it and you're still sitting here," she said with a small smile. "You still with me?"

Meg smiled back her encouragement. "All the way to the end."

Norma nodded and picked up her tale. "Finally Bob admitted he missed the 'exciting' Norma. The hostess everyone raved about—the society wife who dressed to the nines and looked great on his arm. He said I was no fun anymore since I quit drinking and found God."

Meg couldn't help but chuckle at the irony of it.

Norma smiled ruefully. "I gave it my best, but nothing I did was quite enough for him. Bob said he was through, so we agreed that living apart was the best solution—as long as we stay legally married, I can keep the boys. He was good about that."

Meg wanted to tell Norma about Joe . . . it was on the tip of her tongue, but she couldn't do it. She couldn't admit that she thought her own husband had a drinking problem. He probably wasn't actually an alcoholic, since he only drank on weekends, but she worried that if she said any of it out loud, that would make it real . . . make it true.

Meg cleared her throat. "I would imagine it goes on in more houses than you'd think."

Norma looked at her. "That's true. Alcoholism doesn't discriminate. It can hide in some families for years until one day, the family just can't hide it anymore."

Meg looked into the empty water glass she held in her hands. "They get tired, I'll bet. Tired of keeping up with the secret—tired of working around it and through it, tired of the way it sits in the room with them."

Suddenly Meg realized that she'd shared more of her worries than she'd meant to. She looked up to find Norma studying her and quickly jumped to her feet. "You ready to keep pretending we're both eighteen and this isn't hard work?" Meg asked.

"Only if you're ready to think of me as a country girl again," Norma replied.

Meg lifted her eyebrows. "Are you saying that city girls don't routinely open holes in their walls?"

"I'm saying some of them don't even routinely open their own drapes at the windows," Norma said with an amused smile.

"Then here's to all those pampered city girls who are missing out on the satisfaction of swinging a mallet into a wall!" Meg said as she raised hers.

Norma raised her own mallet. "Pampered city girls—this is for you!"

They crashed through the wall at the same time, sending broken bits and pieces across the room. Meg looked over at Norma and grinned through the mist of white dust that floated around them. "I'd say you've officially turned in your city-girl credentials."

"I'd say that was an answer to prayer." Ferguson's words were like a steady chorus in Joe's head as he automatically reached up to touch his medal before he started his roll down the dirt strip in the Stearman.

He was airborne in a matter of seconds. The climb to altitude was uneventful and something he'd never take for granted again. He'd been worried that his inability to fly that morning had as much to do with shaky nerves as it did with his superstitious need to wear his medal. But now, in the air where he felt the most comfortable, the most at ease, he didn't care anymore what the reasons had been. The point was that he was back in the air. Back in the groove. Back where he was supposed to be. It wasn't a navy jet—but it was his own plane, and that made for an actual gratitude-filled moment.

He executed a slow bank toward the Simpson farm, keeping an eye out for Hiram's place. He would pass directly over the field with the strange "shorn corn" and get an aerial view of the spot's actual size.

He saw the field in the distance and could even see the large, naked patch of ground that had been plucked clean. He squinted through his goggles as he flew right on top of the field. *What in the world . . . ?* What was that? He looped a wide circle above the field as he stared at the ground below. He pushed his goggles up onto his helmet to better view the sight below.

The area was cut into a shape that looked like butterfly wings. *No—wait. It looks like those snow angels we made as kids. Like angel wings?*

He made one more circle above the field. *An answer to prayer.*

Chapter 14

Joe was exhausted as he tied down the Stearman and set the chocks. He didn't want to admit even to himself that the last few days had taken a toll on him. As hard as he tried to push the jumble of thoughts from his head about what had happened, he just couldn't do it. Bits and pieces of images circled like gnats through his mind when he was awake and invaded his dreams when he slept. His body actually ached with the tension. He was waiting for the other shoe to drop—and he didn't know where it would land. The only familiar and comforting thought was that Meg would have dinner ready as soon as she heard him come through the front door. Then a half hour in front of the television watching the evening news would be the ticket. Whatever the news, good or bad, it would be a welcome diversion from his own life. *I promise to be a better man, God. Soon . . . as soon as I can figure things out. . . .*

As he made his way to his truck, he passed the FBO shack and saw Ernie in the window motioning for him to come inside. With a sigh, Joe entered.

Ernie held up a piece of paper. "Meg called and asked me to give you a message."

This was new, he thought. Meg never called to leave him a message. Except for that time she was ready to go to the hospital to have Christy.

Joe frowned. "What's the message?"

Ernie looked at his note. "She said to tell you she's working late at the Meiers' place and you should go home and get supper on for the kids. They'll be home by the time you get there," he reported.

Joe's frown deepened. "Yeah, okay. See ya in the morning," he said, closing the door behind him.

He made his way toward his truck. *Now what's going on with Meg?*

When Joe got home he found Christy reading a book and Danny putting together a model car at the table in the kitchen. The room was surprisingly empty without Meg. It had rarely happened over the years that she hadn't been home to greet him at the end of the day. He remembered a few times the kids had come home without Meg being there—when she'd been tied up at a doctor's appointment or helping someone from the church. But this was the first time he'd ever been asked—ordered, actually—to get supper on the table.

"Mommy's not at home." Christy still had a way of stating the obvious, Joe thought. "She called to say she's still helping at the Meiers' farm."

"So I heard," Joe said.

"Do you know how to make anything for supper?" Christy asked, looking up at him skeptically.

"Depends on what I've got to work with," Joe said briefly as he opened the fridge door and peered inside. He spotted something he *did* know how to make and pulled out a package of hot dogs.

"Now, these *are* my specialty," he said, warming to his task as he opened them up.

Christy made a face. "Hot dogs for supper? Mom only makes hot dogs for lunch."

"Mom's not here," Joe said, trying to control the irritation in his voice. He opened cupboards, looking for a saucepan. "There's no kind of order to this kitchen," he muttered.

"The pans are under the stove," Danny said without looking up.

Joe slid open a drawer under the stove and pulled out a small saucepan. "Now we're in business," he said, dumping the hot dogs into the saucepan and running some water from the tap to cover them.

"Danny, look in the pantry for a can of beans," Joe said while he tried to light the gas burner under the saucepan—but was rewarded with nothing.

"C'mon, light, doggone it!" he grumbled under his breath as he held a match to the burner.

Danny put a can of pork and beans on the counter next to the stove.

"It hasn't been working right—remember?"

Joe detected the small dig of sarcasm. "Fine, open that can, and we'll have cold beans and hot dogs."

"Yuck," Christy interjected, "that sounds awful."

"It's like a Boy Scout camping supper," Joe said. "Right, Danny?" He dumped the water off the hot dogs and prepared three plates with the makeshift meal.

"Yeah, that's right, squirt," Danny said with a disapproving glance at his dad. "We eat cold beans and weenies all the time on our campouts when the dads can't get a fire started."

Christy wrinkled her nose as Joe slid the plate in front of her. "I'll try it, but I'm not gonna like it," she warned.

Joe started to tuck into his own dinner, but Christy reminded him they hadn't yet said grace.

"Oh, right," he said as he bowed his head. "You can say it tonight, Christy."

She folded her hands and bowed her head. "Thank you for this food, Lord. Even though it's beans and weenies, we're grateful. Amen."

Joe stacked the plates and the saucepan in the sink and looked at the clock over the stove. *It's after seven.* What in the world was taking her so long? This wasn't like her. She was never out in the evening. *Maybe she's had car trouble. It's been a while since that Bel Air's had a tune-up. It won't hurt for the kids and me to take a ride out toward Norma's to make sure Meg isn't walking along the road looking for help. I'm doing this strictly for her. . . .*

With the kids crammed into the cab of the truck with him, Joe drove the five miles out to the old Meiers place. He told the kids they were going to surprise Meg. Besides, he added, he hadn't had a chance to see Miss Norma since she got back into town.

"You can see her in church when you go with us on Sunday, Dad," Christy volunteered as Joe made the last turn that would take him to Norma's. "Remember you said you'd go to church and then we'd have a picnic?"

But Joe wasn't listening to her—he was too busy wondering why Luke Ramsey's fancy new truck had just stopped in front of Norma's house. Joe rolled to a stop just behind a stand of oaks planted along the road in front of the drive. Luke was honking the horn, and Meg and Norma came out onto the porch.

"There's Mom and Miss Norma," Christy said, excited. "Why did we stop?"

But Joe didn't answer. He tried to figure out why Luke was pulling a wicker basket out of the truck.

"Hey—looks like a picnic," Christy said.

"It's too late for a picnic, squirt," Danny told her.

Luke must have said something that made both Norma and Meg laugh, and then he followed them into the house carrying the basket.

When Joe saw the front door slam shut, he dropped the truck into reverse and hit the gas.

"Where are we going? I thought we were going to surprise Mommy," Christy protested.

"We'll see her at home," Joe said tersely. "She's obviously still working."

I've been waiting for that other shoe to drop. And it just landed with a great big stinking thud.

Luke put the basket down on the kitchen counter and then turned to them both with a smile. "Guess this makes me the Welcome Wagon."

"Don't tell Mrs. Germiniski you've taken over her job," Meg joked.

"I won't if you won't," he said, reaching into the basket for a Mason jar filled with dill pickles. "Cucumbers from last season so big you'd think they weren't real. In fact everything in here came from one of Vanguard's corporate farms," he added proudly. "We're producing crops that will feed the world—more nutritious because we can afford to cultivate the land the proper way."

"Vanguard manager, salesman, and one-man welcoming committee?" Norma observed. "You must be one busy man."

Luke smiled and cocked an appraising eyebrow at the women. "Looks like you two have been plenty busy yourselves."

Norma brushed at the dust covering her sleeveless blouse. "We've been doing a little remodeling upstairs."

Luke took a step closer to Meg and reached to pull a small piece of wallpaper from her hair. "Prettiest remodeling crew I've ever seen," he said easily as Meg blushed and smoothed a hand over her hair.

"Can I have the tour?" he asked. "See what you've been doing?"

Norma led the way up the stairs, where they could hear her three boys being boys. "Sounds like the house could come down around us," Luke observed.

"They were going stir-crazy in the hotel, so we're camping out while we fix the house. They're supposed to be buffing the floorboards in Zach's new room," Norma explained.

"Sounds like they might be buffing it with Zach," Luke chuckled as he followed her into the hall.

"Whatever's most cost-effective," she quipped as they stopped in the doorway to a bedroom. Sure enough, the two younger boys each had one of Zach's legs, and they were sliding him around the bare oak floors on his back.

Norma grimaced and shook her head. "Remember Mr. Ramsey?" she asked them, and the three stopped their horseplay and dutifully nodded and greeted him politely.

"Keep up the good work," he responded with a wink and a thumbs-up for them.

Luke stood on the threshold of the next bedroom, painted a pale blue, and took in the simple brass bed, maple dresser, and highboy. "Looks like you're all set in here," he commented.

"It was Meg's idea to do this room first," Norma explained.

"All mothers need a refuge, a place to have a few quiet moments," Meg added, and as if to prove it, another thud resounded from Zach's room.

The three laughed, and then Luke said, "I don't know how you're going to do it, Norma." He sounded sincere, but all the while he was looking around the room, his gaze finally lingering on the closet door.

On the way back down the stairs, Luke put a friendly hand on Meg's shoulder. "Be a true friend to her, Meg, and help her see there's no way she can handle this big place on her own."

"I think she's doing great," Meg said, skillfully maneuvering from under his hand.

"Yeah, but remodeling isn't the hard part," Luke argued.

"Hey, I'm still here," Norma protested over her shoulder. "And I'm not alone—I've got the boys."

Luke shook his head as he stepped over sheets and tarps on the furniture in the living room. "Three boys raised in the city who don't know a corn husk from a sheaf of wheat? Be realistic, Norma. This place was too big for your grandfather to farm with a lifetime of experience under his belt. How do you think you can do it?"

"We'll figure it out," she said stubbornly.

"I'm just trying to provide an option for you, and that's what Vanguard is all about. When we come into a community, people have choices—people like Joe, for instance—"

"Joe?" Meg broke in.

Luke nodded. "I can't tell you how happy I am that it looks like he's going to take us up on our offer."

It was easy to see from the expression on Meg's face that this was news to her.

Luke was chagrined. "Oh, Meg," he said with a concerned frown. "He hasn't told you?"

"No, but I haven't . . . we haven't . . ." Her voice trailed off.

"I think I've just ruined a surprise," Luke said with a contrite shake of his head. "I'm sorry—please don't tell him I said anything. He probably wanted to drive up in that new company truck he's gonna get and show you for himself. . . ."

"New truck?"

"One of the perks with Vanguard," Luke said. "And there are plenty of others." He looked at Norma. "As long as I'm talking about options, there is one we didn't discuss in Kansas City. You could sell the majority of your land to Vanguard but keep enough for you and the boys to farm yourselves. That way you'll have a steady income, this house, and—"

"Thanks for the basket, Luke," Norma said with a small smile.

Another thud from above had them looking at the ceiling. "If those boys don't settle down," Norma said with a sigh, "I'm going to end up with *accidental* holes in the walls." She walked over to the kitchen entrance and hollered in the general direction of the stairs. "Hey, guys, keep it down to a dull roar up there, okay?"

Luke smiled. "Okay, I get the hint. I'm leaving—but I just want to say one more thing. First instincts are generally right, Norma. I'm just asking you to revisit your original decision about selling."

"Well, you did bring me dill pickles," she said wryly, "so I'll think about it."

He beamed. "That's all I'm asking."

After the front door closed, Norma crossed to the counter and started to unpack the perishable items from the basket to go in the fridge.

"What did Luke mean when he said 'revisit your original decision'?" Meg held out a hand and Norma gave her the Mason jar full of pickles.

Norma issued a tired sigh and pushed a hand through her hair. "At one time, Bob and I had agreed to sell this place to Vanguard."

Meg started to set the pickles on a shelf in the fridge and turned with surprise. "Really? For some reason I thought the plans concerning the land around Greenville were fairly recent for Vanguard," she said. "At least that's how Luke made it sound to me."

Norma shook her head. "No . . . it's been in the works for a while. It's no secret that I've got the most acreage in the county—and it sits right in the middle of all the neighboring farms. He told me he's been getting the *Greenville Gazette* sent to him for years . . . and when he saw Granny's obituary in the paper, it wasn't much of a leap for him to assume I'd inherited the property. He tracked me down in Kansas City and made an appointment with Bob to talk to him about selling the land."

"And Bob wanted to sell?" Meg asked.

Norma took a head of lettuce and a small sack of potatoes from the basket and put them next to the growing pile of produce. "Actually . . . I was the one who wanted to sell," she said. "As you can imagine, I never thought I'd fit in here again."

"So you told Luke you'd sell?" Meg prompted.

Norma nodded. "He was in the middle of drawing up the contracts when I sobered up and had my change of heart . . . and soul."

"I'll bet he wasn't too happy that you changed your mind," Meg observed.

"He was furious. He couldn't show it, of course, but I could tell. He made an appeal to Bob's business sense and tried to get him to sell anyway. But he didn't count on the fact that Bob's an honorable man and said that even though we were married, this was my property to do with as I saw fit."

Norma stopped unpacking the basket and leaned on the counter. "Suddenly, I couldn't get here fast enough—embrace the past, find the best parts of myself again, and show the boys a side of life they've never seen before. I felt like God was giving us all a chance to change."

"So you packed up the boys and moved," Meg said.

Norma turned her attention back to the basket and reached inside. "Yep. And then right on our heels, Luke turned up here," Norma said, then frowned when she pulled a bottle of wine from the basket, "like a bad penny."

Meg also frowned at the bottle of wine. "Does he know . . . ?"

Norma nodded. "Yeah, he knows."

"That bottle probably got in there by accident."

"Last I heard, Vanguard doesn't have any corporate *vineyards*," Norma said wryly as she carried the wine across the kitchen and dropped it into the trash. "And Luke Ramsey doesn't do anything by accident."

Chapter 15

Meg carefully closed the front door to the quiet, darkened house and made her way to the stairs, feeling like a teenager sneaking in late after curfew. She couldn't remember the last time she'd actually been out in the evening without Joe or the kids. Even though she'd been working hard tearing down a wall, she still considered it time for herself—something *she* wanted to do that didn't involve anyone else in the family. And that brought some guilt. *Coming home at almost ten at night*, she thought—*now that is a bit of rebellion*. She crept up the stairs and saw the light under the door to Danny's room. She entered quietly to find him fast asleep, an open book over his chest, which she eased from his grasp and turned off his light. She went to check on Christy and gave her sleeping daughter a kiss on the forehead before she made her way to her room.

In the moonlight, Meg could make out Joe's shape in the bed. She found herself disappointed to find him sleeping—she had a lot to tell him. *Tomorrow*, she promised herself. *Tomorrow he can hear all about the work we're doing at Norma's, and maybe he'll tell me about his talk with Luke*, she thought.

In minutes she slipped into bed beside Joe. For a second, she thought she heard his breathing change.

"Joe?" she whispered. "Are you awake?" She listened for a second, then turned on her side and closed her eyes.

Meg may have been the last to go to bed, but as usual, she was the first up in the morning. She saw the dirty dishes stacked in the sink and realized that supper the night before had been a scant affair. *Everyone's going to be hungry this morning*, she thought as she made bacon and eggs on the single burner she was able to coax into lighting. She started a plate of toast and set the table.

A few minutes later she heard her family stirring on the floor above. Danny's steady tread back and forth across his room, Christy's lighter footsteps, and then the morning debate about whose turn it was to use the bathroom first. She cocked an ear for the familiar sounds that belonged only to Joe in the morning—the clunk of the bathroom door and the water pipes in the walls that pinged with expansion when he turned on the shower. But she didn't hear either and glanced at the clock over the stove. *I should make sure he hasn't overslept. I'm sure he told me he has a busy day today.*

Meg took the bacon out of the skillet and piled it on a plate. She was in the middle of covering the plate with a tea towel to keep the bacon warm when she heard someone coming down the stairs—and then out the front door. She looked out the kitchen window to see Joe heading toward his truck. With a frown, she grabbed a lunch pail from the counter and hurried out after him.

"Joe!" she called as she ran across the yard to the truck. He looked over the hood of the truck toward her but opened the driver's door anyway.

"Wait a second," she said. "You forgot your lunch." *And forgot to tell me good-bye! What's going on?*

"I'm running late, Meg," he said brusquely.

"Too late to say good-bye?" she asked, arching her eyebrows.

"Good-bye," he said and slid behind the wheel of the truck.

She grabbed the handle of the door and held out the lunch box. "Here," she said.

"I probably won't have time for lunch," he said, pulling the door closed. "And don't plan on me for dinner tonight. I'll get something somewhere."

"If this is because you're mad I wasn't home for supper last night, then I'm sorry, Joe. But Norma and I really got a lot of work done. . . ."

He stared at her for just a moment, then turned the key to start the engine.

"Some of us define work a little differently," he said. "I'll see you when I see you."

She watched him back down the driveway and whispered the words she always said when she knew he was going to work: "Fly safe." She turned back to the house, bewildered at his attitude and the cold anger in his voice.

The kids were coming down the stairs when she got back inside, and she dished up their breakfast, trying to keep her tears from showing and greeting them as matter-of-factly as she could.

Danny was usually quiet in the morning, but Christy woke up talking and never seemed to stop. As Meg poured herself a cup of coffee, Christy launched into a description of Joe's makeshift supper.

"I'm starving," Christy complained, "and I don't like cold hot dogs at all, even if Danny does eat them when he's camping with the Boy Scouts."

"I'm sure Dad was doing the best he could," Meg said quickly. "He's not used to finding his way around the kitchen." Meg put their plates in front of the kids. "You were supposed to do the dishes, Christy. It was your night."

"When we got home from our drive, Daddy told me to leave them and go to bed," Christy explained defensively.

"You took a drive?" Meg asked.

"After supper," Danny mumbled.

"We drove to Miss Norma's to surprise you, but when we got there, Daddy just turned around and drove back home."

"You should have come to the door. I would have shown you what we've been doing to the house."

"I wanted to say hi, but when you and Miss Norma went into the house with Mr. Ramsey, Dad said you were working," Christy said.

While the kids ate their breakfast, Meg turned away so they couldn't see her face. Joe's cryptic comment whirled through her mind. *"Some of us define work a little differently."*

Meg held her breath as she carried the frying pan over to the sink and blasted water over it. Hot spatters of bacon grease burned her hands as much as her anger burned her heart. *In all the years we've been married, he has never had one reason to be jealous or insecure about me! What's the matter with him? How does he manage to take something that's good and make it seem like I'm doing something selfish and bad? Well, I'm not quitting. I'm going to see this thing through with Norma, and if he has to make another meal of cold hot dogs again, so be it. And as for Luke Ramsey—*

"It's bookmobile day, Mom. Can I go with Katie?" Christy asked, interrupting Meg's raging thoughts.

"Sure. Just round up the books you got two weeks ago. We don't want any overdue fines."

"I'm going to the ball field. Some of the guys are getting a game together," Danny told her over his shoulder.

"Okay, but make sure you're home by suppertime."

"Will you be here when I get home later?" Christy asked.

"Yes. I'll be here."

I'll be here because this is where I always am. I'll be here because this is where I'm expected to be. Meg sat down at the kitchen table with her cold coffee and leaned her head on her hand.

It was twilight when Joe walked into Barney's after parking his truck in the alley behind the building. He didn't want Larry—or anyone else for that matter—getting into his business and baby-sitting him. What he did want was to forget the image of his wife walking into Norma's front door with Luke Ramsey. *One look at him and Meg probably knows how much better her life could have been. I wonder how many times she's sat in our tired old living room, looked at yearbook pictures, and wished she'd done anything but marry me. She could have done a lot of other things—gone anywhere—if she hadn't been chained to a loser like me.*

The light in the bar mirrored the faded light outside. Joe's gaze raked over the few patrons. Two young couples sat in separate booths toward the back of the place, eyes locked on each other, oblivious to the pitfalls of life and love. Joe made his way to what he thought of as his stool and climbed aboard. Marsha threw a smile in his direction.

"Coming at you, Joe," she said, waving a mug. She filled it and slid it down the bar toward him. He captured it easily with a quick hand.

"Thanks, Marsha," he said, even as she turned to draw another beer from the tap. She walked the mug to Gunny, who was perched on his usual spot at the opposite end of the bar from Joe.

"Why don't you ever slide it down the bar to me, Marsh?" Gunny complained as she dropped a coaster from her pocket onto the counter and centered the glass on top.

"We tried that, remember, Gunny? Too messy for me and way too expensive for you."

"Oh yeah," he shrugged, then looked over at Joe. "How ya doing tonight, Joe?"

"Fine, Gunny," Joe said in a flat tone that he hoped would indicate he wasn't in the mood for talking. *Guess Gunny is a regular on Friday nights along with Saturday nights too. Doesn't he have any other place to be? Is he even married? Where does he live? Why do I care? Fact is—I don't.*

The first splash of beer washed down his throat, and then Joe quickly set about the business of losing track. The goal wasn't to count how many beers he had—the goal was to *forget* he needed the beer in the first place.

Marsha flipped a hand towel over her shoulder and brought Joe another beer. He gave her an offhand little salute as she put the glass in front of him. "Thanks, Marsh, just keep 'em coming," he said with a thick tongue.

"Whatever you say, Joe," she said, then raised her brows as she looked over his shoulder. Whatever she saw moved her quickly to the other end of the bar.

"I wondered if you'd come here after work." Meg's familiar voice behind him was soft but heavy with disappointment. "I was hoping, though, that you wouldn't." He looked into the mirror to see her standing right behind him. He took in a quick breath and swiveled on the barstool to face her.

"Meg! Welcome to Barney's," he deadpanned.

She took a step closer, lowering her voice even further. "Have you forgotten everything you promised? Is it really so easy to just step over what happened to you, Joe?"

"Don't make a federal case out of this, Meg," he said in a loud whisper. "I just stopped for a couple of beers."

"I'm going home," she whispered tersely, "and I'm asking you to come with me."

Joe slid off his barstool. "I can't go home," he said over his shoulder as he made his way toward Gunny. "It might look like I'm just sitting around and drinking beer—but I'm really *working.*"

He threw his arm around the man's shoulder. "Me and Gunny were discussing the problem he's having getting a kite to fly," he said, "and I've been trying to tell him about Bernoulli's principle a' flight—right, Gunny?"

"Ben—nooli . . . Bernini's . . . That's right, Joe. Stupid kite won't fly," Gunny said with a crooked smile at Meg. "We're working hard."

"See? Working," Joe said, slapping Gunny on the back and pasting on a grin for Meg's benefit. He saw her eyes fill with tears before she turned and walked away. His smile vanished, and he slowly made his way back to his barstool.

"Hey, Joe!" Gunny said loudly. "Thought you was helping me figure out how ta get my kite ta fly."

"Shouldn't drink and fly, Gunny," he said, grabbing his mug. "You could hurt someone." He settled back into his familiar place.

Barney wiped the wet rag over the counter in front of Joe and looked at him with the practiced, critical eye of a bartender who had seen more than his share of patrons who'd had one too many. Joe leaned heavily against the bar, hands wrapped around his glass. The usual theme from *The Tonight Show* with Jack Paar filled the background and signaled the lateness of the hour.

"So, Joe—no fields to spray in the morning?" Barney began, voice carefully neutral.

Joe pursed his lips, knit his eyebrows together in concentration, then shrugged.

"Not on Sunday," he said thickly.

"Tomorrow is *Saturday*, Joe."

Joe paused, then nodded in agreement, stopping quickly and putting his hand to his head. "I think you're right. That makes this Friday."

"Yes, it does," Barney agreed. He caught Marsha's eye. She nodded.

"I think I might have a booth in the corner with your name on it tonight, Joe. Gunny doesn't seem to mind the vinyl—says it's pretty comfortable."

Joe grinned. "You running an inn now, Barney?"

"Only for my very best customers," he replied easily. "I'll be happy to hold on to your keys for you until morning."

"Like a valet?"

"Sure. Like a valet at a swanky hotel in Wichita."

Joe shook his head. "Have you seen my truck, Barney? She's a beaut. No way I'm turning my keys over to anyone." His voice went from loud to a mumble. "Scratched up . . . paint, dings . . . she's a real beauty. Beauty full of junk . . ."

He pushed back from the bar and held on to the edge for a minute. "Okay, that's bunk. I lied," he called out to everyone.

Barney dropped all pretenses. "You're in no condition to drive, Joe. Give me your keys, and I'll drive you home later—or like I said, you can sleep it off here."

"Relax, Barney. This is a round trip I'm making. Here—to the men's room and back. Beer's goin' right through me."

"Oh. Okay, then," Barney said, "maybe I'll set you up with one of Chief Larry's root beers. Or maybe coffee."

"Good idea," Joe agreed amicably and then turned and made his way unsteadily across the bar. When he rounded the corner toward the men's room in the back, Joe stumbled right past it and out the back door.

His truck was parked a few feet behind Barney's in the alley, between a telephone pole and a large metal dumpster. Joe squinted at the distance between the truck and the objects on either end. *Piece of cake for the Red Baron of Bugs to get that thing out of there. Been in tighter spots before. . . .*

The handle on the driver's door of the truck had been known to stick, and he had to struggle with it for a few seconds before he finally managed to pull it open. The metal protested loudly in the quiet of the alley, and Joe issued a sharp "Shh!" to the truck before he climbed into the cab and settled behind the wheel. Putting the key in the ignition presented its own challenge, and he made several stabs at it. A knock on his window made him yell out in surprise, and he looked through the glass to see a hulking form of a man who could easily look over the top of the cab—and then the man leaned down, craning his thick neck so he could peer through the window.

Is that Hiram's guy, what's-his-name—Ferguson?

"Hello, Joe," he said. He was imposing enough in stature and form to make Joe lean away from the glass.

"Hello."

"Are you in need of help?" Ferguson asked clearly through the window.

"No." Joe frowned. "Are you?"

"As a matter of fact, I am," Ferguson said with a nod. "I've got a heavy load I can't manage alone."

Joe blew out a puff of air between pursed lips. "Don't we all?"

Ferguson put a hand on the door handle. "Do you mind?" He didn't wait for an answer but opened the door of the truck. "Ah. Much better. I can see you clearly now."

"Tough luck for me," Joe mumbled as he made another stab at getting the keys in the ignition—this time with success. The truck sputtered, coughed, started.

"Going home now," Joe said, "be seein' ya."

Ferguson stepped back from the truck as Joe pulled the door shut and popped the stick into first gear. The truck lurched forward and hit the trash bin. He changed gears again, hit the gas—and the telephone pole behind him.

Ferguson stood with his arms folded over his chest and watched him crash into the bin again.

Joe stopped and opened the door. "Load up your stuff. You can drive." He climbed out and watched as Ferguson began placing a pile of junk into the truck bed. Joe shrugged and felt his way around the cab to the passenger side and climbed in.

Ferguson finished and wedged himself behind the wheel. Joe heard the old shocks of the truck groan and held on to the handle of the door as the driver's side of the cab actually sank under Ferguson's weight. Suddenly Joe felt crowded in his own space and watched in dismay as the big man wrapped hands the size of baseball mitts around the steering wheel.

He turned and looked at Joe. "I've wanted to do this for a long time," Ferguson said with a grin.

"Do what?"

"Drive," Ferguson answered with another grin.

"You mean you don't . . . you've never . . ." Joe gave up. "Don't let me keep you," he mumbled. "Drive."

Joe watched Ferguson tap the fuel gauge and speedometer, flip the switch for the windshield wipers, and pull out the knob for the headlights. Two cones of light bounced off the trash bin in front of them.

Joe put his hand up to protect his eyes, then turned to stare at Ferguson. "I can walk home faster than this," Joe said, concentrating on the words. "And I'm in no condition to walk." He laughed at his own joke and watched as Ferguson lowered his head to look at the clutch, the brake, and the gas pedal.

"Pretty stand . . . standard equipment there, ol' Ferg. You got the clutch, the stick, and the gas. Use 'em."

Ferguson moved the visor to the side so it wasn't in his field of vision, then flexed his hand on the wheel.

"You *can* drive, can't—?"

The truck shot forward, jamming Joe against the door as Ferguson made a hard left to avoid the dumpster. Ferguson's stuff in the bed of the truck slammed against the tailgate as they practically shot out of the alley and onto the street.

The moon, curtained by clouds, left the night black—except for the round beams of light bouncing around from the headlights of the truck as it careened around corners and over bumps in the asphalt. But in rather short order, Ferguson seemed to find the rhythm of the gears. "Wonderful sense of movement—isn't it?" he asked as he looked over at Joe.

"I could do with a little less movement," Joe muttered as he gripped the door handle. "Keep it steady, will ya?"

"Without movement, we'll never arrive at our destination," Ferguson said. But the truck hurtled down the road in what seemed a serpentine pattern that had Joe breaking out in a sweat.

"I'm not kidding!" Joe said forcefully. "Knock it off!"

"It's just a matter of getting a feel for the wheel," Ferguson said cheerfully as they careened along back and forth across the dividing line.

Joe dragged the back of his hand across his forehead and the beads of cold sweat gathering there. The view out the window was swimming sickeningly, and he felt the heat of his own body signaling that his stomach was getting ready to rebel.

"I need . . . some . . . air," he said, struggling to roll down his window. The breeze rushed into the open space and filled the cab as the truck swerved across the road again. Joe hadn't been sick from drinking in a very long time but knew that streak of luck was about to end. He tried to fight it and leaned his head back against the seat, then closed his eyes. "Pull over," he groaned.

"What's that, Joe?"

"Pull over!" he shouted, then clapped a hand over his mouth.

Ferguson swerved to the side of the road and stomped hard on the brake—and Joe nearly collided with the windshield. He opened the door and practically fell out of the truck to his knees and heaved.

Ferguson looked patient as he waited for Joe to drag himself back into the cab.

"Are you ready to continue on?" Ferguson asked, sounding sympathetic.

Joe raised a limp hand and gestured forward. Ferguson slid the truck into gear and pulled smoothly out onto the road to glide along the asphalt like a skater on a glossy sheet of black ice. Joe managed to lift his head off the back of the seat and take stock of their location.

"Take a right at the next turn," he said. "My house is just up the . . ."

Ferguson notched up the speed, and they sailed right past the turn that would have led them to Joe's house.

"Hey!" Joe said indignantly. "You missed it."

"I have some things that need to be unloaded first," Ferguson said calmly. "Remember?"

Joe let his head fall back against the seat again. "Oh yeah," he muttered, exasperated. "Should have taken my chances and driven myself home."

"That wouldn't have been wise"—Ferguson shook his head—"given your queasy condition."

"I'm never 'queasy' after a few beers," Joe said. "Me tossing my cookies is from your crazy driving." Joe looked out at the road and then over at Ferguson. "By the way—I've noticed your driving has improved a lot."

"A little motion is much more effective than coffee—wouldn't you agree?"

"You were *trying* to make me sick?" Joe was incredulous.

"You're going to need your wits about you," he said. "There are some things you need to do without the buffer of alcohol."

"Oh, I get it."

"I don't think you do."

"Sure, sure—you need my help. My *sober* help. But just so you know, I can unload junk while I'm . . . well, loaded," Joe said. "You didn't have to give me the Tilt-A-Whirl treatment."

"I won't be in need of your help, Joe."

Joe took in the size of the man sitting next to him. "I guess not."

Suddenly, Ferguson slowed the truck and pulled over to the side of the road next to a field of long prairie grass.

"We're here," he said and turned off the engine.

A half moon had appeared from behind a cloud, and Joe looked around at the vast amount of *nothing* as far as the eye could see. Ferguson clambered out of the truck while the cab groaned and leveled itself again. Almost as an afterthought, the big man reached back inside the cab and removed the keys from the ignition. "I'll be swift," he said.

Joe leaned his head back against the window of the cab and closed his eyes. "I'll be here."

It was the crunch of gravel under the tires of the truck that woke Joe from a sound sleep. He opened his eyes to find himself in his own driveway. Ferguson turned off the key, and the uneven sound of the truck engine abruptly stopped, leaving the song of a few crickets to fill the quiet.

Joe looked at the dark house, where just the porch light burned. *Everyone's in bed—the way's clear to go in.*

"Hey, Ferg, how're you going to get back? You should a' woken me up and let me drive myself home."

The man just shrugged and smiled.

"It's a long way out to Hiram's place," Joe said. "There's a cot in our garage if you want to sleep there tonight."

"It's a generous invitation," Ferguson said. "Thank you."

"I'd invite you inside, but I wouldn't want my wife or kids to get up and find a stranger in the house in the middle of the night," Joe explained.

"The cot will be fine."

"And just in case you're interested—I've got an outdoor shower rigged up behind the house," he added through a yawn. "Used to use it when I'd come home covered in fertilizer."

"Thank you very much—a shower would be appreciated."

Joe yawned again, then shook his head. "All I want to do is climb into bed and put this night behind me," he said as he started across the yard toward the house.

"Joe?" Ferguson's voice floated out of the darkness.

"Yeah?" Joe turned to see the large silhouette in the yard.

"You are never truly alone."

Joe frowned, then waved in Ferguson's general direction. "Don't I know it," he quipped and continued up the steps into the house.

Once inside, Joe flipped off the porch light and made his way up the stairs to his bedroom in the dark. Now that he was safely home, he was grateful that the effects of the beer were wearing off. He didn't have the stamina to face Meg with a foggy mind. He crossed the floor of his room at the same time the moon made another appearance, and a silver light filtered through the curtains across the double bed—that was still made. *Meg? Where is she? Downstairs waiting for me? She must have fallen asleep on the couch. . . .*

He went back into the hallway to Christy's room. The door was ajar and protested quietly when he pushed it open, but Christy wasn't there and her bed hadn't been slept in. He hurried to Danny's room and didn't even bother with trying to be quiet as he threw open the door to find the same thing—an empty bed. Sick with worry now, Joe ran down the stairs and turned on the lamp near the couch. *Where are they? Something's happened and nobody could find me. Stupid, stupid—I'm so stupid.*

He hadn't noticed a dim light coming from the kitchen when he entered—the light in the range hood over the stove. He rushed into the room, flipped on the overhead light, and raked his gaze over the familiar room. Everything in its place as was Meg's custom before she turned in at night. Nothing out of the ordinary. Nothing different.

Except what? A note.

He snatched a folded piece of paper with his name on it off the table. The worry he felt when he found his family missing turned into a stone-cold rock in the pit of his stomach. The house had been dark, the beds empty, because they had left him.

My family is gone. He dropped the note back on the table and groped his way to the stairs. *Meg has finally had enough of my broken promises.*

Chapter 16

Joe held stubbornly to the last threads of sleep before surfacing from his fitful slumber to face the day. He felt the heat of the morning in the bedroom and a strip of sunshine working its way around the curtains at the window and across his face. But he wasn't ready to open his eyes. His head throbbed with a familiar, almost comforting beat in time with the pounding of his heart. *So I'm still in the land of the living.*

He sure wasn't ready to retrace the events from the night before—wasn't sure he'd ever be ready. And his family? *What am I going to do?* His eyes popped open. *Bacon? I smell—bacon and coffee and—biscuits?! A dream! She's back? That's it! Thank you, God!*

He found himself on his side facing the bedroom door, and it was only a second before reality settled over him. He was still dressed—the bed was still made. *Maybe she came home early this morning. She'll say she overreacted and made a mistake. She'll tell me, "Let's have some breakfast and talk about this, Joe. . . ."*

He pounded down the stairs, ignoring the pain behind his eyes, and all but flew into the kitchen. He stopped short. "You?"

"Good morning, Joe," Ferguson said as he gestured to a table set for two. "I've made breakfast."

Joe rubbed absently at his temple and frowned in Ferguson's general direction. "What are you doing here—in the kitchen?"

"I thought I just made that clear," Ferguson said as he brought the coffeepot from the stove toward the table and filled a cup for Joe. "Strong and black," he said. "Not as good as Meg's, I'm sure, but I think it will suffice."

"Suffice"? Who is *this guy?* Joe dropped into a chair and picked up the note still lying on the table. While Ferguson sat down and bowed his head over his own plate, Joe slowly opened the note and stared at the words. He had to read it again before they made any sense. *Well, they do make sense,* he had to admit.

At her mom's . . . bet Sylvia is having a heart attack over this. His mind grabbed at whatever it could to keep from facing the reality staring at him from the page. *At least Sylvia's heart's still in one piece—unlike mine. I need to go get them and bring them home. Tell them how sorry I am and that I'll never do it again.*

"Would they believe you?" Ferguson asked.

Joe looked up from the paper to find Ferguson's piercing blue eyes regarding him. "What did you just say?"

"Will your family believe that this time you are really remorseful and want to change?"

Joe scowled. "What makes you think you can read someone's private note!"

"I didn't read your note, Joe," Ferguson said simply. "I didn't have to." He gestured with his fork to the food on Joe's plate. "You really should eat," he said. "You'll feel better and—"

"The only thing that'll make me feel better is getting my family back home." Joe pushed back from the table. Finding the bottle of Bayer in the cupboard, he shook out a couple of the small white pills, turned on the faucet at the kitchen sink, then bent low under the stream of water to wash them down.

Moving slowly, with leaden feet and an even heavier heart, Joe made his way back to the table, where Ferguson had already made a sizeable dent in his own meal.

"I'm sorry for you that your family is broken," Ferguson said sincerely.

"It's not . . . broken," Joe responded. "It's just . . . just . . ."

"You know something I've observed? Weddings are easy; *marriages* are difficult."

"Look, last night is a little fuzzy for me," Joe stated, "and this morning is proving to be one of the worst in recent memory."

"One would think that would make a case for not drinking," Ferguson observed.

"One would think," Joe said flatly. "Now, am I crazy, or did you know that I was coming home to an empty house last night?"

"I tried my best to prepare you for what I knew was going to be a shock," Ferguson said.

Joe stared at the large man sitting opposite him at the table. Everything about him spoke of power and strength, but in his eyes Joe saw a depth of compassion that was unsettling.

"Who *are* you?"

Ferguson leaned forward in his chair. "I *am* an angel, Joe. I was yesterday, I am today, and I will be tomorrow."

The clock over the stove ticked loudly in the quiet that followed the declaration. Joe didn't know what to say—what to make of it. Ferguson didn't look crazy, at least not what Joe would have thought crazy would look like. *It must be me. I'm the crazy one. It's finally happened, and today is the day I finally snapped. . . .*

"Uh-huh. An angel. So I guess the next thing you'll tell me is that you cured poor Sara, saved Hiram's crop, and now you're here to help me?" Joe shot back skeptically.

"No, I can't say any of that."

"You're not here to help me?"

Ferguson simply shook his head.

"You tried to help me last night," Joe argued.

"I did help you last night—but it's not why I'm here," Ferguson answered.

"Oh yeah? Then why *are* you here?"

Ferguson swallowed down the last morsel of food on his plate. "We are connected, Joe. Our lives have intersected, and something was set in motion."

"Just because you happened to be in the alley last night . . ."

"No, before that. Conditions that I should have—but *didn't* resist. The beautiful clouds building like mountains against the wide expanse of sky, the coolness of the day, the serenity of the moment until . . ."

"Until what?"

"I didn't see you until it was too late," Ferguson said. "I can't lie. It was my fault entirely."

"What are you talking about?"

"It wasn't a bird that day in the clouds, Joe. You hit—me."

The statement hung in the air between them. Joe heard the flutelike song of a meadowlark outside the window as he stared into the clear, unblinking eyes of the man at the table.

"That's even better than saying you're an angel," Joe finally said. He waved his hand impatiently. "And now you're done. You can leave my house because I don't have the energy for this. I've got enough on my plate without a nut case telling me he and I had a head-on collision thirty-five hundred feet in the air!"

Joe got up from the table and stood next to Ferguson's chair. "Time to go. Thanks for stopping by. Thanks for breakfast."

Ferguson stood. "There are things we haven't discussed yet, Joe," he said as he made his way out of the kitchen with Joe on his heels, "things that should be recounted."

"I'll take my chances," Joe said. They crossed the living room toward the front door. He opened the door and gestured for Ferguson to step out ahead of him.

Ferguson turned toward him with a purposeful look. "You've got one more day, Red Baron. But I worry that you'll squander the next twenty-four hours and the next twenty-four hours after that."

Joe stared at Ferguson. "Lots of people around here know that nickname."

" 'Help me, God, please! I don't want to die. Just give me one more chance. One more day.' "

The words—*his words*—flattened Joe back against the door. "How could you know that?" he whispered.

"You knew the answer to that before you even asked me the question," Ferguson said.

Joe shook his head. "No. It's not possible. You . . . you must have spoken to Meg. I told her some stuff after the accident. I told her, I said—"

"It was accidental, but while we were both spiraling toward earth *I heard* you pray, Joe. You had regrets and wanted to fix them. You understood what you were about to lose and didn't want your life to end that way."

"But you're standing in my house," Joe said. "Looking human."

"Human for now. You see, angels are spiritual beings and have no physical form, unless needed. I know that humans are very curious about angels, but we too are very curious about humans. We observe you constantly, wanting to understand what it is you think and feel. The clouds provided an opportunity for me that day—a cover so I could take a physical form to *feel* the mist, the cool air washing over me. And for this lapse I will remain human until I have finished my mission."

"I . . . I can't buy this. This is crazy," Joe said, shaking his head for emphasis.

"You don't have to *buy* any of it. It's called faith, Joe. Sometimes there are no rational explanations—no physical signs or reasons that provide explanation. How *do* you explain Sara's newfound health? Hiram's flourishing fields? You—standing here breathing in spite of the uncontrolled spin that should have taken your life?" He paused a moment to look deeply into Joe's eyes, but Joe looked away.

"Whether or not you believe I am who I say I am—doesn't matter," Ferguson continued. "We both know you made a promise to God to be a better man and live every day as if it were your last. You asked for one more day, and He spared you. Who I am doesn't change that truth."

Joe couldn't deny it—any of it. He remembered the exact way he'd felt as he pleaded with God to spare him, pleaded with Him for another chance at life.

"I don't know what to do," Joe finally said, his voice barely audible even to him. "I don't know where to start."

"Start by doing one thing at a time. One foot in front of the other. Always aiming toward being the man God intended you to be. Keep your promise in actions and deeds, Joe. Ask yourself if you're becoming less or more."

Ferguson pushed back the screen and stepped out onto the porch. "In my curiosity about being human, I believe I did you a favor, Joe Daley. Take advantage of that."

Chapter 17

Meg paced barefoot across pink roses woven into a gray rug that stretched the length of her mother's rather formal living room. A sleepless night combined with four cups of coffee since dawn had left her with more nervous energy than she could handle. She glanced at her watch and calculated she had a little more time before Joe's hangover would allow him to actually get out of bed—let alone make the drive to her mother's.

She pulled her chenille robe tighter around her waist and stared out the window. He would be mad—*really mad*—that she had left with the kids. But for the first time in her marriage, she wasn't backing down. He had put them in this position, and she wasn't letting him off the hook. All the years of keeping things calm and on track had come to an end for her when she'd walked into Barney's and seen him sitting on that barstool.

She could still feel that sudden realization she wasn't looking at her husband at all—rather some stranger who had such total disregard for her feelings it had made her weak with despair. And then the anger had kicked in. Before she knew it, she had found herself at Norma's, pouring out her heart—and fears. Norma had listened without interruption, without judgment—even without pity. Norma let her voice the unthinkable out loud.

Norma told her God walks the hard roads with us—leading us the right direction if we listen. Thinking back on it, Meg knew now it was in the safety of telling the truth to someone who understood what the truth could mean—that it was then she had come to her decision. She barely remembered the drive home from Norma's house, walking into the house and calmly telling Christy and Danny to pack their bags. They were going to stay at Grandma Sylvia's for a while. *Danny knows what this is about—but Christy will have to be told . . . something,* Meg reminded herself, dread sweeping over her again.

She heard the sound of Joe's truck approaching. "He's here," she said aloud as she started toward the door and pushed her way through to step out onto the porch.

Joe parked and slowly got out. As he approached she tried to tamp the flip of nerves in her belly, but everything that had been building up for months—for years—spilled over her before he could even walk up the driveway to the porch. She stepped out on the front steps and shook her head at him in warning.

"I'm not coming home with you, Joe!" burst from her lips. "I'm tired of all this. Tired of lying to myself that things are going to get better. You never make the effort to change. That day they told you that you were 4-F became the defining moment of your life—not the day you became a pilot, or we got married, or even the days our children were born. You've let the fact of not becoming a navy pilot dictate who you are and everything else! It can't always be about your needs and what you think you're missing. Once, just once, I need to be able to share some of my burdens; sometimes I need you to make things better for *me*." She was looking everywhere except Joe's face. *Don't cry! Don't cry!* she kept telling herself.

Meg took a deep breath. "I don't want to walk on eggs worrying that a look, a comment, or a broken appliance will be another reminder of your disappointing life. I think you like being miserable. I think you're afraid to be happy because then you'd have to admit how many blessings God has given both of us." Then the tears she could no longer hold back slipped down her cheeks, and she wiped at them with the back of her hand. "I'm all used up, Joe. I can't save you from yourself anymore—right now I'm just trying to save myself and our kids."

He looked up at her from the bottom of the porch steps, and she could see tears in his own eyes.

"You're right," he said quietly. "And I'm sorry I drove you to this."

She stared at him. He had shaved, pressed his shirt and pants, maybe even had a haircut?

"How are the kids?" he asked quietly.

"They're still asleep. We didn't get here till late, and I'm not going to wake them."

"You're right . . . let them sleep," he said. "And how about if you come back home with them and let me find somewhere else to stay? It makes more sense to have the three of you there."

Another surprise, she thought, but then shook her head. "I need this change, Joe. I feel like this is the right place for us for now."

"Are you sure?" he asked, a worried frown reaching beyond just his expression.

She nodded. "I'm sure. I'm just not sure how long we're going to stay."

"Stay until you see a reason to come home," he replied, then lowered his chin and studied the ground for a few seconds. She thought she heard a sniff—he rubbed at his eye and then sucked in a steadying breath as he lifted his eyes to her.

He cleared his throat. "What . . . what did you tell Christy and Danny?"

"Nothing to Christy yet, but I told Danny you needed some time alone in the house to get some things fixed."

"And he heard the truth," Joe said, surprising her again.

Where's the ranting and raving and put-upon Joe? Where are the angry outbursts and the man who heads for Ray's or Barney's or the skies? Where's the man I'm ready to do battle with?

"Danny will be angry with me," Joe said.

"He's been angry for a long time. You've broken too many promises, Joe."

Meg kept her voice even, but she could see the hurt on his face. *Good. Wake up and fight for your son! Fight for your daughter and your wife. Fight for the life we could have together!*

"This time you won't hear promises, Meg. But you will find promises in what I do," he said earnestly.

From the second-story window, Danny kept his eyes on his dad as he turned and walked away from the porch. He'd been awake ever since he heard the distinctive sound of the old Ford as it approached his grandma's house. He had watched his dad move toward the porch and stop. *Mom must be out on the steps*, he thought. He was awfully glad it was finally morning. What a long night it had been. He couldn't seem to get comfortable on the spare bed in Grandma's sewing room. His feet hung over the edge, and the sheets didn't feel or smell like the sheets at home—he felt like he'd had his nose in a flower bed all night long. He couldn't hear what his parents were saying, but he guessed there would be a lot of "I'm sorry" and "I'll try and do better" from his dad.

He couldn't believe what had happened over the last twelve hours. One minute he and Christy were listening to *The Jack Benny Show* on the radio, and the next minute his mom was telling them to pack a bag because they were going to Grandma's house.

"But why? Are you and Daddy going on a trip somewhere?" Christy had asked. Danny thought about the look he had seen on his mom's face and the knot that had formed in his stomach as he watched her trying to hold it together. He immediately thought that something had happened to his dad. He'd asked the question before he could stop himself. "Dad didn't crash . . . ?"

Meg shook her head and pasted a smile on her face. "No, honey. Dad's fine. He's at his . . . meeting." The worry he had felt only moments before quickly dissolved into anger as soon as he knew his dad was all right. *At Barney's again.* The next thing his mom said made Danny realize things were about to change.

"I thought the three of us would have a sleepover at Grandma Sylvia's tonight," Meg said as she carefully avoided his eyes.

"What about Daddy?" Christy had asked. "Won't he be lonely all by himself?"

"He'll be fine. He won't be home until much later, and he'll go straight to bed," Meg said. She finally looked Danny in the eye, and he saw more than he wanted to.

He put his arm around Christy. "Let's go pack your pj's, squirt," he'd said, trying not to notice the grateful look from his mom.

From his vantage point at the window, he'd only been able to see his dad's face during their conversation—and only the low murmur of their voices. When his father walked back to his truck—alone—he wasn't sure how he felt. On the one hand he wanted to go home and pretend last night had never happened. But on the other, he was tired of the knots in his stomach every weekend. He was tired of trying to pretend he wasn't mad at his dad. Because he was. *If I still believed in Santa . . .* He shook his head once and lay back on his makeshift bed.

Meg entered the kitchen and found her mom in her "baking apron," pulling flour and sugar canisters out of the cabinet above the stove. "You went out there looking like that? No lipstick, and in your bare feet?" Sylvia protested.

Lipstick and bare feet?! Seriously—this is her worry? Meg looked at her mom: there wasn't a hair out of place; her lipstick was fresh, her back rigid with expectation.

"I'm going to make an apple pie for Danny," Sylvia announced.

"He loves your apple pie," Meg assured her as she went to pour herself another cup of coffee.

"You can always take the leftovers home to Joe," Sylvia said with a quick sideways glance.

Meg carried her coffee to the table and tucked one leg under her as she sat down.

"You need to realize, Mom, that this isn't something that's going to fix itself overnight," she said with a sigh.

Sylvia wiped her hands on her apron and then cracked an egg into a yellow bowl with painted apples on the side, one that Meg remembered well from her childhood. She stared at it, thinking about her dad and how much she missed him. *Maybe Mother would not be so unbending if Dad had lived. . . .* She shook her head once and turned her attention back to her mother's voice.

"If you ask me, it's not your marriage that's broken, Meg," Sylvia was saying. "It's your attitude. I still say this is Norma's doing—she always was a bad influence on you."

"This doesn't have anything to do with Norma," Meg protested, trying to keep her anger in check. Any hints of those feelings would only be chalked up to her "attitude."

Sylvia turned from assembling the piecrust and lifted her right eyebrow—a sure signal that she was about to dispense more unsolicited advice.

"You and Joe have been married sixteen years, and not a peep out of you about being unhappy. Norma breezes back into town, and first chance you get, you run out your own front door and don't look back."

"No one says I'm not looking back," Meg said quietly. "This is the hardest thing I've ever done."

Sylvia's expression softened, and she went to sit at the table with Meg. Suddenly, Meg could see every line on her mom's face. The worry wrinkles around her mouth from years of pursing her lips, crow's feet at the corner of her eyes, the deep lines in her forehead from years of concerned frowning. *She's just worried about me. What would I say to Christy if she were in my kitchen like this sixteen years into her marriage?*

"All a mother can ever ask for is that her child is happy, healthy, and believes in God," Sylvia said. "I've always been blessed by you, Meg. I just don't want you to make any rash decisions. Any choices you will regret."

"I won't," Meg assured her, "because this was the right thing to do, Mom. I'm not doing Joe, the kids, or me any favors by pretending things are fine." She looked her mother full in the face. "Things are not fine. Why should Joe ever have to make an effort to make things better if there aren't any consequences for his actions?"

Sylvia sighed. "It's just not biblical to separate a union that formed in a church. The women will be gossiping about this before the day is out, and I just hate that you and the kids are going to be talked about that way."

"Let them talk," Meg said with more bravado than she felt.

"Joe's a good man," Sylvia argued. "He's always provided for you and the children. You have a lovely home, clothes on your back, and food on your table." She paused, then said, "He's not the only man in town who warms up a barstool once a week."

"Once a week is turning into twice. Soon it'll be three. . . ." Meg stopped at the creak of a floorboard upstairs. One of the kids must be awake.

"Remind me to tell Christy and Danny not to leave wet towels on the sink," Sylvia said briskly.

Meg nodded. *We've invaded her nice, neat, quiet house. . . .* "I'll tell them, Mom. I know this is an imposition, and Joe offered to move out of the house. But I know he'd have a harder time staying with his folks. I made the decision to do this, and I'd like to be here for a while . . . if that's all right."

Sylvia laid her hand over Meg's. "If you can't impose on your own mother, then who?"

Meg smiled. "Thanks, Mom. Right now I just want to keep things as normal as possible for Christy and Danny. And it will make me feel better to know they're here with you when I'm working over at Norma's."

"You're still going to do that?"

Sylvia's disapproving tone made Meg realize she'd dropped her guard too soon. "Yes. It's something I really want to do."

"Oh, Meg, you're a wife and a mother. Can't that be enough?"

"No. Right now it can't. I'm good at decorating, and the money Norma is paying me will come in handy . . . whatever happens."

"You walk out on your husband, live with your mother, and now you've taken a . . . job," Sylvia said with a long-suffering sigh. "You really are making sure the gossip train has a good long ride, aren't you?"

"They have to talk about someone," Meg said lightly. "Might as well be me."

Something different. Something better. Something's going to change.

Joe made his way into the empty kitchen and looked around. He felt as lifeless as the house did without Meg and the kids. If only he would have appreciated those moments strung together over the years that had made up his family—his life. *Sunday mornings, family suppers, chores, car trips, decorating the Christmas tree . . .*

He took a deep breath and looked around the room again. *Okay, what's next?* He went about the task of making coffee, filling the pot with water. He knew he had to make this day, and every day, count. But the question was how to go about it.

He put the coffeepot on a burner and went to light it—then soon remembered it wasn't working. He tried two other burners, sighing when he got the same result. He held another match to the last burner on the stove, stubbornly holding the knob until the flame finally caught under the coffeepot. He wondered how many times Meg had dealt with this very thing every morning for weeks . . . or months? *How could I have just ignored it for so long . . . how could I have ignored her for so long?* He leaned both hands on the stove and stared at the ring of blue fire. *She deserves better than this and so much more. . . .*

Chapter 18

Norma stood just outside the back door and plucked her cotton blouse away from her skin. She felt as if the weather were sitting on her. *A Kansas kind of hot and humid*, she told herself.

She kept her eyes on the barn door—waiting and watching. She had sent her boys and Danny into the barn to get tools to help them clean up the neglected garden. And then she immediately worried that some small thing—something said in jest, or not—would escalate into a fight. It had happened frequently between the boys since she'd taken them in—she just didn't want Danny getting caught up in all that. She had told Meg some of the boys' history—the neglect and beatings they'd endured, along with the stealing and aggressive behavior. But Norma knew Meg couldn't really fathom the things that had affected the boys—nor had she completely thought through the influence they might have on Danny. *I'll just worry enough for the both of us*, she decided, staring at the barn.

The sound of Christy chattering away to Meg filtered from the kitchen through the screen door. She thought briefly about how different it would be to have a girl in the house. If Christy was any example, girls seemed to have a lot more to say than boys.

Finally the four—JP, Zach, Frankie, and Danny—stepped back outside the barn carrying an assortment of gardening tools. They started toward the garden at the back of the house. Norma was relieved to see they were doing okay, even though it was evident that Danny was the outsider. It seemed to her that the other boys had shouldered him out of their circle. She decided that could be good or bad depending on the point of view. Good because her three had bonded to some extent in the months since they'd been with her. Bad because they didn't have a great track record when it came to dealing with other boys close to their age. She was just grateful they all seemed to be getting along right now—at least this minute. *One step at a time,* she thought as she opened the screen door and went back into the kitchen.

The smell of fresh paint permeated the room. Meg was using her brush to cover the last bit of white on the wall with a sunny yellow color. Christy, using her own brush, stood so close to Meg that Norma didn't think a piece of paper could be squeezed between them. Meg moved over—Christy did the same. Meg dragged her paintbrush down the wall and actually collided with Christy's hand, painting a yellow streak across her wrist.

"Mommy—you painted me," Christy accused as she held up her hand.

Meg stepped back from the wall. "You're too close, Chris. I can't make a move without running into you."

"I'm helping you."

"I know. I know you are. You're doing a good job. I just need a little space—a little elbow room."

"But I'm getting the places you miss," Christy argued.

"Maybe I missed some places on the other walls. Why don't you check?"

Norma knew Meg's decision to leave Joe was weighing heavily on her. She could hear the impatience and edginess in Meg's voice—even if Christy couldn't.

"But I want to paint with *you*."

"You'll still be painting with me—just on a different wall."

"But, Mommy—"

"Please just do it!"

Christy looked surprised and pained at her mother's tone.

"I was just about to ask Christy to do *me* a favor," Norma put in. Meg turned and looked at her, and Norma could see the worry and fatigue on her friend's face.

"What favor, Miss Norma?" Christy asked.

Norma went to the old refrigerator that—miracle of miracles—still worked, and opened the freezer. "I was thinking about the best way to motivate all those boys out there to get that garden ready," she said as she pulled out a box, "and then I remembered that all boys love to eat."

Christy eyed the box. "Girls like to eat too."

"That's what makes this a good plan," Norma said with a smile. "I told the boys I'd have a cold treat for them when they finished the garden—and if they see you eating one of these banana popsicles, they'll be motivated to get done that much quicker."

Christy looked at Meg, then the frozen treat. "Couldn't I just stay in here and eat it?"

"No," Meg jumped in, "no, you can't."

"It's just that popsicles can be really messy, and we wouldn't want it to drip all over the floor," Norma explained. "And the point is for the boys to *see* you enjoying it."

She held the popsicle out to Christy. "If you sit right there on the back porch, we can see you through the screen door. And the boys can see you from the garden."

Christy hesitated. "You'll stay in the kitchen, Mom?"

"Planted like a tree," Meg said wryly.

"Okay."

After Christy stepped outside, Meg watched her go and shook her head. "I don't know if I can do this," she said, keeping her voice low.

"What?"

"My mother—she thinks I've made a huge mistake, and I'm ruining everyone's life—including my own."

"What does she think you should do?" Norma asked.

"She thinks I should start by making Joe a pie and taking it home with the most humble apology I can think of."

"Seriously? That's *seriously* her advice to her only daughter?"

Meg crossed the kitchen and dug a printed article out of her purse. She waved the paper at Norma. "She gave me this right before I came over here. Advice on marriage. And she made me promise I'd share it with you."

Norma raised her eyebrows. "Me?"

Meg nodded. "I've got the rules here for how to be a good wife. My mom found it in a magazine—let's see, it's from *Housekeeping Journal,* the spring 1955 issue."

"Well, it's three years old, but let's hear it."

Meg made her voice prim and proper with an instructional overtone. " 'Have dinner ready. Plan ahead, even the night before, to have a delicious meal on time. This is a way of letting him know that you've been thinking about him and are concerned about his needs.' "

"Hmmm . . . can't argue with that, especially since it was our cook, Matilda, who must have been thinking of Bob and his needs," Norma quipped with a grin.

"It gets better," Meg said. " 'Take fifteen minutes to rest so you will be refreshed when he arrives. Be a little gay and a little more interesting. His boring day may need a lift.' "

Norma started to giggle, then laughed outright. "So boredom is only a problem for men."

Meg went on, " 'Clear away the clutter and prepare the children. Minimize the noise. Be happy to see him and greet him with a warm smile. Make him comfortable and speak in a low, soothing, and pleasant voice.' "

At this, Meg held up an index finger, teacher-style. "*But*, 'Always let him talk first. Don't complain or greet him with problems. Don't complain if he never takes you out to dinner or other places of entertainment—instead try to understand his world of strain and pressure, his need to be home and relax.' "

Meg looked over the paper in her hands at Norma, who was still grinning. She said, "I sure did flunk Good Wife 101."

Meg laughed but quickly turned serious. "What if I *am* wrecking our lives? What if my mother is right?" She wadded up the article in her hands and tossed it onto the counter. "But right or wrong, she's eating away at me! And I'm going crazy that she's able to get under my skin like this. And Christy won't let me out of her sight, and Danny . . . well, Danny's just plain mad. At me. At Joe. At the sun coming up in the morning. The kids both look at me like I'm some *stranger,* and I can barely manage being in the same room with them at times because I feel so guilty! I probably *have* made the biggest mistake of my life and uprooted my family to move into my mother's house, where you can't even leave a glass sitting in the sink and the bed has to be made before you're even out of it and where a homemade pie cures everything and my husband probably thinks I'm the witch from *The Wizard of Oz*—not the good one, but the bad one—"

"Whoa. Take a breath."

Meg turned huge eyes on her friend. "What have I done? What was I thinking?! I should have just kept doing what I've been doing. I had a roof over my head—food on the table—a husband who came home most nights and did his job to provide for his family. I'm an idiot! I miss my own kitchen. My own bed. My own clothesline in the backyard!"

Meg turned away from Norma to brush at the tears filling her eyes. "This is too hard," she said, her voice breaking. "I don't know if I can do it. All the possibles and unknowns are driving me insane!"

Meg took a big breath and turned back to Norma. "When Joe talked to me that first morning, I almost believed there was something different. . . ."

"Time will tell," Norma said. "Those old habits die hard, our grandmothers used to say. What you practice is what you get good at."

Meg wiped at her cheek with the back of her hand. "But what if he *doesn't* change? What if he *can't* change? What if he ends up *liking* his freedom? What if the kids get all messed up and never feel secure again? What if Joe's incapable of being happy with or without alcohol? What if I end up living with my mother and we turn out to be two old women who start to take in cats?"

Norma's smile was both amused and sympathetic. "You know what I think the definition of insanity is?"

Meg shook her head.

"I think insanity is doing the same thing over and over and expecting a different outcome," Norma said. "You're not going crazy, Meg. You've made a change, and it's a *painful* one. The pain can make you question . . . everything. It's scary. But *insanity* . . . insanity would be for you to keep on living a life you know is a lie. That Danny knows is a lie. That Christy eventually would know is a lie."

Norma and Meg glanced through the screen door at the same time. Christy was still out there, her back to them.

"So I'm not a lunatic to worry like this?" Meg asked, sounding just a bit relieved.

"No. When I was going through the whole sorrowful mess with Bob, I prayed my heart out. I think I had a direct line to heaven and was overloading the circuits. Most of the time I didn't even bother God with the usual formalities. It was just, 'Hello, Lord, it's me again. . . .' "

Meg smiled and sniffed.

"And be sure to tell your mom I appreciate the steps to being a good wife. It answers all those burning questions I had about why my marriage failed."

"I'll tell her. She loves to be helpful," Meg said, and they both laughed.

It hadn't seemed like too hard a task when Norma had asked them to turn over the soil in the garden behind the house, but Danny soon realized it would be tougher than any of them had anticipated. It all boiled down to who was the one in charge—and that had yet to be determined. Tools were limited to two shovels, a hand trowel, and a spade.

Danny sized up the boys he was being forced to spend time with. He'd never met anyone like Zach before, and truth be told, he was a little worried about the guy. Zach had entirely too much confidence for someone who was the new kid in town and didn't belong.

Zach grabbed one of the shovels. "I'll start at this end," he announced with a note of authority. Danny knew Zach was a year older than he was, and a good two inches taller, but he wasn't about to let him assume he was going to run the show.

"Have you ever turned soil in a garden before?" Danny asked, picking up the other shovel.

Zach pushed the tool into the dirt. "Yeah. Did it all the time at that swanky resort they sent me to."

Danny frowned. "Resort?"

JP laughed and jabbed his elbow into his younger brother's ribs. Frankie was the quiet one.

"Yeah. He's been on vacation," JP said with another laugh. Frankie just stared at the hard-packed black dirt beneath his feet.

"I'm talking about juvey, Einstein," Zach growled and stomped hard on the edge of the shovel. "You wouldn't last two minutes in a place like that."

"I don't plan on ending up in a place like that," Danny retorted. He watched Zach attack the ground with a vengeance.

"We're not digging holes to China," he commented. "Just loosen the soil." He looked at JP and Frankie. "You guys can use the trowel and spade and come along behind us."

"I don't think anybody voted you the boss," JP shot back.

Danny shrugged. "I'm the only one who's done this before."

"Pushing around dirt ain't something I'd brag about, Farmer Dan," Zach sneered.

Danny decided to let the farmer comment slide. He worked his shovel like a pro and moved quickly through the hard dirt.

"What'd you guys do to get in trouble anyway?" Danny asked.

"Stuff you can't even think about without breaking into a sweat." This from Zach.

"I was a pretty good thief," JP boasted, "and Frankie ain't bad either."

"I can hot-wire a car quicker'n you can spell your own name," Zach said as he worked his own shovel with nearly as much skill as Danny.

Danny stopped turning the dirt and stared. "You're lying."

Zach stopped and leaned on his shovel. He shook his head slowly. "I don't lie."

"No. You just steal," Danny said, all he could come up with for the moment.

JP and Frankie had yet to pick up a spade or trowel. JP doubled up his fist, though he let it hang at his side. Frankie looked expectantly between JP and Zach.

"You think you're better than us?" Zach demanded with an edge to his voice.

"*I* don't steal," Danny said.

"Neither do we anymore," Frankie piped up. "We wouldn't do that to Norma."

"Sure. Okay. Whatever you say." Danny started turning the soil again. Zach crossed the hard dirt to stand closer, the shovel dangling from one hand.

"I know what's going on with your family," Zach said. "I know you're living in one house and your dad's living in another. Whether you like it or not, we're the same."

"I don't think so," Danny said as he took a step backward.

"Sure we are. We're all from broken homes," Zach said with a smirk.

Danny felt the heat rise up his neck and spread across his cheeks. He wanted to push Zach's face right into the black dirt below their feet.

"My home's not broken," he shouted, "and I'm *nothing* like you."

Zach spit into the dirt and took another step closer, the shovel gripped in his hands.

"My mistake—we aren't alike after all. I can accept the truth about my family. Broken beyond repair."

"Mine's not," Danny said through clenched teeth.

"Whatever you say, Farmer Dan."

"Shut up."

"Oooh. Mama's little church boy said 'shut up.' Won't God get you for that, Farmer Dan?" Zach taunted.

Danny stepped closer and his hand shot out to shove Zach's shoulder. It must have caught Zach off guard, and he took a couple of unsteady steps back.

Danny thought he detected a look of surprise on Zach's face. *Good. Let him think twice before he calls me Farmer Dan again.*

"You don't want to do that, Farmer Dan," Zach said, his voice low and menacing. JP and Frankie moved to stand behind Zach.

Danny didn't know how he'd gotten to this point, but he knew he couldn't back down now. "Don't call me Farmer Dan."

"Farmer Dan doesn't want us to call him Farmer Dan anymore, boys," Zach told JP and Frankie.

"Sorry, Farmer Dan," JP said with a grin.

Danny's hand shot out again, and he shoved Zach. This time, Zach was ready and stood his ground.

"I told you not to do that." Zach dropped the shovel, then slowly raised his clenched fists chest level in front of him. Danny swallowed, looked at the fighter's stance Zach had assumed.

The sound of approaching vehicles got their attention. Danny watched as Zach turned toward the two trucks.

"Looks like company," Zach commented, then went back to his section of the dirt.

Danny felt relief and then shame at his own relief. He hadn't been sure he could hold his own with someone like Zach. *He's probably got a lot more experience fighting than me. I wonder if that fight I had with Johnny Simpson in third grade counts?*

Norma leaned against the railing of the porch and looked at the small contingency of neighboring farmers who'd come to pay her a visit. After some polite small talk about the way the place was shaping up, Jerry Trader, a weathered farmer with a permanently sunburned nose, removed his John Deere hat and mopped his forehead with a bandanna.

"You know how much I respected your grandparents, Norma," Jerry said as he shoved the cloth back into his pocket. "I learned most a' what I know about farming from your grandpop."

"That's nice of you to say, Jerry," Norma said. "I know they thought you were a real good neighbor."

Tom Simpson, the oldest of the group of five men, planted a worn boot on the bottom step of the porch and leaned over his leg. "We want to talk to you about the offer Vanguard's making to the farmers in the area."

"What about it?" she asked.

Tom looked at the faces of the other men. "Well, we think it sounds like a good deal." He glanced around again at the men with him, and they bobbed their heads in agreement. "We know you're . . . you know . . . alone, without a man to help guide you on these things, and that's why we thought you ought to know we think Luke's offering decent money—which will help with some of the headaches that have been troubling us for years. I know I'd like to think about next year's crop without getting a knot of worry in my belly," he said. The rest of the farmers grunted their agreement.

"While I appreciate your . . . *guidance* . . . I still have to make up my own mind about this." Norma looked at Adam Malloy, the youngest man in the group. "I can't believe you want to sell, Adam," Norma said. "You and Helen have worked for years to make that farm what it is."

"Yeah. We have," Adam agreed, "but the worry about the land and the crops is wearing Helen down. Luke Ramsey says he can take that worry right off our shoulders—and he can do the same thing for you."

"I've barely been back long enough to worry about more than the color I'm painting the kitchen," she said. "I want to make a go of this place. I've got three boys to help me, and I just can't imagine turning over Granny and Pop's place to some corporation."

"Then hang on to just a workable piece for your own," Tom suggested, "and sell the rest—the bulk of it. You need to be realistic, Norma. A woman alone with three boys can't do it. Not without a man's help."

Norma raised her brows and let her hand ride her hip while she stood her ground. An uncomfortable look circled around the faces in front of her.

"We'll just say it straight out, Norma," Jerry said. "This might be bigger'n just what *you* want. You got the biggest parcel of land, and Luke's made it clear he don't need the rest of our farms 'thout yours. He needs this place to bring the total acreage up to Vanguard's minimums."

"We're just asking you to think about Vanguard's offer, Norma, that's all," Adam said.

Norma nodded. "Thanks for coming by," she said. "I'll think about it." She watched them drive away, then went back into the kitchen with a frustrated sigh. "Nothing like feeling ambushed by my own neighbors."

Meg's smile was sympathetic. "I don't think they mean to make you feel that way."

"I don't know about that," Norma said. "I know Luke's right about the size of the land, and I know the boys and I can't handle it alone. There are a million things around here that need to be repaired. Half the tools are broken or missing. The tractor runs at full speed or not at all, the barn door is rotten and falling apart—and I could go on and on. Bob gave me a fair amount of money when we separated, but it won't last long past the repairs I need to do."

“So then you are really thinking of selling?” Meg asked carefully.

Norma picked up her paintbrush and shrugged. “Two weeks ago I wouldn’t even have entertained the possibility . . . but now . . . now I honestly don’t know what to do.”

Chapter 19

It was almost dusk when Joe arrived at Sam's hardware store. He had just managed to slip inside before closing time—something Sam reminded him of with a tap on his watch and a frown.

Now, as Joe stepped back outside with a paint can and a box of nails, he heard the deadbolt slide across the door and looked over his shoulder to see Sam flip the "Closed, Please Come Again" sign in the window. He secured his new purchases next to the assortment of lumber in the back of the truck before slamming the tailgate and heading around to the cab. He climbed in and glanced down the street just as the light for Barney's Tavern blinked on. *Barney's. It's Saturday.* He'd been kind of busy the past few days doing good turns for friends and strangers—fixed two flat tires, picked up a trailer for a neighbor, helped an elderly woman find her lost dog, delivered groceries, and sprayed two fields—gratis. He hadn't had time to even think about Barney's—but here he was in town, just down the street from his Saturday-night haunt. And now, he realized, there was something else he needed to do.

Hands sweating and heart pounding, Joe stepped inside to the strains of the Penguins singing "Earth Angel" on the jukebox, and in spite of his nerves it made him smile. He took a quick look around and saw the usual Saturday-night crowd was there. Ralph and Bo Gene shooting pool. Eddie and Clyde in the back booth—and Gunny perched on his usual barstool. It suddenly occurred to him that he was the only man in the place that was married. The only one who had a family waiting at home. *Did* have a family waiting for me, he revised. He pushed the thought down. *One step at a time. The man God intends you to be.*

He had started across the room when he saw Marsha making a beeline in his direction.

"Hi, Marsh—"

She hooked her arm through his and spun him away from the bar.

"I'd think twice before bellying up to the bar right now, Joe," she warned. "Barney's still plenty steamed at you." She looked a little closer at him. "Nice haircut," she added.

Joe frowned. "He is?"

She nodded, and Joe watched her throw a quick glance over her shoulder toward the bar. Barney was nowhere in sight.

"You bet he is. You did the dash, Joe. You know he hates that."

Joe had totally forgotten how he had ducked out of Barney's and slipped away the last time he'd been there. Barney was very protective of all his customers—especially the regulars. He never let anyone drive if they'd had one too many.

"He won't serve you—and he told me I couldn't serve you," Marsha continued.

Joe nodded. "Good. That's good."

She raised her eyebrows. "It is?"

"Yeah. In fact, Marsh, I need you to do me a serious favor."

"Don't ask me to go behind Barney's back, Joe," she said with a shake of her head.

"No. No, it's nothing like that. In fact, I want you to promise me that under *any* circumstances, you won't ever put a beer down in front of me again."

He saw the surprise on her face, and the skepticism. "Please, Marsha? This is really important to me . . . and, frankly, I'm worried about my own willpower."

"New leaf?" she finally asked. He nodded and watched her smile. "Good for you, Joe. You'll get no beer from me." She looked over her shoulder again at the bar, where Barney had just settled a tray of clean glasses.

"I better get back to work," she said as she started toward a booth in the back.

Barney looked up and frowned as Joe approached and took the empty stool next to Gunny.

"Hey, Joe, visiting my neck of the woods tonight?" Gunny asked jovially.

"Thought I might, Gunny. Is that all right with you?"

"Sure, sure. Some guys need to shake up the view every now and then," Gunny said. "But me—I like the view of the tap from this stool. Guess I'm just a creature of habit."

Barney materialized in front of Joe and scowled. "You slink in here, sit on a different stool, and look like you're going to Sunday services. You think I won't recognize you for the liar and cheat you are, Joe?"

"Listen, Barn—I'm sure sorry I ducked out the other night."

"Sorry wouldn't have cut it if I'd had to tell your wife you killed your drunk self driving home from my bar," he growled. "Sorry would be something I'd have to live with for the rest of my life. You can apologize till the cows come home, Joe, but I'm not serving you."

"Good. Fine. I don't want anything to drink," Joe said. "Well, maybe a Coca-Cola."

"That's a good one, Joe," Gunny chuckled. "Coca-Cola."

"I'm not buying it for a second," Barney said. "You're just trying to con me into serving you."

"No, really, Barney. Just a Coke," Joe insisted.

"You on some medication can't mix with alcohol?" Gunny asked. " 'Cause I'm here to tell ya they put that warning stuff on the pill bottles just to scare the pants off us. I've washed down plenty a' pills with beer and ain't dropped dead yet," he added.

"No medication."

Barney looked puzzled. "You know you can get soda pop at the lunch counter in Woolworth's, Joe."

"Woolworth's isn't open, Barney. Got any peanuts?"

Barney threw a dish towel over his shoulder and turned to fill a mug with beer. He unceremoniously plunked it down in front of Joe.

"Okay, here you go. But if you *ever* pull a stunt like you did the other night—"

Joe barely had time to register the beer in front of him before Marsha was there grabbing the mug handle and lifting it out of his sight.

"Hey, Barney. Stick to your guns! You said you weren't serving him!" she chided. "You cave in for Joe and everyone'll think they can walk all over you."

Gunny lifted his eyebrows in astonishment. Joe caught her eye and tried to convey his thanks. Barney watched as she marched away—beer still in hand.

"Didn't know I was such a role model," Barney mumbled. "Give it a second, Joe, and I'll pour you another."

Joe shook his head. "I really just want a Coke. But I appreciate the forgiveness, Barn."

Meg turned and drove slowly down Main Street. She wasn't in any hurry . . . wished in fact she hadn't come to town at all.

She noticed a few couples strolling along the storefronts window-shopping. Three teenage girls turned to go into the theater. A large—really large—man in a pair of overalls rolled a car tire down the sidewalk.

She couldn't remember the last time she'd been on Main Street on a Saturday night. *Wait—yes I do. It was Larry and Anne's anniversary celebration in the church fellowship hall. I went by myself—as usual.*

She wasn't proud of the fact that she had left her children home with her mother so she could carry out this quest. She'd mentally fought over whether she should check up on Joe—but in the end, she felt she had to know. Were his words just more empty promises—or did he really mean what he said about changing?

She passed the cinema and Greenville Hardware, then looked ahead to Barney's. *No! No! No!* She slammed on the brakes, stopping the car in the middle of Main Street. She stared out the window at Joe's truck parked right out there in plain sight under the sign at Barney's. *I'm so stupid! So gullible! He's never going to change—why did I think he'd change?*

She didn't even realize she was crying until the streetlights blurred. Someone in a car behind her honked. Meg moved her foot from the brake to the gas and slowly passed Joe's truck. She felt the crushing disappointment fill her chest till the air was squeezed out of her. She felt used up. Drained. Exhausted. Brought to her knees.

I wanted to know, and now I do. This time it's good-bye.

Marsha did what she had promised—and Joe was grateful. She kept all beer mugs out of reach—including the last full mug Barney again had tried to serve him, compliments of Ralph Hutton. "For helping me pick that load of lumber off the road yesterday, Joe!" Ralph called over. Joe just waved in acknowledgment.

"Hey, Barney," Bo Gene said as he stepped up to the bar beside Joe and slid a companionable arm around his friend. "Pour one for my best pal, here." Bo had obviously had more than a few, Joe noted. *Yeah, easy to spot when you're not drinking yourself.*

"No, don't, Barney. Thanks anyway, Bo."

"Heard about you and Meg," Bo said. "It breaks my heart, Joe. You and Meg! Since high school. Since the day I was there and helped you pull off the most romantic proposal in history, man!"

"It's going to be fine," Joe tried to assure him. *I hope. . . .*

Barney started to settle two mugs in front of Joe and Bo Gene, but Marsha was right there again to intercept.

"Thanks, Barn. Clyde and Eddie are waiting on these," she said, whisking the mugs away.

"Hey!" Barney protested. "Bring those back." He turned to fill two more. "What's gotten into her tonight?" he grumbled as Marsha made tracks toward the back with the beer, leaving Bo with a confused look on his face.

"There goes my beer. I'm off like a dirty shirt, Joe. If you need to talk—or a shoulder or, you know . . ." Bo said, a bit too loudly.

"I know. Thanks, Bo."

"Need more peanuts over here, Barney," Gunny called. Joe pushed his bowl toward Gunny. *One step at a time.*

"You know, Gunny, I've been sitting down the bar from you for a good long time now, and I don't know much about you," Joe said, looking at the rather disheveled man beside him.

Gunny's lips vibrated as he blew out an amused breath. "You ain't missed much."

"I'll bet that's not true. What do you do for a living?"

"An appliance repairman," he said, his lips moving carefully around the syllables.

"You work for yourself or a company?" Joe asked.

"Me, myself, and I," Gunny answered with a little grin. "Fact is, I enjoy the work most of the time. I like fixing stuff."

"Where do you live?"

"Emporia," Gunny said. "Bought a house there when I married Barbara."

Joe couldn't hide his surprise. "I didn't know you were married, Gunny."

Gunny drained the last of his beer and tapped his empty mug on the bar a couple of times. "We're running behind here, Barney. Let's pick up the pace a little."

He turned and looked at Joe. "Barbara died a year after we were married. A drunk driver hit her," he said and took another long swallow of his beer. "Promised myself after that I'd never put myself behind the wheel after I'd been drinking."

"I'm sorry, Gunny," Joe said as Barney put two mugs down—yet another beer in front of him, right next to his Coca-Cola.

"It's from Clyde back there," Barney announced in an offhand manner. "To thank you for helping him with that flat he had on the road the other day."

Joe stared at the mug, then reached for it—and pushed it away. *I finally quit drinking and everyone wants to buy me a beer!* "No thanks," he said just as Marsha came around the bar. He saw her smile of approval.

"You're not coming back here next Saturday . . . are you, Joe?" Gunny asked in an unusual moment of clarity.

"No. I don't think so. I'd like to be clear-eyed when I look at Saturday-night moons from now on," Joe said quietly, "and it would be nice to wake up Sunday morning without a dull ache behind my eyes and a mouth that feels like a deserted beach. I'm going to start going to church again." *Okay, I did it. I made it. I sat at this bar and didn't drink.*

Joe raised the soda to his lips and caught his reflection in the mirror behind the bar—and for once he didn't avoid looking into his own eyes. He saw Larry Ledet come up behind him and put a hand on his shoulder.

"How ya doin', Joe?" Larry asked. Joe spun his barstool to look Larry in the eye.

"Doing good, Larry. How 'bout you?"

"Can't complain," he answered. "What are you doing sitting here? This is Gunny's territory."

"He's sharing the meaning a' life with me." Gunny's wry comment was followed by a burp.

"Is that right?" Larry asked, turning to look carefully at Joe.

"Yup," Gunny said, popping his lips. "Ya know, it kinda makes sense."

"You gonna have the usual, Lar?" Joe asked.

"I guess so," Larry said as he took the stool next to Joe. He signaled Barney, who was at the opposite end of the bar.

"Be right with ya, Chief," Barney said.

Joe threw a couple of dollars down on the bar. "It was good talking to you, Gunny."

"You would a' liked Barb, Joe. She was something," Gunny said sadly, staring into his mug.

"I'm sure she was," Joe agreed as he got off the barstool.

Larry quickly got to his feet. "You're leaving?"

"Yeah. Calling it a night," Joe said as he started toward the door.

"Wait. I'll walk out with you."

Larry's patrol car was parked right next to Joe's truck. As was their custom, Larry followed Joe to the truck and then waited for him to get in and try to start it. But this time, Joe stopped at the hood and lifted it.

"What're you doing?" Larry asked.

Joe held out his hand. "I'm gonna need the coil wire, Larry," he said with a grin.

"What do you mean?" Larry stammered.

"I mean you've been a better friend than I could ever hope to deserve—but tonight I'm stone-cold sober and drank nothing but Coke," Joe told him.

Larry reached into his pocket and pulled out the coil wire. The two men were silent as Joe unscrewed the distributor cap and put the wire back where it belonged. After he slammed the hood of the truck, he extended his hand to Larry.

"Thanks, Larry. I'm giving you and Anne back your Saturday nights."

Chapter 20

Luke was filled with resentment at being summoned into Vanguard's corporate office in Kansas City, but he made sure it didn't show. Steve and Earl, the reps who had been working the smaller farms in Greenville, had arrived with him, but he knew they didn't feel any of the same pressure he felt. They weren't playing the game at the level he was—they didn't have as much riding on the Greenville deal. In fact, no one in the room knew how badly he wanted to deliver what he had promised—Greenville and the surrounding properties on a platter to Vanguard.

The conference room was bypassed in favor of the boss's personal office, a space big enough to accommodate the six men who had gathered in Don Dushell's paneled inner sanctum. The charts, maps, and hand-drawn graphics on the walls spoke of acquisitions in hand and those yet to come. The atmosphere of the place carried the same air of power as the big man behind the desk.

On the other side, Luke forced himself to lean back casually in his chair and meet the direct gaze of his boss. At fifty, Don

Dushell had enough age on Luke to make him feel young and inexperienced, something Luke would never let the older man know if he could help it. Known for a forthright manner and keen business sense, Don put in long hours and expected his employees to do the same without complaint. Despite the fact that Vanguard was all about agriculture, Don made sure he would never be mistaken for a farmer, favoring expensive suits and polished shoes to the work boots and pants most of his employees wore.

"So, basically, you're telling me you still don't have Norma Meiers on board—is that about it?" Don summed up bluntly.

"Well, technically, I'd have to say that's true," Luke said, steepling his hands in front of him. "But it's only a matter of time. I can see she's waffling."

Don reached under his glasses and rubbed his eyelids. "We've already given you more time on this deal than anybody else, and I'm losing my patience."

Howard Walker, sitting to Luke's left, piped in with, "Maybe we should just write off the time and money we've already spent trying to get this thing to come together here and head to the east end of the state like I wanted to do in the first place—you know, move on to greener pastures—"

"I'm telling you, I can get the Meiers place," Luke broke in as he leaned forward in the chair, "and we're *not* wasting time. Steve and Earl have gotten handshake deals with more than half the farmers around Norma's land."

"He's right, boss," Steve confirmed, "and we think we can convince the rest of them in pretty short order. That'll give us everyone but the Meiers woman."

Don leaned forward and planted his elbows solidly on the desk. "What's the deal with you and Greenville, Ramsey?"

Luke's brows drew together. "I told you—I grew up there. You know, hometown boy and all that."

"Yeah, yeah. I remember that part of the story—and I remember something about your father losing his job and your family having to move before you got out of high school," Don said, looking around the table.

Luke shrugged. "Same story for hundreds of families across the country."

Don opened the top drawer of his desk and pulled out a yellowed newspaper. "I think your story had a twist you forgot to tell us about," Don said, shoving the paper across the desk toward Luke. "Like the fact that your old man was putting the screws to the farmers, and they almost lynched him in your *hometown.*"

All eyes were fastened on the newspaper, and Luke felt bile rise in his throat as he saw the headline splashed under the *Greenville Gazette* logo: "Ramsey Indicted on Embezzlement Charge." His eyes blurred as his vision tunneled through the paper, through the desk, back through the years.

"What have you got to say, Ramsey?" Don pressed.

"Well! Say something, Ramsey!" The voice was like a razor blade, sharp and intimidating. He peered around the hallway corner, to where a single lamp burned in the living room, but shadow after shadow cut its power as men came through the door, pressing in on his father, their faces contorted in anger beyond control.

Mom's crying somewhere. Mom? There was unrecognizable fear on his dad's face, and then a hand shot out of the group, and he saw someone grab his dad by the collar and yank him forward into the furious assembly. . . . Dad!

"Don't touch him!" Luke spat out, eyes wild as he stared at the headline.

Don's brows shot up, and the other men in the room turned confused looks on each other.

"Luke!" Don's voice cut through the icy silence.

Luke's glazed, unfocused eyes swam back to reality. "What?"

"What are you babbling about?" Don demanded. "I hate games!"

Luke wiped beads of sweat from his forehead as casually as he could, then pushed the newspaper back across the desk. "I hate games too," he said, his voice sounding rough in his ears. He took a deep breath. "Unless I win—which I do. Always. I closed the last two deals in Nebraska—the same two deals that are bringing in higher revenue than we'd anticipated."

"I won't have you use *my company* for your own personal reasons," Don said firmly, leaning forward, "and I won't have you wasting valuable company time and resources so you can pander to your own ambitions for that town, whatever they may be." The man leaned back in his chair and waited.

"Look, Don," Luke finally responded, keeping defensiveness out of his tone, "you're just going to have to trust me on this. I had the deal locked up with Norma once, and it's true—she walked. But I know I can get her to go back to our original deal—and soon."

Don shook his head. "I think Howard may be right. We should just cut our losses, and I'll put you on the survey team for western Iowa."

"No! You can't do that—not now, not when I'm so close." Luke knew he was begging, but he was desperate. "I've never let you down, Don. You owe me this," he concluded, then immediately worried he'd gone too far.

"I *owe* you?" Don snarled. "Carl Baker was productive for this company for ten years, and I cut him loose last month because he lost his edge and led me and everyone else in this room on a wild-goose chase. You don't get the title of regional manager by letting days and weeks slip through your fingers when we're in the business of seasons!"

The threat vibrated in the silence from the other men in the room. Don slowly picked up the newspaper on the desk and folded it in half, then put it back in his top drawer. "I'm giving you one last chance here, Luke. You can either write this whole Greenville fiasco off and I'll never bring it up again, or you can stay the course and try to close the deal. The catch is this: if you pursue this—and botch it—you're going to wish you had never stepped foot in Greenville. Do I make myself clear?"

"Loud and clear," Luke answered with a hard glint in his eyes. "But I have no intention of joining Baker in the unemployment line. I'll deliver the Meiers place just like I promised."

Steve and Earl followed Luke out the door of the nondescript brick building located just east of the business district in Kansas City. It was now dusk, and the lights in the parking lot cast a dull yellow glow on Luke's shiny truck and the older Ford model parked next to it.

"Dushell's pretty worked up, Luke," Earl remarked as they approached the vehicles.

"You guys keep doing your job—and I'll do mine."

"What if she doesn't change her mind?" Steve asked.

"She will," Luke said confidently, "especially if we tip the scales in our favor and show her just how much easier life could be with Vanguard."

"How do you plan on doin' that?" Earl asked.

"I'm full of ideas," Luke said. "I just have to narrow it down to the right one."

Chapter 21

Meg heard the truck door slam shut, and she stepped through the screen door onto her mother's porch, surprised that he actually had come for the kids. After returning from church that morning, she had thrown on an old T-shirt of her father's and some faded pedal pushers. She avoided looking at herself in mirrors these days—shadows around her eyes hinted at sleepless nights and made her look older than her years.

She tried to ignore the thudding of her heart and shoved trembling hands into her pockets. She had never dreaded anything as much as the conversation she was about to have with Joe. She watched him make his way toward the house, and she met him at the bottom of the steps, her arms folded across her chest.

"Hi," Joe said. "You doing okay?"

"I didn't think you'd come." She knew this sounded blunt and rude, but she couldn't help herself.

"I understand." Joe's tone wasn't defensive, and she looked at him carefully.

"Do you?"

"Trying."

He looks pretty rested for a Sunday. No hangover pallor or bloodshot eyes—no sunglasses against the brightness of the day.

"I wanted to talk to you before the kids came out," she said.

"Yeah, okay."

She hesitated and drew in a breath. "I think it's a good idea that you find someplace else to live. . . ."

"Yeah, sure I will. That's what I wanted to do. . . . I want you and the kids to—"

"Joe, no!" she said, cutting him off. "I mean for good."

She waited while her words sank in, saw the moment when it dawned on Joe what she meant. She could see him swallow hard, looking pale and shaken.

"I thought you were going to give me one more chance—"

"I did, Joe. It's over. We're . . . over."

"But I don't understand. What did I do? What didn't I do?"

"You made me believe again. That's what you did. And I just don't want to do that anymore. Never."

They could hear Christy calling to Danny in the house. The two would be out any second.

His eyes brimmed with tears. "Okay, Meg. I'll do as you say. I'll find a place. But . . . but I need to tell you . . ." His voice cracked. "I'm not giving up. Even if it means trying until I take my last breath. You know why? Because you deserve at least that much from me. I'm not giving up. Never."

Meg wiped her own tears with a shaking hand and saw him struggle for some kind of composure before he had to face the kids. She knew she could have done this differently, a better time—a better place. But when and where would that be? Was there ever a good time to say a marriage was finished? Could you ever be prepared to hear those words out loud? She didn't think so. And now she was done—the words were out there, the wheels set in motion.

Christy burst through the screen door. "Daddy! You're here!" She launched herself at him, and he caught her and held her tightly. He looked at Meg over Christy's shoulder, and she had to look away. Danny came out onto the porch, scowl firmly in place.

Joe cleared his throat as he put Christy down. "You guys ready to go fishing?"

"Yes, Daddy! " Christy exclaimed.

"I don't have any of my fishing stuff here," Danny grouched. "It's all at home."

"I . . . I thought that might be the case, and I brought everything with me," Joe said.

Danny looked surprised, then quickly covered it with a brief nod as he walked past Meg and down the porch steps.

Christy ran back to Meg. " 'Bye, Mommy," she said with a hug. "Are you sure you don't want to come too?" Meg shook her head briefly and managed a smile. Christy headed toward the truck, hollering back over her shoulder, "C'mon, Daddy, let's go!"

Meg stood on the bottom step a long time after the truck was out of sight and the dust had settled.

Meg's declaration played over and over in Joe's mind as he drove. Christy had chattered nonstop from the time he had closed the door of the truck, all through the drive to Carter Lake, and continued as they walked along the shore to stake out a good fishing spot. She'd covered all the bases from her grandmother's strict rules about toothbrushes on the sink to the Sunday school lesson she'd learned that morning.

But Danny had barely said two words since Joe had picked them up. Now he stood silently under the umbrella of shade provided by huge maples, his line in the water, the bobber floating lazily on the surface. Joe felt his heart lurch when he thought about not ever living with his children again. He couldn't bear the thought of telling them that they might not be a family anymore. *It can't happen . . . I won't let it. I'll prove to her that I am different. . . . Somehow I'll prove it to all of them. God, help me. . . .*

Joe forced his thoughts away from his conversation with Meg to Christy. She was standing over the bucket of live minnows. He watched her wrinkle her nose as she edged her hand toward the bucket.

"Are you sure you don't want some help with that?" he offered again.

"I can do it," she said, more determination than confidence in her voice, and then bit her bottom lip in concentration.

Joe smiled. "Sometimes you remind me so much of your mom. We used to go fishing before you guys were born, and she never let me bait her hook. Even though I know she hated picking up the slimy minnows. She always wanted to do it herself."

"She's good at doing things for herself," Danny said sullenly. "She has to be."

Joe felt a stab of guilt and sadness. *That's okay,* he reminded himself. *I need to allow him to get some of this stuff off his chest.*

"If we catch enough fish, we could have a fish fry," Joe said.

"Tonight?" Christy asked, eyes wide, as she finally pulled the hook through the minnow with a shudder of disgust.

"We can't," Danny put in quickly. "We're having pot roast at Grandma Sylvia's for supper tonight."

"Maybe save the fish in the fridge for when we come back to our house?" Christy asked hopefully.

Joe felt his heart constrict. "Sure, we'll have a real fish fry in the backyard, and Mom can make her potato salad and coleslaw."

"When is that going to be, Daddy?"

Joe glanced over at Danny, but his son seemed focused on his bobber.

"I don't know, sweetie. The truth is . . . things like this take some time to sort out. I'm sorry."

"It's okay," Christy said solicitously. "We understand."

"I don't," Danny announced flatly. "I don't understand it at all—and I think it stinks that we're crammed into Grandma's house while my room is empty and that my friends know my family is *all messed up*! Nobody else has to do this. They have normal families. Normal fathers who don't come to *visit* them. They *live* with them!"

"I know this is a tough situation," Joe began, "and I am sorry. . . ."

"Sorry doesn't fix it," Danny said tightly as he stared at his bobber.

Joe took a step toward him. "I know that," he replied, "and I also know that I can't change what's happened in the past. . . ."

Danny threw an angry glance in his direction. "No, you can't. There's a thousand games we didn't play—just being together, going fishing. Other guys had dads who helped them with their soapbox derby cars, but not me. *Grandpa* showed me how to knot a tie. When was the last time you watched me play ball? I'm a good pitcher, Dad, and you wouldn't even know it. And most Saturday nights my stomach hurts because of where you are instead of with us."

Joe stayed quiet. Though every word sent a knife through his heart, he knew Danny had to get the pent-up pain out in the open. Christy took a nervous step toward them.

Danny turned to face his father squarely, his chin thrust forward in defiance. "You couldn't miss your 'meetings,' could you, Dad? Couldn't stand the thought of giving up your Saturday night to spend it with me when I needed you too!"

"Leave him alone, Danny," Christy said, her voice trembling. "He can't help it if he has meetings to go to—"

"Tell her about the meetings, Dad!" Danny shouted. "Tell her where you really go on Saturday nights!"

"That's enough, Dan," Joe said, trying his best to keep his voice even.

"I don't think so," Danny said. "It's not enough. I think she needs to know what the rest of the town already knows—that you're a dru—"

"Enough!" Joe's sharp command cut Danny off, but the unspoken word hung darkly in the air between the man and the boy who suddenly seemed older than his years.

Shoulders stiff and chin jutting, Danny swung back to the still, calm water of the lake. Joe couldn't help but notice the contrast between their surroundings and the bitterness Danny was feeling.

Suddenly Danny's bobber jerked under the glassy surface of the water, and he put his emotions into reeling in his line—fast and furiously. A large pike twisted and struggled on the hook when he yanked it out of the water, and before Joe could react, Danny sliced across the line with his pocketknife and the fish splashed back into the water.

"We'll figure this out, you guys, really we will," Joe assured them, putting his arm around Christy's shoulders. Danny leaned his pole against a rock and moved away to sit under the shade of a tree.

"You'll keep coming to visit us until we're all together again?" Christy asked, looking trustingly up at her father.

Joe couldn't speak around the lump in his throat. He nodded and put his other arm about his daughter to give her a hug.

He looked at Danny, who was poking a small stick into the dirt. "We'll do it as often as we can. Maybe next Saturday we can have supper at the Burger Shack in Emporia."

Danny looked at him, and Joe could see absolute disbelief in his son's eyes.

Keep trying. One foot in front of the other.

"Okay," Christy said with a tremulous smile. "That'll be fun."

Help me . . . and help them, God.

It was late in the afternoon when Joe stood in his driveway and pulled the fishing gear out of the rust-streaked truck bed. He'd held on to his emotions so tightly that now he felt his control start to crumble along with the bands of tension across his shoulders. Suddenly, his own limbs felt too heavy, and he moved clumsily across the yard with the rods under his arm and the tackle boxes in hand.

The two-story detached garage at the back of the lot behind the house looked two-toned—faded paint on the front, new white paint on the sides. *A few hours tonight and I may get the outside finished. . . .*

The garage smelled like turpentine and the insect spray Meg put on the kids to keep the mosquitoes from eating them alive in the summer. Joe sent a cursory glance at the cot in the corner, neatly made like a military bunk, and then moved by rote through a maze of worn-out furniture—a chair Meg wanted to reupholster, a couch her mother insisted they have. A broken bentwood rocker, where Meg had cuddled babies, was spread in pieces over Joe's workbench, and a pair of shiny brass hinges lay on top of an old hope chest that was next to the wall where he normally kept the fishing gear.

Joe's muscles ached as he turned to squeeze past a Ping-Pong table that had doubled as a hobby table for Danny. The kid loved to put together puzzles—*big, long puzzles,* Joe thought with a little shake of his head—and the game table had proven to be the perfect spot. Joe glanced briefly at his son's work in progress as he dropped the tackle boxes near a wall and the poles slid out from under his arm and clattered to the floor. *Looks like a thousand-piecer,* he noted idly.

Suddenly it was as if every raw emotion of that day had banded together for another go at him, and he leaned against the wall for support, unsure if he could remain upright. It was then he heard the distinctive sound of running water and realized Ferguson must be using the outdoor shower. *An angel who showers,* he thought wearily. Hiram was right when he said Ferguson was odd—with just a bit of crazy thrown into the mix. Here was a guy who claimed he was an angel—*one who collects junk, cooks breakfast, and dispenses advice. Advice that turns out not to be so crazy, along with knowledge of things he shouldn't know.*

Grabbing on to whatever was in reach for support, Joe moved along the wall to the window that offered a view of the side of the house and backyard. Sure enough, Ferguson was standing under the makeshift showerhead Joe had attached to the back of the house. His face was turned upward into the spray, his large frame towering above the fenced-in area designed to provide privacy for an average-sized man.

Ferguson shifted his position under the water, turning so that his massive back was visible, and Joe was presented with a startling sight. Ferguson's broad back was marred with raised red scars that ran from shoulder blade to shoulder blade—crisscrossing his skin like a grid that spoke of things Joe couldn't imagine. He felt his stomach constrict and wondered how on earth Ferguson had survived whatever had caused all those scars. *Who is this guy? Wounded war veteran maybe? Someone with a past so unspeakable he can't bring himself to remember it? Maybe that's why he thinks he's an angel.*

Joe felt he was seeing something that was none of his business and was about to turn from the window when he heard strains of . . . singing. A beautiful, rich baritone voice flowed out of Ferguson, who stood under the man-made rain and lifted his eyes toward heaven. With some difficulty, Joe slid the window up, and the melodic voice filled the space around him. He didn't understand the words—*It sounds like Latin!*—but he didn't need to. The meaning was clear and universal—and Joe knew he was hearing a pure form of love. Worship so beautiful he began to feel tiny inklings of—what was it?—freedom?

The crushing weight on him seemed to lift just a little—along with his spirit. Suddenly, his knees buckled, and he began to weep, tears running unchecked down his cheeks as the melody reached a crescendo of perfection.

Joe woke with a start and tipped his neck back to get the kinks out. He had no idea how long he'd been asleep on the garage floor. He pulled himself to his feet and looked out the window, but Ferguson was gone. Joe felt a bit awkward after having seen his guest's scars, so he hoped to avoid the man—the angel?—for a while.

Joe walked across the yard carrying a couple pieces of old wood under his arm. *So far, so good,* he thought. *Maybe he's left.* Joe turned the corner and nearly collided with that tall, strong figure.

"Hey!" Joe hollered as he dropped the wood, stumbled backward, and landed on the ground with a thud.

"Don't be afraid, Joe," Ferguson said and offered him a hand up.

Joe ignored the hand and shook his head. "You . . . you just startled me, that's all."

Ferguson raised his eyebrows at Joe and pushed his hand out farther, leaving Joe little choice but to grab hold of the big mitt. Ferguson almost pulled him off his feet.

"Uh, thanks," Joe said, brushing himself off.

"I have to thank you for the use of your shower," Ferguson said. "The water was the perfect thing to wash away my fatigue. This exhaustion I was feeling is something new for me."

"Yeah, well, working hard will do that to you," Joe commented as he bent to retrieve the wood he'd dropped.

"You look like *you're* working," Ferguson observed.

"I was just bringing this to the pile I've got going over there."

Ferguson turned to look at a good-sized pile of junk—splintered wood, old furniture, empty paint cans, a few pieces of a broken picket fence, a lawn chair with torn webbing.

Ferguson looked from the junk pile to Joe and smiled. "I think I could use all that . . . junk."

"I had a feeling you might say that." Joe shrugged.

"It's another heavy load," Ferguson said, eyebrows moving up in a question.

"Had a feeling you might say that too," Joe said reluctantly. "I guess we can take my truck."

Ferguson's answering grin was wry, but Ferguson just turned to his task.

The sun had started its slow, lazy exit with a copper glow over the landscape. Joe drove with Ferguson beside him on the two-lane road that would lead them to what Ferguson was calling his field. Joe leaned hard on his side of the cab, away from the man who seemed to wear gentleness and war wounds with equal ease. He cast a sideways glance across the seat and quickly averted his eyes when he saw that Ferguson was looking right at him.

"You saw my scars," Ferguson noted. "And you're wondering about them?"

Joe felt a twinge of unease. *What's going on?* It was like his mind was an open book and Ferguson could read all the pages at will. Where was he getting his information? "Yes," he finally admitted.

"I have many battle wounds," Ferguson said. "But then, we all carry scars, Joe. Some visible, some not."

Joe felt some sense of reality return. Here was an explanation for something he could understand. *Battle.* Ferguson had been a soldier. *Not so fast . . . ask him. Ask him about the battle. . . .*

"It must've been the Korean War, then?" Joe said.

Ferguson smiled easily. "Think about what I have told you, Joe."

Joe frowned. "What do you mean?"

"Sometimes it's a war that can be seen, but it's *unseen* wars that I fight."

Joe heard the humming of the tires against the asphalt. He swallowed and threw another look in Ferguson's direction—the sheer size of the man was intimidating, and his countenance was impossible to dismiss.

"You're talking about the angel thing?"

"Yes, that's right. I'm an angel of judgment."

"An angel of judgment," Joe repeated, grasping the steering wheel harder than necessary. "What does that mean?"

"I fight for good. For Him." He nodded, his face turned upward.

Joe breathed out a nervous sigh and instinctively tried to edge himself farther away from Ferguson, but there was no place to go—surely not when he was driving.

"You wanted to fight for God and country," Ferguson reminded him.

"That's right. That's all I ever wanted to do," Joe said in a quick burst.

"But you feel that God didn't give you that chance," Ferguson continued.

Joe's slightly hysterical laugh embarrassed him. "You could say that. He made me 4-F."

"Unfit to fly."

" 'Medically unfit to fly,' according to the military standards." Joe's voice sounded bitter in his own ears.

"Maybe the truth of what happened to you is other than you think."

"No. It's very clear—black and white. A matter of record," Joe said firmly.

"The truth *is* black and white. But sometimes to get to the truth you must go through all the other colors. Like a painter searching through a palette of hues to find one true color."

"Then why would God put it in my heart to fly and fight—just like you say you do—and then stop me from having the chance?" Joe argued.

"Maybe God spared you from the war so you could fight for something else. Something more precious to you."

"Meaning I would have died had I gone to war?"

"I can't tell you that," Ferguson said, "but what I *can* tell you, Joe, is that what you need is faith. This means trusting the One who created you—along with me, and everything else. Seen and unseen. Trust that He loves you and watches out for your good."

"That's easier said than done."

"Faith makes things possible—not easy."

"Meg's lost her faith in me," Joe said honestly. "My whole family has."

"They didn't lose it overnight," Ferguson pointed out. "Just keep doing what you're doing, Joe. Righting wrongs, helping those who need help, strengthening relationships with loved ones . . . becoming *more*. And trusting God."

Suddenly Ferguson put his hand out the window and pointed to the side of the road. "That's it. Pull over there."

Joe eased the truck onto the shoulder, and the engine coughed to a stop. He looked at the flat landscape edged in tall prairie grass along the road.

"Now what?" Joe asked.

"Now we unload." Ferguson got out of the truck and walked around back to open the tailgate.

Joe helped Ferguson carry his cache to the edge of the field, past the tall prairie grass, and then stopped to gaze at the circle of open land in amazement. There was junk everywhere. All sizes, shapes, and colors. Rows of stuff crisscrossed all over the flat acreage.

Ferguson moved into the field carrying a beat-up tricycle that used to be Christy's and placed it carefully at the tail end of a long line of junk.

"I can't get over how much stuff you've dumped here. What's it all for?" Joe asked.

"I'm fulfilling my mission, Joe."

"Your mission is to fill a field with worn-out junk?"

"Remember, Joe. Faith."

Ferguson swept his large arm in an arc over the field. "On earth there is no heaven—but there are *pieces* of it."

Chapter 22

Righting wrongs, helping those who need help, strengthening relationships with loved ones . . . becoming more. The litany of phrases, now becoming as familiar as his own hand, circled through Joe's mind as he tucked an errant tail of his shirt into his jeans and smoothed a hand over his hair.

Taking a deep breath, he paused at the front door of Hiram's house and knocked. He briefly considered leaving. But it was too late. He could hear someone approaching the screen door.

"Why, hello, Joe! What brings you out our way?" Hiram greeted him from behind the silvery mesh, then pushed open the door.

"Afternoon, Hiram. Hope I'm not bothering you."

"No bother at all. I just finished having a bite to eat with my girl," Hiram answered with a smile and a glint in his eye. "Are you hungry? Sara would be happy to fix ya something."

Joe shook his head. "No, thanks just the same."

Hiram stepped outside and shoved callused hands into the pockets of his overalls, then looked up at the sky. "Heat like this makes a man appreciate the clouds—wouldn't you say?"

"Sure does," Joe agreed. He cleared his throat and an awkward silence grew as he searched for just the right words—the perfect way to tell Hiram he regretted the way he'd so heartlessly disregarded the situation when Hiram came to him for help.

Just be honest with the man. "I'm sorry, Hiram. Before—when you came to me about spraying your fields—I was a jerk. A selfish no-good jerk who was putting value only on money—and not on your circumstances. I hope you'll forgive me."

Hiram didn't respond—didn't move a muscle. He just stared at Joe. He finally smiled and pulled his hand out of his pocket and offered it to Joe.

"I appreciate the apology, Joe. I figure you've got harder feelings about yourself than I ever did. Consider it all forgiven," he said, his tone warm.

"And Sara? Maybe I should tell her how sorry I am. . . ."

Hiram shook his head. "Ain't no need for that. Sara never heard a word from me 'bout our business talk."

Joe felt his shoulders relax. "She's still feeling fine?"

"Right as rain in spring," Hiram said with a grin. "We feel like we've had as many blessings as we've got cicadas in the trees, and that's a bucket load."

Joe smiled back at him. "The corn still free from the beetles?"

"Sure is. Haven't seen nary a one—and I've been checking it, believe me. Like I said before, I really need a good crop come fall. I'm not getting any younger, Joe, and with every year I get under my belt, an acre feels a little bigger to walk."

Hiram glanced up at the sky again. "I don't think there's rain in those clouds—do you?"

Joe shook his head. "No. Nice shade but no rain. And we could use it."

"Yes sir, we could. I've got a pump on the fritz that I was just headed over to see 'bout if I want to get my north field irrigated."

"Can I help?" Joe asked.

Hiram studied him. "You ain't got a debt to repay here, Joe."

"I appreciate that. But I'd really like to help you fix that pump, Hiram."

"I'm walking out there."

"Fine by me."

"Let me just tell my girl I'm stepping out to the field," Hiram said as he turned back to the house.

Joe had to work to keep up with Hiram as they walked along the road that led to Hiram's field toward the north of the house.

"I heard from Ferguson that he's bunking out to your place these days," Hiram said with a twinkle in his eye.

"Yup, he is," Joe replied.

Hiram chuckled. "I think that fella has a bit of the gypsy in him—a *big* gypsy—and I do believe we lost our luster when we ran out a' junk for him."

"Could be," Joe said, trying not to sound winded. *He has to have thirty years on me.* "You ever think about driving your truck out here, Hiram?"

"I started out as a young man walking my fields, and I find that still suits me."

"How long have you and Sara been farming this place?"

Hiram reached out and yanked an outer husk off an ear of corn and examined it as they walked.

"This was my granddad's farm before it was mine. Sara and I moved on the place in the early twenties. For a time the crops were good."

"I remember the dust bowl years. You obviously weathered a tough time."

"Yes, sir, that we did. We did a lot of praying during the thirties. Didn't think that drought was ever gonna end. I remember watching black dirt clouds a thousand feet high rolling in and settling over everything. It would make the sky so dark the chickens would go to roost midday. I don't believe I've ever *experienced* dirt like I did back then. That dirt was so fine it would sift through the keyholes of the front door and get into the cupboards, so we'd have to wash it off the plates."

Hiram made an abrupt turn down another long row between the crops. Joe did a double step to stay with him.

"When the weather granted us some favor again in the forties and the rain came back, we told ourselves we'd never complain about anything again." Hiram laughed. " 'Course, that's a promise easily made and rarely kept."

"I kinda know what you mean. Did you ever think about selling—doing something else?"

"Did you ever think about being something other than a pilot?" Hiram countered.

"Nope—never have," Joe admitted.

"It's in your blood, I suspect, like farming's in mine. It's what we do. It's what we love, and I think a man who can feed his family doing something he loves is a blessed man indeed."

"Some men aren't that fortunate," Joe said quietly.

"And then again, some men find the blessings in what otherwise may seem like a curse," Hiram offered. "Like your pa, for instance. There's a man who loved to fly—and by all accounts was an awful good flyer but came home from the war with an injury that might have made another man—a lesser man—give up. But not Harold. No sirree, he found something else he was good at—politics, of all things—and made a difference in so many lives around here I can't begin to count 'em."

"He was a fine congressman," Joe agreed, wondering where this was going.

"You know, when he uncovered what Frank Ramsey was doing, I was about washed up with my farm. I couldn't understand why the wheat I was growing back then wasn't turning me a better profit. I trusted Frank like the rest a' the farmers around here. Trusted the railroad officials too until we found out that's who he was in cahoots with. A couple a' crooked fellers was giving Frank the kickbacks. Thank the good Lord your pa couldn't make Frank's math work—and he looked into the whole ugly mess. He saved a lot of farms—and a lot of dreams."

Hiram looked over at Joe. "It's a compliment to your pa when I tell you he's always reminded me of my own father." He shook his head. "He's been gone fifteen years, but I still miss him. What I'd give for an afternoon with my dad."

An afternoon with my dad—I won't have my mom and dad forever. . . .

"Anyhow," Hiram said, "in spite of Frank Ramsey, I'm still walking through my field today."

"Has Luke Ramsey been to see you yet?" Joe asked.

"Yep," Hiram confirmed, "and so did a flood of memories come along with him. Called up that ugly night for me in such vivid detail it was like I was living it all over again."

"I remember my dad saying things got pretty heated," Joe said, "but he never said much more about it."

"That's because your dad's a modest man, and he didn't want to blow his own horn. But the truth a' the matter is that he stopped a mob of angry farmers from carrying Frank Ramsey right out his door to make him face down-and-dirty justice," Hiram said with a shake of his head. "I'm ashamed to admit I was part of it. But at the time, all I could think about was how that man had robbed us blind—and when you're in a group of men that angry, ones who have been scared about losing everything for that long—well, you might be able to understand why it's a good thing your dad came along with the sheriff and convinced us all that Frank Ramsey wasn't worth the heaviness that would lay on our conscience if we'd had our way with him."

"And that's the same night the Ramseys left town?" Joe asked.

Hiram nodded. "Up and left in the middle of the night with nothing but the clothes on their backs. Before the bank auctioned off their house, they found a pile a' government bonds stashed in the attic. Seems Ramsey had been buying the bonds with the cash he'd been skimming from the farmers. He had himself a paper savings account. Anyway, the judge who'd presided over everything ordered the bonds be divided up between the farmers according to acreage. As it turned out, George Meiers had the biggest chunk of land, and he got the lion's share of the bonds."

Joe shook his head. "I heard about the bonds, but I could never figure out why Frank Ramsey would have left them behind."

Hiram shrugged. "It's a mystery. Some folks speculated that he was afraid of being stopped on the way out a' town by farmers still looking for revenge, and he was afraid they'd find the bonds in the car. Others thought he was just too scared to think straight and didn't remember them until it was too late."

"You think Luke is sincere about wanting to right his father's wrong? Bringing Vanguard to Greenville?" Joe asked.

"I won't hold the sins of his father against him," Hiram said, "but I'll admit it was strange getting the offer from Frank Ramsey's son."

"If you don't mind my asking, are you considering it?"

Hiram heaved a sigh. "An offer like that gives a man pause when he gets to be my age. Sara and I don't have children to pass this place down to—never were blessed that way. Guess the best way to explain it to you is that I'm letting the thought of selling roll around in my head to see if I can get it to not feel so foreign. Have you ever had to do that with something?"

"As a matter of fact . . . I have." Joe nodded slowly.

Hiram stopped at a small clearing where a windmill sat next to a well and an irrigation pump. "I'm thinking the pump has thrown a bearing," he said as he peered into some machinery. "It's lost the horsepower to get the water out a' the well and into my fields."

"Do you have a new bearing?"

Hiram nodded, gesturing to a tractor parked a few yards away. "It's in my toolbox on the tractor. Wanna get it for me?"

"Sure." Joe walked over to the gray tractor—and then something caught his eye. Joe moved around to the front of the tractor, and painted across the engine cover was the manufacturer's name and logo: Massey Harris Ferguson. *"I've found that a name is important." Ferguson. Is this where he got his name?*

Joe chuckled at the thought as he rooted around in the toolbox balanced on the steel seat of the tractor. When he found the bearing, he walked back to Hiram. "Have you spent much time talking to Ferguson?" Joe asked as he squatted beside Hiram in the dirt.

Hiram watched as Joe efficiently began replacing the bearing on the pump.

"Truth be told, Joe, I think I spent so much time running on and on 'bout Sara and the cornfield, I didn't give poor Ferguson much chance to get a word in edgewise."

"So I guess you never heard him mention . . . well, angels?" Joe asked as casually as he could.

Hiram frowned. "Angels?" He shook his head. "No—but like I said, I was a little preoccupied. Maybe he did and I just missed it."

Joe turned his attention back to the pump. "I doubt that." He pushed the new bearing into place. "Give a tug on the starter and see what happens."

Hiram yanked a retractable cord, and the pump sprang to life.

"We never know the worth of water till the well is dry," Hiram said. "Thanks for your help, Joe."

"I know you didn't really need it," Joe said sheepishly. "Thanks for letting me help."

"I know you needed to do it," Hiram said matter-of-factly, "and that's what counts."

Chapter 23

The air was thick with humidity, just like the claustrophobic worry that had been filling Danny's insides. He stood on the sidewalk in front of Butterick's Fabric Store and listened as his mom and Miss Norma ran through a checklist of things they needed to buy. He looked at his mom and thought about how tired she looked.

Anyone can see she's falling apart—even though she tries to smile. She's not eating, she cries at night—she looks worried and sad and mad at the same time. Danny's gaze shifted to Zach, JP, and Frankie. He figured they were about as unhappy about being there as he was. The only one with a smile was Christy—*probably because she gets to stay glued to Mom's side,* he thought, *and shop for all the stuff girls seem to like.*

Norma lifted a few pieces of fabric from a small box in the back of her truck and then turned to Zach, JP, and Frankie. "I don't know how long it's going to take to pick out upholstery fabric, but I don't want you disappearing on me, okay?" They nodded dutifully.

Seeming to move at half speed, her voice barely above a whisper, Meg handed Danny a dollar. "Why don't you take Zach, JP, and Frankie over to the Tastee Freez and buy everyone a cone?" she suggested.

"Oh, Meg. I can give them some money," Norma protested.

Meg grinned crookedly. "I'm a working woman now. Besides, it was my idea to buy everyone an ice cream."

"What about me?" Christy chimed in.

"You stay with us—but I'll get you a cone before we go home," Meg promised, then looked at Danny. "Meet us back here in half an hour."

"You boys stick with Danny, okay?" Norma asked, in that way parents have of asking a question that only has one answer.

"Yes, ma'am," Frankie agreed solemnly after the other boys had passed on their chance to respond. "We will."

Danny led the group along Main. So far, this was the worst summer he could remember. The strange situation with his dad, Grandma Sylvia's insane rules about keeping everything perfect, the sideways looks his friends gave him when he saw them at baseball practice or at the creek. He had never wished for summer to end before—but if his mom kept sticking him with these kids, he'd rather be in school. He didn't want to stay at his grandma's during the day—and his mom wouldn't let him go home alone. So he was stuck tagging along on girl errands with boys who didn't want to be with him—any more than he wanted to be with them. *Life's not fair,* he thought, and stepped resignedly into the street toward Jeeter's Tastee Freez.

As he stepped up to the window to place their order, it dawned on him how the place might look to an outsider—cracked cement patio out front and the giant plastic ice-cream cone with the twirled top that had been cracked by lightning two summers ago—and which owner Roy Jeeter refused to fix. He said it gave the place character. To Danny, the place looked rather old and run-down—but Mr. Jeeter still served the best ice cream he'd ever had.

"What can I do you for, Danny?" Roy asked from behind the screened window.

"I'd like a chocolate swirl, Mr. Jeeter." He looked at Zach, JP, and Frankie. "It's the best," he told them. The boys shrugged. Danny turned back to the window. "Make that four swirls, please."

There seemed to be an unspoken agreement about not speaking while they waited for the cones. To a casual observer, they would appear to be four strangers in line.

When the screen window slid up, Roy set out a small box with four cones wedged inside. Danny pushed the dollar across the small counter. "Tell your folks I said hello," the man said as he gave Danny the change.

"I will. Thanks."

The boys started back the same way they had just come, now eating their cones as they walked.

"So I guess in a small town like this everyone knows your business, huh?" Zach finally asked around a large bite.

Danny shrugged. "I guess."

"Don't you get sick of that?"

"I've never known anything different. Guess it doesn't matter to me," Danny said.

"Seems to me like if you just burp wrong you're gonna get some old lady tattling to your parents that you've been a bad boy," Zach said.

"I don't burp wrong," Danny said. "It's that simple."

Zach raised his eyebrows and offered up a belch anyone within earshot could hear. JP and Frankie laughed.

"Oh-oh," Zach said as he looked around. "Does this mean the burp police are gonna pick me up?"

Danny rolled his eyes and stepped up his pace.

They arrived back at the store and Norma's pickup. Danny could still see his mom and Christy through the window while Mrs. Lundgren piled bolts of fabric on the table in the center of the place for Miss Norma. Danny figured they were in for a wait and dropped the tailgate of the truck to sit on.

He stuffed the last bites of his cone into his mouth and watched JP and Frankie do the same. Zach, however, flicked the rest of his cone into the street.

"You didn't like it?" Danny asked.

"It was all right. But not exactly what I wanted," Zach said offhandedly. "What's behind this place?"

"An alley runs behind all the stores, but you have to go to the corner to see it," Danny said.

Zach patted his breast pocket. "I'll be right back," he said as he started toward the alley.

"We're gonna be leaving soon," Danny called out.

Zach turned around, now walking backward as he looked at JP and Frankie. "You guys coming or what?"

"It beats sitting here," JP said. "You want to come with us, Farmer Dan?"

Danny shook his head.

Zach laughed. "He's a choirboy. Why would he come with us?" JP and Frankie quickly ran to catch up with Zach.

Exasperated, Danny shook his head and swung his legs off the tailgate. He didn't think the foster three would last through the first quarter of the school year if they kept acting like such jerks. Not that he cared. He had plenty of friends and didn't need the aggravation.

As if his very thoughts had come to life, two of Danny's friends banged on the side of the truck from behind and startled him.

"Made you jump!" Ron Tidwell said as he rounded the corner to stand in front of Danny. Danny grinned at his two best friends. Ron, the oldest of the three of them by two months, was also the smallest. What he lacked in stature he more than made up for in attitude. He thought he was huge. No one—including the coach—had been able to convince Ron he was too small to play football.

Jeff McGraw was the serious one of the trio, always telling his friends he'd be a doctor someday. He did his homework, studied for tests, even read books on his own time, but there was no one Danny would rather have in his corner. Jeff had been Danny's friend since the two of them had been in the church nursery together.

"What are you doing sittin' here?" Jeff wondered. "Whose truck is this? Is that chocolate swirl on your T-shirt?"

Danny grinned at the rapid-fire questions, Jeff's trademark. "The truck belongs to a friend of my mom. They're in Butterick's, and I'm waiting for them, and yes, it is chocolate swirl." Danny looked down at the dollop of brown in the middle of his formerly clean white T-shirt.

"So just you and your mom and her friend are doin' some shopping?" Ron looked through the store window and grinned. "Looks like your sister's along for the ride too. That's sweet."

Danny lifted an irritated brow. "I got dragged along with those new kids I told you about."

"Then where are they? Looking at patterns?" Jeff asked, laughing at his own joke.

"They're back in the alley," Danny told the two. "Maybe they don't have those in the city."

"Let's have a look at 'em," Ron suggested.

"What for?" Danny asked.

"Never saw foster kids before," Ron said, starting toward the corner with Jeff at his heels.

"They look just like any other kids," Danny called after them.

Jeff and Ron didn't slow down. Danny hopped off the tailgate and looked over his shoulder at the fabric store. His mom was nowhere in sight, and he hurried after his friends.

The hard-packed dirt that made up the surface of the alley ran the width of about twenty-five feet and two street lengths behind the downtown buildings. Back doors led inside all the businesses, and trash receptacles, discarded cartons, and wooden crates were stacked against the brick walls.

Ron and Jeff with Danny right behind them came around the corner and saw JP and Frankie standing a few feet from Zach behind the Greenville Hardware Store. As they got closer, Danny figured out the sudden trip to the alley. He could see a cigarette dangling between Zach's fingers, and they heard JP chiding Zach for the habit.

"You know Norma doesn't like you to smoke," JP was saying, and he turned when he heard Danny and his friends approaching.

"So you just wanted to come back here for a smoke?" Danny asked.

Zach shrugged. "Want one?"

"No. And you shouldn't either," Danny chided.

"It's a free country. He can smoke if he wants to!" JP shot back in an abrupt about-face on the issue. Zach grinned as he wedged the cigarette between his lips for another pull.

Ron and Jeff stood behind Danny. The boys all sized each other up in a matter of moments.

"You guys from Kansas City?" Jeff asked. "Are you staying here for good? Do you like Greenville? Is it a lot smaller than where you left? What happened to your parents?"

Zach frowned at Jeff. "You writing a book or something?"

"Yeah. That's it. He's writing a book, and it's all about you," Ron quipped.

"I guess this is what a Greenville posse looks like," Zach sneered.

JP laughed. "It ain't a posse if you're a farmer. It's a herd. Isn't that right, Farmer Dan?"

"Who's Farmer Dan?" Ron frowned in concentration. "I don't know anybody with that name." He looked at Jeff. "Do you?"

Jeff shook his head. "Nope." Jeff and Ron shifted and stood on either side of Danny. Frankie and JP flanked Zach. The lines were drawn.

Zach casually put the cigarette to his lips, and the others watched the ember on the end brighten.

"Norma did you a favor taking you in," Danny said, "and this is how you repay her? By smoking?" He knew his voice sounded self-righteous and judgmental, but he couldn't help it. These guys just got under his skin.

"You don't know anything about us—so maybe you should keep your mouth shut," Zach said, his mouth curving downward.

"I know enough. You've been in trouble, and this is your second chance," Danny threw back at him.

"You're a real boy scout—ain't ya?" Zach said. "Some kind of goody-goody if you ask me."

"Nobody asked you," Ron said, moving forward a half step.

Zach took a step forward in front of Danny and let the cigarette ride his lip. "Here's the thing. Norma doesn't need to know I smoke. And she *never will*—unless you're a farmer *and* a snitch."

Danny, keenly aware of Jeff and Ron beside him, knew they expected him to stick up for himself and would think less of him if he let this new kid mouth off. With a flash of his hand, Danny plucked the cigarette from Zach's lips and tossed it on the ground. He crushed it into the dirt with the toe of his sneaker—nervous, but determined to get the upper hand.

"You shouldn't have done that, *Farmer Dan,*" Zach growled through clenched teeth.

"You know what? I'm not the one who's going to be planting wheat come fall. It'll be you, *Farmer Zach,"* Danny said as he gave a hard shove against Zach's shoulder.

Zach shoved him back. JP started toward Danny, but Jeff reached out and grabbed the neck of his T-shirt. "Oh no, you don't. We fight fair in Greenville."

Danny took a swing at Zach, his knuckles just glancing off Zach's chin. Zach aimed low and caught Danny right in the gut. The air whooshed out of him and he doubled over.

"Get up, Dan! Straighten up!" Ron yelled.

Zach danced around Danny, fists clenched and held high in front of his face. Danny got his wind back and, in one fluid motion, threw an uppercut at Zach's chin. Zach easily deflected it and moved around Danny, forcing him to turn just to keep his eye on him.

"Hit him again, Zach!" JP hollered. "Give it to him!"

Jeff, who still had hold of JP's shirt, yanked hard and nearly lifted him off his feet. JP, Frankie, Ron, and Jeff were all yelling advice like spectators at a prizefight.

Danny came at Zach again and grabbed for his shirt. He caught the neck of the T-shirt and ripped it. Zach ducked to loosen the hold Danny had on him and jabbed hard at his face, catching him in the left eye. The hit dropped Danny to his knees just as the back door to Greenville Hardware opened.

"Hey! What's going on here?" Sam Williams demanded, coming out the back door of his store with a sack of trash.

Zach ignored the man and jumped on Danny. As he straddled him, he threw punches, one after another. A left. A right. Another left. The best Danny could do was shield his face with his forearms.

Zach was jerked off Danny. "Stop! Off!" Sam yelled as he shoved Zach to the side. He looked down at Danny, who rolled onto his hands and knees in the dirt.

"You okay, Danny?" Sam asked.

Danny, struggling to catch his breath, stayed on the ground. He was spitting blood. "Yes, sir," he managed.

"Somebody want to start talking?" Sam demanded.

"It's nothing," Zach said with just enough attitude to raise Sam's eyebrows.

Danny felt his breath start to even out. His eye smarted and he held the bottom of his shirt up to his bleeding mouth. *This is bad. Beat up by the new kid. Beat up in front of Ron and Jeff.* He noticed a shiny piece of metal sticking out of the dirt, about a foot from his hand. *It's some kind of chain.* He had glimpsed something around Zach's neck when he'd grabbed his shirt. *That must be Zach's.*

"Don't tell me it's nothing, young man. Got some boys brawling behind my store in the middle of the day and it's not nothing," Sam said sternly to Zach. He looked at JP and Frankie. "Never seen you boys before. You from around here?"

"Just moved here, sir," JP answered.

"From Kansas City," Frankie added. "Sir."

"First impressions count, son. Better try hard not to let this be the first impression you give everyone here in Greenville. Folks won't like it. Won't like it one bit."

Zach looked straight at Sam, opened his mouth, and burped loudly.

Sam stepped closer and bent to look in Zach's eyes. "People around here don't like smart-alecky kids."

"Guess I won't sleep tonight," Zach said just under his breath. JP and Frankie kept their eyes on the ground. Sam looked dumbfounded and frustrated.

Danny slowly got to his feet and winced. Sam looked over at him.

"What's this all about, Danny?" Sam asked.

"Just something stupid that got out of hand, Mr. Williams," Danny said through his swollen lip, then looked at Zach. "We're sorry."

"You're gonna be more'n sorry when your parents see that black eye you're gonna have," Sam warned. "This alley isn't any place for you kids. Skedaddle on out of here, and stay out of trouble."

"Yes, sir." Danny's shirt was full of dirt and blood. He could already feel his eye swelling along with his lip, and he'd torn the knee of his jeans. How to explain this to his mom?

He looked at Zach and was happy to see he looked almost as dirty—and he had a nice cut across his cheek. Ron and Jeff had already put distance between themselves and the back of the hardware store.

Zach sidestepped around Sam and walked away. "I hate this stupid town," he said loud enough for all to hear.

"Shut up, Zach," JP hissed, "you've said enough." JP and Frankie started after him.

Danny cast one more furtive glance at the small metal object stuck in the dirt and followed the boys out of the alley.

Chapter 24

Every mile that brought him closer to his parents' house quickened Joe's pulse. He'd had a couple of awkward phone calls from his mom along with her quiet declarations that she loved him and was praying for him—and for Meg and the kids.

He hadn't spoken to his dad, but that wasn't unusual. In recent history, he'd made a point of not speaking to his dad whenever he could avoid it—but thanks to Hiram, that was about to change. The stony silence between them had gone on too long. He wanted to dismantle the years of polite greetings, civil talks about the weather, brief answers to inquiries about his flying.

As the truck bumped over potholes, Joe realized he really did *want* to spend afternoons with his dad. Longed to sit down in front of the radio and listen to a ball game together. Maybe sing along with "The Star-Spangled Banner" as they did when he was a kid—they'd yell for the outfielder who snagged the ball, give advice to the pitcher when he walked too many batters. Cheer for the victors at the end, a little louder if it was a favorite team. He wanted that relationship back.

The first thing Joe noticed when he pulled up to the house was that the shutters had been painted. That small detail made the whole house look new again—and that made Joe inexplicably happy. He hadn't realized on his last trip here how much the peeling paint had bothered him—maybe a symbol of his relationship with his father. But now—fresh paint. Fresh start.

He ran up the steps to the door and was about to knock but thought better of it. He turned the knob and entered. "Mom?" he called out. "I'm here."

She appeared in seconds, wiping her hands on her apron and looking both worried and happy to see him. "Joey," she said as she put her hands on his arms and looked into his eyes. She never used his nickname from childhood if anyone else was around, and it caught him off guard, and he felt his eyes well with tears.

"Are you all right?" she asked without preamble. A mother's probing, loving, and all-important question.

He nodded, cleared his throat. "Yeah, Mom. I'm okay. Really." He looked past her. "Is he . . . is Dad busy?"

"He's out in back. I didn't tell him you were coming," she admitted.

Joe looked into her face. "Why?"

A small, embarrassed shrug. "Just in case . . ." she said as she took his arm and pulled him away from the door. "I talked to Sylvia," she went on, "and she's just as upset about what's happened between you and Meg as I am."

"I know . . . and I'm sorry to worry both of you."

"What can I do?" she asked with such care and sincerity he reached out and hugged her tight.

"Just keep praying for me, Mom," he said quietly. "Keep praying I'll do and say the right things to bring my family back."

She took a step away to more clearly see him, nodded, pulled her ever-present lace handkerchief from her apron pocket, and wiped at her eyes. "I can do that."

Joe was strangely comforted by her simple promise.

As they entered the kitchen, Joe could see she'd been busy cooking. Tins were stacked upon tins, casserole dishes and glass jars full of food ready for storage.

She gestured to the counter. "I'm sending you home with some food," she said.

"*Some* food? An army couldn't eat all this," he said lightly.

"Mothers worry," she said. "If this doesn't help you, it helps me."

He leaned down and kissed her cheek. "Thanks, Mom." He looked over her shoulder again, toward the back door of the kitchen. "What's he doing out there anyway?"

"I'm not sure. He's got some big project going. I just hope he's not overdoing it. Painting the shutters and all. He won't admit it, but his leg is bothering him some. He's not a young man anymore," she said with a shake of her head. "I'm just not sure he realizes it."

Joe released a deep, nervous breath. "Guess I should go say hello to him."

"Yes, that would be good. I've made some iced tea. You can take some out for both of you." She matter-of-factly handed over the cold glasses as if he visited every day and shared iced tea with his dad. He loved her for that.

In Joe's opinion, the view out the back of the house had always been the best. A lawn of lush green rolled downhill to the shoreline of a good-sized lake. Officially on the map it was Greenville County Lake, but unofficially, Joe had always thought of it as Wally's Lake—for the huge walleye he caught the spring of his tenth year when he'd been fishing with his dad and Robby. Since their acre was mainly treeless, his parents had an unobstructed view to check on them when he and Rob would spend hours fishing and then ice skating when the lake froze solid every January.

Joe spotted his dad surrounded by piles of lumber in the middle of the yard. Harold was busy measuring something on the ground and didn't notice Joe's approach.

"Some project you've got going here," Joe said.

Harold looked up and squinted into the sun. "Joe. No fields to spray today?"

"I doubled up my schedule tomorrow so I could have the day off," Joe answered. "Here . . . Mom thought you might be thirsty," he said as he held out the glass.

Harold hesitated.

"Don't worry. It's iced tea, not prune juice," Joe said with a chuckle.

"Then I'm thirsty." Harold gave him a half smile. "Thanks." He downed the glass in one long swallow.

"Sure hot out here. What are you doing anyway?" Joe asked as he walked over toward the assembled piles.

Harold set the glass down on top of a pile of wood. "Building something called a gazebo."

Joe raised his eyebrows. "A what?"

Harold moved toward him, and his dad's limp was more pronounced today, Joe noted. Harold pulled a set of folded drawings out of his back pocket and spread them across a wide plank of wood resting between two sawhorses.

"I saw one of these things advertised in the Sunday paper," he told Joe. "I sent away for the instructions on how to build one."

Joe leaned over with his dad until they were nearly shoulder to shoulder over the sawhorse. *So far so good.* He watched his dad trace the outline of the building with his index finger.

"See? This gabled roof here will give it plenty of height so you can stand up in it comfortably. I'm going to put pavers in for the floor to make it nice and level and some fancy latticework like this here around the top."

"Wow. Nice."

"And that's not all. I'm putting a swing in here especially for your mom, and I'm tacking screen all the way around to keep the mosquitoes and other bugs out. That way, she can sit out here and look at the lake in peace. It's always been her favorite view, you know." Harold straightened up and Joe saw an honest-to-goodness smile on his dad's face.

"That's a great idea, Dad. She's going to love it."

"I think she will. She's always wanted me to put up a swing. The woman works too hard for her own good. I don't think she realizes we're not as young as we used to be."

Joe smiled. "I'd like to help."

Harold's brows creased together. "Oh no, you don't have to—"

"No, I'd really like to. I've never built a gazebo before," Joe said. "And I happen to have some time today."

Harold folded the drawings back up and stuffed them into his back pocket.

"There's an extra hammer in my toolbox over there."

Joe headed that direction. "Hey, Dad," he said over his shoulder, "I think I should warn you that Frank Ramsey's son is in town."

"Thanks for the warning, but you're too late," Harold replied. "He was here."

"What? When?"

"The other day. He showed up on our doorstep and said he wanted to apologize on behalf of the Ramsey family." Harold shook his head. "I told him there wasn't any need. It was his dad's wrong—not his. He was barely more than a boy when all that happened."

"He must feel some responsibility," Joe said.

Harold rubbed absently at the back of his neck. "A man can feel overshadowed by his father—whether he was good or bad."

You can say that again, Dad. . . . "I think Luke's really trying to make things right."

"You mean with this Vanguard thing?" Harold asked.

Joe nodded. "You hear the mayor's called a town hall meeting to talk about it?"

"That's what I heard," Harold said. "Are you going?"

"I thought I would since Luke's offered me a job." Joe looked for his dad's reaction, but Harold merely lifted his eyebrows.

"Is that right? What kind of job?"

"A manager's position over the dusters. Good steady pay, health coverage for the family. They're bringing in some fine planes that make the old Stearman look like a bucket of bolts."

"So you're thinking of accepting?"

"I think it's a good offer," Joe said, "so, yeah, I'm thinking about accepting."

Harold set a nail into a board and drove it through with two whacks. "Just think it through carefully, Joe, before you accept any offer from Luke Ramsey."

"You just said what happened wasn't Luke's wrongdoing." Joe frowned.

Harold set another nail on a two-by-four. "That's true, but I have to say there's something about this whole thing that doesn't feel right to me."

"What whole thing? The corporate farming thing? Or Luke offering me a job?" Joe tried to keep the irritation from his voice.

"All I'm saying is to be careful of that man, son. Sometimes the apple doesn't fall too far from the tree." Harold went back to driving nails.

They worked side by side for nearly an hour. Joe wasn't sure which was louder, the hammering of his heart or the nails he was driving. The frame of the gazebo was rapidly taking shape. He looked at his dad and realized his face was flushed red from both exertion and heat. *Say you're sorry. Say it.*

"Dad? Can I talk to you about something?" he asked.

Harold pounded another nail into the wood and then pulled a bandanna from his pocket and wiped at his forehead. "Yeah, I suppose we should talk about Meg," he said. "I wanted to bring it up, but I wasn't sure what to say—"

"Yes, I would like to talk to you about what's going on with the family," Joe said, "but I think I need to start with an apology to you, Dad."

"Joe—"

Joe held up his hand. "Please, let me just get this out."

Harold turned to look at the lake while Joe continued in a rush of words. "I'm sorry I've been such a lousy son to you, Dad."

Harold, eyes still on the lake, shook his head. "Please, Joe, don't—"

"You can't even look at me, Dad," Joe said, the timbre of his voice rising. "I know my life is nothing like you hoped it would be. I know I haven't done great things like you and Robby did for our country. My drinking . . . I've even failed at marriage and probably embarrassed you and Mom more times than I can count. But I'm changing. I've . . . I've changed. On the inside. I'm trying hard not to let my past rob my present any longer."

Harold turned to face him, pain etched all over his face. "You don't understand, Joe."

"I understand that everything between us was different since the day I got the news I was 4-F. I was your only living son, and I couldn't even carry on the family legacy of military service. Since that day, all I ever see when you look at me is . . . disappointment."

Harold closed his eyes . . . then opened them and focused on Joe. "It's not disappointment you're seeing in my eyes, Joe. It's . . . it's guilt."

"Because you taught me to love my country? Because you instilled in both me and Robby how important service is? Because you introduced me to flying?" Joe frowned.

Harold's eyes welled with tears. "Because I'm the reason you didn't get into the navy." He reached out to lean on the sawhorse for support. "Oh, Joey . . . it's all because of me."

Joe couldn't breathe. Couldn't swallow. *What's he talking about? This is* my *time of confession.* He finally found his voice. "No, my heart murmur. That was the reason. That captain, the navy doctor that gave me my physical, wrote 4-F on my medical form. He's the reason."

Harold seemed to age in front of Joe's eyes. "That was Captain Francis O'Connor."

"How do you know his name?"

"We were in the first war together. We stayed in touch." Harold drew in a deep breath.

"I didn't know that," Joe said slowly. "You never told me that. How come you didn't tell me, Dad?" *He's going to say something that makes sense now. Go ahead, Dad. Say something. . . .*

Harold shook his head and turned back toward the lake. "The day before you planned to enlist, I saw something that was private. Something that affected me . . . that shook me up real bad. Your mother was on her knees beside our bed and she was sobbing, crying out her distress—yes, her anger—at God for taking Robby from us." Harold shuddered. "This woman—this strong woman who never faltered in her faith—was suddenly lost in anger and grief and fear." He turned to look at Joe. "She pleaded with God, Joe! No—she *begged* God to spare you from the war. She told God her heart couldn't take another loss—couldn't hold up to the grief she already knew as paralyzing. I listened to her praying, and it was like she was speaking for both of us."

Joe couldn't move. He couldn't believe he was hearing this from his father. He gripped the hammer in his hand until his knuckles ached. "What are telling me?" His voice sounded hoarse.

"I had to protect your mother, which meant I had to protect you, Joe." Harold's voice had dropped so low Joe could barely hear the words. "I couldn't imagine what it would do to her—to both of us—if you were killed in the war too. I got in my truck that day and drove to Kansas City. I found Francis and asked him to give you your physical. I had never used my congressional office for anything personal up to then, but I was prepared to make my request as 'Congressman Daley' if I had to. As it turned out, I only had to appeal to Francis as a friend."

Joe couldn't quite grasp what he was telling him—didn't want to understand, actually. "So . . . your old navy buddy gave me my physical," he finally said. "He's the one who found the murmur." Joe watched his father take a deep breath, then slowly turn to face him.

"Francis and I gave you the murmur on paper, Joey. You didn't—don't—really have one."

Joe recoiled as if his dad had sucker-punched him in the gut. He shook his head. He tried to swallow—then tried again. Harold moved toward him, but Joe threw his hand, palm forward, in the air.

"Hold on! Just wait!" His jaw clenched in anger, Joe stepped away from his father.

"I'm so sorry, Joe," he whispered, tears in his voice. "I did it, and I've lived with it ever since. I've lived with the lie between you and me—and between me and your mother. The only excuse I can offer is that I couldn't face putting your mother through the loss of another son. I couldn't bear to see you killed."

Joe stared at his father. "I've been slowly dying for years, Dad. You've had to see it anyway."

"I don't know how to ask for your forgiveness," Harold said, tears on his face and voice choked with emotion.

"Then don't," Joe said abruptly. He walked away in a world that had just turned on its axis—nothing made sense, and he was helpless to stop the tumbling sensation in his head. *So much for bridge building, God! So much for prayers!*

Chapter 25

Escape was a refrain in Joe's head from the minute he left his father standing in the skeleton gazebo—broken, and looking as if he were a hundred years old. On some level Joe knew he should worry about his dad—after all, as both his mom and dad had pointed out, they weren't young anymore. But he felt too angry, too betrayed, to muster up sympathy for the man who had let him live a lie all these years.

How? How could he look at me and know what I was going through and not tell me? Of course—he never really looked at me. He never really wanted to hear about my miserable life, because he caused it. The anger he was feeling terrified him—but there was no softening it, no keeping it at bay. Like a fire burning through dry wood, the rage threatened to consume him. He knew what he needed.

He sped down the road toward town, trying to outrun bits and pieces of the stunning conversation he'd had with his father—the man he had thought nearly perfect, the man, the *pilot* he had wanted to emulate from the time he was just a boy.

I remember like it was yesterday. . . .

"Joe! Joey! Wake up! Happy birthday, son!" He opened sleepy eyes to find his dad standing over him, grinning from ear to ear. "Get dressed. I've got a surprise for you."

"What is it, Dad?"

"Your first flying lesson."

He'd been asking for over a year for his dad to teach him to fly. He'd been on plenty of flights as a passenger—sitting in the front of the tandem seats in his dad's plane affectionately nicknamed Betty, after his grandmother. He dressed in record time—too excited to eat the blueberry pancakes his mom had made in honor of his thirteenth birthday. Too excited to even speak on the ride to the airstrip. Through the window of his truck, his dad had pointed out a Great Lakes biplane that had just taken off. "That's going to be us today, son. You and me surrounded by blue and looking down on the earth like a couple of eagles."

Joe had nodded mutely—aware that this was the day he had to prove to his dad that he *could* fly. He could be a pilot just like his dad and like Robby. He sent up a quick prayer for help. He just wanted to do well enough to have a second lesson, then a third and a fourth. He wanted to solo more than he had ever wanted anything in his life.

God had answered that prayer, and he had flown the plane with an innate ability that had surprised him—and stunned his dad.

"You're a natural-born pilot, Joey. It's going to come easy to you, but I want you to remember a couple of things. Pilots are cocky—but they cannot be careless. They have to be confident—but not cavalier. You can't be afraid to be in the air, but you won't live long if you're never afraid. Do you understand, son?" his dad had asked when they landed after a nearly flawless flight.

"Yes, sir. I understand." Joe grinned. He heard the words, but it would be some time before he made them his own.

As they walked away from the plane, Joe looked up at the man beside him, the father he respected and admired. "I'm going to be a naval aviator, Dad. Just like you were."

"You can be anything you want to be, Joey. Anything at all. I'm proud of you, son."

A pothole in the road jolted him out of his reverie, back into the roiling anger that demanded some kind of justice. If there was ever a time he deserved a drink, this would be it! *Find out my own father ruined my life—and for what? He was so sure I wouldn't make it through the war, he kept me from going! I could have been an ace—defended my country with honor and heroism and valor!* He hit the steering wheel with his fist.

I need a couple to wash away the taste of all the lies . . . maybe three to pretend I can go on being a bug killer when I . . . I could have been more. . . .

"How about that, God?" He was shouting out loud now. "How about this backward way I've lived my life? At least if I'd died fighting for my country, Meg might've had a reason to be proud of me!"

Quit thinking, quit thinking, quit . . . Joe reached over and cranked up the radio, then screamed at the top of his lungs.

The heat rising off the asphalt gave the illusion of standing water over the road. Joe squinted in the distance and could see something moving slowly along the shoulder. As the distance shortened he could see it was someone—Ferguson—pulling a large cart full of more junk. Joe pulled alongside him and slowed the truck to match his pace.

"Okay!" he yelled through the window. "I'm done with the double-talk! Who are you—really? How do you know it wasn't God who ruined my life? And what about the prayer? How did you know the exact words I prayed? *Who told you?*"

Ferguson was slowing down. "Don't try to dodge me, Ferguson!" Joe shouted, glancing quickly at the road in front of him. "You might be big, but I'm—"

He looked back through the side window—but Ferguson was gone. He slammed the steering wheel in frustration. *Where did he go! How did he do that?*

The truck rolled a few more feet, and Joe looked into his rearview mirror. He hit the brakes and bolted out of the truck. Ferguson was lying on his back on the side of the road next to his precious cargo. Joe knelt down next to him. "What happened? Are you okay?"

"Is this what 'okay' looks like?" Ferguson countered but without a trace of sarcasm. Beads of sweat rolled down his temples, and he had unnaturally bright spots of color in his cheeks.

"No. Definitely not what okay looks like. I'm sorry, Ferguson," Joe said. "Did you trip—fall? Is anything broken?"

Ferguson closed his eyes. "The only thing broken is my energy. I'm so . . . tired. Bone-tired."

"I've got some water in my truck," Joe said as he stood. "Don't move."

"Don't worry," Ferguson replied.

Joe ran back to the truck and grabbed a thermos of water he'd thought to bring with him that morning. He raced it back to Ferguson, who had now maneuvered himself into a sitting position. Joe propped a foot on the edge of the cart and watched as he drank every last drop.

"You know, you're pretty pathetic as a human," Joe observed but without malice.

"I know. And you'd make a pretty pathetic angel," Ferguson said, also without malice.

"You need to slow down, Ferguson."

"I want to get home, Joe."

"And I want my family home."

"You saw your father today," Ferguson said quietly.

Joe nodded miserably. "He had me 4-F'd! My own father got me declared unfit! All these years I've felt like a complete failure, my dreams nothing but a pile of rubble! I wanted my life to count for something. I've just been kidding myself. I'll never be anything more—just a failure. And I have my own father to thank."

Ferguson got to his feet, and Joe was again astonished at the sheer stature of the man. He dropped his big hand on Joe's shoulder. "I know you won't believe me when I tell you this, my friend, but I've gotten just as much satisfaction collecting other people's castoffs and placing them in that field as I do fighting for Him."

"You're right. I don't believe you," Joe said. "C'mon. I'll help you load this stuff into my truck."

"Listen carefully to me, Joe." Ferguson looked directly into Joe's eyes. "I have spent centuries observing mankind, and the one thing I've seen over and over again is that people continually look for their own glory, not the glory that comes from searching out the one who alone is God."

Joe let the words sink in as he and Ferguson loaded up the rest of the stuff from the cart into the bed of his truck. *I wanted my life to count for something. For whom? For what? Who knows what I could have done if I'd had the chance and things had gone like they were supposed to. I could have been . . .*

A yell of victory echoed over the Pacific just as the last Japanese fighter plunged nose first into the sea. On the horizon, where the sea met the sky, a cloud stretched lazily across the expanse of blue. . . .

The citizens of Greenville lining each side of Greenville's Main Street were there to pay homage to the returning war hero.

They cheered as the convertible slowly motored between them, police car providing a dignified escort. American flags waved, and three lovely young women called and blew kisses.

As the Greenville High marching band, playing "The Star-Spangled Banner," stepped smartly behind him, he waved his hand in time to the music. There was his dad wearing the old navy uniform and looking at him with unmistakable pride in his eyes. His mom was enjoying the spotlight, her expression lit with joy. Confetti rained down on everything—the street, the procession, the car, the shoulders of his uniform. *Glory—it's all for my glory!*

Suddenly the man in uniform, the one sitting high on the backseat, turned. It was Robby.

"*Whose* glory, Joe?"

The sight of his brother's face startled Joe awake, and he sat bolt upright. Swinging his legs over the side of the bed, he sat there as the realization hit him. The dream he'd been having for years was never meant to be his. It was *Robby* who'd worn the uniform and who should have come home to a hero's parade. It was *Robby* who had done his duty, served his country, and made the ultimate sacrifice. All *without* accolades or attention.

His brother's words resonated through his mind. *"Whose glory, Joe?"*

Joe moved efficiently between the dresser and an open box on the bed, trying to focus on the task of packing his belongings rather than on the empty feeling he got every time he sorted out the contents of another drawer. He felt Ferguson's presence even before he turned to find him standing in the bedroom door.

"Seems you've been up for a while," Ferguson said, looking at the boxes Joe had already packed.

"There're not enough hours in the day anymore," Joe admitted. "I want to get things finished up around here as quick as I can so Meg and the kids can move back home."

"They need to be home," Ferguson said with a nod.

Joe dropped some T-shirts into the box on the bed and then sat down. "I know now what I've been living for, Ferguson," he said. "*I* wanted the glory. I wanted to be the hero who came home to the cheers of my family and friends . . . everyone. I wanted to be the guy who got all the attention for saving the day."

"Living for your own credit and fame," Ferguson said, "is something most men try to do, but few will admit to—and it can make for an unfulfilling life." He smiled.

"I always thought my passion for flying was a gift from God," Joe said.

"It is," Ferguson agreed, "but most people want to use their gifts to glorify themselves instead of glorifying the One who gave them the gift in the first place."

"Is it too late, Ferguson?" Joe asked, his voice low. "Is it too late to use the gift He gave me for Him . . . to glorify Him?"

"I told you I get just as much satisfaction collecting junk and placing it in that field as I do fighting for Him," Ferguson said. "But I must warn you, once you start living for His glory instead of your own, the enemy will be at your doorstep."

Joe frowned. "What do you mean?"

"I mean you need to keep your guard up, Joe," he said solemnly. "Something dark is coming, and you need to be ready."

Chapter 26

In Greenville vandalism was virtually unheard of. There might be the occasional painting of the sidewalk in front of the high school by a graduating class marking their year for posterity, Halloween pranks involving wet toilet paper and shaving cream, or the carving of names into the trunk of someone's favorite maple tree by dreamy young romantics.

But actual, destructive vandalism where the perpetrator means to do someone or someplace harm simply doesn't happen around these parts, Larry concluded with a frown. He didn't use siren or lights, but the cruiser was moving as fast as was safe on Main Street.

He made his first stop at Jeeter's Tastee Freez. It didn't take but a moment to see what had happened at Roy's. The ice-cream cone that had been a Greenville fixture ever since Larry could remember was gone. And spray-painted across the front window of the place was "Closed for the Summer." Roy was pacing out in front when Larry got out of the squad car.

"Well? What are you going to do about this, Larry?" Roy was obviously fit to be tied. "Someone stole *my ice-cream cone.* Can you *believe* it? That thing was over twenty years old! It's a piece of history! A piece of this town! What kind of maniac would take *an ice-cream cone*?" Roy sure had built up a full head of steam.

Larry kept his face expressionless. "Calm down, Roy. We'll get this figured out. When was the last time you saw—the cone?" *Oh boy,* he thought. *Am I gonna have to put out an APB for a giant plastic ice-cream cone?*

"I closed up at seven last night like I usually do," Roy rushed to explain. "The cone was right where it always is—was." He pointed to his window. " 'Closed for the Summer'—you see that? If that's someone's idea of a joke, it isn't funny! No sirree! Not funny at all. I'll be losing business by the hour. I'm gonna have to scrape that paint off there with a razor blade!"

"Is there any other damage—how about inside?" Larry asked.

Roy shook his head. "They didn't get in. But they did enough out here to make up for it," he said, teeth gritted.

"You got any ideas of who might have done this, Roy?"

"It has to be someone from out a' town," Roy said with certainty. "Everyone from around here loved that old cone as much as I did. I can't imagine a Greenviller doing something like this."

Larry nodded his agreement. He had to admit, the people of Greenville did love that cone. He felt as if a piece of his childhood had been vandalized. "Don't worry, Roy," Larry soothed. "We'll find out who did this and get the cone back. Let me nose around a little. In the meantime, I've got a few other stops to make right now."

Viv's Diner was next. Larry parked in front and could see dozens of broken eggshells and their gooey yellow contents littering the sidewalk. The door itself was covered in egg drippings. The morning sun had already done its work drying the crusty yolks and egg whites onto the wood. The large picture window in the center of the diner looking out over Main Street had been painted black. *Somebody's gone to an awful lot of trouble—eggs and paint cost money* was Larry's assessment as he climbed out of his vehicle.

Viv stood in front of the diner, hands on ample hips, an angry scowl across her face. "I want the hooligans that did this caught, Larry! Caught and tried in a court of law!"

Larry put a sympathetic hand on her shoulder. "Anything happen inside, Viv?"

"No." She shook off his hand and swung her arms around. "Isn't this enough? Eggs ruin paint, you know! They were already dried on there by the time I got here this morning. I'm going to have to scrape that window and repaint the door—and I'm an old woman!" Viv wouldn't have called herself "old" in any other circumstances, Larry decided. And neither would he—she was pretty spry for her age.

"We'll get you some help," he assured her. "Seems there was a whole rash of vandalism last night."

"My customers won't want to eat in a place that smells like rotten eggs," she said, and he noticed her eyes looked a bit teary.

She went on, "I don't know anyone who'd do something like this—do you?"

Larry put his arm around her shoulders and gave her a squeeze. "No, Viv, I don't. But I'll get to the bottom of it. I need to check on Sally's place, and it sounds like Sam may have been hit too."

One thing for sure, Larry thought a while later, *the vandal or vandals sure were creative.* Poor Sally Lundgren had been mortified to find some of the wooden letters on her sign had been removed. "Butt Fabric Store," it read. Larry had removed the offensive letters and promised to help her restore the proper sign.

He drove slowly down the rest of Main Street looking for any other possible damage that might not yet have been reported. From several yards away he saw a gaping hole in the front window of Greenville Hardware. He had thought it lucky that so far none of the businesses had actually been broken into—but it looked like luck had just run out. Besides the smashed front window, the front door of Sam's store was hanging open.

Once inside, it was clear Sam hadn't been there yet to open the shop. Larry stepped around the shards of broken glass littering the floor. He cast a keen eye over the place looking for any gaps in the inventory—anything else unusual besides the obvious.

Then something caught his eye on the floor a few feet from the window. He knew what it was immediately. He had a set of his own in a bedroom dresser drawer. He picked up the long, beaded chain with an oblong piece of embossed metal on it. His mind went back to his own army days and the name, rank, and serial number litany he had learned early in his training. The name stamped in the metal was "First Lieutenant Benjamin James Reed." Government-issued to help identify military casualties. Dog tags were issued in pairs with one tag staying with the body, the other at times going to the next of kin. This chain held only one tag, so Lieutenant Reed was likely deceased.

"I was afraid of this!" Sam shouted as he roared through the front door. "I saw the damage to the other businesses and was afraid what I'd find here!"

Larry slipped the dog tag into his pocket. "Sorry, Sam. Looks like you might have gotten the brunt of it. Vandalism's worse here than the other places I've been this morning."

Sam shook his head—angry, then sad, then angry again. "What a mess! What an awful mess!"

"Someone was really busy last night," Larry agreed. "This is the fourth stop I've made today."

"What'd they use to smash up the window?" Sam asked, looking around.

"Haven't found it yet."

Larry followed Sam through the aisles of the store. The store owner fumed and muttered as he walked, head down, ears red with emotion. "Here ya go. Looks like a small boulder!" Sam pointed to a large rock at his feet. Larry bent to retrieve it, but Sam put a hand on his arm to stop him. "Wait! Don't you want to dust it for prints before you touch it?" Sam demanded.

Larry went ahead and picked up the rock. "Well, maybe if I had a fingerprinting kit I might do that, Sam, but I don't. Good thinking, though."

Sam grabbed a broom that was leaning against the wall and started to sweep. "I've listened to *Perry Mason* on the radio for years, and now I watch the TV show once a week. I've picked up a few police tricks here and there," he assured Larry.

He felt the weight of the rock in his hand as he walked toward the large shattered window. He figured whoever had chucked it had to have carried it from somewhere else specifically for the purpose. *But why?*

"You better check to see if anything is missing from the store, Sam," Larry instructed. "Cash. Tools. Anything at all. Though most likely you're missing a can of black paint and a brush or two."

Sam looked around. "I'll get out my inventory sheet and figure out exactly what's missing. I don't keep cash here overnight, so I know they didn't get that." He shook his head. "Hoodlums! Why would someone go and do something like this?"

"That's the question, Sam. I'm gonna have to do some digging."

"I'll help if you want," Sam said seriously. "Like I said, I've learned a thing or two about detective work, plus I'm a pretty good authority figure, if you know what I mean."

"I'm sure you are."

"I gave some boys *what for* yesterday when they were out back in the alley tussling around. Broke up the fight and sent everyone packing."

"What boys?" Larry asked.

"I only knew three of 'em. Danny Daley and his buddies Jeff McGraw and the Tidwell boy."

"Who were the others?"

"New kids in town. Said they just moved here from Kansas City."

"Might be the boys Norma Meiers has taken in."

"The oldest one had a sassy mouth on him—but I didn't take any of his lip. I told them to stay out a' my alley and get on home," Sam said. "Danny looked like he'd have at least one black eye." He paused to look at Larry. "You don't suppose it was those new boys who ran amuck in town last night—?"

"I don't know," Larry said quickly. "I hope not. I'll keep my ears open and see what I can find out."

"I'll have to order the glass for the window from Emporia, but in the meantime would you give me a hand with a piece of plywood to keep the mosquitoes and the flies out?"

"Sure, Sam. Be happy to," Larry said. Sam found a sheet of plywood at the back of the store, and the two of them picked it up. As they carried it to the window, they saw Ferguson cross the street with a large, rusty weather vane.

"Are we loading up on strangers around here all of a sudden?" Sam wondered.

"Hiram Edwards introduced me to that guy the other day—said he was staying at their place for a while. Name's Ferguson—something or other," Larry said as he hefted his end of the plywood off the ground, requiring Sam to do the same. "Let's get your window boarded up."

Norma stepped off the front porch and turned to survey the work JP, Zach, and Frankie had done—and she was impressed. For city boys, they had taken to wielding a hammer pretty well. The loose boards on the steps had been repaired, and now the whole porch had been whitewashed until it gleamed. JP and Frankie stood behind her.

"Looks good," JP said. "A lot better'n before."

"I like the white. Makes everything look clean," Frankie observed.

Norma relished everything that came out of Frankie's mouth. It had taken months for him to start saying much of anything. Now she was hearing him chime in to the conversations more and more, and she was grateful. Maybe he was finally starting to feel safe and at home.

"It does look great," Norma agreed. "I'm so proud of the work you've all done."

Zach came up behind them carrying a coffee can. "Found the turpentine in the barn just like you said, Norma. You want me to clean the paintbrushes?"

"Thanks, Zach. You can do it over there in the grass," she said, pointing, and then noticed a police car coming up the drive. The boys followed her gaze and watched as Larry parked the car and got out. They instinctively moved closer together, she noticed.

"Hey, Norma!" Larry waved.

"Hi, Larry." She smiled her greeting.

"I just thought I'd take a drive out and see how you're all doing."

"We're doing fine. The boys and I have been painting the porch."

"I haven't officially met the boys yet," he said, looking toward the three.

Norma called them over and wished they didn't look so reluctant, but their past experiences with the police had never been pleasant.

"Boys, this is an old friend of mine who also happens to be the police chief here in Greenville. This is Mr. Ledet. Or Chief Ledet, I guess." She smiled. "I haven't gotten used to saying that yet." She gestured toward the boys. "This is JP, Frankie, and Zachary."

Larry nodded at them. "Nice to meet you young fellows. How do you like Greenville so far?"

Zach shrugged. "It's okay, I guess. Pretty quiet."

"Yeah, we like it all right," JP added.

"Probably a lot different than what you're used to," Larry said.

Norma frowned. "Is this really a social trip, Larry—or is this about the skirmish the boys had in the alley behind the hardware store?"

"I'll admit Sam mentioned the fight to me," Larry acknowledged. "I heard Danny might be sporting a shiner, and I just thought I'd make sure everyone here is okay. Introduce myself. Let the boys know I'm available if they ever have a problem."

"We appreciate that, Larry, don't we, boys?" Norma said meaningfully.

JP nodded. "Thanks." Frankie's head bobbed up and down too.

Larry smiled. "Besides, boys will be boys, I guess. I sure had my share of fights when I was a kid."

Norma laughed. "I think I remember a couple of those."

She raised an eyebrow for the benefit of the three young ones. "But this kind of skirmish won't happen again with these boys. They've promised me."

"Good to know," Larry said. He looked toward the porch. "Looks like you've been working nonstop around here."

"We've been putting in some pretty long hours," she confirmed.

"How about last night?" Larry asked evenly.

"We generally quit at suppertime," she said, then cocked her head to the side. "What's this really about, may I ask?"

"Just wondered if you'd been in town and happened to see anything."

The three boys glanced at each other. Norma could see how closely Larry was looking at them. She crossed her arms over her chest. "No. We weren't in town last night. We were all right here," she said firmly.

"Well, anyway, Anne and I want you all to come to supper some night. You let us know what will be a good time, and my wife will make the best Salisbury steak you've ever eaten."

"That would be nice, Larry. Thanks," Norma said gratefully.

"And, boys—I hope you're going to love living here. I was a military pilot during the last two wars and have seen a lot of the world—and Greenville is still my favorite place on earth."

Zach spoke up then. "My dad was a pilot in the service."

"Is that right?" Larry said warmly.

"He was a war hero," Zach said, then abruptly closed his mouth, obviously not planning to say more.

"Why don't you boys go clean those brushes before the paint gets hard," Norma suggested. When the boys were out of earshot, Norma stared at Larry expectantly. "What's going on?" she asked, raising her eyebrows.

"Okay, so there's a little more to my visit," he confessed, "and I'll admit it's leaving me pretty uncomfortable."

"Just spit it out, Larry," she said impatiently.

"Zach's dad—the war hero? His name wouldn't have been Benjamin Reed, would it?"

She nodded slowly. "That's right. How did you . . . ?"

Larry pulled the dog tag out of his pocket and held it up. "I found this inside Sam Williams' hardware store. Along with some vandalism."

She recognized it immediately. "Zach always wears this," she said, her voice low. "This looks bad, doesn't it?" Her shoulders slumped wearily.

He sighed. "It doesn't look good, that's for sure. I found that in the middle of all the damage, but I haven't said anything to anyone yet."

"Why not?"

"Look, Norma, I respect what you're trying to do with these boys, and I don't want to pull the rug out from under you before you even get settled," he said. "I'll give you an opportunity to talk to Zach and see what you can get out of him. But just so you know, the mayor has called a town hall meeting tonight to discuss this whole Vanguard operation coming to town. I'm going to have to have some answers about the vandalism—folks are pretty ticked off. It'd go a lot better for Zach if he'd confess and then take some responsibility for putting things right."

"I already planned on being at the meeting," she said, "and I hope I've got some answers for you by then."

Larry moved the tag closer to Norma, who reached for it, then hesitated a moment. He dropped the chain into her hand, then turned toward the cruiser.

Chapter 27

Zach focused on a couple of flies outside the kitchen window flying in crazy patterns around each other. At the long oak table, Norma, JP, and Frankie were looking at him, waiting for his reaction to what Norma had just said. But what he'd rather think about was how many flies he could keep alive in a Mason jar. *Ten? Twelve? Maybe fourteen?* His cheeks blew out in a long breath. *I can't believe she thinks I did it.*

"Zach? Don't you have anything to say for yourself?" Norma asked.

He glanced at her hands, folded together on the table, then watched her clenching and unclenching them. He crossed his arms over his chest and hoped his face wouldn't give away his conflicting emotions. "I already told you I didn't do it," he said flatly. "What else is there to say?"

"What if I told you that Chief Ledet has some evidence that says maybe you *were* in town," she said.

"I'd say that I didn't have anything to do with the vandalism," Zach retorted, "and that's the truth."

Frankie and JP looked at each other with worry written like a billboard all over their faces. Zach could see their look wasn't lost on Norma.

"Well?" she asked him again.

He hated the way Norma was staring at him like those people in the group home used to do. Like he was some kind of juvenile delinquent who was going to explode at any minute. He should have told her about going into town to look for the missing dog tag, but he hadn't. Now he'd sealed his own fate. She would never believe that he'd been in town the same night as the vandalism—but had nothing to do with it. And why should she? If he lied about sneaking out, he could very well lie about the vandalism. It's not like he hadn't lied to her before. But he'd changed—was changing—and he hoped Norma would realize he wouldn't stab her in the back after all she'd done for him. He was in a terrible spot.

"Look, Zach, the store owners are giving you an opportunity here. You need to apologize to all of them, clean up the damage and repair what you can repair—or . . ."

JP frowned. "Or what?"

Norma propped her elbows on the table, closed her eyes, and rubbed small circles on her temples.

"Or I'm going to have to buy a bigger bottle of aspirin," she muttered.

"I didn't do it," Zach said stubbornly.

"So you were here all that night? You never left the house?"

Zach turned his attention back to the flies.

Norma looked at Frankie and JP. "How about the two of you get washed up for supper," she instructed, nodding toward the stairs.

Zach wished he could go get washed up with them. What he'd really like was to be in his own room right now—the one

Norma said used to belong to her as a little girl. He just wanted to climb into bed and forget the last couple of days had ever happened. He'd been in trouble before—lots of times—but never with someone he cared about. Never with someone who had an opinion that mattered to him.

He moved his gaze from the window back to Norma and found her looking at him, her eyes wet.

"I want to stay here, Zach," she began, her voice a bit shaky, "but I can't stay in a town where people don't trust us. I want you and Frankie and JP to come to think of Greenville as your home. No matter where you go when you grow up, where you move to, whatever you do in your life, I want this place to be as special to you as it is to me. I want you to feel cared for here—I want you to know that you matter." She reached a hand across the table toward his but stopped before she could touch it.

"I'm sorry if you're mad or upset about something and I didn't realize it," she continued. "I've been so busy getting the house ready and settling in that maybe you felt you couldn't talk to me about whatever has been bothering you."

"Nothing is bothering me," he burst out. *It's not fair! You want me to admit to something I didn't do!*

"We can't make this work if you won't be honest with me, Zach," she said, the disappointment in her voice far more painful to him than the words. He turned to the window. He didn't have anything else to say to her.

In a matter of moments, he heard Norma push her chair back. "You might as well go and get washed up as well," she said. He heard her place something on the table but kept his eyes on the window until she left the kitchen. Zach finally looked at the table—and saw the missing dog tag.

He climbed each step methodically, his footfalls creating their own noises to add to the other sounds in the house. Each step increased the anger that had been brewing like a wildfire. He berated himself for being so needy and gullible. He had almost bought it. The whole homespun deal. Norma, caring for him in a way his own mother had never been capable of. He'd almost thought of Frankie and JP as brothers. *I let down my guard! Why did I do that? Stupid, stupid! I knew it was too good to be true, and I believed it anyway. A home like this can't last for someone like me. So what if they found my dad's dog tag? They would have blamed me with or without evidence.*

Zach figured it was only a matter of time before he'd be sent packing—back to the group home, where he could hang in there until he was old enough to be kicked out into the world.

It's no different here than the other places I've been. As usual, I'm the one who doesn't fit. Frankie and JP have each other. Norma didn't question them—didn't even ask if they'd had a hand in the damage. I'm not gonna let her kick me out—I'll just leave this dump before anybody has a chance! Who cares anyway? I don't need them. I don't need anyone.

Zach started down the hall to his room but stopped when he heard his name. He paused to listen through the closed door.

"But we *know* Zach was in town last night," he heard Frankie say. "Should we tell Norma?" Zach leaned closer to the door. *The little sneaks would have told on me anyway!*

"Nah. He wouldn't snitch on us—and we won't snitch on him," JP said.

"Do you think he wrecked those places?" Frankie asked.

"I guess he could have," JP answered. "I just don't know *why* he would have done it. I don't think Zach wants to go back to the group home anymore'n we do."

"Norma *could* send us back, you know." Frankie sounded worried. "If everyone in town is mean to her because of us, I wouldn't even blame her if she did."

"I don't think she'd do that," JP said without much conviction. "Do you?"

"I don't think she'd want to. I don't mind it if people are mean to us, but Norma's too nice for that. It wouldn't be fair. All she's done is try to help us," Frankie said, an uncharacteristically long speech.

"Let's just see what happens. All I know for sure is that we can't snitch on Zach. He's like our brother now, you know. You don't rat out your own brother—even when he acts like a jerk."

Zach stepped back from the door and moved lightly down the hall to his own room. "*He's like our brother now. You don't rat out your own brother*" sang over and over through his mind.

Norma lay on her bed fully dressed for the town hall meeting. She kept her eyes closed as the evening sunlight spread farther into the room and across her face. Her thoughts pressed in on her, one concern spilling into another. *I'm losing it. I don't know what I'm doing. The money is going to run out—and I don't even have a crop planted yet. What if we can't do it? Maybe Luke was right. I should have just sold the place. I thought Zach was happy here. I missed something . . . what did I miss?*

She forced her eyes open. They felt so heavy—she felt so heavy. "Okay, God—I'm in trouble here. I gave up the life of money and parties and drink. I even lost my husband over it. Now I feel like it's all too much—my head's spinning more than it did with the booze. I'm not sure I'm up to this task you've given me. Please help me."

The clock on her bureau ticked off the seconds. Subconsciously she counted the ticks—*fifteen, sixteen, seventeen . . . change is very hard. Change can bring you to your knees.*

She slid from the bed onto her knees and buried her face in her hands.

Norma stepped into the kitchen to see the three boys.

"Fine," Zach said without preamble. "I'll do it."

She felt her eyes well with relieved tears, but a lump in her throat prevented her from answering aloud. *Thank you, God.*

"Norma? Did you hear me?" Zach asked.

She cleared her throat and moved toward the boys, seeing that Zach had the dog tag around his neck. "I did," she said. "And I'm proud of you for taking responsibility, Zach."

He dipped his head and studied the black checkerboard floor, where he could just make out a reflection of his face. "Thanks," he mumbled.

After a hug around Zach's shoulders, she pulled a bowl from the cupboard. "It's got to be quick tonight. I'm making eggs for supper. Scrambled or sunny side up?"

Zach started toward the refrigerator. "Scrambled, I guess."

"Us too," JP said, and he and Frankie began to set the table without being asked.

Norma cracked the eggs into the bowl. "You two will have to handle Zach's chores tomorrow when he's busy in town."

The boys glanced at Zach. He met their eyes for a moment, then turned to get the glasses out of the cupboard.

"We can't be the ones to do Zach's chores," JP said, silverware in hand.

Norma raised her eyebrows. "Is that how you feel too, Frankie?" she asked.

"Yes, ma'am," he said quietly. "It can't be us."

"I've got to say I'm surprised. We're a family now, and everyone in a family helps out—and sometimes that means picking up the slack for someone in the family who has another obligation." She was bewildered. "It's not like Zach usually has to paint the house or something. It's not laundry day, so you don't have to strip his bed. His chores would take you next to no time. How hard is it to sweep the porches, water the garden, and take out the trash?"

"It's not that hard. Even my chores and Frankie's chores aren't that hard," JP said stubbornly.

"*Excuse* me? You're refusing to—?"

"Well, I figure we'll be too busy helping our brother clean up Main Street."

Zach stared at them, looking stunned. Frankie and JP had moved a little closer to their brother.

"Well, if that's what you want, I guess I can handle the chores alone for a day," Norma said, stunned herself. *Maybe this is going to work after all.*

"That's good," said JP firmly. "Because it's of the utmost importance that everyone in a family stick together." He raised his index finger and waggled it at Norma, obviously doing his best to imitate her tone, her way of phrasing things. "We need to get up and get cracking every morning. Lollygagging doesn't get the job done. Beds don't make themselves, dishes don't wash themselves, and porches full of dust don't welcome guests! When the house has order—life has order!" He put his hand on his hip. "And that's all I have to say on the subject—today."

Norma started to laugh. Frankie looked carefully at her, then joined in. It was contagious and rippled across the room in a wave that caught them all off guard. It was exactly what they needed—what *she* needed. *It's music to my ears. The load's a little lighter now, Lord. Thank you, thank you, thank you.*

Chapter 28

The citizens of Greenville who piled into the high school gymnasium were unusually noisy, speculating about all the goings-on in their little town. *What of Vanguard and Luke? Who had sold out, and who was still holding on? And what about the awful vandalism?*

The crowd buzz swirled around Joe as he paused in the doorway. It had been years since he had attended a town hall meeting.

". . . did you see the board over Sam's window?"

". . . turn over your land and you're turning over your headaches."

". . . had to actually rummage in the field behind the Tastee Freez for the ice-cream cone! Shameful."

". . . interested to hear what *Frank Ramsey's son* has to say."

Rows of folding chairs had been placed over the school mascot, a tiger painted in the center of the wooden gym floor. Yellow-and-green pennants were suspended from the ceiling for every year the school had won a football, basketball, or baseball championship, and a large clock hung on a brick wall beside the American flag.

Joe found an empty chair, and as he sat down he spotted Meg and Norma making their way toward some seats near the front. Most of the merchants in town were in rows near the front, as well as Pastor Don and his wife, Virginia. Joe saw that a contingency of farmers had consciously or unconsciously migrated together—Adam and Helen Malloy, Hiram and Sara Edwards, Tom Simpson, Ralph Hutton, and Clyde Evans were all clients of his. Chip Armstrong sat next to Ernie and was talking the older man's ear off.

Joe sat up straighter as Luke leaned down to say something to Meg. *She's my wife, Luke. Don't forget it.* His heart twisted when she smiled up at Luke. The man found a seat near the front next to someone Joe didn't recognize.

Larry took his seat next to Anne just as Tom Stevens, the mayor of Greenville, asked everyone to stand and recite the Pledge of Allegiance. They turned to face the flag and joined their collective voices in the way they always did at any public gathering. The rumbling of conversation started again almost as soon as everyone had taken their seats.

"Okay," Tom called out, "let's quiet down and get to why we're all here tonight."

"I'm here to find out what you're gonna do about my store, Tom!" Sam Williams shouted.

"And mine!"

Ralph Hutton stood. "Let's not muddy up the issues here—"

"Muddy, my foot." Roy Jeeter stood and pointed a finger at Ralph. "First things first, Ralph."

"Let's simmer down here," Tom said. "I know you're upset about the vandalism."

"You bet we are!" Sam said.

"Must have been a stranger," Viv said loudly. "That's what I think."

"Maybe that new guy who goes around collecting junk," Sam speculated.

"It wasn't Ferguson," Hiram called out. "I'll vouch for him."

"But how do we know—"

"I agree with Hiram," Joe said, on his feet. "It couldn't have been him." This got their attention, and silence fell over the crowd.

He sat down as Larry stood and turned to face the gathering.

"While I'm not prepared to name any names right now," Larry said, sounding authoritative, "I will say that I've got a solid lead I'm working on. I'll get this resolved as quickly as possible and have the damage to your stores repaired by the guilty party."

"So if we can move on," Tom said quickly, "we've got guests here tonight who came to address us. As you've all heard by now, Vanguard Industries is interested in setting up shop here. I'm going to let Luke Ramsey, regional manager, tell you about Vanguard and how it would affect our community."

Luke shoved his hands into the pockets of his nicely creased chinos and let his gaze roam over every person in the gym.

Joe thought the man looked comfortable in front of the group—a man completely at ease with the circumstances and himself. Joe couldn't help but be impressed.

"There are thousands of acres of farmland in this state," Luke started, "but when the head of my company, Vanguard Industries, asked me where I thought our next corporate farm should be located, I told him without hesitation that it should be here—in Greenville. I pushed hard to get my boss to go along with this for two reasons. One is that I believe the farmers and people here personify hard work and integrity—and the other is a little more personal. Put simply, folks, I'd like to make up for what my father had a hand in doing to this community seventeen years ago." He waited a moment, dipping his head humbly until the rustle of whispers had ceased.

"Most of you in this room know what I'm talking about," he continued, nodding at a few, "and for those who don't, suffice it to say I'd like to bring some pride back to the Ramsey name by giving you here the best opportunity that's ever going to come your way."

Luke started to pace in front of the group, as if his excitement couldn't be contained, and his arms were now gesturing to match his words. "I'm talking about embracing progress and prosperity—and letting go of anxiety," he said sincerely. "I'm talking about an expanded economy for this city, a bigger police force, more tax revenue because of Vanguard, more time for people like Norma to spend with their families instead of worrying about how they're going to pay their bills because last season's crop was too small. More time with children and less worry translates into happy families. Families who can feel pride that they're contributing to feeding people in this country and around the world."

"Not everyone in this room is a farmer," Viv Hatfield put in. "I just don't see what Vanguard has to do with us."

"It's a ripple effect," Luke explained. "Vanguard will have to hire more people as we expand. More people in the community means more business for store owners," he said, making eye contact with Viv, Roy, Sally, and Sam. "Diners, real estate agencies, hardware stores, movie theaters—you name it, and it's affected in a positive way. Vanguard doesn't want to just operate a company here—we want to *belong* here. We want to call this place home too. Make the town better. Replace the playground equipment in the park on Birch Street. Repaint the steeple on the church, fix the potholes on County Road 7."

The buzz began again as members of the audience picked up on their favorite issues.

The guy knows how to deliver a sales pitch, Joe concluded with reluctant admiration. He could practically hear the optimism in the room—see it on the faces of his friends and neighbors.

But Luke wasn't done. "I'd like to introduce you to Jack Riley, a friend of mine who has directly benefited from corporate farming. He's from Dry Creek, not far from here." Jack, a middle-aged man in a pair of dark blue dungarees and a white T-shirt, awkwardly stood in the front row. Luke said to him, "I don't mean to railroad you into a public speech, Jack, but maybe you'll share with these folks the merits of Vanguard in your community."

Luke sat down as Jack turned to address the crowd. "I only sold a portion of my land to Vanguard and kept the acres around the house. Pride of ownership, I think it's called. I didn't have to worry 'bout farm equipment no more. Vanguard *gave* me everything I needed. I didn't concern myself about the market value of my crops—Vanguard always gives me a steady income. I didn't lie awake nights anymore wondering if I'd have money to fertilize my crops or spray to get rid of pests—Vanguard was my saving grace."

Jack nodded around to the crowd and took his seat.

Jerry Trader now stood with a glance at Luke. "I'm convinced," he said to the audience, "and I've been convinced for weeks now. Luke's figured out a way for me to have it all. I'll keep my land, but all my crops will automatically go to Vanguard. Seems to me it's just like an insurance policy. I'll always have a buyer at a fair market price. But from what I understand," he added, pausing meaningfully, "Vanguard won't be interested in the rest of us without the Meiers place. It's the piece of land that ties everything together."

Luke quickly stood to his feet. "I don't know if it's fair of us to put this burden on Norma right now." He looked at Norma but not too long.

Looks a bit set up to me, Joe thought.

As Norma stood, she said, "It's all right, Luke." She clasped her hands in front of her, eyes sweeping the people in the room. "I love this town. I came back here because I want to raise my boys here with the same sense of community that I had, the same work ethic, the same feeling of belonging somewhere." Norma looked over at Larry, and Joe thought he saw an almost imperceptible nod. "I'm sorry to say my son, Zach, was involved in the vandalism." She dropped her head as a few comments were heard through the gym.

"I knew it."

"Bring troublemakers to town and you get trouble."

"Not a surprise . . ."

Norma lifted her head and straightened her shoulders. "I don't know why Zach would do something like this," she said, face composed, "but I've spoken to him, and he has agreed to make things right. I'll personally supervise the cleanup."

Another ripple of conversation ran through the gym, but Norma wasn't finished. "I also want to say that as far as Vanguard's offer goes, I'm ready to go along with whatever decision the community makes."

As Norma sat down, Mayor Tom moved back to his spot in front of the group. "I figure we can take an unofficial poll with a show of hands to see how many here are in favor of bringing Vanguard into Greenville."

A majority of the people in the room raised their hands. Joe put his up too.

"Since I'm speaking to a farming community," Luke now said to the collective group, smoothly picking up from the mayor, "I don't have to remind anyone of the importance of time. We'd like to get moving as quickly as possible in order to take advantage of the next growing season. I'd like to suggest a group signing—a celebration of our new venture—tomorrow on the steps of the church."

"After our stores are cleaned up!" Sam called out.

Luke smiled. "Right. After, it is. How does five o'clock sound?"

Tom looked out over the assembled group of bobbing heads, voices murmuring in agreement. He reached out to shake Luke's hand.

"All right, then—five o'clock it is!"

Joe watched as Meg and Norma walked toward the door with a group of people all headed the same direction. He wanted to go after her—just talk to her. He yearned to make some connection with her, but the fact that she hadn't sought him out made clear she wasn't ready. Instead, he made his way toward Luke and the small band of farmers who had lined up to shake his hand. One by one, they had a word or two with Luke, nodded at Luke's guest, and then ambled out of the gym.

Joe was last in line, and he stuck out his hand toward Luke. "I just wanted to say it took guts for you to stand up here tonight and say what you did about your father."

"Thanks," Luke said as he shook Joe's hand.

"And I don't know if this is the time or place, but I'd like to take you up on the job you offered me," Joe added.

"That's great, Joe! I'm really glad you decided to come aboard," Luke enthused as he gestured toward Jack. "I want you to meet Jack Riley. Jack, this is Joe Daley. Soon to hold the position of chief pilot for Vanguard Industries. Joe and I go way back to high school days."

Joe pumped Jack's hand, then drew his brows together in puzzlement. He looked down as Jack suddenly released his hand and self-consciously flexed it before shoving it into his pants pocket.

"Nice that you could make it to our meeting tonight," Joe said. "What brought you through Greenville?"

Jack flicked a look at Luke. "Oh, well, I had some business this way and thought—heard—well, knew Luke was in the area, so I decided to stay over. A man can drive only so many miles in a day, you know what I mean?"

Joe's eyebrows rose slightly. "I don't meet many traveling farmers. Guess your setup with Vanguard lets you have more free time, eh, Jack?"

"That's for sure. It's the perfect setup. In fact, I wish we'd had this opportunity years ago. Would have saved me and my wife a lot of needless worry."

"Well, at least the rootworm beetles have been eradicated from this part of the country," Joe said, "so no more worries there."

Jack offered a wan smile. "That's right. Check that off the worry list," he agreed.

"Listen, Joe," Luke inserted, "I realize you and I don't have any land documents to finalize tomorrow, but I'm hoping you'll be at our ceremonial signing. After all, your future is with Vanguard now."

Meg and Norma said their good-byes in front of the gym. As Norma walked away, Meg fished in her purse for the keys to the car. She didn't want to be standing here when Joe came out. Being in the same room surrounded by a crowd was hard enough—but facing him alone was something else entirely. *Keys, keys . . . finally!* She pulled them out of her purse and turned to leave just as Larry and Anne came out of the school, followed by Clara Jenkins.

"I appreciate the ride home, Larry," Clara was saying.

"No problem at all, Clara," Larry replied as Clara lifted an eyebrow in Meg's direction, followed by a polite nod.

"Meg," she said archly as she sailed past.

"Evening, Clara," she answered.

Anne stopped next to Meg with that unintentionally sympathetic yet quizzical smile that Meg was getting to know all too well from friends who knew that she and Joe were not living in the same house.

"Let's have coffee soon, okay?" Anne said.

Meg nodded. "That sounds good, Anne. Thanks."

Larry put his hand on the small of his wife's back and leaned in. "Why don't you and Clara go on to the car, honey. I'll be right there."

As soon as Anne and Clara were out of earshot, Larry looked Meg in the eye.

"How're you doing, Meg?"

"I'm okay."

Larry raised his brows. "Really?"

She nodded. "If you're going to worry about someone, then worry about Joe. I hate the thought of him driving after he's been at Barney's, and I know he's still going there."

Larry shook his head. "Hmmm. I don't think so, Meg. It's not what it might look like."

"I think some habits die hard. He told me he'd quit drinking, and then I saw his truck at Barney's last Saturday night," she said. "It broke my heart, Larry." And her voice broke on the word.

"He *was* there—but he wasn't drinking," Larry told her. "He was just talking to Gunny when I went in. He didn't have a drop of alcohol that night—in fact, I'd swear that he hasn't had a drink since you left with the kids. I'm telling you, he's not the same old Joe. Something *has* changed, Meg."

Stricken, Meg turned quickly to see if she could find Joe. She felt terrible that she had let his past dictate an automatic conclusion of guilt. She wasn't ready to let down her guard quite yet, but she could acknowledge she'd jumped to a conclusion about why he'd been at Barney's on Saturday night—and she needed to apologize for that. The last thing she wanted was to be the reason Joe slipped back into his old ways, just because she failed to give him a chance.

I need to tell him I was wrong, that I know he's trying. She ran back into the gym, but the room was empty. Joe was already gone.

Chapter 29

Meg hadn't been to their house since the night she'd packed up the kids and gone to her mom's. Lost in thought, she drove through the quiet streets of Greenville hoping to get to Joe before he left for work. She had spent a miserable night tossing and turning and going over the apology she hadn't been able to deliver at the meeting. Finally, just before dawn, she got out of bed, dressed quickly, left a short note, and slipped out of her mom's house before anyone else awoke.

She made the turn onto their road and thought back to the morning when she'd told Joe it was over. The look on his face had almost been her undoing—his simple questions—*"What did I do? What didn't I do?"* After all the years she'd prayed for him, she hadn't even told him what had finally sent her packing—seeing his truck in front of Barney's. He had kept his word about trying, and she'd dismissed his effort based on her own false conclusion.

"I'm not giving up, Meg. Even if it means trying until I take my last breath. You deserve at least that much from me. I'm not giving up. Never."

She knew she hadn't gotten there in time before she even turned into the driveway. His truck was gone. *Maybe I can catch him at the airstrip before he takes off,* she thought as she rolled the Bel Air onto the gravel driveway. She glanced at the house before she shifted into reverse—then quickly glanced back again. It looked different somehow . . . maybe the way the sunlight was just starting to climb over the roof. Maybe it was . . . *the new paint*?

She stood transfixed in her own front yard and stared at the transformation that had taken place. Sparkling white paint, redwood-stained porch with every slat in place, and baskets of flowers suspended over the railing. *He's never been interested in flowers before,* she marveled as she took in the potted flowers on the steps, marigolds filling every space of her garden and lining the path to the house, grass freshly cut, even a new bird feeder hanging from the biggest tree in the yard.

Meg was speechless, and helpless to resist the urge to go inside. She ran up the porch steps, past two new lawn chairs, and into the house.

It smelled of lemon furniture polish and . . . *wild flowers*? She stood in the doorway and took in the living room in a long, sweeping glance. The wooden floor had been waxed and polished, rugs had been cleaned, pillows on the sofa were fluffed and placed just so. Vases filled with blue indigo and phlox, purple morning glories, and pink hollyhock graced end tables and the coffee table.

She could see evidence of a caring hand everywhere she looked. She hurried toward the stairs. Even the banister had been buffed and polished to a mirror sheen. She went into the kids' rooms and stared in wonder. On Christy's desk there were wild roses and two new books. In Danny's she found a box with a kit for a model airplane and a landscape puzzle of a lake with deer drinking at the edge.

Meg took a deep breath and pushed open the door to their bedroom. The first thing she saw was her hope chest—but given new life with a coat of varnish. In the corner of the room was her old rocker from the garage—the graceful line of the arms and the back had been stripped and stained, the seat recaned. She sat down in the rocker and remembered how it felt the first time Joe had leaned down to hand her Danny when he was just five days old. She could almost feel the weight of him in her arms. . . .

"Oh, Joe . . ." The words were nothing more than a breath in the room that gleamed with his efforts. She rocked back and forth as the tears streamed down her face. More flowers, her grandma's Bible on the nightstand, new lace pillowcases met her gaze. *He's even cleaned off the dresser. Oh, Joe . . .* she sobbed.

Wait . . . the dresser. He didn't just straighten it up. She wiped her face and crossed quickly to look at the empty spot where their wedding picture used to be. She snatched open the drawers on Joe's side of the dresser and found they were all empty. She hurried to the closet—his clothes were gone. *I asked him to find someplace else to live . . . I asked him to leave so the kids and I could come home. . . .* Her shoulders shook with emotion.

Meg mentally gauged the time it would take her to get to the airstrip as she hurried down the stairs to the living room.

"This time you won't hear promises in anything I say, Meg, but you will find promises in what I do. . . ."

Stopping abruptly, she turned and ran across the room into the kitchen, past the table covered with her favorite tablecloth, across the waxed floor—to the stove. With the simple strike of a match and turn of the knob, the flame on the burner sprang to life.

Heart pounding, Meg drove breathlessly to the airstrip, hoping against hope Joe hadn't taken off yet. But as soon as she made her way past Ernie's office, she could see she was too late. The Stearman was gone.

"Meg?" Ernie came out of his office, pulling on his baseball cap.

"Morning, Ernie," she said, trying to keep her voice normal.

"Joe's gone." Ernie looked toward the empty spot where Joe's crop duster was normally tied down.

"I can see that," she sighed. *I can't believe I missed him again.* "Maybe I'll wait for him."

"Suit yourself," he said, "but it could be a long one, since he's headed toward the state line."

"Why? What for?"

Ernie shrugged. "He said somethin' about checking out things in another town."

"He didn't say anything else?" Meg pressed.

"Just that big changes need some investigation first," Ernie said importantly, no doubt liking the sound of the big word.

He fixed up our house, took all his clothes—looking for a new life in a new town?

"You got any idea what he's up to?" the man inquired.

Meg felt an icy knot form in her stomach. "I hope not, Ernie."

It was a fact of life that farmers had rough hands—callused and muscular with dirt under their nails that no amount of scrubbing could vanquish. Joe had shaken hands with plenty of farmers, and he was almost positive that Luke's associate, Jack Riley, was no farmer. His hands were as smooth as a baby's bottom and so clean he could be cooking at Viv's Diner. That unsettled, *something's wrong* feeling had started as a nudge after he'd shaken that gentleman's hand; then it became a push after he'd seen the blank look in Jack's eyes when he'd mentioned the rootworm beetle that every *true* farmer knew was an epidemic in Kansas.

Joe was doing the only thing he could think to do—he was going to Dry Creek to check out Jack Riley's utopia farmland.

Zach lined up the glass Mason jars on the shelf in the hardware store and glanced over at JP and Frankie, who were painting the trim on the inside of Sam's newly replaced front window. *The one good thing that's come out of this whole mess,* he thought, *is that they stuck up for me—like real brothers.*

Norma stood off to one side of the store, watching but rarely commenting on the job they were doing. Any directives or comments came from Sam Williams, who had kept an eagle eye on them since they'd started the clean-up job over two hours ago.

"You sure you got all those little shards of glass off the shelves, Zach?" Sam asked from his post behind the counter. "I don't want my customers getting cut when they reach for the merchandise."

"I'm sure," Zach mumbled.

"What's that you say, son?"

"Yes, sir, I'm sure," Zach said more clearly.

Sam bobbed his head. "That's better."

Zach retrieved a broom propped against the wall and started to sweep the floor. His thoughts turned once again to figuring out how his dog tag had ended up in the hardware store in the first place. He was sure he'd lost it during his fight with Danny, but that didn't explain where it had been found. Zach cast a sidelong glance at Sam, wondering if maybe the old guy had set him up. Zach knew he'd been pretty mouthy, and his burp had been good—but disrespectful, he admitted to himself. *Would that be enough to make the man—he's a respected member of the town—trash his own and other people's stores just to make me look bad?* He dismissed the theory as quickly as it had crossed his mind. Sam might be mad enough to do some damage to his own place, but Zach was positive he'd never damage anyone else's. *I may never know how the dog tag wound up here,* he thought, *but at least I have it back—and that's all that matters.*

"It's looking pretty good, boys," Sam said approvingly. "I'd have to say the place is put back together like it was—only cleaner now."

Norma smiled and the sight gave Zach some encouragement. He wanted her to be proud of him.

"All right, boys, I think we can move on, then," she said. "As long as you're satisfied, Sam."

"Just missing one thing," Sam said, looking pointedly at Zach.

Zach swallowed his pride, took a breath, and stepped up in front of Sam. "I'm really sorry about the damage to your store, sir. It should never have happened." *Every word true,* he thought, *though it's someone else who should be apologizing.*

Sam stuck out his hand. "Apology accepted, Zach. It takes a real man to admit he's done something wrong and then make good on it."

Zach sighed and his shoulders drooped as he shook Sam's hand. *One down—three more to go.*

With the aid of an unrelenting tailwind, Joe found himself in the vicinity of Dry Creek by midmorning. He dropped altitude as the visual references on the ground told him he was nearing the Graham County airstrip. Preparing to land, he could see that the fields for miles were bountiful—it seemed as though every square foot of available earth had been planted. Joe had hopes that in spite of what he suspected about Jack Riley, corporate farming would turn out to be a good thing—that Luke really did have the best interests of Greenville at heart.

When he was on the ground, Joe took note that the old dirt runway he remembered as pocked and full of rocks was now as smooth as a long strip of varnished wood. He taxied to the end and motored over to the tie-down area. His jaw dropped at the sight of four shiny new planes, identical to the plane in the photograph Luke had given him, lined up side by side on the tarmac. He could barely take his eyes off the aircraft as he brought the Stearman to a stop. He slipped off his goggles and stepped out of the cockpit onto the wing as two men ran up to the plane.

One of the men hollered at him. "This is a private airstrip, mister. You can't tie down here."

The men, standing just off his wing tip, both wore sunglasses and sported matching shirts with *Vanguard* stitched over the breast pocket, along with their names—*Doug* and *Al.*

"I thought this was the Graham County airstrip," Joe said.

"Not anymore. This is the property of Vanguard Industries, and like I said, you can't tie down here," Doug, the bigger of the two men, repeated.

"I need fuel," Joe said, "and I can't take off until I get some aspirin and something to eat. I've got a headache that's giving me tunnel vision." *All true,* he said to himself.

"I don't care what'cha got," Doug said. "This is a—"

"Private airstrip. I heard you the first time," Joe said, jumping the few feet to the ground, then gripping his head. "Just passing by. Got some work waiting for me. A buddy who needs some help spraying as bad as I need a job."

"Nice plane. Retired war bird, isn't it?" Al asked as he nodded toward the Stearman.

"That's what the guy who sold it to me said," Joe answered. "For three hundred bucks and a few more to fit it with a hopper, I was in business."

Joe swung his head toward the planes on the tarmac and started toward them, leaving Doug and Al little choice but to follow.

"So what'cha doin' out this way?" Doug asked.

But Joe was far enough ahead that he didn't bother to answer. *Luke wasn't kidding—those things are beautiful! Beautiful strip, beautiful planes . . . Things are looking good. . . .*

"Sleek machines," Joe said admiringly, close enough now to reach out and run his hand reverently over the leading edge of one of the wings. He looked up to see the Vanguard logo on each of the tails.

"Top-of-the-line dusters," Doug said proudly. "Brand new."

Joe moved toward the nose of the first plane, but Al stepped toward him.

"I don't want to sound like a broken record, but like we said, this *is* a private facility. If you want fuel, I guess we can do that, but . . ."

Joe was ready to accept their offer—just fuel up, head back to Greenville, and daydream about flying one of the beauties he was actually touching, but then he remembered the farmer he'd shaken hands with in the gym. . . .

"Without food and aspirin the fuel's not gonna do me any good. I shouldn't fly with this headache," he said, rubbing his temple again.

Doug studied him. "I guess Al can drive you into town, and you can get what you need."

"I'd really appreciate that," Joe said gratefully.

"Not at all," Doug said, then looked at Al. "Make sure you stick close to our guest, seeing as he's feeling under the weather and all."

Al grinned. "I won't let him out of my sight."

Nobody could see Danny in his grandma's backyard, where he stood in her flowered apron beating the dust from the rugs that hung over the clothesline. He'd tried to talk her out of the apron but finally figured it was more trouble than it was worth.

Like a batter intent on a home run, Danny whipped the long-handled broom back over his shoulder, adjusted his hands, and swung at the braided rug next in line.

"He swings! He hits! The ball is up, up! Over the backfield fence, and it's another home run for Dan Daley!" he called out in his best imitation of radio sportscaster Mel Allen.

"Way to go, slugger!" And, "You show that dust who's boss!" Familiar voices behind him joined the sports chatter.

Danny froze. The last two people on earth he wanted to see right now were Ron and Jeff.

"Nice apron, Daley—bet it goes real nice with your black eye," Ron said with a chuckle.

Danny turned slowly. "Hey." *I'm in my grandma's apron,* he thought, *with nowhere to go and nowhere to hide. Kill me now.*

"Your grandma told us you were back here," Jeff said, grinning like a Cheshire cat. "But she didn't tell us that you were dressed so . . . so *purrrty.* Do you feel purty, Dan? Do you like doing housework? Does that eye hurt as bad as it looks?"

Jeff and Ron laughed and slapped each other on the back while Danny struggled to untie the full-length apron.

"My grandma made me wear it. She doesn't want the dust from the rugs to get on my clothes 'cause then I'll bring the dust back in the house," he explained, then wished he hadn't.

"Whatever you say, Matilda," Ron laughed.

"What're you guys doing here anyway?" Danny asked, hoping to change the subject.

"We're supposed to go out to the creek today, remember?" Jeff said. "You do remember, right? We all said that today we'd go to the creek—"

"Yeah, I remember," Danny said.

"We thought we'd go down Main first," Ron said. "There's something you just gotta see."

"I don't need to see the vandalism," Danny said quickly.

"No, no, justice in action," Ron said. "So are you coming, or maybe you'd rather stay here and play dress-up in your granny's clothes?"

Danny yanked off the apron and wadded it up. "Let me just tell my mom I'm leaving."

Joe sat in the passenger seat of a truck that was the mirror image of Luke's. *I'd love to have one of these,* Joe thought. *No shaking, shuddering, or groaning when he shifts. Very nice.* Al had told him they were headed for the only place in town that had both edible food and aspirin.

The scenery out the window was standard Kansas issue—long lines of telephone poles and barbed wire ran along the edge of the road. Sandy yellow shale looked as if it had been sprinkled in the bare spots between the thick clumps of prairie grass that went on as far as the eye could see. Joe had to admit, it looked like Vanguard was living up to everything Luke had promised. The fields he had seen from the air were thriving, the airstrip was one of the nicest Joe had ever landed at—and even his "escort" seemed friendly enough now that they had things sorted out.

And then a few miles from the airstrip they passed two empty farmhouses, and then a third whose clapboard walls had flaking paint and windows boarded over.

"Looks like a glut in the real estate market out here," Joe observed. "That's the third empty house we've passed in just a few miles."

Al yawned, long and noisy. "That's how it goes."

"What do you mean?"

"Nothing." He shrugged.

Norma had to admit the boys had worked hard—Zach hardest of all. She was proud of how he went about each task as a personal quest. Even JP and Frankie seemed to take special satisfaction as they replaced the letters in the Butterick's Fabric Store sign and swept the sidewalk. They had polished the glass in her window until Sally was "sure many a bird will try to fly right through, it's so clean." With the aplomb of a grandmother who had grandsons visiting, she had even brought homemade cookies and lemonade for the boys when they were finished. Zach then made his dutiful apology to her, using nearly the same phrasing he had with Sam.

Viv Hatfield was ready and waiting for them when they arrived at her diner—hands on her hips, hair shellacked into her famous beehive that had JP and Frankie looking at her with unabashed curiosity. She gave Norma a cup of coffee and a newspaper, then told her she could wait at the lunch counter. Norma knew better than to argue, though the boys looked a little worried to be left under Viv's watchful eye.

Viv was all business, her voice cross and impatient as she handed Zach a bucket and gloves and told him not to breathe in the ammonia he'd be using to get the black paint off her window. But by the time the window was shining and they'd given her front door a fresh coat of white paint, Viv was telling them stories of her days as a girl in Greenville—and how she was caught stealing a chicken from a neighboring farm because someone had dared her.

"Everybody makes mistakes," she said to Zach. "The point is to fix 'em when we can and apologize from the heart."

"I really am sorry that your window got painted and your door got egged, Mrs. Hatfield," Zach said sincerely. "You're too nice a lady to have that happen to you."

Viv patted Zach on the shoulder. "Thank you, Zach. I'm sure you've learned your lesson." She chirped on, "I'd be happy to have you and your brothers come in for pie anytime. I'm famous for my sour cream apple, you know."

Joe looked out the passenger-side window toward Graham County Drugs and Dry Creek Hardware, two stores with boarded-up windows and "Out of Business" signs on their doors. Thelma's House of Beauty was open, but if the disheveled-looking woman sweeping the sidewalk in front of the shop was Thelma, Joe thought she might just be scaring away her own patrons. Garden Market at least had a customer going through the door, but that was more than Joe could say for the County Bank, where a placard on the door read "Open Monday and Friday."

Al pulled into a vertical space in front of Martha's Café, a small brick building where the largest collection of vehicles was parked.

"This is about it, as far as food goes," Al told him. "But Martha does make a fair stack of pancakes and a decent BLT, and I know she keeps a spare bottle of Bayer under her counter."

Doug stood on the wing of Joe's plane and grabbed the rib of the long white feather to pull it out from behind the altimeter. He'd seen a lot of superstitious rituals, but this one was a doozy. *Crazy pilot—wonder how long it'll take him to notice it's gone.* He casually dropped the feather over the side of the cockpit. He turned his attention back to the clean, minimally equipped cockpit and the registration slip taped to the side of the air speed indicator. Doug leaned in closer to read the name and address of the registered owner: Joseph Daley, Greenville, Kansas. He pulled a pen and piece of paper from his pocket and copied down the information and the tail number of the plane. He had a phone call to make.

Chapter 30

Joe followed his guide into Martha's, where a handful of old men in dungarees and overalls sat in booths or at the lunch counter. An older woman with a pencil tucked behind her ear, an impatient scowl permanently adorning her face, was sliding a sandwich in front of an equally surly-looking man seated at the counter.

"Here, Zeb, if it ain't right this time, don't bother telling me about it," she groused at him.

"I won't eat soggy bread, Martha, you know that," Zeb retorted, "so if this bread's soggy, you'll be making me a new sandwich, or I'll take my business elsewhere."

Martha snorted. "Be my guest. I think The Blue Parrot is still open for business if you want to drive a hundred miles. By then you can get yourself supper instead a' lunch."

Al gestured to an open booth. "We can sit there." But just then someone hailed him from a booth in the back.

"Go ahead," Joe said. "I'll just sit here close to the aspirin."

"Suit yourself," Al said as he headed to the back of the diner.

Joe took a seat at the counter on the other side of Zeb. Martha brought a tepid glass of water and a food-stained menu.

"I'm kinda between breakfast and lunch, so take your pick," she said without preamble.

"How about two aspirin with a short stack on the side?" Joe asked.

"Careful she don't bring you no soggy pancakes," Zeb muttered next to Joe. "In humidity like this, the woman needs ta learn ta keep things closed up in containers."

Martha rolled her eyes and disappeared though a door into the kitchen.

Zeb eyed Joe. "You passing through town?"

"Yep," Joe said.

Zeb looked toward Al. "You one a' Vanguard's people?"

Joe shook his head. "Nope."

"You came in with one," the man said bluntly. By the look of his hands, Zeb was a farmer.

"I needed a ride into town from the airstrip," Joe said. "He drove."

Zeb studied him, then nodded and went back to his sandwich.

Martha served up two aspirin and a short stack of pancakes. "That'll be forty-five cents."

"I thought I might look up a friend while I'm in town," Joe said quietly to her as he dug into his pocket for the coins. "Is Jack Riley's place close by?"

Martha frowned. "Jack Riley? No one by that name around here."

"Are you sure? He's a local farmer."

Martha shook her head. "Lived here all my life, and I can tell you there's no farmer with that name in these parts. Now, we got a *Jake Wyley* that goes door to door selling doodads none of us want or need," Martha added as she pocketed Joe's money, then moved on down the counter to refill someone's coffee.

Joe knew the answer to his question before he even turned to the man sitting next to him, but he asked it just the same. "You wouldn't happen to know a Jack R—"

"Nope," Zeb interrupted. "Never heard a' him."

"Do you own a farm around here?" Joe asked.

"If you want to call it that," Zeb said, his voice bitter. "I'm what ya call a *corporate farmer* now."

"What does that mean?"

"It means I'm a contracted employee of Vanguard. I'm a worker in my own fields." Zeb practically spat out the words.

"Less stress, they say, less headaches—more modern equipment," Joe offered.

Zeb shook his head in disgust. "I bought that load of horse manure three years ago. I'd take back the stress and the headaches in a second if it would mean I could have some say-so about the crops I grow on my own land. Some say-so about how they're sold and to who and for what price!"

Zeb wadded up his paper napkin and threw it onto his half-eaten sandwich. "I'd like to turn back the clock, is what I'd like to do," he said as he pushed off his stool. He grabbed an old straw hat on the rack by the door and plopped it on his head before he moved outside.

Martha came by to clear Zeb's dishes. "The pancakes are good," Joe told her as she wiped down the counter.

"Appreciate your saying so," she said. "The BLT is good too, but Zeb Hanson's too ornery and irritated to know it."

"Some folks just have a bad day once in a while, I suppose," Joe offered.

She sighed. "Folks around here would be thankful for a bad day—instead of a bad couple of years."

"The town does seem a little . . . well, forlorn," Joe suggested.

"The town's drying up and fading away, is what it is," she said, her tone also forlorn. "Farmers left in this area are nothing but a shell of who they were. At least the ones who kept their homes and leased out their property to Vanguard."

"Yeah, but the way I heard it, they collect a steady paycheck now," Joe said. "No more depending on the market value of the crop, no more shelling out big dollars to spray their fields and keep up with their equipment."

Martha leaned a little closer. "I don't know how much you know about working the land, son, but my late husband was a farmer, and he'd be spinning in his grave if he could see what these corporate farmers are doing to the land around here."

"I saw the crops from the air," Joe argued, "and the fields looked amazing."

Martha's face looked grim. "For now. But there's no crop rotation—no rest for the soil—no care for the land to sustain generations long after we're gone. They're just wringing every last nutrient out of the soil, and when the land is dead and doesn't have anything left to give—they'll move on. It's already happened in places just like this. You mark my words—Dry Creek won't exist in a few years."

"You ready to go?" Al's hand came down on Joe's shoulder and made Joe jump.

He turned on the stool. "Yeah, I think I got what I needed," he answered.

Doug hung up the phone in the fixed base operator's office at the Vanguard airstrip and turned to Andy, a stocky man who sported his own Vanguard logo shirt.

"So? What'd he say?" Andy asked.

"He said if we keep Daley here he may not get us fired for letting him go into town," Doug said with a disgusted frown.

"How're we supposed to do that?"

"He don't care—we're just s'posed to make sure he don't get wheels up until after one o'clock. That way this Daley don't make it back to Greenville until the deals are signed."

Doug walked out of the office to keep an eye out for Al. If Luke said Joe Daley needed to stay put—then they would see to it. The one thing Doug knew for sure was that Luke Ramsey wasn't a man to trifle with.

Norma and the boys arrived at Roy's place to clean up. But he wasn't quite as amiable as the other store owners had been. He was of the mind that JP and Frankie, while well intentioned to be helping out their foster brother, shouldn't be doing any of the work. When Frankie and JP assured him they wanted to help, he held up a hand to stop all arguments. "No, sir. I want Zach to do the work—and only Zach."

Norma watched Zach's expression and prayed he had the good sense not to say what surely was on the tip of his tongue.

"Fine by me," Zach muttered as he picked up a bucketful of soapy water. He started with the window where the words "Closed for the Summer" had been painted, while Frankie, JP, and Norma sat at a patio table under the shade of a big umbrella. Then Zach moved on to wash the caked dirt and mud from the giant ice-cream cone. Something across the street caught his eye. Danny Daley and his buddies Ron and Jeff had stopped their bikes on the opposite side of the street to watch him. Zach felt his cheeks burn. He turned his back on them and went on with his task.

Danny stood over the bar of his bike and watched Zach clean the ice-cream cone. Ron and Jeff were laughing.

"That's right, big-shot city-slickin' burper—buff that cone till it shines!" Ron joked.

"Serves him right. What kind of a creep does stuff like that anyway?"

Danny looked down at the ground under his bike. It was one thing for him to vandalize those businesses and hope they would pin it on Zach. But it was quite another to actually see Zach paying the price for what was his own crime. He thought back to his conversation with his mom when she'd come home from the town hall meeting and told him Zach was the one suspected of doing the damage to the stores. Danny had felt a tiny victory. *Take that, Zach,* he thought. *Don't tell me we're the same—don't tell me my family is as messed up as yours was!*

"You think he's got a conscience?" Jeff began his usual string of questions. "You think no one's ever taught him right from wrong? You know what I heard? My mom says his mom was troubled. Troubled by what? What does that even mean?" came in rapid-fire succession.

"It means he can't help that he's a low-life loser," Ron sneered. "Right, Dan?"

"Yeah, right," Danny said, looking away just in time to see Luke Ramsey step out of the barbershop. Luke tossed a quick look at Danny, then turned and walked in the opposite direction.

"You think he's as messed up as people are saying he is?" Ron asked, still staring at Zach.

Jeff chimed in instead. "My mom says the person who did all that vandalism must be one very angry person. So, yeah, I guess you could say Zach's pretty messed up."

"Are we going to the creek or not?" Danny asked impatiently.

"Yeah . . ."

Danny pushed off on his bike. "Then let's go."

Zach watched Danny and his friends ride away. He was hot and tired and ready to put the whole ugly incident behind him. Satisfied he had done everything he could to "polish" the old ice-cream cone, he found Roy Jeeter and offered up the obligatory apology. "I'm really sorry about all the damage that was done to your place, Mr. Jeeter."

Roy cast an appraising eye around the patio and at the cone, then shook Zach's hand. "A man's property is sacred, son," he said. "I don't want to ever hear a whisper around town about you misbehaving again."

"You won't, sir," Zach said.

Joe wasn't sure if it was his imagination or not, but he could have sworn there was some kind of secret communication going on between Al and Doug when they returned to the airstrip. A cocked eyebrow, a long glance, a small nod between the two.

"Topped you off with thirty gallons," Doug told him.

Joe reached into his pocket. "Let me throw in a buck for the ride into town," he offered. "The food made all the difference."

"The ride was compliments of Vanguard," Al assured him. "The company with a heart."

Joe's imagination kicked in again, and he could have sworn Al's tone held something like a sneer. Joe needed to get going so he could get back home and let Norma and the other farmers know what he had found out. Vanguard seemed like a shiny present on Christmas morning, but at the end of the day the price of the gift might be more than anyone could afford.

Joe counted out some money and handed the bills to Doug. "Well, thanks again," he said. A man he hadn't seen before walked out of the office and nodded to him. Joe nodded back, then started toward his plane with Doug pacing alongside him.

"You know, I've always wanted to fly a Stearman," Doug said.

"You're a pilot?" Joe asked, and noticed out of the corner of his eye that Al and the new guy were following right along behind them.

Doug laughed. "No, I've just always wanted to fly *in* a Stearman. Shoot—I've always wanted to get up in a plane like that, period."

"It's never too late," Joe said as he continued toward his plane. He sent a practiced glance at the windsock near the end of the strip and was relieved to see it floating casually on the breeze. The same tailwind that had pushed him here could have made his trip home twice as long. Flying into a headwind could be like trying to walk against a wall.

"Heading out, then?" Doug asked. "You say you got work someplace?"

"That's right," Joe said.

"Who's gonna do your work in Greenville?" Doug's question held the barest hint of a challenge.

Joe kept his answer casual. "Did I say anything about Greenville?"

"No, but your registration does."

Joe's chest tightened as Al moved closer to the wing and crossed his arms over his chest.

"Hey, Joe, you didn't get a chance to meet Andy," Doug said, pointing to the new guy. "He's our security officer."

Joe started to step around him to remove the tie-downs from the plane. "How ya doin', Andy?" he said as lightly as he could over his thudding heart.

Andy stepped into his path. "Real good, Joe."

"How about a cup of coffee?" Al said. "We'd like to hear how it is to fly one of these barnstormers."

"Another time," Joe said, lifting his watch. "I need to get on my way."

Joe tried to duck under the wing to untie the plane, but Doug placed himself in the way. "Funny thing," he said, "but the airstrip just closed for takeoffs."

Joe lunged for the closest tie-down, but Andy was on him in a second and punched him in the gut. Joe dropped to the ground, the air gone from his lungs.

"Don't make me do that again," Andy growled.

Hands on his knees, Joe gasped for breath and stared at the ground through watery eyes. *When Ferguson said to keep my guard up, I didn't think he meant literally. . . . Hey, that's my feather.* The white plume was just a few inches from his hand. Still working on taking even breaths, Joe slowly reached for it—*ouch*—but quickly pulled his hand back as if he'd been burned with a hot poker when he felt a slice across his fingers. His mind spun back to the first time he'd seen the feather—*felt the feather*—and cut his fingers.

Carefully now, he reached again for the feather and lifted it by the rib, then sat back on his heels and held it up. He had almost forgotten about the three men intent on keeping him from taking off.

"Look! It's Dumbo's magic feather!" Al mocked.

"Hey, pal, does the feather give you the courage to fly?" Andy chortled.

Joe ran his finger, softly this time, down from the top of the feather—ruffling the quills in the opposite direction. He then carefully started up again with his thumb. *Sharp as a knife.*

"It worked for Dumbo," Doug ridiculed, "and he's not nearly as big as an elephant!"

Joe held the feather up and twirled it slowly in the sunlight, creating his own light show. Suddenly he was free-falling again through clouds of blazing light—"*You didn't hit a bird that day, Joe—you hit me. I'm an angel.*"

"Ferguson," Joe whispered, "I believe."

Determination was etched on his face as he got to his feet, feather in his hand.

"Hey, now . . . that's one big feather," Al said jovially. "Maybe you can take your act on the road. Just you and the Stearman and the feather."

Joe faced the three men. "You're breaking the law by keeping me here against my will."

"We're just supposed to show you some Dry Creek hospitality a little longer, that's all," Doug said comfortably.

"Was it Luke Ramsey who told you to keep me here?"

The three men looked at each other as if to determine whether they should answer—which in itself was the answer.

"What did Ramsey promise you?" Joe asked. "New truck? More money? One of those houses that the farmers can't keep anymore?"

"*Mr.* Ramsey don't promise us a thing, wise guy," Doug said.

Joe turned and sliced the edge of the feather down through the heavy rope of the tie-down as if it were a pat of warm butter. He turned back to the men, who stood staring wide-eyed at the rope.

Doug took a step toward Joe. "Hey—what the . . . ? How'd he get a knife?"

Al shook his head. "I don't know."

"He ain't holding no knife," Andy said. "Just the stupid feather."

"Remove the other tie-down," Joe said, "or I'll have to do it myself."

Andy started toward Joe. "Okay, fun and games is over."

Joe backed up and sliced through the second tie-down in one clean sweep with the feather. Dumbfounded, the men stared at the thick rope that now lay in two pieces on the tarmac.

"That's impossible," Al said.

"I'd back up if I were you," Joe warned, "or I might have to show you some Greenville hospitality." He turned with the feather and the sun hit its edge with a glint like steel. The men tripped over themselves to back up as Joe moved toward them.

"You're the security guy. Stop him!" Doug said as he shoved Andy.

"*You* stop him," Andy shouted back. "You're the idiots who took him to town."

Joe climbed onto the wing, stepped into the cockpit, and then dropped into his seat, laying the feather across his lap.

"Clear!" he shouted.

The men scrambled out of the way as the radial engine roared to life. Joe taxied the Stearman past the slack-jawed men and steered onto the smooth dirt strip.

He pushed the stick forward—felt the shudders and shakes, heard the high-pitched whistling of the wing wires as the Stearman careened down the strip at full power. He pulled back on the stick to launch into the air. The wind swirled through the cockpit and caught the feather, lifting it up on an invisible cushion of air. Joe couldn't stop it—knew instinctively he wasn't supposed to stop it. He watched it sweep away in a blur of radiant light. He throttled the Stearman to its maximum speed as he banked south.

Chapter 31

Small-town America at its finest, Luke thought sardonically as he stood on the top step of the church to survey his handiwork. Things were nearly perfect. Beautiful weather—not too hot, not too humid—an azure sky with just a hint of gold to suggest the afternoon was lengthening into early evening. The freshly cut dark green grass of the churchyard lent a sweet scent to the air and contrasted nicely with the red, white, and blue bunting hanging around the table set up just off the steps.

He let his eyes sweep over the group assembled below him on the lawn. He had to stifle a smile when he thought about how they were all playing their parts to perfection and didn't even know it. They had been handled—manipulated—orchestrated to be there. *Revenge isn't sweet,* Luke thought—*revenge is power.*

The layers of his plan had been seventeen years in the making—ever since that fateful night when he'd sat in the backseat of a '35 Plymouth sedan and listened to his mom sobbing hysterically as his dad sped out of Greenville and into a future that was destined to be spoiled by the past.

Luke glanced at Hiram Edwards chatting with Clyde Evans, and he called up the hate and anger he felt at the men who had driven his family out of town, his home, the life he knew. Stolen the rest of his senior year—even stolen his chance at being with the only girl he'd ever loved. Luke hadn't known seventeen years ago *how* he would exact his revenge—only that someday he *would*. He'd been working for this day his entire adult life—and now it was finally at hand.

He had one objective left, and that was to get the contracts signed—legally and irrevocably. Then it would be the long good-bye for Greenville, years of watching from the sidelines as the town withered and died. Because he knew that was Greenville's future, as it was the future of every other community Vanguard had seduced.

Norma walked into his sight line, and Luke wished he could look George Meiers in the eye one more time as his granddaughter signed away his farm. Glancing at his watch to see it was five o'clock on the dot, he made his way down the church steps and stopped midway. He clapped his hands together and pasted on the charming smile that had helped him get to this very spot.

"Ladies and gentlemen," he called out. "It's time to get started with our ceremony. I want to thank you all for coming this afternoon," he said in a clear, confident voice. "And I'd like to take this opportunity to introduce the president of Vanguard Industries, Don Dushell."

A light scattering of applause followed Don Dushell, impeccably dressed in a lightweight summer suit, as he moved up toward Luke, who secretly reveled in the fact that his pompous boss had to look up at him as he climbed the steps to address the group. Don got to the step just below Luke and cocked an eyebrow at him. "I had my doubts, Ramsey, but it looks like you're gonna pull this off," he said quietly.

"I always cross the finish line, Don," Luke answered with a smile as he stepped aside so the older man could stand next to him. "Always."

"Thank you, Luke," Don said loudly as he turned to face the group. "As Luke told you, I am Don Dushell, owner and founder of Vanguard Industries. I wanted to come here today to welcome you all to the Vanguard family! We hope the association is long and—*bountiful*." There were smiles and a few polite chuckles. "We want to *harvest* nothing but good will and will go out of our way to *cultivate* your friendship."

Luke did a mental roll of his eyes at the farm references Don cleverly threw out. He knew the rest of the speech by heart, knew when to smile, when to look serious, hopeful, and thoughtful. His mind wandered as Don continued his well-traveled speech, and he looked at the faces turned toward them—so full of hope for the future. The mayor standing next to Larry Ledet, who stood dutifully attentive—Greenville's answer to law enforcement and war hero all rolled into one, Luke thought derisively. Norma's boys stood by her side a few feet from Larry.

Luke wasn't sure if he was relieved or irritated that Harold Daley hadn't turned up at the signing ceremony. Though he didn't have any property to sell to Vanguard, Luke had thought he might come just out of curiosity.

While Don droned on, someone else caught Luke's eye. Meg was making her way across the church lawn toward Larry. For a brief moment, a wrinkle of annoyance creased Luke's forehead as he was reminded of Joe Daley. The blundering idiot was way out of his league in Dry Creek with Doug, Al, and Andy. They'd keep him there until it was too late for the fool to do any kind of damage to the signing—though he would be a pesky fly in the ointment when he finally came back to town to tell his tale of woe about Dry Creek.

But Luke wasn't worried. Too little, too late would be Joe's theme song. Luke took a surreptitious glance at his watch and tried to focus on Don's speech to figure out how long before he could line everyone up at the table in front of the collated contracts. *Just a few more boring comments about crops and feeding the world and we'll be in the final stretch,* Luke decided as he looked once more in Meg's direction.

All day Meg had worked hard at keeping her fear at bay, but when she approached Larry, she wasn't sure she could get the words out without falling apart.

"Have . . . have you heard from Joe today, Larry?" she asked in a whispery voice that she could not keep from trembling.

"No," he said, looking at her carefully. "Is something wrong?"

She wrapped her arms around herself and blew out a breath. "I don't know. I think so—I mean, I can't find him. He told Ernie he was headed to the state line, but he didn't say why—and I just spoke to Ernie, and I know he's not back yet." She could feel her nerves taking over, roiling around inside her and causing the helpless panic that was getting worse by the minute.

Norma appeared at her side and slipped an arm around her waist. "Anything?"

Meg shook her head and swallowed. "Not a word. Even Ernie's worried. I just talked to him, and Joe's not back yet."

Larry put a hand on her arm as Don started to wrap up his speech. "Look, Meg, I'm sure he's okay," Larry said, trying to comfort her.

"I've had this horrible feeling of dread all day long that I can't shake," she said, on the verge of tears.

"Think of how many hours Joe has logged, Meg. He's just gotten hung up somewhere," Norma said, looking at Larry to back her up.

"Norma's right. You know as well as I do that Joe doesn't take any chances."

"Really?" she shot back. "What about Saturday nights, Larry? We both know Joe would have climbed behind the wheel of his truck if you hadn't disabled it every weekend."

She could see by the look on Larry's face that she'd struck a nerve.

"Like I said last night, he's changed, Meg."

"Right! That's what I'm saying! He's been on a self-destructive path for years, and when he finally gets it right—"

"He wouldn't do anything crazy, if that's what you're thinking," Larry said bluntly.

Hearing the words out loud made her knees weak, and she was glad for Larry's arm under her elbow. "If he went and did something, I'd live with it every minute of every day," she whispered. "Help me find him, Larry, please. . . ."

He nodded. "I'll head back to my office and make some calls," he said, glancing upward at a sound in the distance.

Meg heard it too.

The Stearman swooped in low over the trees and buzzed the whole group. A couple of the women screamed as it passed, then looped back up to come around again.

"It's Joe!" Meg breathed her relief as she ran to the edge of the lawn and watched him approach again. Zach, JP, and Frankie hurried to stand beside Meg as Joe set up for another approach. She saw Zach's jaw drop in awe as the Stearman came back up the street fifty feet off the ground. The engine roared to the accompaniment of the whistling wing wires. The crowd gasped as Joe passed the church going low and slow.

Meg was positive he'd raised his hands over his head and crossed them at the wrists as he passed by. She turned to Larry. "He wants us to stop!"

The current of air off the wings of the biplane swept across the church grounds and sent the carefully stacked contracts into a small whirlwind—scattering them all over the lawn.

"What's the crazy man think he's doing?" Luke shouted, leaping down the stairs in a futile attempt to retrieve the papers.

"Man's obviously been tipping the bottle again!" someone shouted back.

"That's the neatest thing I've ever seen!" Zach's eyes shone with admiration for Joe's acrobatics.

"Thank you, God," Meg said between deep, hugely relieved breaths. "Thank you."

Luke was sweating bullets—and making plans to fire Doug and Al while he scrambled over the lawn gathering up the contracts.

"A little help here, folks," he said, trying not to sound as panicked as he felt. "Let's get the paper work together and continue." He could still hear the drone of the Stearman's engine—and then it whined to a stop. In the sudden silence, Luke heard Larry say, "He landed."

Luke lifted his head to watch Meg hurry over. "He's right, Luke," she said as she came up. "Joe's landed somewhere close by. He wants you to wait for him."

Luke forced a laugh. "Other than blowing my paper work all over the place, that stunt was planned." He continued his paper collection.

Meg frowned. "Planned?"

Don looked at Luke. "A nice stunt, Ramsey. Added some pizzazz."

Luke barely acknowledged his boss as he finally found the signature page of Norma's contract. He slapped it down on the table. "Norma! Here's your contract. Why don't you start us off?"

Norma hesitated. "I thought we were all going to sign together," she said. "A symbolic gesture—isn't that what you called it?"

Luke put on a smile that actually hurt. "Yes, that's right—symbolic." He riffled through the pages and tried to do in two minutes what had taken him two hours to do the night before—collate the contracts into sensible stacks.

The first three farmers were lined up in front of their contracts—Norma in the middle. Luke handed them each a pen. "Signatures on the dotted lines," he said with another smile, "and your lives will change."

Norma hesitated, then bent over the contract. Just as she put the pen to the paper, Joe ran into the churchyard.

"Wait, Norma!" he wheezed, breathless from his sprint. People on the lawn shook their heads, murmured comments.

Meg ran to Joe as he leaned over, hands on knees.

"Are you okay?" she asked, putting her arm around him as he grabbed at the stitch in his side.

"Has anyone signed yet?" he gasped out.

She shook her head.

"I've got information," he told her between breaths.

Joe got his second wind and made his way toward Luke. "I've got something to say."

"We're in the middle of something here, Joe," Luke said tersely. "You're too late."

"No, Luke, I'd say that in spite of your best efforts to the contrary, I'm just in time."

"What are you talking about, Joe?" Norma asked.

Joe turned and faced all the farmers and their families gathered on the lawn. He glanced at Luke, taking note of the steely set of his jawline.

Joe raised his voice. "I've just been to Dry Creek—a Vanguard community—and seen the future of our town if we partner with this company," Joe said. "I have to tell you—it's not what Luke has described. Not even close."

When Norma and the two farmers standing on either side of her took a step back from the documents on the table, Joe plunged ahead with what he'd found on his visit to Dry Creek. He talked about Jack Riley, Martha's Café, and Zeb Hanson, a farmer who'd give anything to turn back the clock.

Luke felt as if he were standing on the edge of a cliff that was gradually falling away, inch by inch, from under him. He refused to cower under the scrutinizing glares of the farmers as they heard Joe's detailed description of what he'd discovered at Dry Creek. Luke could see them slowly embracing the concept that controlling their own lives and land, no matter what the cost, was preferable to being an employee with no opinion on the farms they would continue to work, with no consideration of land conservation.

He heard the murmuring when Joe talked about the abandoned community and the hopeless frustration of the few business owners left in what would most likely become a ghost town in a few short years. It felt surreal as Luke heard Joe suggest they all do a little more investigating before entrusting their own community to a company that put profit and the bottom line ahead of everything else—including the very survival of the participants.

The bottom dropped out from under Luke when Norma stepped up to the table and ripped her contract in half. She turned to Luke. "I didn't trust you in Kansas City, and I shouldn't have trusted you here," Norma said. "From now on, I'm going with my own instincts—and right now they're saying 'no deal.' "

Luke shook his head with a smirk. "You're giving up the opportunity of a lifetime because a disgruntled bug killer, who gets his courage from a bottle, tells you to?" He couldn't help the angry finish to his query.

Don Dushell straightened his tie and stepped over to Luke. He didn't even attempt to keep his voice down. "You missed the finish line here, Ramsey. You've got twenty-four hours to get your company truck back to Kansas City. You're fired."

"Fired?" Luke shouted back. "You can't fire me, Dushell, because I quit!" The people who had gathered were all staring at him. Don shook his head disgustedly and hurried to his car.

Luke did a sweeping point of his finger at the group. "You're all crazy. I don't need any of you—and I don't need this crummy town! You're a bunch of hayseed hicks who don't know a good thing even when it hits you between the eyes! You don't deserve an ounce of my effort—you never did!"

Joe quickly put in, "Just a minute, Luke—"

"Shut up, Daley! Just *shut up,*" Luke spat out. "You're a rabble-rouser just like your old man."

"Get out of here, Ramsey," someone yelled from the group.

Luke raked his hand over what was left of the paper work on the table, ripped at the bunting, and threw it all into the air. He heard the cacophony of disparaging comments as he stood glaring at the group.

In one collective moment, the farmers dismissed him and crowded around Joe, who had become the man of the hour. The blistering anger and humiliation Luke felt rose up and took over. In a few strides, he stood in front of Meg.

"We didn't deserve it to end like this, Meg," he said, using all his self-control to keep his voice even. "It was supposed to all be different this time."

She frowned and took a step back. "What are you—?"

Joe stepped between them and put a hand on Luke's chest. "You're done here, Luke," he said tightly.

Luke set his jaw and pushed Joe's hand off his chest. Out of the corner of his eye, he saw Larry Ledet coming toward him. Luke abruptly swung around and strode away.

Joe and Meg spoke each other's names at the same time—then smiled. She put a hand on his arm.

"I've been looking for you all day," she said quietly as another group of people began to press in on them. "I wanted to tell you I'm sorry. I'm so sorry I doubted you—"

"I didn't blame you, Meg," she heard even as several farmers were reaching between them to shake the hand of their hero. She saw him blink away tears, and her heart constricted with her feelings of sorrow for her doubts and gratefulness for his love in spite of it all.

Meg stepped back and watched as Joe tried to answer the questions and accept the congratulations and thanks of his friends and neighbors. She heaved a huge sigh.

Luke drove out of Greenville with no thought of direction or destination. His fingers ached from gripping the wheel of his truck—*his* truck. He had no intention of ever going back to Kansas City. *Don can write off the truck like he's writing me off,* he raged. The bitter taste of defeat was new for him. He'd been the golden boy for years, on the fast track to upper management at Vanguard, but all aimed at one purpose. His purpose. To bring the people of Greenville to their knees to avenge what they had done to his family. And now years of plotting had vaporized right under his nose *because of Joe Daley*! The seed of anger grew with each revolution of the tires down the black asphalt road.

"Get out of here, Ramsey! Get out of here!" echoed through his mind, further fueling his emotions. He remembered as if it had just happened. . . .

What's that pounding? Who's pounding on the door? The sound was loud and insistent and soon multiplied—many fists hammering on the wooden door of their Greenville house. Luke, just about to drift off to sleep, propped himself up on his elbows and listened to the panicked voices of his mom and dad in the other room. *What's going on?* The young teen got out of bed and slipped into the hallway. He could hear his mom's nervous, high-pitched voice pleading with his dad not to open the door, but Frank was having none of it. He wasn't going to let a few lunatic farmers disturb his family!

Luke crept farther down the hall and heard someone shout, "Get out here, Ramsey! Now!"

"You can't come barging onto my property in the middle of the night," his dad shouted back as the front door opened. Luke got to the end of the hall just as an angry bunch of farmers pushed their way into the room. He watched in disbelief at the scene—his mother, one hand over her mouth, the other fluttering awkwardly in the air, was backing away from the men. His dad had both hands out, palms up, as if the gesture could stave off the advancing group.

"This is illegal," Frank said, but in spite of the implied threat, Luke heard his dad's voice quake. "You can't just force your way inside—"

"You ought to know, Ramsey!" George Meiers shouted. "You been stealing from us and sitting beside us at church! You're a snake of a man. . . ." Luke couldn't believe Norma Meiers' grandpa had it in him to shake a fist at his dad.

". . . good-for-nothing, low-down coward!" another one shouted.

Luke moved into the room toward his mom, icy claws of fear grabbing hold. Angry voices stacked over themselves like a chorus of unruly children clamoring for something.

". . . see the inside of a jail cell, Ramsey!"

"Liar and a cheat—should have seen it!"

". . . you can't sit here in this house while we may lose our own homes!"

". . . law won't do justice, but we will! You're coming with us!"

Luke stood beside his mother, but he was sure she wasn't even aware he was there. "Get out of here! Leave him alone! Leave us alone!" she finally shouted. The raw, naked anguish and fear in his mom's voice made Luke's heart tumble further with dread.

The men were pressing in on Luke's dad, and he was begging—to be spared, imploring them to leave. "We can work this out," he was trying to tell them, still denying his guilt. George Meiers' hand shot out of the group, snagged Frank by the collar, and practically hauled him off his feet.

"That's enough, George!" Harold Daley limped his way through the men with the sheriff. George Meiers didn't turn, but they all knew Harold's voice.

"We want some justice, Harold, and we're gonna get it!" George announced loudly as he tightened his grip on Frank's shirt.

"I've known every last one of you for years," Harold said calmly, "and I know this isn't how you want your justice. You do something foolish tonight, and you'll be paying a lot bigger price with your conscience than you ever paid with your crops."

Luke felt the blood pounding in his head, and his mom finally reached over to grab his arm. He could feel her nails digging into his skin as Harold Daley finally brought some semblance of calm to the melee and convinced the farmers they would receive some recompense for the losses they had suffered.

It was hours later that Luke found himself in the backseat of the family car as they drove away from Greenville under the cover of night. There were two things he was sure of—his dad had been railroaded into admitting something he didn't do. And somehow, someday, those people would pay.

Danny pedaled his bike slowly along the road that would eventually bring him back to his grandma's front yard. He was sure Norma and the boys were long gone from Main Street now, and he was glad. He didn't think he could stand another reminder of what he'd done. Removing the letters from Mrs. Lundgren's Butterick's Fabric Store sign didn't seem funny anymore.

Spending the day with the guys at the creek had been good. He had a cut on his heel, a blister on his hand from the rope that they had used to swing across the creek, and a sunburn across his shoulders that screamed for a heavy coating of sour cream to take away the sting. They'd raced their bikes from the creek all the way to the road where Ron and Jeff turned to go home. Now, even though his legs were starting to feel like rubber, he picked up the pace. Danny was starved and knew pot roast was in the plans for dinner.

As he moved over to the side of the road to let a car pass, he glanced over his shoulder. His spirits plummeted when he saw a blue two-tone truck. He swiveled his head back around and moved farther to his right, keeping his eyes straight ahead. The last person he wanted to see was Mr. Ramsey.

Luke motored past him, and he felt instant relief. But then Luke slammed on the brakes and made a sharp left across the road. Danny had no choice but to stop his bike. His stomach clenched up as he watched Luke get out of the truck and stride over to him.

"Well, aren't you just the picture of a carefree young man," Luke said maliciously as he leaned over and placed his hands on the worn grips of Danny's handlebars. "Where're you headed?"

"Home."

"What home would that be, slugger? Your home, or Grandma's home? Or maybe you're going to Miss Norma's to spend some time with that poor sucker who took the rap for you." Luke smiled, and Danny shivered.

"I need to go," Danny said as he tried to back up his bike, but Luke kept his hold on the handlebars.

"Not so fast," Luke said, tightening his grip.

"I'm late," Danny said. He hated the quiver he heard in his voice. "My mom is expecting me home."

"Your mom is expecting her *good son* home. How would she feel if she found out her precious boy was the one who broke windows and painted buildings and caused all that damage to those stores in town?" Luke shook his head. "It would tear her up—especially with the tough times she's going through right now. The last thing she needs is a juvenile delinquent for a son who *let an innocent boy take the blame.* And don't get me started on your dad. How's he gonna feel when he finds out he's got a liar for a son? Why stick around for a kid like that?"

"You said you wouldn't tell on me!"

"Yeah, but keeping your secret came with a price—remember? What did I say the night I caught you doing all that damage? Someday you'll owe me a favor. Well, today's that day."

Luke's words penetrated Danny's mind and soul like a knife.

Luke pulled Danny's bike closer. "What's it going to be, sport? Do me one little favor, or I spill my guts to your folks."

Danny hesitated. He could hardly bear to look at Luke. "What's . . . what's the favor?"

"I've got to lay low and can't be seen anywhere around here. I need to know when Norma and those boys will be out of their house."

"Why?"

"Because that's when I will even things up between us," he said with a steely edge to his voice. Luke released his grip on the handlebars. "I'll wait to hear from you, kid. Don't even think about finking out on me." His flat hand against the side of Danny's head held just enough force for the message to be unmistakable. "Won't be worth it to you or your family."

"How . . . how will I find you?"

"Not to worry—I'll find *you*."

Danny angled around the truck he once thought was so cool and pedaled away as fast as he could. He wished he'd never seen the truck or its owner.

Chapter 32

A light breeze skipped over the surface of the water and ruffled the cattails along the marshy edge. It was an idyllic fishing hole, and on any other day Danny would have been happy as a clam to stand there with his line in the same pond he'd fished with his grandpa over the years.

Instead he was looking at Zach, JP, and Frankie, and he felt as though he could have used his conscience as a line sinker. The weight of what he'd done—two things he'd done—was driving him crazy, and twice JP had to ask what bait he should use on his hook. Danny had talked himself into thinking this was just fishing with some buddies—as he'd done countless times before. It wasn't his fault things happened to have fallen into place—his mom and Miss Norma going to talk to Pastor Don at the church and suggesting he take the boys fishing. On his way to collect the guys, who should be waiting out on the road for him, leaning against his truck?

Danny was quaking inside, as much for his family and friends as for himself as Luke demanded information. "They—the

Meiers—should be out of the house this afternoon," he'd told Luke after one look at his expression.

"Should be—or will be?" Luke insisted.

"They will be," Danny affirmed quickly. "This makes us even now, right, Mr. Ramsey?" For a second, Danny wondered if he'd be blackmailed for the rest of his life.

"Yeah, kid. We're even now," Luke finally said.

Now here they all stood, poles in the water. But today, all Danny could think about was Luke. *What's he up to?* had no answer he could even consider.

"Dan! You must be up in the clouds somewhere. I've asked a question," Zach said.

Danny turned with a start. "What?"

"I asked what kind of fish are in this pond," Zach said.

"Oh yeah, sorry. Mostly bluegill I guess—and a few bass." Danny glanced at the container of fish eggs on the ground between Zach and Frankie. "You know, I brought the wrong kind of bait for bass," he said suddenly. "I know where I can get some live crayfish. You guys stay here and fish—and I'll be right back." He sprinted for his bike.

Luke pulled up in front of Norma's house and parked his truck. *The kid'd better be giving me the straight scoop.* He headed toward the back door and knocked loudly, ready with a phony story if someone should be there. He peered through the small window in the door. The kitchen was deserted, and he hadn't seen Norma's car anywhere—just that old heap of a truck she drove once in a while. Luke tried the knob—this was rural Kansas, after all—and grinned his way inside.

Danny was winded from the breakneck two-mile ride to the Meiers' place. His heart sank when he saw Luke's distinctive truck parked in the driveway. He had to know what Luke was up to.

Danny stepped off and rolled his bike to the side of the house. He moved around the house, peering in windows. Suddenly through a window in the front, he saw Luke coming down the stairs with a thick brown envelope in his hand. He ducked—then carefully peeked in again. *What's he doing? What's he stealing? Tell somebody—hurry up and get help. What do I do . . . what can I do . . . ?* He almost groaned aloud. *He'll come out and find me. I can find Dad first—maybe the police. . . .*

Danny raced over to Luke's truck and, as quietly as he could, opened the driver's door. He spotted the keys hanging from the ignition and jerked them out just as he heard a door slam from the direction of the house. He moved the truck door almost into place and started for his bike, but then realized he'd never make it—Luke would see him for sure. The barn was only twenty feet from the truck. Danny ran in a crouch toward the double doors.

Luke was whistling as he pulled open the cab door—*I must not have shut it all the way*—and threw the brown envelope onto the seat. Things were turning his direction again. It was a stroke of luck he'd remembered a childhood discovery—some government bonds, along with some cash and bank books at the Meiers'. He knew the bonds wouldn't have matured during George and Florence Meiers' lifetime—but they were due to mature in a year or so and would bring a fair amount to the one who had them.

He sneered as he thought about the old farming mentality—they didn't trust banks or safety deposit boxes. He'd recalled how surprised he'd been when playing hide-and-seek at Norma's house when they were all kids. He'd hidden in her grandpa's closet and leaned into a loose board in the wall. He'd pried the board off and discovered that George Meiers had stashed some cash and bank books in that nook in the wall. *Handy little place to stash a treasure.* He'd thought so then, and he sure thought so now. He would look for the bonds there first. *Sure glad you didn't rip out* that *wall, Norma,* he thought with a satisfied smile.

He settled behind the wheel and reached to turn on the ignition—but his keys were gone. He looked on the floor, on the seat beside him—even in the visor, where he'd been known to stash them a time or two. His good mood was souring in a hurry.

He slammed out of the truck to retrace his steps. As he went around the side of the house, looking at the ground, he stopped when he saw a bicycle leaning against the wall. That wasn't here a minute ago—was it? He put his hands on the handlebars to have a closer look. He'd felt those worn-out grips before—*this is Danny's bike.*

"I want my keys back," he bellowed. "And I mean *now*!" He returned to the truck and flipped the seat forward, then pulled out a shotgun. "I know you're here somewhere, Dan! Just give me my keys and we'll both get on with our day!"

Danny closed his eyes and tried to calm down enough to come up with some kind of plan. He couldn't give the keys back to Luke—he couldn't let him get away with whatever the man was doing, no matter how scared he was. Maybe if he could still get to his dad or Chief Ledet and stop Luke, it would help make up for everything he'd done to get Zach in trouble.

Luke was still yelling, and Danny put his eye up to a knothole in the wooden door. Luke was standing by his truck with his feet planted hip-distance apart and a shotgun cradled in one arm. Danny swallowed hard and looked over his shoulder at the interior of the barn. He had to think of a way out. . . .

"Hey! I've got one—I've got a bite!" Frankie yelled. "What do I do?"

JP was in the middle of baiting his hook. "Pull him out of the water," he yelled back, "before he gets away."

Zach dropped his pole. "I'll get the net." He ran to the area where Danny had been fishing while Frankie reeled in the fish. They all yelled when a large bass broke the surface.

"Quick, Zach—put the net under him!" JP said, holding the container of fish eggs he was using for bait.

"I'll grab it," Zach said just as Frankie pulled at the line, and the fish crashed against JP. The container of fish eggs splashed all over Zach.

"Hey!" Zach yelled, wrinkling his nose against the fish odor.

"Would ya move over there?" JP asked with a grin. "A little farther—right now you don't smell so good!"

"Actually, I can't stand myself." Zach dropped his pole. "I'm going to ride back to the house and change."

"Go ahead, but you better hurry," JP said. "We may catch all the fish in the pond before you and Farmer Dan get back."

"Just stay put," Zach said, "but leave a fish for me, okay?"

Every muscle in Luke's body was rigid as he stood in the yard and listened for a sound—any sound at all that would tell him where the Daley kid was. He shifted the gun over his shoulder and looked around. *The barn.* His smile was as cold as his heart as he took wide strides toward the barn, shotgun at the ready.

"I know you're in there, you little weasel—now get out here or else!" he yelled. He frowned at the sound of an engine turning over.

Danny came barreling through the wooden doors on a green John Deere tractor. He slammed his foot down on the gas as he passed a wild-eyed Luke. He heard Luke yell, then, in the rearview mirror, saw him heft the shotgun and point it at him. Danny heard the blast of the gun just as he maneuvered the bucking machine around the corner of the house. If he could just make it to the field, maybe Luke wouldn't be able to follow as quickly.

Another blast and Danny ducked—certain now shotgun pellets would eventually find their mark. A third splatter of pellets and a bellow of rage from Luke as a picket fence around the garden shattered.

Danny hit the gas and jerked the wheel hard to the left. It felt like slow motion as the tractor tipped and dumped him into the dirt below, pinning his left foot under a tire. He screamed in pain and frantically tried to free his foot. He could smell dirt and gasoline and could hear Luke laughing as he struggled. The rearview mirror ingeniously wired onto the tractor was lying at a forty-five-degree angle in the grass, the bright sun glinting off the glass and making him squint.

In seconds, Luke stepped into his line of vision, his face grim and threatening. "Give me my keys, you little turncoat," he growled.

"Help me first," he said desperately. "My foot is caught."

Luke put the shotgun to Danny's temple. "My keys."

Danny pulled his head as far away from the gun as he could. "In my pocket," he stammered.

Luke reached into the pocket of Danny's jeans, yanked out the keys, and turned to leave.

"Wait! You can't just leave me here," Danny yelled at his retreating back.

"Uh, yeah, kid. I can—and I am. You'll be fine until Norma shows up—and by then, I'll be long gone," he said as he tossed his keys in the air and caught them. "Tell your mom," he began, then shook his head. "Never mind. Someday I'll tell her myself. . . ." Danny watched as Luke walked to his truck, started the engine, and left in a cloud of dust.

Zach made the ride home in record time and was stripping off his stinking shirt even as he ran into the front door and up the steps to the bathroom. A quick shower and he could be back with his pole in the water in no time. He lifted the dog tag from around his neck and hung the chain over the towel bar. Just as he was about to turn on the faucet for the shower, he heard something. He stopped to listen. *I told those guys to stay put.* He heard it again. Someone was yelling. Zach opened the bathroom door to hear more clearly.

"JP? Frankie? Is that you?" he called down the stairs. The only answer was the faint cry he'd heard twice before. In jeans and no shirt, he ran down the stairs and listened again. *Someone is yelling for help. . . .*

He ran out the back door, and it took him a while before he saw the tractor out in the field—on its side.

"Help!"

Zach ran barefoot to the tractor.

"Are you all right? What happened?"

"I'll tell you after you get me out of here," Danny groaned. "My foot's stuck. You'll have to dig it out."

Zach ran for the shovel in the barn and was back at Danny's side in a matter of moments.

"Hang on. . . ." Zach dug into the dirt around the tire and then noticed a trickle of gas coming out of the engine.

"There's gas leaking from the tank," Danny told him through clenched teeth.

A spot of grass lit by the sun's reflection off the mirror began to smolder—then a spark caught. They both saw the small fire at the same instant.

"Zach! Is there water—?"

"No hose back here," Zach said between his teeth as he frantically beat at the fire with the shovel head. The flames leaped up in the wind and licked at Zach's legs. He yelled out and swung back to Danny for another frantic attempt to dig him free. The flames were now devouring the dry grass in a line toward the house.

"It's almost free!" Danny shouted as he pulled at his foot once more.

Zach turned out one more shovelful of dirt, then dropped the tool, grabbed Danny under the armpits and pulled as hard as he could.

Danny screamed as the foot slid out from under the tire. Zach helped him to his feet at the same time the wind picked up and flames began licking at the back of the house. Dense, black smoke clouds filled the air around them.

Danny started to hobble away. "C'mon! We have to get away from here," he shouted.

Zach put his hand to his neck. "I have to get something." He raced away to the front of the house.

"Zach!" Danny screamed as he limped after him. "Don't go—"

An explosion behind him dropped Danny to his knees. He turned to see the tractor completely engulfed in flames—and the back of the house going up like dried kindling.

Zach heard the explosion as he raced up the stairs. All he had left of his dad was in that bathroom—he'd grab the dog tag and be back outside in seconds. He heard a window shatter on the floor below—and then another one. He snatched up the chain and swung back into the upstairs hallway.

But smoke had already thickened into black curling tendrils that made visibility nearly zero. He dropped to his knees to stay below the smoke and crawled toward the stairs. Flames rolled over the drapes, furniture, and rugs and licked at Zach's bare feet. He screamed and stood to run, but the smoke overcame him. He only reached the top of the stairs.

Zach had been gone too long, and Danny had to find him. He could see the roof of the house was already smoking.

He hardly felt the pain in his foot as he limped as fast as he could through the front door and dropped to his knees. The smoke filled his eyes and made him choke as he peered through it for some sign of Zach.

"Zach!" he screamed over the roar of the fire. "Zach!" From his knees in the foyer, he could barely make out something on the top of the stairs. He scrambled his way upward in a crawl.

Danny grabbed for Zach's arms and pulled him down a couple of steps. More windows exploded, and now fire was licking at Danny's legs from the side of the staircase. Fear for Zach and for himself fueled his adrenaline, and he pulled Zach down the stairs with strength he didn't know he had.

With the house in flames behind him, Danny collapsed and held Zach in his arms as tears ran down his blackened face.

This can't be, can't be, can't be happening. . . . Help. Someone help. God, help!

Chapter 33

Joe ran toward the hospital entrance. He spotted Larry pacing just outside the building, and another wave of panic swept over him.

"Larry? Meg called me. Danny's okay, right? He's all right—?"

"Danny's doing fine. He's in the waiting area, and Zach's still hanging on," Larry said with a hand on Joe's arm. "Listen, Joe, you should know Luke Ramsey is somehow involved in all this."

"How do you—?"

"Danny's told me everything," Larry said. "He's pretty upset."

Joe blew out a breath. "What . . . what's happening with Luke?"

"We'll get him," Larry said. "He's not going to slip away."

Joe nodded as he headed inside.

"Wait." Joe turned back, and Larry opened up his palm to reveal Zach's dog tag. "We found this on the ground at Norma's. Zach wants to be a pilot, Joe. I saw it in his face when he watched you fly—saw the same look I used to see in your eyes when we were kids." He held the chain out to Joe. "Give it back to him—will you?"

Joe hurried along the institutional green tile floor, following the signs on the sterile white walls. He turned a corner and heard his daughter call out to him.

"Daddy, you're here." Christy rushed into his arms, and he hugged her tightly. Frankie and Joe were in one corner of the waiting area, and Danny sat in another corner, bent over his knees, his head between his hands. Joe could see one foot was bandaged.

Joe leaned down so he was at eye level with Christy. "You okay?" he asked her.

She hesitated—tears welled in her eyes, and one spilled over and ran down her cheek. "Yes, Daddy, but I'm scared for Zach."

Joe gently wiped the tear with his fingertips.

"Me too," he whispered. "Where's Mom?"

"In Zach's room," she said softly. "I've been staying with Danny. Don't be mad at him, Daddy. It wasn't his fault."

Danny looked up at them, and Joe saw abject misery in his son's eyes. Besides the Ace bandage wrapped around the foot, he also had a gauze bandage on his left hand. Otherwise, Joe was incredibly relieved to see that the boy had no other visible injuries.

Christy held tightly to Joe's hand as they walked toward Danny, but she held back and sat down a few chairs away when Joe dropped to one knee in front of his son.

"You all right, son?"

Danny stared down toward the pale green tile under his feet and barely shook his head.

"Your mom told me you pulled Zach out of the house. That was really brave," Joe said, putting a hand on his son's knee.

Tears dripped onto Joe's hands, and Danny merely shook his head again. "It should be me in there." Joe could barely hear him.

"Do you want to talk about it?"

"I can't right now," he whispered, sniffing.

"Then later," Joe said with a pat on his leg. "I'm going to check on Zach, but I'll be back soon, okay?"

Danny couldn't say anything more to his dad—he felt frozen by his own shame. He watched as his father walked out of the waiting area.

"Dad?"

Joe turned back to him.

"After you see him, please don't hate me."

Christy's lower lip trembled and tears ran down her cheeks as her head moved between her brother and her dad. In a few quick steps, Joe was back in front of Danny, his eyes filled with intensity and unmistakable love.

"Now you listen to me," he said in a voice husky with emotion. "I've been a jerk, neglected you, been far less of a father than I should have been." Joe knelt down. "Missed you. Loved you. But I will *never* hate you. Never. You are my son. *My* son. And no matter what you do . . . I will always love you. Do you hear me? Always."

Danny felt sobs rise in his throat. "I'm so sorry, Dad." He felt arms around him, and he slowly reached up and put both his own arms around his father.

Meg was the first person Joe saw when he entered the room. She moved toward him, face wet with tears, and they embraced. Over her shoulder he saw Norma beside Zach's bed.

"The doctors aren't very hopeful, Joe. They say it could be anytime," she whispered. "Norma's trying to stay strong."

Joe approached the bed. "Norma?" he said softly.

She turned, and he opened his palm with the chain. She took in a ragged breath and nodded at him, then stepped back so he could get closer to Zach.

Zach had his head mostly wrapped, and his eyes looked large and dark. An IV pole next to the bed held a line running under the white sheets that covered him. A monitor's steady *bleep, bleep, bleep* was the only sound in the room. The curtains pulled over the window kept the lighting dim.

Joe tried to smile as he leaned closer to Zach. "I heard a rumor you might want to be a pilot someday."

"Yeah." Zach's voice was hoarse and barely audible. His eyes fluttered shut, then opened again. "Like my dad."

Joe lifted the dog tag in front of Zach. "You'll want this, then."

Zach's eyes teared up. "Thought it was gone. . . ."

Joe gently put the chain into one of Zach's hands, and the boy curled his fingers around it. "I think I'm going to see my dad," Zach said. He looked at Joe. "I asked Jesus to forgive me for all the stuff I've done wrong, like Norma's always buggin' us to do." He dragged in a breath. "I asked for real, from my heart. You think it worked? I don't want my dad knowin' the bad stuff I've done. I want to see him look at me like I remember from when I was little."

Joe could hardly speak. "He will, son. He'll look at you with pride in his eyes, and the two of you will fly like the birds of the sky. Together."

Zach swallowed, lifted a corner of his mouth to smile. "Just like I've always wanted to . . . I'm gonna fly. . . ."

"That's right. You're gonna fly."

"Dad . . ." Zach closed his eyes, and his fingers around the chain relaxed.

Chapter 34

While the daily crop report on the radio played in the background, Joe put away the groceries he'd picked up to fill the empty fridge and pantry. He'd already taken his suitcase over to Larry and Anne's spare room, where he'd be staying. He grabbed a few items from the counter and glanced around, satisfied with his morning's work. He'd dusted and mopped—even replaced the flowers in the vases throughout the house. He wanted everything in place for Meg and the kids when they got back from their trip to Kansas City with Norma and her boys.

Meg had gone to lend moral support while Norma attended to paper work she had to file with the foster care program. The two women had been inseparable since Zach's death, with Meg doing everything she could to help Norma cope with her incredible loss. She had helped Norma navigate through the difficult process of planning Zach's funeral, sat with her in the family pew at the front of the church, and held her hand as they sang Norma's favorite hymns. Joe had seen Danny slip out of the pew as soon as the recessional was played and had followed him to the back of the church, but Norma found him first. Meg and Joe had both watched as Norma held their son in her arms while he sobbed.

Joe finished with the groceries and thought about the long-distance phone conversations he'd had with Meg since she'd been away. There had been so much to talk about—so much to reflect on. But the main thing was that they were feeling their way with each other again, finding their way back. He thanked God for that. When Meg asked about Luke Ramsey, Joe had to admit they were still looking for him. He assured her that Larry said they weren't going to let him vanish into thin air like his old man had done.

Vanish . . . like Ferguson. Joe had made several attempts to locate the big man who'd done so much for him, but without success. A visit to the field that Ferguson had called his mission had left Joe scratching his head in frustration. There were even more "castoffs" in the field than at his last visit, but no Ferguson. Joe resigned himself to the likelihood that Ferguson had left his life just as mysteriously as he had come into it.

Joe clicked off the radio on the kitchen counter and took one more look around the room. Meg had promised to call when they were headed back to Greenville. *Now everything's in place.*

He frowned when he heard something hit the side of the house with a thump. Another thump . . . and then once again. He hurried out of the kitchen and through the front door.

The tree branch had cracked just enough that the breeze swung it back and forth against the house. *More irritating than damaging,* Joe concluded as he made his way to the garage to find a saw.

He flipped the light switch and watched a mouse scurry across the floor. *That's not good. There's never just one. . . . I guess now that I've straightened things up in here, the mice have room to run.*

He climbed up to the loft to get the saw that was hanging just over the edge of the platform floor. But when he turned to go back down the ladder, he stopped when something below caught his eye—Danny's half-finished puzzle on the old Ping-Pong table. From his vantage near the ceiling, he noticed the pieces were formed like a Ferris wheel.

On the floor with his saw, he stopped to look at the puzzle again. *Can't tell what it is anymore from here. They're just a bunch of colored pieces that don't make any sense. Just pieces . . .*

On earth there is no heaven, but there are pieces of it.

Joe reversed direction again and practically ran up the rungs of the ladder to look again at the puzzle.

Hiram's field. Angel wings . . . The field is cut in the shape of angel wings.

Joe was amazed as he looked over the side of the cockpit at the field below. *How could I have missed this all the times I've been in the air?* he pondered. *Because I wasn't looking for it,* he concluded. He circled the field three times, and with each pass he saw something new in Ferguson's junk. One man's junk is another man's . . . message? Hundreds—no, thousands of objects were lined up in a precise pattern to form letters that stretched from one side of the clearing to the other.

He knew I'd see it, Joe thought. *Ferguson spent days, walked miles, tested his physical body to its limit because he knew I would see this—and that I'd know what to do once I found it.*

Joe banked the plane one more time around the field, and as he did, the sun reflected off the metal on the pieces below—some rusty, some awkward looking, some broken—illuminating them so the whole was a radiant, sparkling, fluid symphony of glittering light. It read, "FAITH GIVES SECOND CHANCES."

It had been over two hours since Joe had enlisted Chip Anderson's help with a second plane. Word of Joe's discovery had spread. Between the two of them, Chip and Joe had crammed people in where the hoppers had been and ferried a dozen people each over what was now known as Ferguson's Field. To think they'd all driven past that field day in and day out and never once seen the simple but profound message, Greenville's citizens marveled over and over.

Joe stopped to refuel and taxied the Stearman off the strip toward the fuel drum at the edge of the tarmac. Barney waved as he passed. He saw Pastor Don and his wife and grinned as Chip helped Viv Hatfield climb into the front cockpit of his Kaydet. Joe made a mental note to check if Viv's beehive hairdo would stand up to a hundred knots in the air.

He rolled the Stearman to a stop and stepped out of the cockpit. When he climbed off the wing, there was his father.

"Dad."

"Hello, son," Harold said. "Folks are saying a stranger left a gift in the field."

Joe nodded. "He was an answer to a prayer."

"I'd like to see what the commotion's all about."

Joe could see the remorse in his father's eyes. Harold's shoulders sagged with regret when Joe didn't answer, and he started to turn away. But Joe put his hand on his dad's shoulder. "It would be my honor and privilege to show you, Pops."

Joe made it to their destination in under ten minutes. He tapped his father on the shoulder and pointed below just as he banked into the turn. Like all the townsfolk during their rides, Joe's father gazed down in amazement, unable to take his eyes off the sight. And at that very moment, Joe realized how much he loved his dad. Loved him deeply, more than he would be able to put into words. Tears welled in his eyes just as Harold turned to him, his eyes also looking teary, and they shared a smile. Love perfected in that moment. Joe knew the *feeling* would not last—disagreements, heartache, the ups and downs of life would make the emotions come and go. But he also understood that this life only showed us glimpses, pieces of heaven, and they were to be held on to as tightly as possible.

His mind drifted back to the young boy lying in a hospital bed, clutching his dad's dog tag and yearning to fly. *He physically died, but he also lives,* Joe reminded himself. Two realities. One truth. And only faith could bring them together. Faith for broken relationships, for healing, for a better tomorrow, for a boy now flying in the heavens with his father.

I believe. Thank you, Ferguson.

Chapter 35

Leaning against the hood of his truck, Joe waited patiently in front of the charred remains of Norma's house. He'd purposely been vague when he'd told Meg they should come straight to the farm when they got into town. He looked down the road, where a small cloud of dust trailed a vehicle coming toward him. Joe checked his watch and smiled. Right on time.

He raised his hand in a wave as Norma's car drove up, heads in every window.

"So you have some people who are interested in the property," Norma called as she climbed out, Meg and the kids all scrambling after her.

"I definitely do," Joe said with a smile.

"Well, who is it, Dad?" Danny asked. "We were trying to guess on the ride back."

"I don't care who it is," JP said quietly. "They'll never like this place as much as we did."

It was Frankie who got their attention, pointing to a long line of vehicles coming up the road and turning onto Norma's property.

"I don't understand. What's this all about?" Norma asked.

"It's about faith," Joe said. "Faith and second chances, Norma. Faith in what you're trying to do for JP and Frankie. Greenville wants to help you rebuild. The community agrees this is your home and where you belong. You came back here because you thought this was a place full of people who care—and you were right."

"Oh, Joe, thanks, but I can't afford this. My money is nearly gone and—"

"It's all taken care of," Joe assured her. "All you have to do is say you want to stay."

Norma's eyes filled with tears. "I don't know what to say. I want to stay, but I'm not sure I can now because of Zach. The memory of what happened—"

"Zach loved it here," Frankie announced, his voice high and clear. "He said it was the first time he felt like he had a real family. He even told me when he grew up he wanted to stay and farm the land and be close to all of us. He would want us to stay, Norma. I know he would."

JP nodded. "Frankie's right. Zach would want us here."

Joe smiled. "And you'll have the support of a whole community who want to do this for you."

"I can't believe this," Norma said, her voice husky. "But why?"

"Perspective." Joe grinned. "Let's just say we all have the same perspective now."

Cars and trucks full of lumber and supplies were pulling onto the property. Friends spilled out the doors, calling to each other and waving at Norma. She started to laugh. "Remember what we talked about, boys? 'Be worried for nothing,'" she reminded them. "God is with us!"

Doors slammed as Norma and the boys got out of the car behind the Daleys. But in Joe's truck, no one moved. Finally, Meg looked at him.

"Can you wait just a minute?" she asked.

He nodded. "Sure."

From behind the wheel of his truck, he watched as Meg and his kids disappeared into Sylvia's house with Norma and the boys right on their heels. He heard a squeal of excitement from Christy and realized how much he'd missed hearing that sound and all the noisy chaos that a family makes together.

It was only minutes until Meg came back through the screen door, approached the truck, and opened the door. He was surprised when she slipped back inside.

"So, Norma and the boys are going to stay here with my mom until their house is done," she said.

"Really? That's . . ."

Meg grinned. "Unexpected—right?"

He smiled back. "A little."

"When I asked Mom about it, she insisted," Meg said. "Especially since she has more room here than we do at our house. It would be a little crowded with the four of us along with Norma and the boys."

"The four of us?" he asked with a catch in his throat.

She had tears in her eyes as she answered him, but it was the pride and trust he saw reflected there that squeezed his heart. "Yeah, the four of us."

He sucked in a breath, almost afraid to believe what she was saying. Christy and Danny pushed through the screen door, overnight bags in hand, and ran toward the truck. Before he could process the turn of events, the kids were squeezing into the cab of the truck with them. Danny slammed the passenger door. Almost simultaneously, Joe got out of his side of the truck.

He felt a rush of tears fill his eyes and pushed his fist against his mouth to stifle the sobs he felt rising. The enormous relief and gratitude was overwhelming, and he had to lean on the truck for support. *Home. They are all coming home. . . . Thank you, God.*

He pulled in small gulps of air to collect himself, then blew it out in one long steadying breath. He got back into the truck and settled into the driver's seat. He looked over at his family. "Let's go home."

Meg and Joe walked slowly together toward the house and smiled as they heard Christy and Danny calling to each other while running through the house, noticing all the little things Joe had done.

They placed their feet at the same time on each wooden step. The sun slid past the horizon with a flourish of color as they stood together on the porch. They laughed when they heard Danny yell to Christy, "Guess what, squirt?! The stove works!" Feet thundered up the steps and bedroom doors banged closed. Cicadas started to sing in the trees beside the house.

Joe took a step closer to Meg—let his hand touch the small of her back in that familiar, intimate way. She leaned toward him, rose on her toes to give him a soft kiss, then reached back to take his hand in hers.

She held tightly to his hand as she led him into the house. Their house.

The trill of a meadowlark outside the bedroom window slipped into Meg's dream and drew her from sleep. She was lying on her side facing Joe. He was fast asleep, a half smile on his lips. The clock on the nightstand beside the bed told her it was early—only six o'clock. Being careful not to wake Joe, she slipped from the bed and grabbed his sweatshirt from the back of a chair.

The front porch, with a cup of coffee, had always been her favorite place to start the day when the weather permitted. The morning was cool, and the breeze had prompted her to pick up the quilt from the rocker and wrap it around her shoulders. Meg moved to the edge of the porch and tipped her head back to look up at the sky. *Looks like a storm is coming,* she noted idly. In spite of the gathering clouds, she felt that a morning had never been brighter. She felt contented. Cherished. Valued. She felt loved.

She sipped her coffee and let herself revel in the utter peace she felt in her soul. She knew the days ahead wouldn't be perfect, but she wasn't looking for perfect. She wanted a real life with the man she'd loved all her life. Closing her eyes, she breathed in deeply.

And then her world went black.

A clap of thunder woke Joe, and he couldn't believe he had slept until eight-thirty. *Peaceful mind, happy heart.*

Christy and Danny were in the kitchen eating cold cereal.

"Morning, kids," Joe said. "Where's Mom?"

"We thought she was still asleep with you," Christy said.

Joe frowned. "No."

Another clap of thunder echoed through the room. Joe turned on the radio on the counter and then looked out the kitchen window. The Bel Air sat where it usually did.

"Guess she took a walk," he said.

"She does that sometimes," Christy said. "You want some cereal too, Daddy?"

Joe dropped a kiss on her head. "No thanks, sweetie. I'm just going to have some coffee."

They all listened attentively when a tornado watch was issued over the radio.

"You think there will be a tornado here, Dad?" Danny asked.

"We better keep an eye out," Joe said. "You guys listen to the radio, and I'll go check around for Mom."

Stepping out onto the porch, he first noticed the quilt in a heap on the floor and trailing off the edge. Just to the right of it was a turned-over coffee cup, its remnants staining a dark patch on the wood. Joe reached down to touch it and realized it was almost dry.

As the air crackled around him, Joe was overwhelmed with a feeling that something was wrong. Very wrong. He called out Meg's name. And then he spotted something on the gravel just below the porch steps. He scrambled down the steps and scooped up a small cotton cloth. A distinct odor made him bring the cloth to his nose. *Chloroform.* A whisper broke through his lips. "Meg."

Chapter 36

Notorious for spring storms and summer lightning, Kansas was making yet another spectacular proclamation with streaks of color fanning out in all directions across the horizon. Backlit with shades of purple and green, the entire sky looked like an abstract watercolor painting. Thunderheads building to the east and west resembled mountain ranges piercing into the clouds above.

Joe pushed his truck beyond any speed he'd ever gone before. He was hardly conscious of the weather. He cared about one thing—Meg. There was no doubt in his mind that Luke had taken her, and Joe was going to get her back. Anger at Luke and fear for his wife raced neck and neck, propelling Joe into action from the moment he knew Meg was gone.

Joe figured more than an hour had elapsed since Luke had boldly kidnapped Meg. He had no idea which direction Luke had taken her—but he knew how to find out. He cranked the steering wheel hard, and the truck fishtailed into the turn at the airstrip. He floored the gas pedal and raced through the gate.

"Something dark is coming, and you need to be ready. . . ." So this is what Ferguson was warning me about. . . .

"I'm coming, Meg! Hang on—I'm coming to get you!"

Luke stomped his foot on the gas of the Chevy and gripped the wheel so hard his knuckles turned white. He tried to reassure himself things were right on track. Meg's trip to Kansas City with Norma had put a hold on his plan for a few days, but it had given him a chance to think things through while hiding out in an abandoned farmhouse he'd found while researching the area for Vanguard. He looked at Meg slumped against the passenger door, and he tried to ignore the icy ball of anxiety in the pit of his stomach. It was one thing to plan a kidnapping but quite another to actually do it.

He could see just by looking at her that the chloroform he'd used was still working; her eyes were closed and her breathing remained shallow. *But for how long?*

He had cursed himself when he'd realized he'd left the chloroform and the rag behind in his haste. *Who knew slim Meg would be so hard to get into my truck? Must be what they mean by dead weight . . . so now I've done it. Given Joe a taste of what it feels like to have something taken away.*

Turning his attention back to the road, Luke saw the sign for Highway 70 and uttered a single word out loud. "Colorado." It had come to him during his days in hiding that the Rocky Mountains would be the perfect place to disappear—a small mountain town off the beaten path where he could blend in for a while.

Meg groaned and shifted in the seat. He glanced over at her again. She was the only loose end he wasn't sure how to tie up—but he wasn't too worried. He had always been able to think on his feet. It would come to him later. Right now, she was serving his purpose.

He looked up at the roiling clouds above him and saw a bolt of lightning split the sky on the horizon. It would take luck to outrun the weather; heavy rains common across the Kansas plains could slow him down—but would also slow down anyone looking for him. Luke figured Joe would have alerted Larry by now that Meg was gone—and he was banking on the probability they wouldn't think he'd be bold enough to travel the highway right out of town.

At the airstrip, Joe had barely turned the ignition off before he hit the ground and sprinted toward his plane. He didn't even glance at the windsock standing at attention at the end of the dirt strip.

He raced past Ernie, who was bent to secure the tie-downs on Chip Anderson's Kaydet.

"Joe!" Ernie yelled as he stepped out from under the nose of the plane. "I already secured yours!" When Joe didn't stop, Ernie hurried after him. "I put the hopper back in the front bay after the rides yesterday," he shouted, "and filled it and the fuel tank. What—?"

"I'm going up," Joe shouted.

"You're crazy! There's dangerous weather rolling in."

Joe kept on toward the Stearman. "Have to."

Ernie trotted over to the plane as Joe was loosening a tie-down. "You're not serious—"

"I am. Help me take off the tie-downs and move the chocks. Luke Ramsey has Meg, Ernie!"

"What do you mean?"

"I mean he kidnapped her. You need to call Larry and tell him!"

Ernie ran to pull the chocks from the wheels, shaking his head. "Watch for FOD on the strip—this wind might have kicked stuff up, you know." Ernie sounded like a worried father.

Joe nodded as he climbed into the back cockpit. He pulled his leather helmet into place and slipped his goggles over his eyes. His hand automatically went to his St. Christopher's medal—not there. *Don't need it. Faith.*

Joe yelled out "Clear!" and then started the engine.

As the prop sprang to life, Joe maneuvered the Stearman onto the strip to take off. *I need you, Lord. Give me the vision, the skill, and the nerve I need to find her. Give me the courage to do what I need to do. . . .*

Ernie stood off to the right, a troubled frown fixed on his face, then trotted for his office and the phone.

The wind buffeted the Stearman as Joe pulled back on the stick and climbed high enough to see for miles in all directions. The combination of warm air rising from the ground and cold air huffing from thousands of feet above united in oceanlike waves that caught the double wings of the plane. Joe tightened the harness across his chest.

The view from above illuminated black ribbons of asphalt framing fields filled with mature crops that were close to harvest. The ominous-looking clouds rolling across the painted sky cast shadows over the ground and plunged one field after another into dark, indistinct smudges. He heard a crack of thunder over the throaty growl of the Stearman's engine and saw the jagged spear of lightning in the distance. He would stay in the air as long as it took to locate Meg—or until the wind ripped the wings from the plane.

"She's my wife! *My* wife, Luke!" he yelled over the engine. "Where are you? Think. *Think.* Where would he go?"

By now Joe knew that Luke was nothing if not arrogant. Joe soon figured that the man would race across the state the quickest way possible—right down the highway. *East or west?* West would get him to the state line and different jurisdictions sooner. . . .

Joe banked left and looked over the edge of the cockpit at the ground below. The storm had announced its arrival with a voracious wind advancing across the plains like waves battering a shoreline. Tall stalks of corn in the fields shuddered and lay flat as the wind battered the precisely planted rows. Small pockets of debris spun into miniature twisters that obscured some roadways.

Joe throttled the Stearman to ninety knots and hoped he was headed in the right direction. For the most part, the roads below were deserted. It seemed people had heeded the weather warnings on the radio and stayed home.

Then Joe saw what he was looking for—a two-tone Chevy pickup barreling west on Highway 70.

Luke could hear nothing but the sound of the howling wind as he drove for the state line. When thunder rolled across the din of the wind, the air around him seemed electrified—even his hair felt as if it were standing on end. He cast an anxious glance at the tall power poles that lined the highway like sentries standing guard. A lull in the wind created a pocket of silence that Meg filled with a groan.

"Stay asleep, princess. I don't need you waking up on me now," he warned through clenched teeth. He leaned forward in time to see two lightning flashes in rapid-fire succession. The sky was growing darker by the minute, and spatters of rain bounced off the hood of his truck.

"Now I remember why I hate Kansas," he muttered. "Colorado's gotta be better than this!"

Joe was tracking the truck from above, but he was very aware of the deteriorating weather. The raindrops stung his cheeks—fogged up his goggles. The increased turbulence had him bucking up and down. Now that he was literally on top of Luke, he wasn't sure how to proceed. He knew just one thing—he had to get the truck to stop.

He pushed the stick forward and dove toward the ground as he'd done over cornfields countless times, but this time it was a run over a Chevy truck that held his wife captive. Joe dropped his altitude until he was even with the power lines on either side of the two-lane blacktop and just in front of the truck. With innate skill and precision, he kept the speed of the Stearman just on the verge of a stall so he could track with the speed of the Chevy. He glanced back and could actually look inside the cab and see Meg slumped against the window.

"What have you done? What's the matter with her?" Joe yelled out in panic. He again looked behind him—over the back of the cockpit—to see that Luke was not deterred. If anything, he was moving even faster. But all the hours Joe had spent dusting farmers' fields were serving him well now. He pitched up to loop back around and resume pacing the truck from behind.

Luke couldn't believe his own eyes. The roar of the wind had masked the sound of the engine of the plane, and he hadn't seen it until it was practically on top of him. *Joe is actually pacing me!*

"You're a lunatic!" Luke yelled, even as he watched Joe maneuver the plane in perfect concert with the power poles and the wind.

Luke hit the brakes and jerked the wheel hard for a U-turn in the middle of the highway. The truck tilted up on two wheels and thudded back to the ground—finally rousing Meg out of her stupor. She blinked as she looked around, still disoriented and groggy from the chloroform. She looked over at him.

"Luke?" The word sounded thick and slurred. "What's going on? Where am I?"

"We're taking a little trip, Meg. You and me."

"What? Why?"

"Because I wanted to." He looked in the rearview mirror and swore. Joe was back on them and flying straight down the center of the road—only a few feet off the ground.

"You want to play it this way—fine," he sneered. "Let's see you hang on, Bug Man." He slammed his foot down on the accelerator and buried the speedometer.

Meg grabbed the back of the seat and stared out the rear window. "That's Joe! Stop, Luke!" When he ignored her, she reached over and clutched his arm. The steering wheel turned and the truck veered wildly.

"Knock it off or you'll kill us both!" he shouted at her.

Joe saw Luke make a sharp right on a dirt road straightaway from the highway. The terrain below had changed, and he looked north as he banked to stay with the truck. The road was barely wide enough for two cars to pass each other—and it was getting narrower. He was still flying low—only fifty feet off the ground. As much as he hated to move away from the truck and Meg, he knew he had to get high enough to see the lay of the land. He pulled back on the stick and immediately felt the Stearman resist his efforts to climb.

The pressure of the weather system bore down on the plane like a giant weight. The rain turned to hail, which ripped across the plane, pockmarking the fabric of the wings. The windshield of the cockpit cracked, and hail pinged off the prop. The Stearman tried to shoulder through the churning wind, but Joe couldn't get it to rise. He looked up in time to see Luke heading into a narrow canyon—maybe two hundred feet deep and two hundred feet wide.

He had been in narrower places, had turned sharper to avoid standpipes and field flaggers. He maneuvered the Stearman through the narrow limestone walls—stayed low, followed the truck as it bounced along the floor of the canyon. They arrived at the end of the chasm at nearly the same time—and the canyon spit them out into air grown thick with dust and black Kansas soil.

"I don't believe it!" Luke yelled. "Has he got nine lives?" He looked around and realized he was between several hundred acres of cornfields. He made an instant decision and steered the truck into a field—right into the eight-foot-tall cornstalks, hoping they would hide them from view. He realized too late that the field sloped, and before he knew it, he was sliding down an embankment into a five-foot-wide irrigation ditch. He swore some more and hit the steering wheel with both fists, then jammed the pickup into reverse.

"You're the one who's gonna kill us, Luke! Stop the truck," Meg yelled over the storm's roar. Luke ran his hand over the stack of government bonds that had been shaken out of their envelope onto the seat between them.

"I'll stop when I'm good and ready. These bonds are gonna give me the new start I need."

"I'm not going with you!" she shouted.

"Oh, yes you are."

Through force of sheer willpower Joe urged the Stearman upward as he saw Luke turn into the cornfield. The greenish-purple color of the thunderheads towered four miles straight up into the sky, promising more than rain and hail to the helpless Kansas landscape. The plane vibrated and rocked with the wind as Joe circled high over the cornfield looking for Luke and Meg. Joe dipped his wings one direction and then the other to get a better look. He finally spotted Luke's truck jouncing along the dirt path next to the irrigation culvert and went after him again.

He had executed this dive hundreds of times, and he settled into a rhythm as natural as breathing. He felt the plane respond to the slightest pressure on the stick, knew when the vibration under his seat meant he was just low enough. At the precise time, he pulled the handle on the hopper in front of him, and Luke's truck was covered in dark green granules that stuck to his wet windshield like a blanket of grass. Joe watched as the truck came to an abrupt stop and Meg's door swung open.

"That's right! Get out, Meg! Get out now!"

But the truck started again—the windshield wipers smearing the green sludge from one end of the windshield to the other—and Meg's door slammed shut.

"No!"

Joe circled back around and watched Luke, like a rat in a maze, turn off the pathway. He maneuvered the truck right across the rows of corn, mowing the stalks down as he drove like a madman across the terrain.

Luke adjusted his grip on the pistol he had wedged between his hand and the steering wheel, and glared at Meg. "Don't ever do that again!"

"I promise . . . I promise I won't try to get out again," she said fearfully. "I'm sorry." She held a trembling hand to her lips.

He shoved the gun under his thigh and pressed the truck as fast as he could through the rows of corn. The small bits of ice that had been hitting the truck turned into golf ball–sized hail that pinged and dinged the hood of his truck. The noise inside the cab was deafening—like someone beating on an amplified snare drum. The air smelled of hot summer rain and wet hay. Protected in the middle of the cornfield, the gale force of the wind lessened, and Luke assumed that the worst of the weather was over. It seemed that Joe had left—Luke couldn't see him overhead anymore. *Probably running low on fuel.*

Luke just needed to make it to the end of the cornfield and out onto a proper road, and he'd be home free.

"Please just stop and let me out . . . please, my children. They need me," Meg begged. He barely glanced in her direction. She sat with her hands braced against the roof of the truck to keep from being thrown all over the cab.

"Not my problem. And Joe's long gone—probably out of gas. Now sit tight and hang on, 'cause it's just you and me," he said with a wicked grin.

Joe flew a wide circle to the south of the cornfield over a windswept bluff capped by a carpet of wild flowers. The sun that had valiantly played hide-and-seek with the storm disappeared completely and plunged the world into an otherworldly gloom. When Joe made another pass over the cornfield, he saw Luke's truck cutting straight across—into the path of a huge funnel cloud.

Joe's heart was in his throat as he saw the funnel touch down over a barn, timbers exploding into kindling and disappearing into the vortex of the twister. The mass of black was so large Joe could barely comprehend it. Another twister came out of the clouds, and fingers of black spiraled toward the ground and reached like an outstretched hand ripping up everything in its path.

Joe dove lower, the Stearman riding the currents of wind like a wave getting ready to break on the shore. He could see debris in the funnel cloud spiraling across the ground, cornstalks pulled out by their roots in the churning wind. He didn't think twice about flying through the edge of the storm to get to Meg.

The thick, black Kansas soil whirling in the air stuck to his windscreen, his face, his clothes. He spit out the dust and grime even as he sent the Stearman toward the ground to stop Luke's truck. He cut the engine and glided over the top of the crop until he saw the Chevy.

He felt the corn snap under the belly of the Stearman as he dropped into Luke's path. The nose of the plane plowed into the dirt and stopped just as Luke's truck came through the tall stalks of corn. Joe could see the flash of panic and fear on Luke's face as he yanked hard on the wheel. The truck fishtailed, and Joe had a terrifying view of Meg's wide, frightened eyes before her side of the truck slammed into the plane.

By the time Joe crawled out of the cockpit and off the collapsed wing, Luke had thrown open his door and scrambled out, with the gun held at the ready in a bloody hand.

Joe ignored it. "I'm taking Meg out of here," he shouted and began to limp toward the truck, his eyes locked on the cab, where he could see Meg slumped in her seat next to the mangled door.

With a steely glint in his eyes, Luke cocked the gun and trained it right on Joe. Then suddenly his expression changed as his frantic eyes fastened on something above and beyond Joe's head. Luke staggered back and looked upward as if squinting at the sun, shaking his head in wild-eyed terror. He dropped the gun just before he turned and ran in the opposite direction.

Joe swung around at the sound of a roaring freight train to see a massive funnel cloud heading right at them. Pieces of wood, sheets of dirt, and branches from trees spun in a chaotic collage. Ignoring his injured knee, Joe sprinted to the truck, weak with relief to see that Meg was conscious, with a hand pressed to her head. He half crawled into the cab through the open driver's side door.

"Meg!" he yelled as he reached for her. "We have to get out of here!" He helped her from the cab as the wind screamed around them. They raced away from the truck and then Joe pulled her down next to him in the dirt and held her. The apocalyptic wind whipped around them, flinging needle-sharp dirt and rocks against their skin.

It was only a moment before the deafening roar of the storm began to sound muffled. The ground under Joe and Meg shuddered—then stilled. Debris still spiraled in the air all around them, but now the sound of the storm was nothing more than a low rumble—and suddenly Joe knew.

He turned his face into a blazing light, and his eyes traveled up over gleaming white wings marred with battle scars, up at least twelve feet to a face with eyes he recognized. Ferguson, now dressed in all his majestic, massive glory, had his wings wrapped around them, sheltering them.

Joe still held Meg tightly in his arms, and her face was buried against his chest. He slowly looked around at land picked clean by the twister but littered with government bonds. The Stearman's prop lay near Joe's feet. The swath of destruction left a wide path back through the field. Luke was nowhere to be seen.

When Meg moved in his arms, he tipped her head back to look at her face. Her forehead was bleeding a bit, and he pulled out his handkerchief to wipe the blood away. "Are you okay?"

"I'm fine—just a bump," she said, lifting a hand to feel the injury.

Joe looked into Meg's eyes. "You can't resist me, Meg Johnson Daley."

The corner of her mouth lifted ever so slightly. "I know it. I just wish *you* didn't know it."

Chapter 37

Joe stepped outside his front door and limped to the end of the porch. The deep cuts across his left cheek were sure to leave scars, and he was certain his knee would cause him problems for some time to come. From the edge of the porch, he looked up at a sky that offered hints of daybreak. The moon hung low on the horizon, and the stars had faded to what Joe only imagined he could see. He loved this hour—not quite night, not quite morning.

The weather was perfect. A puff of a breeze stirred the autumn leaves of the trees, and the final push of a long Indian summer suggested the day would require a sweatshirt in the morning and a T-shirt by afternoon. Joe heard the rattle of the milkman's truck on a nearby street and made his way back across the porch and inside.

The last bit of moonlight slipped over Meg as she slept. Joe gazed at her for just a moment. He reached out and brushed the hair off her face, revealing a bandage across her forehead. He brushed a kiss on her cheek.

"Wake up," he said softly.

She smiled sleepily in the moonglow and closed her eyes again. He touched the tip of her nose.

"Meg. *Really.* Wake up," Joe said again.

Meg opened her eyes to squint at the alarm clock on the nightstand next to the bed.

"What's wrong?"

"Nothing. Everything's good."

She lifted her left arm out from under the covers. A heavy white plaster cast had locked it in a bent position at her elbow. She propped herself up and looked at Joe.

"You know what time it is—right?" She spoke softly so as not to wake the kids.

"Yeah. I know. C'mon. Get up. You don't want me to throw a rock, do you?"

Carrying their shoes, Joe and Meg made their way along the dark hallway from their bedroom toward the stairs. As he made the turn to descend the stairway, Joe stubbed his toe on the bottom of the wooden banister.

"Ouch!" Joe hissed.

Meg flinched. "Are you okay?"

He nodded and put a hand on the small of her back to guide her down the stairs ahead of him. In spite of Joe's limp and Meg's cast, they managed to get down the staircase without hearing anything from their children.

In the living room, Joe stopped and pulled a piece of paper out of his back pocket.

"A note for the kids," he said. "Just in case they wake up before we get back." The propeller, the only thing left from his plane that had disappeared in the twister, held a place of honor across the mantel of the fireplace. He propped the note against the grain of the wood.

Meg pulled two leather jackets from the coat tree in the entryway.

"I've got the jackets," she said quietly. "You're sure Chip doesn't mind?"

"I'm sure. He said, 'My plane is your plane,'" Joe assured her. "C'mon."

The front door complained with a nasty screech when they opened it, and they stopped to listen for any sounds from upstairs. Satisfied the kids were still asleep, they stepped into the new morning.

The squeak of the front door brought Danny out of a sound sleep. He threw back the covers, went to his window, and inched the curtain aside. In the waning moonlight he saw his parents walking across the yard toward his dad's truck. His dad opened the driver's door and tossed in a couple of jackets. Then he joined his mom at the hood of the truck. Between his mother's broken arm and his dad's bum leg, they obviously were struggling, but eventually they managed to push the truck down the driveway.

"What's going on?" Christy said sleepily in his ear as she came to stand beside him at the window.

"Look." He moved the curtain aside a little more.

"What are they doing?" Christy wanted to know.

"Trying to sneak away from the house without waking anyone," he replied with a grin.

"You mean us?" Christy wondered.

"Yeah, squirt. Us."

"They're not very good at it" was her comment as she left his room as quietly as she had entered it.

Danny watched his parents push the truck to the end of the driveway. Then his dad opened the door for his mom and she climbed into the passenger seat. His dad limped around to the other side and got behind the wheel.

Danny smiled and let the curtain fall back into place. *Crazy kids.* He yawned and turned to climb back into bed.

Joe looked at Meg on the seat next to him in the truck. She smiled, and years melted away. They could have been seventeen again. Full of excitement, full of dreams—full of love for each other.

"Are you ready?"

"Ready."

"Is your arm okay?"

"Yeah. How about your knee?"

"Good. I'm good."

He turned the key in the ignition and nothing happened. He tried again. A click. Another try. Another click.

Meg caught her lower lip in her teeth as he made one more attempt.

"Meg? Remember how magnificent the sunrise was from the air?"

"I remember."

"Hold that thought."

They sat in silence for a moment, at the end of their driveway, in a truck that wasn't going to take them anywhere anytime soon. Joe laid his arm across the back of the bench seat and looked at her in the half-light of the morning. "You think we need a new truck?"

"Nah. I like this one. It's got history," she said with a smile.

"Maybe a new battery?"

"I can live with that."

He looked back over his shoulder at the growing light on the horizon. Sunrise wasn't far away. They probably wouldn't have made it to the airstrip in time anyway.

"I've got an idea," he said as he opened his door.

With their legs dangling over the end of the tailgate, Joe and Meg sat in the bed of the truck in their driveway and waited for the sun to make its appearance on the horizon.

"This is good," Joe said. "You, me—one more sunrise."

He slipped his arm around her shoulders and together they watched the saffron streaks of pink and orange announce the beginning of another day.

Acknowledgments

My debts are substantial. First and foremost, I couldn't have written this book without the help and support of my writing partner, Cindy Kelley. And to Tracie Peterson, who got me going on what I discovered is a rather difficult undertaking—writing a novel. I'd like to thank my editor and friend, Carol Johnson, whose indispensable and tireless assistance cannot be measured. My heartfelt gratitude to Gary Johnson and everyone at Bethany House Publishers who has had a hand in turning my story into a novel. Also, a special thanks to my agent, Tom Winters, for getting me started down another path of storytelling.

Most of all, I want to thank my dear wife, Sharee, and our three children, Ashley, Brittany, and Austin. You truly make me the happiest man on earth—*and* above it.

Michael Landon Jr.

About the Authors

Michael Landon Jr. grew up in a family that loved stories and storytelling. His father's *Little House on the Prairie* television series established the Landon name with family-friendly fare. In more recent years, the son has added his personal and distinct stamp to his own films with their spiritual themes and Christian values. His hugely successful work with Janette Oke's *Love Comes Softly* movies has further established his Christian worldview and his audience. His first novel, *One More Sunrise,* follows that path to a similar audience.

Michael and his wife, Sharee, make a home for their three children in Austin, Texas.

Tracie Peterson has loved stories and writing since she was a child, and being a published novelist has been a dream come true. She has gone on to write more than seventy novels, most of them romantic adventures in a historical setting.

She is grateful to Boyd Morgan and Merrill DeGroot for information on crop dusting and flying, as well as to John at Big Sky Stearman regarding Stearman biplanes.

Tracie is a popular writing seminar teacher. She and her husband, Jim, have three grown children and live in Belgrade, Montana.